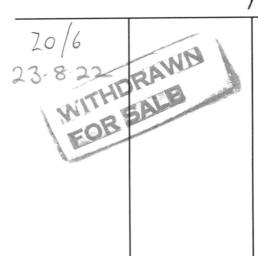
MARK MCLAUGHLIN
G. D. FALKSEN
ALLAN COLE
PAUL D
JOHN GREGO

D1492908

THE EXPANDED "THING" UNIVERSE

Frozen Hell, by John W. Campbell, Jr.
Who Goes There? by John W. Campbell, Jr.

FORTHCOMING

Mars Is Hell, by John W. Campbell, Jr. and John Gregory Betancourt
The Things from Another World, by John Gregory Betancourt

SHORT THINGS

STORIES INSPIRED BY JOHN W. CAMPBELL'S
CLASSIC NOVELLA, "WHO GOES THERE?"

ART EDITOR
EVELYN KRIETE

EDITOR
JOHN GREGORY BETANCOURT

COVER BY
DAN BRERETON

INTERIOR ILLUSTRATIONS BY
MARC HEMPEL, ALLEN KOSZOWSKI,
RAIKY VIRNICID, AND MARK WHEATLEY

WILDSIDE PRESS

CONTENTS

INTRODUCTION

JOHN GREGORY BETANCOURT

You hold in your hands a curious volume, one that was never intended but just sort of happened on its own. It's as if the universe wanted this book to appear.

Let me back up. In 2018, a set of partial manuscripts by John W. Campbell, Jr. surfaced in the archives of Harvard University. Discovered by scholar Alec Nevala-Lee, these works—which had titles like "Pandora" and "Frozen Hell"—turned out to be early, alternate, incomplete drafts of Campbell's classic story, *Who Goes There?* (one of the most acclaimed science fiction stories of all time, filmed first by Howard Hawks as *The Thing from Another World*, then as *The Thing* by John Carpenter, and again as *The Thing* (though this third version is more of a prequel than a remake). And if all goes well, another remake will happen sometime in the next few years.

I manage the Campbell literary properties for the family, and I saw immediately that there were some great possibilities here. When I assembled all the partials into a single cohesive story, *Frozen Hell* turned out to be 45 pages longer than *Who Goes There?* with most of the new material at the beginning. With this amazing new work in hand, I decided the best way to to publish it properly was tp raise the money to do so through Kickstarter.

And that's where *Things* (if you'll pardon the pun) got interesting.

The *Frozen Hell* Kickstarter project took on a life of its own, ultimately garnering $155,000 in pledges to support it. Along the way, we began looking for stretch goals. It started with a single original Thing story (to be written by me). And as we blew past stretch goal after stretch goal, we kept adding stories. And adding stories. And adding stories.

Finally there were enough that I decided to publish them as a book, too. Here are 13 *original* stories featuring the Thing. Writers were allowed to use their imaginations to do whatever they wanted with this iconic monster. Continue the original story? Sure! Venture into space? Of course! Uncover new Things in other lands and times? Definitely!

These stories—with one exception, my own "Nature of the Beast"—are not officially part of the Thing canon, but they are a lot of fun, and I'm sure you will enjoy them thoroughly.

And watch for *more* new Thing novels and stories coming soon!

LEFTOVERS

ALAN DEAN FOSTER

The thing was dead. Fried, carbonized, reduced to a blackened stain. Even the oily smoke that had comprised the only residue was gone, dispersed by the Antarctic wind.

Macready, Barclay, and Norris stood in the tool shed and gazed thoughtfully at what the thing had left behind.

Despite the ragged entrance and broken door that left the interior open to the outside, it was one hundred and twenty degrees Fahrenheit within the storage facility. Hot and humid enough that all three of the survivors began to sweat despite the icy wind outside. Had the shack remained closed up, the heat would soon have suffocated them. Apparently for the thing, the altered climate had been just right.

The shed was filled with piles of material that had been scavenged from the base's supplies: bits and strips of metal, aluminum and titanium fasteners, cannibalized power tools, engine parts, batteries that had been warped and fused together in inexplicable configurations that resembled sculpture more than power sources, bulbs and tubes fashioned from carefully blown glass, and all of it linked together by glistening torons that looked as if they had been excreted rather than braided.

Resting in the center of it all was an alien mechanism composed of crystal, salvaged metal, and metallic glass. It stood next to and partially enveloped a solid block of stone that glowed with an inner blue fire. Approaching with caution, the three survivors studied it warily. As they drew closer it was apparent that the radiant block was the source of the extraordinary warmth that was heating, or to their minds overheating, the shack. Macready leaned toward the block, then straightened and glanced back toward the ruined doorway. Outside, a katabatic wind was rising. Inside and despite the gaping portal, it was downright tropic.

Barclay pursed his lips. "I've seen that blue color before." In response to his companions guarded reactions he hastened to add, "Not in person. In pictures." He turned back to the incandescent block of stone. "It looks exactly like the glow at the center of a functioning nuclear reactor."

"Sure, why not?" Macready grunted. "Give a thing some scrap, some rock, a little time, and hey presto, out comes your ordinary everyday portable nuclear reactor." He pushed his open palms toward the steady, intense blue light. "I wonder if can do hot dogs?"

"We know one thing it doesn't do," murmured Barclay. "It doesn't emit killing radiation. The thing was tough, but it was killable. Not likely it would knowingly subject itself to a radiation overdose. Of course, we have no way of knowing what its physical tolerance for radiation was. I feel like I'm in Aladdin's cave. The alien version, anyway." His gaze narrowed, and he nodded toward the far side of the shed. "I wonder what that is?"

Edging around the luminous stone block and its inexplicable font of heat, the trio found themselves contemplating a collage of metal, glass, and leather that appeared stuck to the ceiling. Though a small part near the center of the agglomeration looked as if it was on fire, no warmth emanated from it. A rat's nest of leather straps and buckles hung downward from the tangle. To Macready it most nearly resembled a demented artist's interpretation of a dead cephalopod. Or a leather-and-metal jellyfish.

Reaching up, Norris grasped one of the dangling straps and tugged. The leather straightened out but the device, if that's what it was, didn't budge.

"Pull harder," Barclay advised.

Norris stepped away. "You pull harder. Let's see if it pulls back."

"That doesn't make sense." Barclay sounded confident. "If the thing wanted to booby-trap this place it could have done so with something less obvious." Moving underneath the apparatus, he examined the underside carefully.

Watching from a distance, Macready added, "If the thing wanted to booby-trap the shed we'd be dead already."

Barclay replied while continuing his inspection. "That's for sure. No, like the heater block, this must have been put together for some advantage." Reaching up, he grasped a strap and pulled. This had no more effect than had Norris's effort. Gritting his teeth and this time using both hands, he pulled on two of the hanging straps simultaneously and leaned back, putting his weight into the effort.

The device detached from the ceiling. Or more accurately, it was pulled downward. It strained in Barclay's grasp, trying to rise. Studying the ceiling, Macready could see a burn mark where the apparatus had rested. The roofing material was scorched but had not caught fire.

Barclay was already securing one strap after another around his body. When he finally ran out of buckles and clips and other attachments he looked like an early twentieth century urban junkman about to start on his morning rounds.

"How's it feel?" Norris asked him. "For something made for an alien body."

"Unnaturally light." Barclay shifted his shoulders against the mass resting on his shoulders and upper back. "Like it doesn't weigh anything, really."

"Not necessarily made to fit an alien body." Macready was peering hard at the now swathed Barclay. "All those straps and ties are of different length. There's enough slack to accommodate any body. Including a human one."

"I don't see any buttons, switches, or any other kind of control." Norris was frowning as he scrutinized the device. "What d'you think it's it supposed to do?"

Barclay twisted to his right, then to his left. Nothing. Experimentally, he gave a little jump. Rising into the air, he had to duck to avoid bumping his head on the ceiling. Macready blinked. Though it looked as if Barclay was traveling in slow motion, in actuality he had traversed the length of the shed so quickly that the crossing had fooled his companions' optics. It was a singular kind of blur, not unlike the effect that makes rapidly-spinning helicopter blades appear to move slowly.

No sound had come from the device. The air within the shed had not been disturbed. Yet Barclay had effortlessly navigated the room to land on his feet on the opposite side.

Norris shook his head in quiet amazement. "Interesting propulsion system. No evidence of ejecta, no noise, no heat. Some kind of anti-gravity?"

"You read too many stories," Macready snapped.

Unperturbed, Norris stared over at him. "You got a better explanation?"

Macready shook his head. "High-energy physics aren't my field."

"Let's try it outside—see what it can do if I give a really good push." Barclay took a step forward.

Carefully, Macready moved to block his path. "Why? Why outside?"

Taken aback, Barclay blinked at him. "Not much room in here." He frowned at his associate. "You look weird. What's up?"

"I may look weird," Macready replied, "but I'm not acting weird." He held his ground.

"You think I'm acting weird?" Barclay's voice was rising. "Because I want to see what advanced alien technology can do?" Seeing that the third member of their little group was now also eying him uncertainly, Barclay turned his attention to the other man. "You think I'm acting weird, Norris?" He tugged gently on one of the fastening straps. "Even if we only get to share in a portion of this discovery, we'll be famous. Also set for life. Tell me that doesn't interest you."

"Sure it interests me." Moving slowly, deliberately, and without taking his eyes off his companion, Norris reached down to pick a large hammer off the floor. "If I have a life to be set for."

Barclay was now genuinely upset. "What the hell's wrong with you? And you, Macready? All I want to do is try out this backpack a little more. Don't tell me you think...you're not implying...." He took a step backward, eyes darting rapidly between the two men. "You're losing it, both of you!"

Moving casually while careful to keep himself between Barclay and the open doorway, Macready removed one of several ice axes from where they hung on a nearby wall storage rack.

"You're the one who compared—or maybe recognized—the blue glow from the block as being like that in a nuclear reactor. You're the one who said, without any proof, that it didn't emit killing radiation. You're the one who explained why the device that's now on your back and the shed weren't likely to be booby-trapped. When Norris couldn't move detach it from the ceiling, you're the one who advised him to pull harder on a strap, and when he declined, you stepped right in, got it down, and onto your back. And you got it to work."

Patently nervous now, Barclay retreated another step. "Either of you two could have worked it. Could work it." Twisting, he reached for a strap. "Here, dammit, I'll take it off. Try it yourself, Macready. What did you think I was going to do, anyway?"

Raising the business end of the ice axe, Macready held it across his chest. "Take a bigger hop, you said. Where? To McMurdo Base? Maybe to New York?" He nodded at the apparatus. "We don't know what that thing is capable of. Maybe you do?" He took a step forward.

Barclay's reply was a mixture of fear and anger. "Crazy! You've both gone crazy! I'm not a thing—the thing. Get out of my way, goddamn it! Let's go back to the lab and I'll prove it to you!"

"Sure," Norris muttered. "Anything to get outside, where you can jump freely. One jump and you're out of here." He looked over at Macready, who was also advancing. "He almost made it, too."

"Insane, both of you!" Barclay yelled. Whereupon he promptly leaped, aiming for the busted portal.

Macready had been expecting it. Swinging the ice axe, he caught several of the leather straps—and promptly found himself lifted off the ground and being carried effortlessly toward the open doorway.

"Norris—before he gets outside!"

The big man was already in motion. Just as Barclay was about to exit the doorway, Norris heaved the heavy hammer. His accuracy was commendable. The hammer slammed into the side of Barclay's head with a dull thunk. Barclay's eyes glazed over, and he drifted sideways, slamming into the shed wall. As he slid downward, a frantic Macready freed his axe. One swing of the titanium tool pierced Barclay's skull. Blood spurted; staining the floor, the alien apparatus, and Macready's boots. Breathing hard, his heart racing, he stood with hands on knees beside the now motionless Barclay, waiting for him to writhe, to change, to transform.

"There's a torch on the workbench!" he gasped. "Get it, fire it up!" They would have to incinerate this latest and final manifestation of the thing before it could get away. One thing Macready was certain of: it wasn't going to get its pseudopods on him.

"I'm on it!" Norris shouted back. But he didn't rush for the workbench. Instead, he stayed where he was, pondering Macready.

Mac never saw the talon that penetrated his neck from back to front. Dropping the ice axe, he grabbed at his throat with both hands. Fountaining bodily fluids, he fell forward, to land atop the falsely accused and already dead Barclay. Choking on his own blood he bled out very quickly.

Behind him, Norris collapsed. As he folded onto the floor his torso split open like an overripe tomato. Emerging from the shell of the dead human, the mass of eyes and tentacles and protoplasm that was the thing's natural form oozed forward to examine first Barclay's corpse, then Macready's. Outside, the rising wind was howling now.

Emerging from millions of years of stasis, it had been forced into an extremely rapid learning curve. But its kind were clever and adept. Before ultimate death and destruction, it had just barely succeeded in learning how to cope with the primitive but lethal bipeds. Initially, it had reacted out of fear and a straightforward need to survive. Time to think, to analyze, to consider alternate methods of defense and survival had been in short supply. It had hoped to escape this very day by utilizing the transport device it had painstakingly constructed. Instead, it had been compelled to defend itself one more time.

Yet the confrontation had yielded invaluable information. As it slid various parts of itself into the lift device it knew it could now transport itself with confidence into the middle of one of the bipeds' swarming metropolitan throngs. It knew now, at last, how best to assemble and assimilate its primeval antagonists. While they were infinitely superior in numbers that it was by itself unlikely to overcome, the recent confrontation had effectively demonstrated that such forthright conflict was not only unnecessary but actually counterproductive.

With a little persuasion and the right wordings here and there, the thing was confident that the resident indigenous species was perfectly capable of self-extermination provided it was abetted by merely the slightest of verbal proddings from something like its own highly adaptable self....

THE MISSION, AT T-PRIME

KRISTINE KATHRYN RUSCH

Fifty ships ringed the planet they called T-Prime. God knows what the creatures called it. No one wanted to get close enough to find out.

Kessa stood on the bridge of her ship, hands clasped behind her back. She studied the holographic images before her.

They weren't that detailed. On a mission like this, she had learned, it was best not to see too clearly.

What she did see—in the real time imagery—was a thriving planetscape on two large continents, both far enough from the equator to thrive despite the hot sun. She half imagined teaming blue masses below, their round orange eyes taking in everything—miniature suns absorbing rather than giving off.

She had no idea how anything could live on a planet filled with telepathic shapeshifters, or what kind of culture they would build.

Again, she didn't want to find out.

Her palms were wet, and she wiped them on the side of her pants. She normally wasn't nervous. She had been given this job because she was calmer than almost any other captain in this cobbled-together mess of ships, dubbed Earth's Defenders by those who had stayed behind.

Because she was normally "emotionally muted," as the psych evals called her, most of her team was as well. Unlike other bridges in the EDF, this one was never filled with raucous laughter or panicked voices. All five members of her main bridge crew (as well as the five who formed the secondary crew) got the job done, efficiently and quietly, before returning to their quarters or going to the handful of public areas on deck three for private time.

Emotionally muted, and uncharacteristically nervous. She almost pinged her commander to tell them that *America's Pride* wasn't up to the job, but she didn't. It was too late. Back before it was too late, she thought her team could get the job done.

And maybe they could.

Maybe she was the only one who couldn't live with the results.

The ships surrounding T-Prime all bore names like *America's Pride*, only with different countries or unions in the title. The European Union was represented, along with the Pan-African Conference, and every organization in between. The smallest of Earth's 200 countries had sent representatives to work alongside the largest.

Finally, the event that had unified the Earth—at least for the moment—had been repeated discoveries of aliens encased in ice all over the planet. After the first discovery over 150 years ago, humans had fought back effectively, mostly by never thawing the creatures out, and eventually jettisoning their ice-packed bodies into space—outside of the solar system.

But it was clear, as the ice caps melted and the Earth warmed, that these creatures—dubbed "The Things" after the term used by that 1930s Antarctic crew—had scattered themselves all over the planet. That they hadn't accidentally stumbled outside their ships and froze nearly to death, but that they had deliberately planted themselves on Earth, to be found at roughly the same time.

No one knew why that was, but world leaders decided—with the concurrence of almost every scientific mind on the planet—that this had been some kind of odd invasion force, and that these Things had to be stopped.

Didn't matter—as some argued—that the plan the Things concocted was millions of years old, and that at the time, humans didn't even exist. Earth had been a primitive place, ripe for colonization. They could have been refugees, accidental survivors of some major interstellar catastrophe or anything else.

But those arguments hadn't held sway, and so Kessa found herself here, light years away from her home—one she would never see again, one that had probably moved on from this major endeavor, thinking it was safe from invaders that had maybe moved on themselves.

She took several deep calming breaths, quietly, so that her crew wouldn't see how nervous she was.

They all had their heads down, working their own holographic screens, making certain that everything was in order.

She checked the telemetry flowing from the other ships, seeing nothing out of the ordinary.

"Reston," she said, "any changes on T-Prime?"

She had asked Reston to monitor the planet, because it had bothered her from the moment they arrived in this solar system, that no one responded to the arrival of such a massive group of ships.

If the Things were truly hostile space-faring invaders, why hadn't they defended their own planet?

"No changes," Reston said. He looked at her over his shoulder. He was a short thin man whom she relied on for any kind of tricky work. His brain worked along a similar line to hers.

They'd already discussed the strangeness of this assignment, late one night after everyone else cleared out of the fifteen-seat area that was labeled as a "bar" by the ship's specs.

Higher-ups had planned the mission. Everything had taken years. Years upon years upon years, as different ships tracked the Things, monitored different regions of space for the strange ships that resembled early 20th century submarines and ran on some version of power that the unsophisticated Antarctic researchers had thought was magnetic. It wasn't. It had been something else, something she didn't entirely understand, and it had a signature that someone discovered and could follow.

Then there was the discovery of another cache of those ships—abandoned, fortunately—near an exploded moon. EDF had spent a few years retrieving information off those ships, figuring out where the ships had been heading, where they had come from, and what their mission was.

That was when the paranoia grew in the EDF, the belief that these Things were actually trying to supplant humanity, and would try to use humanity's resources, including the human bodies themselves, to expand around the globe.

It all rang false to her, and to Reston too. They didn't discuss it with the rest of the crew, because they had been assigned a mission, along with forty-nine other ships, and they were told, in no uncertain terms, that if they didn't follow the mission, the ship—and its crew—would be destroyed.

She had never faced orders like that before, and until she received the details of the mission, she didn't understand it.

She understood it now.

The look he gave her was a helpless *this makes no sense* look. But it did make sense, if the plans the EDF had found were accurate.

She had also read about the attacks on Earth itself. Scary, near-misses. It was almost impossible to defeat a being that was telepathic, smart, and shifted shape. The very idea of it made her skin crawl.

Like this mission. She clenched her fists, then released them, not sure exactly how to move forward.

The idea came from procedures used in the barbaric 19th and 20th centuries to execute criminals. A squad of men—and they were always men—stood in a line and, on command, shot at a tied-up blindfolded criminal, one who had been judged guilty and who deserved to die.

She had made a feeble protest about this mission: she had said that there had been no real proceeding here, no real determination. Just a guess and a lot of fear.

And that was when she had received the warning. *America's Pride* was already heading to T-Prime; she knew the mission; and if she wanted to divulge it to anyone or to protest it, then she and her crew would die.

Their communications array had already been partially destroyed. Not even removed; destroyed. She could only communicate with the other EDF ships around T-Prime. She couldn't communicate with anyone on the planet if she wanted to.

Nor could she send messages back home.

She and her crew had to do that long before they received details of the mission, and she had chosen not to. She was "emotionally muted" after all, and because of that, really didn't have enough friends and close family to worry about.

It was odd that she was worrying about her colleagues now. Before, she might have considered a job like this something they all had to get through, not something that might cause them sleepless nights in their future.

She bent over the holograms, thinking maybe she would get an up-close scan of the planet's surface. Maybe pick one of the well-lit areas, one that clearly had a lot of tech, and see exactly what a Thing community looked like.

Her hand hovered over the virtual controls for just one moment, and then she brought her hand back. If she did that, her rather limited imagination would have something to play with.

She didn't dare give it fuel. She didn't want to regret what she was required to do.

There's no way out of this, is there? Reston asked, just the night before.

No, she had said softly.

What if we're wrong? he asked. *What if they're harmless?*

There was no evidence that the Things were harmless. Every time humanity had encountered one, humanity had won...just barely. And the cost in human life had been great. It was also twenty or more humans to one original Thing entity.

They weren't harmless.

But she didn't say that.

She knew what he meant. He was asking about the life on the planet before. What if the Things that had come to Earth millions of years ago were outliers. What if the Things that had abandoned those ships were part of that outlier fleet?

What then?

"Um, Captain?" Reston said, a wobble in his voice. He was looking at his screens, and his face had turned a weird shade of gray. "You might want to see this."

"No time," she said.

Because as he spoke, she had gotten a timing packet from headquarters. The ships—all fifty of them—would release a small weapon all at the same time.

Some of the weapons were live. They would hit the planet's surface, and send several different kinds of death into the ecosystem. From gas that destroyed the environment that the Things thrived in to flame that would burn off the gas (and everything in its path) to actual bombs that would drill their way into the planet's core and, if all went as the models said it would, would blow the entire planet into tiny pieces.

By then, the ships would already be at the edge of the solar system. That was why the planet-destroying bombs were last, so that the ships had time to escape the destructive force of an exploding planet.

Her hands were shaking now. Imagine if she wasn't emotionally muted. Imagine if she had the full range of human emotions at her command. She wasn't sure if she'd be standing. She was taking part in the destruction of an entire race—and maybe many other races.

An entire planet, and everything that was part of it.

She took one ragged breath, and reminded herself: three different kinds of active weapons, all of them destructive, spread across thirty ships. And three different kinds of *inactive* weapons, none of them destructive, spread across twenty ships.

No one would know which weapon delivered what blow. The members of the EDF firing squad could, if they so choose, believe that they had nothing to do with the destruction to come.

The countdown began on her holographic panel.

"Ready weapons team," she said, her hand near the weapons release command. If no one had the balls to do this, then she would.

Even though, when it came down to it, she didn't believe in this decision. She regretted standing here, regretted being part of this mission, regretted ever volunteering for the EDF.

"Ready," said Dunster and Kinner in unison. She had assigned two team members for the exact same reason there were twenty ships with inactive weapons. Because she wanted each of her team members to have the ability to lie to themselves, to believe they actually had no part of this gigantic mess.

She watched the timer, ticking down, and then she said in her most forceful voice, "Fire."

Not *fire at will* which was what she was supposed to say. But *fire*, so they fired at *her* will, so that, if their weapons were active, *she* was responsible and no one else.

Her heart pounded against her chest, and she felt lightheaded. She watched as the weapons—dots on her holographic screen—dove toward T-Prime, and then penetrated the atmosphere.

"Bunder," she said to her pilot, "take us to the return coordinates."

Her voice remained calm, even though her entire system was alive with adrenalin. She wanted to look closer at that planet, to see what happened when the gas spread, to watch—

And then the atmosphere ignited, just like it was supposed to. Planet-wide—red and blue and filled with flame that they could actually see from space.

Her crew froze for a moment, staring at their screens, all of them knowing what that horrid fire meant.

Nothing could live through that. Nothing.

And the ship wasn't moving.

"Bunder," she said again.

He moved this time, hand floating over his virtual screen, seemingly as calm as she was pretending to be.

The ship moved, finally. They had more than an hour to get to the rendezvous coordinates.

She hoped those were far enough away.

She let out another breath, then shut off all live images from the planet. She would watch the telemetry from a distance. Hell, she might not even watch that.

It would be pretty damn clear when a planet in this solar system exploded.

She needed to think about something else, to *focus* on something else.

"All right, Reston," she said, proud of herself for that even tone in her voice. Proud that she could hold it together in the face what they all had done. "What were you going to say?"

He shook his head. He looked even sicker than he had earlier.

"It doesn't matter," he said.

"Tell me anyway," she said.

He scanned the bridge. Everyone was watching him, rather than looking at the horrors on their screens. Rather than letting what they had been a part of sink into their consciousness.

"You asked me to dig," he said.

"I did," she said. She had asked him to look at the data, see if there was anything in it that seemed a bit off. "But you're right. It no longer matters."

He nodded, then closed his eyes. One finger on his left hand moved, ever so slightly, and she received a notification on her virtual screen.

He had sent her something anyway.

She had the will power to look away from the planet, the will power to ignore what they were doing, but she couldn't quite ignore this.

She opened the file. It didn't make sense at first. She tapped the images that he had sent, watched as shapes shifted, and tiny blobs of blue liquid—like blood—replicated and injected themselves through environmental suits.

All that protection the teams had worn when they had gone into the abandoned ships: that protection hadn't worked.

This entire mission wasn't something dreamed up by human military leaders. The Things themselves were behind it.

Her knees buckled, but she managed to catch herself before she fell.

Reston was watching her. That strange color in his face—was that because he was as appalled as she was or was he one of them?

"Why?" she asked, and he shrugged.

Such a human motion, but something so easily adopted.

She could think of a dozen reasons why, though. They could be destroying other enemies, using human ships to do so, sparking an interstellar war.

Or they could be destroying their own kind, the ones in their world who *didn't* want to attack other species.

Or they could simply be screwing with the already guilt-laden captains, making them doubt whether or not this mission was the correct one.

As if she hadn't had doubts already.

She closed her eyes, took a deep calming breath, remembered that she was emotionally muted. Events like this shouldn't bother her.

But they did.

Oh, they did.

"Bunder," she said. "Return to our earlier coordinates."

"Captain," he said. "We'll be too close."

They would. And it didn't matter.

Because they should see what they had done, up close and personal. They should watch as an entire planet died—just before they died as well.

She saw no other choice. Not because she couldn't handle the emotions of all of this. Not because she was afraid it would bother her for the rest of her days.

But because she already doubted Reston, and the information she saw. And, she would wager, every other captain saw the same information at the same time.

She would give them a clue how to handle it.

She would show them the future.

Finally—belatedly—she agreed with the generals.

The only way to deal with the Things was to destroy everything they touched.

Not because they were shape-shifters or even because they were telepaths. But because they sowed the seeds of doubt into every action.

And there was only one way to remove any doubt.

She felt calmer than she had in days.

She clasped her hands behind her back, stared at the holographic screen in front of her, and watched a planet die.

She didn't even brace herself for what was going to come next.

She didn't have to.

For the first time since she had joined this mission, she finally felt like she was doing the right thing.

HIS TWO WARS

PAMELA SARGENT

Norris opened the door to find McReady standing on the front stoop, towering over him. The big man dropped his duffle bag, grabbed Norris's hand with a firm grip, and shook it.

"Great to see you again, Vance," McReady said with a heartiness that seemed forced.

"Come on in," Norris said as he stepped back. Abby had taken McReady's phone call that morning after his arrival at Hickam Field. The soldier who had dropped him off was already pulling away in his jeep. McReady picked up the duffel and stooped as he came through the doorway. He looked much the same, with the same broad shoulders and bronze hair, but the red beard that had covered his face during their mission in Antarctica was gone.

"Whew," McReady muttered, wiping his face with the back of his big hand. "Kind of a warm day. But I guess you must be used to it by now."

"It'll be cooler outside." Norris had not paid much attention to the weather except to note that it was slightly warmer than expected for Honolulu in early December. "And what brings you to Hawaii?"

"Heading for Manila. Seems MacArthur and his boys can use a meteorologist there. So I figured I might as well stop over for a few days."

"Mac's here," Norris called out to his wife as he led his visitor toward the lanai. Abby followed them outside from the kitchen, carrying a tray with two glasses and two bottles of beer. She glanced toward McReady as he set down his bag. He looked up and gazed back at her with slightly narrowed eyes. Norris was suddenly certain that Abby had secretly talked Mac into visiting them here on his way to the Philippines. She might have written to him or sent him a telegram. Given that he hadn't spotted any long-distance charges on their telephone bill, she might have placed a call to him from her desk at the newspaper.

They both thought he was crazy. Maybe he was, Norris thought. He couldn't even look at the red blossoms on the ohia lehua trees near the house without recalling the red eyes of that creature, the Thing that still haunted him. The damned Thing was still out there, somewhere. He could sense it hiding in the life around him. Up in the trees near the lanai, a myna bird screeched, as if in warning, and another myna cried out in response. The hills below the house were thick with the greenery of plants that might easily camouflage alien invaders.

"Good to see you both again," McReady said as he sat down in a wicker chair and stretched out his long legs, then glanced at the glasses and beer bottles. "You're not joining us?" he said to Abby.

"Can't," she replied. "Promised my editor I'd check in with him this afternoon but I'll be back in plenty of time to join you two for dinner."

"You two pick the place. Dinner's on me. Drinks, too."

"I'll look forward to it, especially since I won't have to cook, and I think I've found the perfect date for you."

McReady frowned. "Another Wellesley girl?" Back in Boston, Abby had set him up on a couple of blind dates with former classmates of hers that hadn't gone too well.

Abby shook her head. "A nurse at Tripler General. Interviewed her a month ago for a story about the hospital and I think you'll like her. See you later." She waved her fingers at them before retreating through the open door to the living room.

Norris heard the front door slam shut. "So Abby's still working," McReady said as he poured himself a beer. Norris could guess at what he wasn't saying, that Abby wouldn't be writing for the Honolulu *Star-Bulletin* if Norris was able to hold up his end, not that they needed the money from her job given what came in from her trust fund. She held on to the job, he couldn't help thinking, largely because it was preferable to spending long days at home with a brooding, shell-shocked husband. "And what have you been up to these days?"

"Tutoring. Basic science and some physics."

McReady frowned.

"A couple of local high school kids," Norris continued. "One of them has a rich dad who wants to make sure he's ready for Yale next year but the other boy shows some real promise."

McReady's ruddy face softened. He was feeling sorry for Norris now, and Norris didn't welcome his sympathy. McReady had stayed with him and Abby in Boston just after their return from Antarctica, when they had been given some much-needed leave time, and Norris had welcomed the other man's company. They had spent their afternoons taking long walks and sitting in on lectures at M.I.T. and their evenings at Boston Bruins games or making the rounds of the nearby bars. They never talked about their time in Antarctica, their battle against that shape-changing alien Thing, the comrades they had lost there, or the report that McReady, with input from the rest of the survivors, had written before it was finally classified and filed away.

McReady had left Boston after a month and a half to visit his parents in New Jersey, promising to visit again soon once he found out where his next assignment would be. Not long after that, Abby discovered she was pregnant and quit her job writing for the Boston *Herald*'s society pages to prepare for the birth of their first child.

And it was then that the Thing had started haunting Norris again. He would wake in the middle of the night, feeling it near him, knowing that if he moved even an inch he would feel the slimy grip of an alien tentacle. Whenever the winter wind howled outside, muffling the sound of the traffic in Boston's streets, he was back at the base in Antarctica, thinking he was again hearing Blair's hysterical gibberings from the shack where the biologist had imprisoned himself before the alien had taken over his body and erased Blair altogether. Lying next to Abby as she slept, Norris would suddenly recoil, imagining that a drop of blood from the Thing had somehow infected him and that something alien now gestated inside his wife's body.

In her sixth month, Abby had fallen on their icy front steps and had lost the baby afterwards. He remembered sitting with her in the hospital as she wept and grieved over their loss and confessed to him that the doctor had told her there was probably no chance for another child. All he could feel was relief at knowing nothing alien could ever grow inside her again.

He didn't remember much about the months after that. There was a vague memory of another visit from McReady, dim recollections of overheard mutterings about battle fatigue and nervous breakdowns, his angry refusal to submit to sessions with a psychoanalyst, and of being discharged from the Expeditionary Force team not long after that. He had been assured no dishonor or stigma would be attached to his discharge, which would officially be labeled an "indefinite leave." Even so, he had felt ashamed, unfit, less than a man somehow. It was Abby's idea to move to Honolulu, where she had a cousin who could get her a job there as a reporter. Maybe she had also been thinking that life in such a tropical paradise might finally heal him.

"…to the Philippines at the wrong time," McReady was saying. Norris forced his attention back to the other man. "The Japs aren't going to tolerate that oil embargo forever. They'll have to make a move sooner or later."

"Let's hope it's later." Or never, he thought. Abby had been saying much the same thing lately. They might soon be at war, according to some of her colleagues at the newspaper.

Norris poured beer into a glass as McReady lit a cigarette. A movement near him caught his eye as a house finch alighted on the railing near him and then flew away.

Norris repressed a shiver. The sight of any bird, even a tiny one like that finch, made him uneasy, reminding him of the albatross he had shot down in Antarctica. Occasionally while walking on one of the nearby beaches, he had seen an albatross circling overhead and thought of how easily they might have lost their battle against the alien. The Thing might not even have needed the antigravity device it had been putting together in order to conquer the world, or any of the alien technology Norris had hoped to study before the rest of the team had decided that mankind wasn't yet ready to be trusted with such knowledge. It might instead have hitched a ride on that big white bird, swallowed the albatross and taken on its form or infected it with one tiny stray drop of blood. Maybe just a molecule would have been sufficient to transform an albatross into a Thing that could threaten all of Earth.

They had been able to win one battle. They had defeated the monster and the alien technology lay hidden under the Antarctic ice. Now he wondered if they had actually won that war.

The front doorbell rang. Norris stood up. "Don't know who that could be," he said, wondering who would be dropping by. Apart from his two students and their families and a couple of Abby's coworkers, he hadn't made that many acquaintances here.

He went to the door and opened it.

Jonathan Nishimoto was outside, clutching a pulp magazine. He was small, with closely cropped black hair, a sixteen-year-old boy who looked no older than twelve. Norris remembered what it had been like for him at that age, when he had been smaller than all of the boys in his class.

"I forgot to bring this back before," the boy said, holding out the magazine, which bore a cover depicting a frightened man and a swath of starry sky above what looked like a telescope. "What a great story."

"Which one?" Norris asked. He hadn't read much pulp fiction during the last couple of years, although he picked up the occasional magazine mostly out of habit. Once the stories had been an escape for him; now they seemed pallid next to what he had experienced.

"'Nightfall,'" Jonathan said as he handed the magazine to him. Norris glanced at the title, printed in red capital letters on the cover, but didn't recognize the author's name. "It's about a planet where there's no night, only daytime, so nobody ever sees the stars, they don't even know there are any stars except for their own sun, but..." The boy fell silent. "Read it yet?"

Norris shook his head.

"Then I better not give away the ending."

"Come on outside and meet an old friend of mine." Norris dropped the magazine on the coffee table and led Jonathan toward the lanai. "He just got here from the States this afternoon." McReady looked up as they stepped outside. "Mac, meet Jonny Nishimoto. He's the boy I was telling you about, the one who'll be a darned good scientist one of these days." Jonathan lowered his head, as if embarrassed. "Jonny, this is Mac McReady."

McReady tensed, stared at the boy for a few long seconds, and then managed a half-smile. "Hello," he muttered.

"Hi," Jonathan said in a small voice.

"Can I get you a soda?" Norris asked.

"No, thanks." Jonathan turned toward him. "I have to get back home," he went on. "Promised Dad I'd help him weed our garden." He nodded in McReady's direction. "Nice to meet you, Mr. McReady." He glanced at Norris. "Thanks for letting me borrow your *Astounding*, Mr. Norris."

"Any time." Jonny always brought any borrowed magazines back in pristine condition. He was as meticulous in caring for them as his father was with their garden and his mother in maintaining their house, a small and spare but well-maintained wooden structure supported by large beams of teak.

McReady's eyes narrowed as the boy left the lanai. He gulped down more beer. "Maybe you shouldn't be tutoring that kid," he said at last. "You never know. The Japs might—"

"Jonny's as American as you are, Mac. His grandparents came here before ..." He caught himself just in time. "Before the turn of the century," he finished. Before my grandfather got off the boat in New York, he had almost said. Norris had never told Mac about his immigrant grandfather or the father who had decided, probably correctly, that his son would do better in the new country with the name of Vance Norris instead of Vincente Naroni.

Jonny was, Norris thought, a hell of a lot more human than Blair had been at the end. He could look into Jonny's almond-shaped eyes and see a fellow human being gazing back at him, a boy not unlike the one Norris had once been.

* * * *

Norris listened as McReady talked about his future plans. Back in Washington that summer, there had been a change involving American policy toward the Philippines. If the Japanese were going to attack, those islands were probably where they would strike first. For some time, it had been generally accepted that there was little chance of defending the Philippines, with the Japanese holding Formosa and also in control of Indochina. But with a large concentration of American aircraft now based in the Philippines and General MacArthur having been busy building up the Filipino and U.S. forces, defending the islands was now feasible.

There was a good chance Mac would be in the middle of a war once he landed in Manila but he did not seem disturbed by that prospect. Maybe he was thinking that nothing could be worse than what they had already gone through in Antarctica.

"You're still in the reserves, aren't you?" McReady said. Norris nodded. "But you might not get called up."

"Think I can't handle that?"

"That wasn't what I was thinking. I'm worried about you, Vance, and not because I think you're a shirker or a coward. You proved you weren't, back in that frozen hell."

Norris shook his head. "At first I couldn't stop thinking that we didn't kill it all, end it for good. I kept thinking of ways some bit of it might have escaped us."

McReady looked away for a moment. Norris thought he glimpsed an uneasy, almost fearful look on the other man's face, as if he was thinking the same thing. "We got it all. I'm damned sure of that. If there was any chance, if I thought we hadn't—"

"—you would have burned out even more of the place and none of us would have left the station alive," Norris finished. "I know that. It doesn't help. I can't help wondering if that was the only one of their ships, if there isn't another one hidden somewhere, in Antarctica or maybe somewhere else."

"You're just spooking yourself, Vance."

"It's a possibility."

"Okay, it's possible. Maybe there's another Thing buried out there somewhere. Maybe there's another alien ship on its way here right now that we haven't detected. But until we have hard evidence for something like that, I'm not going to sit around worrying about it."

That was what any rational man would do, Norris thought. That was how somebody like Mac, who had surely been as terrified as the rest of them while confronting the alien, would behave.

"And if anything like that shows up again,' McReady continued, "it'll be facing the deadliest species alive—Man. Now show me where I can park this duffel and then maybe we can take a tour of the neighborhood."

"Abby has the car."

"Doesn't matter. We—I can use some exercise."

* * * *

They left McReady's bag in the small room where Abby did her sewing and had set up a cot for their guest, then went for a walk. The narrow road from Norris's house led down a hill to a roadside stand where a few local farmers had pineapples, mangos, and lychees for sale and two boys were selling glasses of fresh tangerine juice. The farmers were Japanese and, like many of the people in the region, had fruit trees and gardens in the narrow plots next to their houses. McReady bought a glass of juice from one of the kids and complimented the adults on their produce, sounding a bit too expansive in his praise.

They left the fruit stand and walked on. To the west, they could glimpse the armada anchored at Pearl Harbor, but McReady kept on talking about the weather, the greenery around them, how tasty the tangerine juice was—anything, Norris supposed, that would distract them from brooding about more serious matters. Such efforts were useless. He was already thinking about the coming war that seemed inevitable. Maybe slapping an oil embargo on the Japs and freezing their assets would finally push them over the edge. He wondered if war could still be avoided, how many opportunities for negotiation and understanding President Roosevelt and his Cabinet might have missed. The Japanese could be as merciless as their soldiers had been in China or they could also be as peaceful and industrious as the farmers selling their fruit and Jonny Nishimoto dreaming of becoming a scientist.

He could guess what McReady would think about such musings, that they were as useless and delusionary as hoping that one could make peace with something as alien as the Thing.

Norris tensed at that thought. Only a few nights ago, he had dreamed he was standing over the Thing again as it lay in its block of frozen ice. The ice had suddenly disappeared and Norris watched, unable to move, staring helplessly at the writhing blue worms on the creature's head. The alien glared at him with its angry red eyes and then abruptly took on the form of Commander Garry, who had led the Antarctic team. The Thing that had been Garry lifted its hand, and it came to Norris that the alien was trying to tell him something, that infecting and taking on the form of the commander and Blair and the others was not an attempt to conquer Earth, but instead a desperate attempt to communicate. If he waited, he might even be able to sense the Thing's thoughts, its plea for help in surviving in a frozen alien environment, on a world that lacked the familiar light of a blue sun.

"Vance." A big hand clutched his shoulder. "Are you all right?" Norris shook off the tendrils of the dream. "Something wrong?"

Norris shook his head.

"You just suddenly stopped walking and got this funny look on your face." McReady peered at him. "Sure you're okay?"

"I'm fine."

They walked on. Norris was thinking of the debriefings they had undergone after their return from Antarctica. The last debriefing had been more like an inquisition, with queries from various bureaucrats representing the War and Navy Departments that were more like accusations of incompetence and bad judgment than questions. They had destroyed an alien artifact before it could yield any of its secrets. They had wiped out an alien life form before being able to determine whether it was hostile or simply acting in its own defense. Norris began to wonder if they were going to be summarily discharged, court-martialed, or secretly consigned to a long stretch in Leavenworth. By the time the interrogation reached its end, McReady's frown had turned into a scowl and his heavy brows were drawn together over eyes narrowed in anger.

"Got anything else to ask us?" McReady said in a low voice. The Assistant Secretary of War, a small, balding man, shook his head. "Now I can't tell you for sure if that creature, that Thing, came here intending to take us over, or only because it got curious about our world, or just ended up landing here by accident, but that doesn't really matter. Whether it was acting in self-defense or out of pure malice doesn't matter, either. We know it had a technology far in advance of ours and that, if it wasn't stopped, it could have infected and taken over and wiped out the entire human race." He paused. "The only safe assumption to make was that it was either the Thing or us, that any species that managed to develop that level of technology, that could whip up an antigravity device using whatever happened to be at hand, that could make it across the galaxy to another planet, was going to arrive at the same conclusion once it encountered us—that it was either their species or ours. Them or us." McReady managed a crooked smile. "I can't even say for sure whether that Thing was even thinking consciously along those lines or just acting on blind instinct, but that doesn't matter, either. When it started taking over, when we found out it was a damned shape-changer, we did what we had to do. We knew we couldn't even trust each other until we eradicated every trace of that creature."

The Assistant Secretary of War scowled. "Even if we grant you that much," he began, "you needn't have destroyed the alien's equipment and deprived us of any opportunity to learn from it."

"Permission to speak frankly, sir," McReady muttered in a sarcastic tone. "Don't be an idiot." He showed his teeth. "If you'd crash-landed on an alien world, what would have been your priority? If you were a scout, which that Thing might well have been, you'd want to find a way to let the rest of your team know where you were. If you'd landed somewhere by accident, if you'd gone off course somehow and ended up God knows where, you'd be fixing to send out a signal. Whatever else that contraption it managed to build could do, I'm willing to bet some sort of communications device was part of it. The alien would have tried to get the word out."

"After twenty million years?" A gray-haired rear admiral from the Navy Department had spoken. "Didn't you determine that the alien vessel had landed here about that long ago?"

"Maybe it didn't realize it had been under ice for that long." McReady folded his arms. "And maybe a civilization that can cross space can stick around for twenty million years or longer. I hope I'm wrong about that, hope they're long gone, along with whatever hellish world spawned them, but you never know." He paused. "Right now our only defense against a Thing like that is to lie low and hope another one never finds its way back to our world again, destroy any evidence that it was ever here, make certain that it couldn't send out any kind of signal and that we wouldn't accidentally send out one ourselves on the device it was putting together. Whatever we might have learned from its technology, any discoveries we might have made, wouldn't be worth the risk."

The meeting had ended with their interrogators muttering among themselves before announcing their decision. The surviving members of their team would be granted a long leave before being assigned to other duties. Their report would be labeled top secret and anybody revealing what had happened in Antarctica to anyone outside that room would face the harshest of penalties. Not that anyone was likely to reveal any secrets, Norris had thought, given that anybody else hearing such a tale would find it unbelievable and consider its narrator nuts.

"What now?" McReady asked, startling him back into the present. "Sure you're okay?"

"I'm fine," Norris replied, keeping his eyes down. He was avoiding any glance at the shrubs and trees on either side of the road, fearing that all he would see there were fleeting hallucinatory glimpses of the writhing tentacles and repulsive red eyes of the Thing.

* * * *

Abby arrived at the house just before sunset after calling to say that she would pick up Mac's date for the evening on her way home. The date, Noelani Wieland, who wore a red silk dress, turned out to be a tall and shapely young woman with long black hair who bore a marked resemblance to Dorothy Lamour. At the sight of her, McReady brightened and quickly ushered her to the lanai, where the two sat down next to each other on the wicker love seat.

"Promised Abby and Vance our night out would be on me," McReady said as he lit Noelani's cigarette. "But I could use some recommendations about where to go."

"Depends on what you're looking for," Noelani murmured in a husky voice. "If you like living dangerously, just head for the bars on Hotel Street near the docks, but I don't think I'd recommend that to any respectable guy." McReady grinned, clearly happy that she didn't sound much like a Wellesley girl. "If you're looking for the swankiest place around, nothing beats the Royal Hawaiian, but it'll cost you. If you want a good steak and drinks and a dance band on the patio, there's Kemoo Farm outside the city. The soldiers at Schofield like to hang out there, but it's a long drive." Noelani seemed very familiar with the island's night life.

"You and Abby decide," McReady said, "and I don't mind spending money for a good time, so if it's the Royal Hawaiian—"

Noelani's face lit up. "We'll have to dress up for that," Abby said.

McReady grinned. "Then it's a good thing I packed my dinner jacket."

That was Mac, Norris thought, always prepared for anything. Abby glanced at him as he thought guiltily of how long it had been since he had taken her out.

* * * *

The dance floor overlooking the beach outside the pink façade of the Royal Hawaiian Hotel was already crowded with dancing couples by the time they arrived. Noelani had recommended that they dine at a Chinese restaurant along the way that had good food and strong drinks at about half the price they would have paid at the Royal Hawaiian. While they ate, Mac entertained them with tales of inventive pranks he had devised as a student at M.I.T. and Norris refrained from pointing out that his old friend had a talent for exaggerating his exploits. They had all agreed that the food was the best any of them had eaten in a while, and even Norris felt his spirits lifting as they left the restaurant.

Norris slipped a bellhop a few dollars to park his sedan, the least he could do since Mac was paying for everything else, then walked toward the dance floor, his arm around Abby's shoulders. McReady, with Noelani clinging to his right arm, was still steady on his feet even after enjoying three drinks at the restaurant. A waiter approached them as they sat down at an umbrella-covered table near the dance floor.

McReady murmured an order to the waiter, who nodded and left them. On the dance floor, Norris spotted a few men in the dress uniforms of Army and Navy officers, although they were outnumbered by those in tails or white jackets. The band was playing "Dancing in the Dark" and he found himself reaching for Abby's hand. She leaned toward him and smiled and he was at peace for the first time in a while. Below them, the incoming waves, illuminated by floodlights, lapped at the edge of the beach.

The waiter returned with four glasses and a bottle of wine in a silver ice bucket. McReady handed a bill to the waiter, waved him away, and poured the wine for them.

"To good times," Mac said as he lifted his glass, "and better days ahead." His glass clinked against Noelani's before he downed the wine in one gulp, stood up, and bowed. "And may I have this dance?"

Noelani laughed as she got to her feet. "Of course." The band segued into "In the Mood" as McReady ushered Noelani to the dance floor. For such a big man, Mac was surprisingly light on his feet. He drew Noelani toward him, then swung her out as she twirled under his arm. They moved into a jitterbug, Noelani following his lead, a Polynesian princess dancing with a Scottish warrior.

Abby reached for his hand and held it. Norris suddenly wanted to pull her to him, press his face against her soft brown hair, and unburden himself of his fears. I had to battle a monster, he would tell her, an ungodly Thing, the stuff of nightmares. We were sure we defeated it but it was still after me, I kept seeing it, sensing it out there somewhere, that's how I became the way I am now, the way I've been ever since I came back, but It's over now, it has to be, I can put it behind me. Abby—

"Vance, what is it?" Her grip tightened and he realized he had said her name aloud.

He shook his head. "Nothing." Abby had never asked him about his experiences in Antarctica. All she had ever said after he had been home for a few days, reluctant to talk about anything, plagued by insomnia, unable to resume their normal routines, was that she was glad he was home, that if he ever needed to unburden himself she would be there for him, and that she loved him. He wondered if he was worthy of her compassion.

"Come on, let's dance." She tugged at his hand and smiled. He couldn't remember the last time they had danced together. Abby glanced toward the dancing couples as Mac dipped Noelani toward the floor, then caught her in one arm.

He stood up and drew her toward him, willing himself to embrace the peace he had felt earlier.

* * * *

On the way home, Norris stopped to drop Noelani off at the small house she shared with her mother and sister. While he and Abby waited in the car, McReady lingered with Noelani in the shadows outside the front door, apparently deep in conversation.

"Looks like Mac's falling in love," Abby murmured.

"If you want to call it love," he replied. She poked him in the arm and then laughed. The door to the house opened to outline the silhouette of a couple locked in an embrace. The two quickly moved apart and the door closed.

Norris got out of the car as McReady approached and waited as he climbed into the back seat. "Thanks for our night out, Mac," Abby said as Norris slipped behind the wheel. "We had a wonderful time."

"Thanks for introducing me to Noelani." McReady paused. "Asked her if she'd care to show me around the island tomorrow afternoon. That is if I can borrow your car."

"Of course," Abby said. "I've got tomorrow off."

They passed the rest of the ride home in silent contentment. Mac passed up their offer of a nightcap and Norris was ready to go to bed, feeling relaxed enough to hope that there would be no bad dreams for him that night.

* * * *

The bedroom was still dark when Norris woke up. Abby's even breathing told him that she was still asleep.

He tried to remember what he had been dreaming. An unseen presence had been following him but he could not bring himself to turn and see what it was. Now that he was awake, he realized that someone else—something else—was in the room with them.

He kept his eyes closed. If he didn't open them, if Abby didn't wake up, if he kept perfectly still, nothing would happen. Something was moving closer to him, hovering over the bed, drowning out Abby's soft inhalations with loud, heavy breaths. He heard the Thing move away and then realized it was on the other side of the bed, preparing to swallow his wife.

He cried out, screaming himself out of the nightmare. "You won't!" he shouted. "Not Abby! You can't!" A wordless cry escaped him as he sat up. "I won't let you!"

"Vance!" Abby clutched at his arm. "What is it?"

"Get away!"

She threw her arms around him, trying to restrain him. "It's all right," she whispered. "It's just a bad dream, it's all right, you're safe."

The door to the bedroom opened and a light went on overhead. McReady stood in the doorway. "What's going on?" he asked.

The bare-chested man in pajama bottoms was not McReady, not any more. He hadn't come to Hawaii just to visit an old friend, but because he knew the Thing was still out there. Mac had come here on the trail of the alien and now it had swallowed him and taken on his form.

"Vance," McReady called out. There was a red glow in the big man's eyes, the suggestion of blue tendrils in his reddish hair. Norris pushed Abby away, leaped from the bed, and lunged at McReady, who knocked him aside. He hit the wall and was suddenly lying on his back, pinned to the floor by two strong hands.

"Vance!" Norris struggled for breath. "Hang on." Norris gulped more air, then took a deep breath. He was fully awake now, outside his dream, and saw concern in the other man's eyes.

Only Mac was there, with nothing else inside him.

McReady loosened his grip and Norris sat up. They were both silent for a while. Abby watched them from the bed, her arms crossed over her chest.

"Bad dream," Norris muttered at last.

"Figured as much," McReady replied in a steady voice. "Maybe we had too much to drink last night. Think we could use some coffee." That was Mac, forming a likely hypothesis, getting the situation under control, and then finding a quick solution to the problem. Norris looked away as the other man helped him to his feet.

* * * *

Abby and McReady were out on the lanai, with breakfast, a bowl of fruit, and the coffee pot on the table, when Norris finally came out to join them. He had washed up and dressed as slowly as possible, reluctant to face them after his outburst. McReady was wearing khaki pants and a loud Hawaiian shirt while Abby had put on a white linen blouse and light blue slacks. They both looked ready for a day of taking it easy. They would be calm, pretending that his display of panic and fear was only a momentary lapse.

The greenery around them looked bluer in the early morning light. A couple of myna birds in the trees behind Mac were already cawing loudly. Abby handed them both plates of eggs and bacon, their usual Sunday breakfast. "So when are you supposed to pick up Noelani?" she said to McReady.

"Told her I'd call first. Don't want to wake her up too early." Both of them went on chattering about their plans for the day in cheerful, brittle voices as Norris picked at his food. Abby was probably already thinking about how to distract him once Mac was on his way to meet Noelani.

In the distance, Norris heard intermittent cracks that might have been gunfire. Maybe the soldiers at Hickam Field were drilling again, although the sounds were louder than usual. The cracking sounds deepened into louder booms and then, just over the trees, he glimpsed small puffs of grey smoke against the clear blue sky.

Mac slapped his plate down and jumped to his feet, then looked west. "Sounds like anti-aircraft fire to me."

Norris stood up as more clouds of smoke appeared. Abby ran from the lanai into the living room. He hurried after her as she turned on the radio.

A singing choir broke off in the middle of a hymn. "This is not a drill," an announcer's voice called out from the radio. "We're being attacked. This is not a drill."

Mac came up behind Abby. "It's started," the big man said.

The cracks and booms were growing louder. "Pearl Harbor is under attack," the announcer continued. "This is not a drill."

Abby grabbed Norris by the arm. "I have to get to the office," she said.

"The hell you do," he replied.

"Vance, I'm a reporter."

"Not a war correspondent."

"I have to cover this story."

He grabbed her by the shoulders and shook her. "And get yourself killed?"

She pulled away from him and darted past Mac to the lanai. Norris followed her outside just in time to hear an explosion from somewhere on the green hillside. The house shook as a second explosion, closer this time, tore through the air. Smoke rose from a neighborhood farther down the hill as a plane rose above the trees. Even from this distance, Norris could see the bright orange circle of the Rising Sun on one wing of the low-flying plane.

Abby ran back inside. A hand clapped down on Norris's shoulder. "Take cover," Mac muttered as he pulled him inside the house.

Abby sank onto the sofa. Norris went to her, sat down, and reached for her hand. The wall behind the radio trembled at the sound of another explosion. McReady paced the room, frowning and looking uncharacteristically agitated. He would be thinking what Norris had already concluded, that the ships in Pearl Harbor and the planes at Hickam Field were sitting ducks.

Norris said, "We might not be safe here." He felt again as though something was watching him from behind, something alien, and forced himself to ignore that feeling.

McReady stopped pacing. Another deafening blast shook the house and he crouched, as if trying to shield himself. Norris could hear another plane overhead but the sound of its engine was muffled. He let go of Abby, stood up, and moved slowly toward the lanai. As he looked outside, he saw flames leap from one of the wooden houses farther up the hillside to the shingled roof next to it.

The Japanese neighborhood where Jonny Nishimoto and his family lived was on fire.

Norris turned. "Mac, come with me. Somebody may need our help. Abby…"

"I'm coming with you," she interrupted. "I'm probably not any safer here than out there."

There was no time to argue with her. He went to the front door, opened it to see their still undamaged sedan parked outside the house, and ran down the short pathway to the car. He opened the door on the driver's side and guided Abby into the back seat as McReady got in on the other side.

The car lurched as he gunned the motor. The sound of gunfire to the west was louder and more constant. He sped up the road and swerved around a crater that was still smoking. Several adults on foot herding children were fleeing from a row of burning dwellings toward the nearby school.

"Japs," McReady muttered behind him. "They're all Japs." The big man's voice sounded unlike him, low and raspy and distinctly hostile. "How do we know they aren't aiding the enemy?"

Norris kept his eyes on the road, ignoring McReady. He braked as a woman ran across the road toward the car and recognized Jonny's mother.

"Mr. Norris!" she cried, waving her arms. Her usually confined black hair was loose around her shoulders and her eyes were wide with panic. He opened the door and got out of the car. "My husband and Jonathan, they're…" She pointed toward her house, where smoke was billowing from a side window. "They haven't come out."

He turned and raced toward the house. "Jonny!" he called out, hoping that the boy and his father were near the open front door. Footsteps pounded behind him. "Jonny!" As he skidded to a stop near a small flower garden, a big hand gripped his shoulder and spun him around.

"Vance."

He looked up at McReady's face. Mac's pale eyes were wild with fury, his face contorted into a grimace. Norris had seen that expression before, in Antarctica.

"Vance," McReady continued, "leave it alone, there's nothing you can do."

Norris pulled away. Mac's face hardened as he gazed past Norris at the burning house. "Leave it alone," Mac said, "the fire'll kill it." He was back in Antarctica, Norris realized, fighting the Thing once more.

"Hiro!" Mrs. Nishimoto screamed. Abby held the weeping woman, trying to restrain her. A few people on their way to take shelter at the school watched from the road.

Mac suddenly swung at him. Norris blocked him with one arm and punched him in the gut with the other. The big man crumpled to the ground. Lucky punch, Norris thought, and ran to the door, smelling smoke inside the house. He stumbled inside, coughing as he struggled to breathe.

"Jonny," he called out, unable to see anything in the darkness.

Somebody whimpered and then gasped. He could barely see through watery eyes stinging from the smoke. A man lay on the floor, arms out, legs pinned under what looked like a long, thick beam. Norris drew closer and saw someone smaller crouching near the trapped man.

"Dad's stuck." Norris recognized Jonny's voice. "I tried to move it but I can't."

"Are you all right?" Norris asked.

"Yes, but—"

"Then get out of here."

"But Dad—"

Norris bent down and grabbed the beam, straining against its weight. "Help me lift this." The boy gripped one corner of the beam but failed to budge it. Tears streamed down Norris's face as he managed to lift the beam just a few inches. Hanging on, he said, "Now let go and pull your dad toward you, fast." He was straining now, holding the beam up with all his strength, as Jonny dragged his father a few inches across the floor. He lost his grip then and the beam crashed to the floor, barely missing Mr. Nishimoto's extended arm.

The smoke was thicker now. Norris thought he heard a moan. He staggered toward Jonny and his father. The other man shook his head as Norris slowly pulled him to his feet, wondering how badly injured he was. With Jonny holding up his father on the right, they shuffled toward the door.

A flaming strip of wood dropped in front of them, sparks flying. Norris inhaled smoke and gasped for air. Mr. Nishimoto let out a moan and Norris struggled to hang on to him.

A large indistinct shape appeared in the doorway. Norris was suddenly lying on the floor, his head throbbing. "Jonny," he called out but heard no response. He slapped the floor with one hand, feeling how hot it was, unable to see anything through the smoke. He blinked away more tears, barely able to keep his eyes open.

Arms lifted him up. "I've got you." That was Mac's voice. The smoke and darkness disappeared and Norris abruptly found himself lying on softer ground. A breeze cooled his face. He opened his mouth and gulped air.

"The kid's okay," Mac said. "His dad, too, but I think he might have a broken leg." A sharp whistling sound interrupted him and Norris heard an explosion farther down the hill. "Now we better get out of here."

* * * *

With the Nishimotos crowded into their car, Abby drove them all to the nearby school, where the principal was offering shelter. A nurse, a young Japanese-American woman, set Mr. Nishimoto's broken leg in a splint and patched up Jonny's burns and scrapes while the rest of them rested on tatami mats in the school's gymnasium.

Others seeking refuge gradually trickled into the large room and Norris soon saw that Abby, Mac, and he were the only white people there. Mac, sitting on a mat next to him, didn't say a word about that or anything else. He had not spoken during the drive, either. Norris wanted to tell his friend that dragging him to safety had more than made up for anything the big man had said or done earlier, but kept silent.

The people around them talked of what they had seen that morning, some in Japanese and others in English. Bombs had fallen all over the city. The local drugstore and a few stores next to it were now only charred ruins. One woman had seen the bodies of a couple of children lying in the road not far from a roadside farmers' stand. Over at Hickam Field, firemen and other volunteers were bringing injured soldiers and sailors to the station hospital and to Tripler General. At least one battleship had been sunk and maybe the whole fleet was lost. Soon a couple of Army officers showed up to announce that Hawaii was now under martial law and a mandatory blackout would begin that evening.

They were at war.

* * * *

The day after the attack, Norris and Abby, along with McReady, were allowed to return to their house, still standing with no damage that he could see apart from a couple of broken windows. By then they had all heard the grim statistics. More than two thousand dead, most of them Navy personnel, although civilians were also among the casualties. The *Arizona* and the *Oklahoma* had been sunk, and other ships had suffered severe damage, while most of the military aircraft at Wheeler and Hickam Fields had been destroyed. A gruff Navy officer ordered McReady to report to Hickam Field, although it didn't seem that he would be going to the Philippines any time soon. Anyone who might be out at night, as Abby often was when getting home late from her office, would need a curfew pass, and there would be limits on what she could publish in the Star-Bulletin.

Within a week, the Royal Hawaiian Hotel was sporting a barrier of barbed wire along its beach, gas masks had been issued to all civilians, and Norris was often out with a team of men conscripted to dig more holes for makeshift bomb shelters. Abby used much of her time at her newspaper desk making calls to the mainland for friends who wanted their families to know they were safe. Mrs. Nishimoto, along with a contingent of parents from Jonny's school, had approached Norris about replacing the current science teacher, who had already decided to enlist in the Army. He told them he would think about it and found himself welcoming the offer. He realized then that days had passed without nightmares, without feeling an unseen threat lurking nearby, without the fear that the Thing was still hunting him.

* * * *

McReady stopped by on Christmas afternoon with a present of Scotch hidden in his duffel. Abby shook her head at this unexpected gift of holiday cheer. A ban on alcohol was already in effect, along with rationing, so Norris did not ask how Mac had acquired a bottle of liquor.

"Noelani wanted to be here, too," Mac said as they sat in the living room with small glasses of Scotch, "but with all the patients at the hospital, she's on double shifts." He shrugged. "I'll head over there later before curfew. Have to firm up our plans before I find out what the powers that be might have in mind for me now." He paused and looked down. "You're still on to be our witnesses, aren't you?"

"Of course," Abby said.

"Good thing Noelani's mother's taken a shine to me and doesn't mind having me for a son-in-law."

Abby finished her drink and stood up. "All we have for Christmas dinner is sandwiches, I'm afraid," she said. "Then I'll have to head over to the office and put the final touches on my holiday story before the censors do their editing." She headed toward the kitchen while Norris led his friend to the lanai.

"Peace on Earth," McReady muttered as he sat down, shaking his head. "I doubt MacArthur can hold Manila." He was silent for a while. "Don't know what got into me before."

"You don't need to explain." They both had another enemy to fight now. Maybe, like the Thing and whatever hellish evolution had produced that alien species, human beings also had their own unconscious need for an enemy to fight.

Norris looked up as an albatross circled overhead. The large white bird dipped its wings and then flew west toward the bright red sun.

THE

CHELSEA QUINN YARBRO

"Who, or what, was that?" Astrogator Calculator Carstairs asked as she watched what looked like a four-foot-in-diameter lawn-bowl roll by, The's compressed sides shining as if made of platinum or some other valuable metal. She had been assigned to the bridge when she first came aboard, and she was trying to become acquainted with the rest of the bridge crew. This was only her second assignment to a fully integrated Worm ship, and she had not yet seen the full panoply of space-going life in the Reconciliation territories; Humans were new to the Reconciliation, and to space travel by wormhole to points far beyond the solar system. Carstairs was excited and tingling with fear at once and this strange being seemed more like a machine than a life-form.

"That's The," said the Helmsman, the translator crackling the effort to convey what it had said, and with whom Carstairs worked. "You'll get used to The."

"What makes it roll?" Carstairs asked.

"According to The, gravity does," the Helmsman said. Appointment to any given space-going ship was based upon the similarity of gravity on the crew's home planet, and no matter what they might look like, all shared a narrow range of gravitational tolerance; to do otherwise would have risked severe health problems among the crew, and deep space travel was demanding enough without that.

The *Star Treader* was preparing to cast off from *Station 8, Quadrant 61,* out beyond the band of solar rubble that hung around the vast field of Terran planets, on the far side of the Ort Cloud

"You'd best pay attention to The," said the captain—at least that was what her translation unit provided by way of identifying the lawn-bowl—who was a multi-limbed creature who might have been a centaur if centaurs had started out as octopuses and crustaceans instead of horses and Humans. "We need The to find our way." One of his arms extruded from his body to emphasize what he was saying.

"So I've been told," Carstairs responded without having to admit that she could not understand the reason why she found The confusing. "In my crew manual."

"This is the first time that you've seen The?"

"Yes." It was galling to have to admit that she had only recently acquired bridge rank and on her first ship, she was limited to the Astrogator calculator, the ship's libraries, and all the rehearsal halls for information of who and what was aboard. This was the first time she had been summoned to the bridge to watch the vast amounts of supplies being loaded into the *Star Treader*. It was a formidable task, she admitted to herself, studying the Bridge Crew monitoring their various displays. They had to coordinate the stacking and boxing and sacking and bagging devoted to the optimal use of limited space on the vast ship. They also looked after the devices that would turn the basic proteins from numerous home planets into the local dishes that the every species in the crew depended upon.

"We all rely on Thes, every Worm-ship in the Reconciliation. You might want to bear that in mind," the captain recommended.

"Yes, Captain; I will." Carstairs knew from everyone on the bridge that she had not been on board the *Star Treader* for very long, that she was still under scrutiny.

"Your evaluation will be completed during this run," the captain reminded her, as if Carstairs needed reminding.

The had stopped rolling and was instead spinning in place; the not-quite-spherical being had no eyes that she could make out, yet it rolled flawlessly through the containers of supplies being put into supply cabinets that lined the walls of the bridge that were not taken up by huge screens and various navigational equipment; they were being loaded without any problems or hesitations as soon as the systems' check began. Chief G#aa kept a close eye on every one of his workers, occasionally making a sharp remark to those not working as diligently as the Chief expected them to.

A half-dozen young midshipbeings were sent off to assist in securing the holds.

"Prepare to begin loading last cargo," said the First Mate.

The emitted a sound that the translator interpreted as something like a purr.

Sachsmatk-tk, the Interior Communications Officer glanced in The's direction, and one of his-2's multitude of limbs working, his-2's massive thorax, a cartilagenous length of finger clusters and oleagenous skin glistening with effort to keep up with all the reports of loading coming into the bridge. The translation pod that hung over his-2's mouth at mid-chest, said to Carstairs, "The's observing you."

"The what?" Carstairs asked, becoming more confused.

"The is the's name, and The's pronoun," Sachsmatk-tk informed her.

"Just The?" She wondered how anyone could tell that this rolling, metallic-looking object as actually alive.

Sachsmatk-tk's translation pod crackled. "The's your superior. The is the Astrogation Unit, and we're lucky to have The."

"Why?" Carstairs could not keep from asking.

"The, like all of Thes, has a part of The's…brain that has a much more sensitive…well…sense of direction than any other space-going species we've encountered yet." Sachsmatk-tk said, and it was apparent to Carstairs that his-2 translation pod was having difficulty with the concepts. "Thes are the only species the Reconciliation has found with such abilities."

"That—excuse me—*The* does? The doesn't even have eyes."

"Not as such, no, but that ring around the slightly flattened central disk on either side of the is a locational organ that not only has a very acute sight function, it also gauges temperature and…angle. Similar to the clusters of hair on top of my back, only many times more developed." He-2 examined the implant on his-2 upper wrist. "The last of the supplies should be aboard shortly. Then we can prepare for cast-off in two standard time units. You won't be needed again until then."

As if to confirm this, a signal from the loading bay brayed through the speakers.

Carstairs consulted her coordinator, selecting the screen dedicated to her duties for the work period. "The shuttle is coming up. Give it ten ticks."

Sachsmatk-tk's translator pod made a sound that Carstairs equated to a load of metal utensils being dropped down a flight of stairs, which she knew, from her dealings with other Matk-tk-tks was similar to laughter. "You'll get used to this, Human, in time. Your species has not been space-going long, and you have not completely adjusted. We should know if you, as a single Human, can adapt to deep-space travel, by the time we're through with this voyage, or to suggest that you try to find something else you could do, rather than serve on a Worm-ship." He-2 entered a column of data onto the screen in front of him-2. "We will be departing in…let me see…two…no, three standard time-units. You'll need to be on hand for cast-off."

Feeling a bit defensive, Carstairs said, "I may be new to the Worm-group, but I can handle Matk-tk-tks like you, and Ouoanau, and Zijhree, and Hods, and even ** Tppm**, and most of the other limbed species—I just have never seen something that rolled like The does."

"Don't get your tdotks up; all of us had to learn to deal with very different species than the one we came into when we went into the Reconciliation. I needed three journey's to get used to you Humans having so many of your sensory organs in that bulbous extension on top of your torsos."

Carstairs nodded, and her translation pod expressed agreement in Sachs-matk-tk. "How many of you Matk-tk-tks will be on this ship?"

"Forty-four. I know there will be nineteen Humans, counting you. Not bad for a new member-species of the Reconciliation."

"How many Thes?" she asked before she could stop herself.

"Just the one," said Sachsmatk-tk. "More than one within a lightyear of each other, and Thes' perceptions tend to jam up."

"How?" Carstairs asked.

"No idea; my guess would be it's something vibrational," said Sachs-matk-tk replied. "Not much information about that."

"But aren't they the reason we can go through worm-holes and get where we need to be?"

"And when," Sachsmastk-tk. "Getting us to a part of space where we want to be, that is relatively easy, but to repeat arriving in the same place *when* we want to be there, and then get us back to this part of the galaxy in our own space and time, that's their talent. That's why all Worm-class ships have Thes."

"Oh," said Carstairs, which her translation pod, collared around her neck, turned into a sort of hum for Sachsmatk-tk. She decided she would use her information Access to learn more about Thes when her watch was done and she had time to concentrate on something other than astrogation, when there were fewer distractions. "Do you need me before then?"

"Not here." He-2 looked toward the captain. "The Astrogator Calculator would like the opportunity to rest for a while. Her watch is almost up, and you won't need her until cast-off. Want to let her have a little down-time? She looks like she needs it."

A whoop warned the crew of the Worm-559#V *Star Treader* that the final shuttle was approaching, and Sachsmatk-tk moved away to his-2 place to record the last of the crew coming aboard, while the Organization Crew got ready for the last round of supplies.

The continued to spin in place.

* * * *

Being a Bridge Officer, Carstairs had been allocated her own cabin on the Ninth Forward Unit of the ship, so that she would be near to the bridge itself. The room was one-and-a-half times her height wide, twice her height long, and one-and-a-third times her height tall; generous space for a Worm-ship. There was a cleaning unit that opened up from the wall opposite the door, which not only provided her cleaning facilities for her clothes and cabin, but for her body as well. In addition, the room had a display in the ceiling that revealed all that was happening outside the ship, as well as enabling Carstairs to access all the informational material available to the crew. She let herself in with a blink of her eyes, closed the door, and went to her bunk, dropping down onto it with a sense of gratitude for the rest mixed with a hint of bewilderment. Why should The be interested in her? What capacity did it have that made it possible for The to astrogate in time and space? What sense did The have to be able to astrogate a Worm ship, and how did it work? She tapped the information Access in her right forearm, and said "Thes" to the air, and waited for the Access to respond.

A dizzying array flashed on the ceiling over her bed, with a formidable mix of languages, images, and narration, a combination that was truly overwhelming.

Carstairs coughed, and said, "Purposes aboard Worm-class starships."

The display began to sort itself out, the chaos of the information resolving into clusters of potential topics, the one at the top if the clusters labeled *The, Humankind, and Astrogation,* in which Carstairs found this disquieting paragraph:

> Attempts to study Thes' remarkable sense of direction have thus far been inconclusive, but current theories include either a keen sense of direction or hearing or perhaps some combination of the two which enables Thes to perceive the nature of space/time in a way that may be unique to them.

Carstairs sighed and began to make her way through the first articles in the file, which described the first contact between Humans and the Reconciliation, and what the first treaties had proposed for the first century of interaction. It was filled with comments and descriptions that Carstairs had studied in school, and so she was tempted to skim over the information she thought she knew, but then made herself peruse more closely, for her ninth-level studies mentor had warned about being careful about things you thought you knew.

"Origins of Thes," Carstairs asked the ceiling.

"Unknown," came the answer, along with a flurry of citation.

"Reasons for Thes' astrogational talents?"

"Unknown."

"Do they have a home planet, or location?"

"Unknown."

"What benefits them and what does not?" Carstairs felt she was running out of questions.

"Unknown."

"What about reproduction?" Carstairs sighed. "Unknown as well. Never mind." She lay back and stared at the ceiling, hoping for some insight, which eluded her. The one question that stuck in her mind was why Thes had not been discussed during her training, since, as an astrogator, Carstairs was required to work with one?

About forty minutes later, she dimmed the display on the ceiling and reached for her English horn case, the one at the top of the shelf, above the oboe, the shawm, and the bassoon below it, and took the very old instrument out, pausing to inspect the double-reeds in the mouthpiece. The Humans aboard the *Star Treader,* as part of their duties as members of the ship, which required all species in the crew to practice a native art as well as attend to the duties of their official positions, had founded a chamber music group, and rehearsal was scheduled in little more than an hour. They were to present a concert in ten days. Tonight, it was to be the Kyses who would be the first to present what Carstairs' translator had called a folkdance. She slipped the mouthpiece between her lips and licked the reeds until they were softened, and then began to play, the plaintive voice of the English horn reflected her mood, and she continued to play with more engagement, searching for the music in the notes, concentrating on the melodic line like the sense of a conversation; music provided context for Carstairs in a way that few other things could, and just at present, she felt an intense dislocation that she had not experienced since childhood.

* * * *

A little while later, there was a signal from the door that someone wanted to be admitted. Carstairs reluctantly set her English horn aside and looked to the door display to see who it was. To her astonishment, The was waiting for the door to open.

A voice sounded in her translator, so mechanical and strange that she had trouble comprehending what was being said. "What is the source of those vibrations?"

"That," she said, pointing to the English horn, adding, "It makes the vibrations."

"What is it?" The asked.

Carstairs sighed again and signaled the door to open. "It's an antique musical instrument from Terra, my home planet," she explained as she sat up and did what she could to make The feel welcome, much as she would have done had she been back on Terra instead of bound for a worm-hole that would take her half way across the galaxy.

The rolled into the exact center of the chamber and stopped. "Tell me more," The said. "This sound is unknown to me."

"It is what is called a woodwind," she offered.

"What is a woodwind?" The asked.

Carstairs decided to begin with the basics. "This instrument is called an English horn, although it's neither English nor a horn; it's this bend here"— she pointed to the bend—"that gives it the name, which actually means the bent horn."

"How does it make sound?" The asked.

"I blow through this mouthpiece, getting the double reeds to vibrate, and then I use these stops to change the pitch." She could not decide if this was what The wanted to know, but she struggled on gamely. "It's had a long and positive history in Western music."

"Can you make it give sound now?"

"Certainly," Carstaris said, wanting to do whatever she could to learn more about The. "Just one note, or sever al?"

"One first, then several," The told her, moving near. "Do not rush production of the vibrations. I want to…appreciate them."

"All right." Carstairs set the double-reed mouthpiece in place on her upper and lower lip, and chose E as her note. The sound filled her room, more loudly than it had earlier.

"Now more," said The, rolling back and forth as if rocking, but if in delight or agony, Carstairs could not tell.

Carstairs thought about what to play, and settled on a passage from *The Nutcracker*, which was easy to play and easily understood for many species. At the conclusion of the excerpt, she took the reeds out of her mouth. "That's the sound."

"A fairly small range of vibrations," said The; whether this was positive or negative to The was undetermined.

"Most wind instruments are like that," Carstairs agreed. "That's part of why there are so many of them."

"How many?"

"Probably many hundreds," said Carstairs, "if you include the folk instruments, many thousands. They're very old in our species; only drums are older." She wondered how much of what she said made sense to The, and waited for more questions.

"What do you call the vibration variations?"

"Pitch," she said, and regretted it, for The was turning around slowly. She decided to try to elaborate. "The instrument has a range of vibrational increments, which musicians call pitch. In order to produce a pleasant sound, all the instruments have to agree on the...vibrational increments, or the results are not pleasing."

"Do all Humans hear pitch?" The increased The's slow spin, turning first to the left and then to the right.

"Most of them, but not all. Why?" This was an unexpected turn in The's inquiry, and Carstairs could not quite figure out what it was that The wanted to know. "There are Humans who have no perception of these vibrations, or very limited oens, and there are those who lose the capacity to hear...perceive them, through accident or age or disease."

The made a noise not unlike a minor explosion in an echoing room.

"Does that trouble you?" Carstairs asked after a long moment.

"It perturbs me," said The. "It confuses me. It stimulates my balance."

"Why?" She wondered if this was going too far, but reminded herself on the regulations about overly inquisitive inquiry.

"I have no words that can tell you, nor would I if I could," The answered, and abruptly left the room.

* * * *

Rehearsal went well enough, but Carstairs was strangely dissatisfied with her own playing, and could not keep her mind on the Bach transcription of keyboard music they were working on. She decided that The's visit to her quarters had something to do with it, but found herself annoyed that such an event could discompose her.

At the end of rehearsal, she returned to the bridge to take over for the Master Astrogator—a burley, bustard-like N'Bsao hybrid with four sets of eyes that protruded along what Carstairs supposed to be its spine—and to plot in the next eight standard time-units of the voyage before going for the last meal of the day. She did her calculations, coordinated them with the Star Treader's current speed and any potential drift, and was about to engage them when she had a moment of light-headedness, as if she had just lost her balance. She cancelled her calculations and started again from the beginning, telling herself that she was being overly cautious, but better to be sure than sorry, as her grandmother used to tell her. She worked steadily, taking time to analyze everything she did, and worked out any irregularity she found, knowing that she would be late to dinner, but her work would bear the scrutiny of anyone aboard.

* * * *

By the time she had entered her new calculations, she was exhausted and famished; she headed for the Humans' mess, trying to shake that uneasy sensation that lingered. For once she had the place almost to herself, and that pleased her; she did not yearn for Human company and conversation, not with this feeling of disquiet taking hold of her. Was there something wrong with the ship's gravitational field? she wondered as she dialed in her selection for the meal and waited for it to appear on the table. She was slightly groggy when her food arrived, but she determined to eat so that she could put an end to the way she was feeling. The food tasted slightly odd, but not unpleasant, and the basic protein slurry from which all Human food was made did occasionally try a new approach to a familiar dish.

It was almost a standard time unit later that she left the Human mess and returned to her quarters, her senses calmed somewhat and were more of what she was used to. On coming aboard, all the Humans were warned about potential reactions to the gravity and air circulation, and to report it to the Medical Crew if they became disruptive; she decided to chalk this up to such an event, and to report it to the Medical Crew if she had not improved in the morning. Entering her chambers, she took a while to bathe in the chemical solution that cleaned, moisturized, and kneaded her skin—a process that often offered her still more tranquility—but tonight that eluded her, and she felt consumed by twitches.

"Overtired," she said to the air, and resigned herself to fidgety sleep, telling herself that she should take the sleeping solution before getting into her bunk for the night, but in the end, gave it up as an over-reaction, then spent almost half the night in restless dozing.

* * * *

For the next day, Carstairs went about fulfilling her duties with dogged determination but relatively little enthusiasm, which she chalked up to a poor night's rest. Her calculations were meticulous, her rehearsal went with precision, and there was no repetition of the peculiar lapse in balance that had plagued her yesterday. Once again, she told herself, the load-in had been more gravitationally upsetting than she had realized, which accounted for the strange sensations. She entered a report to the Medical Crew and hoped that was the end of it.

She did not encounter The throughout the whole of the day, for The was not on the bridge when she was on duty—which she was told was not unusual for The—and when she went to her quarters, she slept peacefully.

* * * *

On the fourth day out, Carstairs was called early to fill in for the N'Bsao, who was observing some sort of religious ritual and could not operate the Astrogational Calculator, so Carstairs did not get to practice her English horn, an exercise that usually got her morning off pleasantly; she arrived on the bridge to find The rolling in a figure-eight pattern in the center of the astrogational equipment.

"It is necessary to correct course by two-point-four degrees upward and one-point-one degrees toward galactic center; I have the coordinates ready to present," The's translator announced.

The Helmsman—this morning it was the multi-finned and ridged Ksy who had been among the folkdancers the first night out; now it handled all the instruments with an array limbs—did a number of rapid calculations and the ship responded in a way that was impossible to detect, although the images on the display screens changed ever so slightly. "Course correction complete. Verify, Astrogator Calculator," the Ksy announced, and Carstairs responded promptly that her astrogation equipment confirmed the turn as executed.

The captain was not on the bridge at the moment, but was due shortly. The First Mate was handling the bridge with its usual pragmatic aplomb, using its highly developed sense of touch to maintain an awareness of the functioning of the various sectors of the *Star Treader*. It was always a pleasure to watch it work; it was embedded in a number of instruments, and functioned by shifting parts of its complex body.

The came to a halt near Carstairs, and made a sound like a clarinet with a faulty reed, then said, "That was well done."

"Thank you," Carstairs said automatically, puzzled by the compliment, if it was a compliment.

"You have a sense of the movement," The told her.

Carstairs tried to hide her surprise. "What do you mean by that?"

"That you understand the movement you measure," said The, as if this were obvious.

"Hey, Carstairs," the First Mate called out through the translator, sounding agrieved. "Keep your mind on your displays. We have to recalculate for drift in a few ticks."

"Right," she said promptly, and added to The, "Sorry. Got to tend to this."

"Naturally," said The, and rolled away.

"I think The likes you," said the Helmsman.

"Do you?" Carstairs said, feigning indifference.

"The pays attention to you," the Ksy added.

"That doesn't mean that The likes me, only that The is curious. The's more curious about the music I play than The is in me." Carstairs had an instant of alarm at the idea that something so alien as The might like her, for she had no idea of how that would manifest itself. She redoubled her calculations, wanting to be sure that she had performed the verification faultlessly.

"Still, The's perplexing, isn't The?" the Ksy remarked in a tone that the translator presented as cynical in delivery.

Carstairs did not dignify that possible slight with an answer; she continued to run her course calculations without further comment.

The First Mate settled down to analyze their speed in relation to the remote systems out in this spiral arm, and order on the bridge was restored.

The left the bridge without explaining anything about The's unusual behavior.

* * * *

Jule Lui, the Midship Coordinator among the Humans who served as their musical leader, stopped Carstairs in mid-passage on her oboe. "Your intonation is odd." They were in one of the practice rooms provided to the musicians, and Carstairs was working on her solo for their concert. "So what's the matter?"

Carstairs took her oboe from her mouth, looked at Lui, and shrugged. "I thought it was okay—not great, but okay."

"But where's that faint overtone coming from?" Lui asked patiently.

This question nonplused Carstairs. "What faint overtone?"

"That octave-and-five above your pitch," said Lui, whistling the note for demonstration. "Don't you hear it?"

Carstairs held back a sharp retort, and answered candidly, "No, I don't."

Lui frowned. "Well, I can, and I think it's intrusive. Is there something wrong with your reeds, or any other part of your mouthpiece?"

"Not that I know of," Carstairs said, trying not to leap to her own defense. "The reeds are vibrating properly."

"I find that hard to believe," said Lui. "You have perfect pitch, and that overtone ought to stick out like a white rat in a coal scuttle."

Carstairs knew that when Lui resorted to old-time expressions that he was attempting to keep his temper, so she thought about her response before she gave it. "Well, I still didn't hear it."

"Are you okay? Do you need to have an ear exam?"

"It's possible," she allowed; ears were associated with balance, and she had had those minor disruptions in balance.

After an exasperated silence, Lui said, "Tell you what—we'll knock off for now, and you can get checked out for hearing. And we'll meet again to-morrow and have another run at this."

Carstairs knew that Lui was being sensible; little as she liked the pros-pect, she was aware that it was a pragmatic approach. "All right. I'll get my ears tested, and I'll go over the oboe. And I'll play the English horn for a while to see if the overtone is present in that instrument, too; it might have to do with some resonance in the ship, and perhaps it varies from person to person." As an improvisation, this was skimpy, but it was better than nothing, Carstairs told herself as she stood up and reached for her instrument case.

"Let me know what you find out about your ears," Lui said as he went to the door.

"As soon as I have a report, so will you," she promised as she removed the mouthpiece from the oboe and put it in its own little compartment in the case, then wiped off the oboe with a cloth and set both in their own position in the case. All the while, she tried to keep her sudden worry at bay, but was not doing it very well. With a cough that was partly a sigh, she left the practice room and began the walk toward the medical suite that served Humans and the Broket population on the *Star Treader*—among them, the cephaloid centaur who captained the ship—doing her best to quiet the dismay that had awakened within her. What would happen to this assignment if she was not allowed to continue play in the musical consort? Would she have to leave the ship? The idea was as repulsive as it was frightening, and it dogged her thoughts all the way to the medical suite.

* * * *

Two of the audiological assessment machines went to work on Carstairs at once, sending all kinds of tones, pitches, and sounds to test what she could hear properly for a Human, at the end of which, the technician who supervised the testing informed her that there was no discernable reason for her failure to detect the sound that Lui had claimed he heard, a report that was relayed to Lui when Carstairs left the suite to return to her quarters.

"Maybe it has something to do with the air pressure," she said as she lay back in her bunk, determined to come up with an acceptable explanation for this most uncharacteristic lapse in her musicianship. The steady sound of her own voice lent her a little relief from the nameless vexations that had been marshaling within her.

She was almost dozing when the speaker in the ceiling informed her that she was needed on the bridge at once. Telling herself this was a welcome diversion, Carstairs got up, checked the room for any other messages, then hied herself to the bridge, doing her best not to worry about why the captain required her presence.

The captain met her just outside the bridge, his array of tentacles moving far more than usual. "Carstairs."

"Sir," she said and saluted.

"We're having a bit of a problem with your equipment. It's going to have to be sent down to tech. In the meantime, you'll have to use the backup Astrogator Calculator. It's a newer model, and we don't know how familiar you are with the most recent models."

Carstairs did her best not to bristle. "I did my training on the last decade of machines, and on three of the most up-to-date prototypes for new ones. I think I ought to be able to handle whatever you have aboard."

"I do hope so," the captain's translator said. "But just to be certain, I'd like you to come and start work on it as soon as it's up and running. I'll have the speaker summon you."

"Of course," said Carstairs, while she wondered why he had to summon her to discuss this rather than use the communicator on her arm, or the speakers in her cabin.

"The thing is," the captain went on cautiously, "the problem may have a more pragmatic origin."

"And that is—?"

"Security thinks it might be deliberate sabotage, a way to throw us off course in small increments, so it would be difficult to detect until we are a long way from where we want to be. I'm waiting for their official report." The captain's tentacles writhed with emotion.

"Is that likely?" Carstairs asked, appalled.

"Security seems to think it's possible."

"Then I suppose you have to be especially careful with the new Astrogator Calculator as well as the old." For a long moment, Carstairs felt a cold lump settle into her chest.

"Security is planning for that," said the captain.

"Good," Carstairs said before she realized she was speaking aloud, not silently thinking. To cover her embarrassment, she went on, "What does The think about this?"

"I don't know," the captain admitted, an expression settling over his malleable upper side that Carstairs took for a frown. "Why do you ask?"

"The seems very much in tune with Astrogators, and Astrogator Calculators, given how The works aboard the ship. and might know if this is sabotage or something more…ordinary." She closed her mouth so as not to be tempted to speak out-of-turn again.

"That's interesting," the captain said in a rumbling tone. "I'll check with Security and ask them. For now, I have to tell you that you do not speak of this to anyone."

"Yes, sir," said Carstairs.

"And for now, return to your quarters and stay there until I order you to the bridge. Do not mention that you have been here."

Carstairs was nonplussed. "Don't you want me to start now? I'm ready to do what I can to—"

"Not yet," he said, much to Carstair's mystification. "I want you aware of what we're searching for, so that you will not blurt out any irregularity you discover. For now, I want you discussing this potential trouble with no one but me. So back to your quarters for now. You may order your food from there, if you're still in the room when the mess begins." And with that, the captain made a gesture of dismissal, turned away, and returned to the bridge.

Carstairs stood quite still for almost six ticks, trying to decide what she thought about what had just happened, but when she admitted that she was baffled, she went down to her quarters and tried to ease her increasing apprehension by practicing her bassoon, taking a degree of comfort from it lugubrious tones.

* * * *

For the next few days, Carstairs spent many extra hours on the bridge trying to help the Security detail search for any sign's of sabotage, but when nothing could be found, she was given an extra day to work on her music, in appreciation of her efforts. With a surge of joy, Carstairs made up her mind to make the most of the opportunity, and set out to practice for the consort's coming recital.

So it was that Risshima Patma, the principal double-bass player, who was also the best soprano in the chamber consort, was in a practice room with Carstairs, working on the very old Mozart *Laudate Domino*, trying to deal with the very long breaths that the piece required of them both, and finding it difficult. They ended up making four false starts before deciding that they would need a different approach to the opening phrases.

Patma stopped in the middle of the *omnes gentes*, shaking her head. "I have to get a breath before the *laudate eius* and *omnes populi*." She was one of the Environmental Monitors, who dealt with everything from the air and gravity of the ship to the psychological state of the crew. "How do you manage your breath, Carstairs?"

Carstairs shrugged. "I have reeds to contend with, and I suspect that makes a difference."

"But you're doing better than I am," Patma declared, then shook her head. "That sounds as if I'm competing with you, but I'm not. I'm surprised that I'm having trouble with the breathing. This piece is a really demanding one, but I don't usually have to struggle with the phrasing." She gave a single laugh. "At least we're not doing the last of the work."

"At least," Carstairs agreed. "Let's take a break. I'm working myself up for no good reason. We'll go along to the Humans Canteen for a cup of something hot, and see what we can work out."

"I feel like that's giving up," Patma said. "But I do need a break."

"Fine with me," said Carstairs, setting her bassoon into its stand after removing the mouthpiece and putting it in a small cup of ordinary water. "I'll do the reserve on this room, so we can come back later."

"Thanks," said Patma, and held the door open for them both.

As they made their way along to the Humans Canteen, Carstairs decided to take a chance and asked Patma, "Have you run into The yet?"

"Not really; I've seen The once or twice, but that's about it." Patma slowed down a bit. "Why do you ask?"

"Well, something about my playing seems to have caught The's attention. I'm trying to figure out why, and what—if anything—it means."

Patma shook her head. "I can't help you there. The is the only individual aboard who does not come to us Environentals for evaluations."

"Why not?" Carstairs asked.

"I don't know." Patma frowned. "I can ask, if you like."

"Don't go out of your way, but if it comes up, go ahead."

They had reached the Canteen door, and as they went into the place where the Humans gathered—a room with chairs and couches and tables with a service area at the far end where food and drink could be had—and made for a pair of comfortable chairs next to the service area. The nine other Humans in the room paid them little notice beyond friendly waves, and that allowed Carstairs and Patma to have a little privacy. There were half-a-dozen Brokets at the other end of the room engaged in what looked to Carstairs like a complicated board game; they paid no attention to the Humans.

"Since you're asking about The," Patma said after claiming a large cup of spiced tea with milk, "is there anything that you want to know about Thes in general?"

"Not especially. I already read up on Thes; the most I learned is that there's very little known about them." Carstairs got up to claim her serving of chicken-flavored salad and a cup of Italian coffee. When she sat down again, she and Patma devoted themselves to struggling with the Mozart, and for the time being, The was forgotten.

* * * *

But two days later, the captain called Carstairs to his office, and said to her, "You've got to keep quiet about what I'm going to tell you. Swear to me that you'll do as I order. What I have to tell you must be in total confidence, with an official seal on it."

Carstairs held up her right hand. "I swear," she pledged as her thoughts filled with alarm.

The captain motioned to Carstairs to sit, and then said nothing; Carstairs' fears increased dramatically, but she remained silent.

Finally the captain did the Broket equivalent of a cough and his translator began. "We've been going over the calculations that you and the other Bridge

Crew members have been reviewing, and I'm seriously concerned that we're a long way off-course. Our Astrogators do not line up with our outside scanners. Therefore, I'm going to need you to work with the Helmsman to try to correct this. We're out of alignment with the worm-hole, and that is extremely dangerous."

"Can't you use The to work that out? Doesn't The have the best sense of direction of any species aboard? Isn't that why The is on the ship?—to keep things like this from happening?" Carstairs asked, the anxiety she had done her best to keep at bay returning in double force.

"No to the first, yes to the second and third." The captain struggled to rise from his hammock-like chair. "The trouble is, some of the Bridge Crew are worried that The may be the source of the drift, and that means, we may not be able to go into the worm-hole safely. I don't like to think what would happen to the *Star Treader* if that happened."

Carstairs nodded, trying to discover when she was supposed to do these new calculations with the Helmsman. "I gather this is urgent as well as secret?"

"True enough," said the captain in a lowered voice. "More urgent than I thought at first."

Carstairs thought this over, then asked, "Why me? I understand about the Helmsman, but you have four other Astrogator Calculators you could call upon; I'm new aboard, and the others aren't." She almost held her breath as she waited for the captain's answer.

"For one thing, you haven't had the opportunity to fully acculturate to this ship yet, which means most of your alliances are with other Humans, and the ones with other species are still developing. Unless one of your species is the cause of this—which I doubt—you are going to be more willing to report accurately what you discover. You can act with independence and implicit loyalty to the ship, which is why I've put so much in your hands."

Carstairs could not come up with a response; she nodded, hoping that was enough.

The captain took her silence with respect. "There are a few among the S'sve aboard who may be allied with a splinter group in their home-system, and Security has been watching them, but I can't imagine why they should want to put eight hundred twenty-nine living beings and sentient machines aboard at such risk. You Humans are new to the Reconciliation, and have no history of multi-species political or economic or religious or territorial disputes as many of the rest of us have. For the time being, I ask you to help me."

"Of course, sir," said Carstairs, not entirely certain how to take this distinction. "Tell me how you want me to handle myself."

The captain hesitated. "As much as you can, maintain your usual schedules of duties; you may continue rehearsing and playing, but then, I will arrange for Security to place a small Astrogator Calculator in your quarters in a locked cabinet, and I ask you to scan every Astrogational calculation from the bridge that will be routed to your machine, and make note of any irregularity when it occurs and how far off it is from the Helmsman's records. I will ask you to give me a daily tabulation of any and all abnormalities you might find, no matter how small."

"That's a tall order, sir," said Carstairs.

"Agreed, but you're the one it falls to," said the captain.

"When is Security going to install this Astrogator Calculator?"

"It should be in place by the time you go back to your quarters," the captain said, offering Carstairs a glowing skin-insert. "Here's your key. Touch the lock with your thumb and this will open and afterward lock it for you."

Carstairs felt the skin-insert settle in beneath the base of her thumb, wondering as it did if it would affect her playing. "Is there anything else, sir?"

"Begin your calculations tonight after mess, and say nothing to anyone about this."

"Yes, sir," Carstaris responded with a salute.

"Then go down to your quarters and await my signal. I'll want to discuss your findings with you in a day or so. Dismissed."

Carstairs repeated her salute and left the captain alone with his musing.

* * * *

The Astrogator Calculator was half the size of the one on the bridge but so densely packed with toggles and displays that it was harder to use than the one on the bridge. Carstairs had rarely had trouble with vision, but after five standard time units on the small Astrogator Calculator, her eyes were sore and she felt as if she had been working for double the length of time that she had. She sent a record of the work she had done to the captain, put the Astrogator Calculator on sleep mode, closed up and locked its cabinet, and returned it to the port in the wall where Security had concealed it, which was on the underside of Carstairs' bunk.

For a standard time unit, she lay in her bunk, resting uneasily as if the Astrogator Calculator was commanding her attention even in sleep mode, but as fatigue caught up with her, she continued to will herself to sleep. After no more than four standard time units, she wakened with a start, and could return to sleep, so she sat up and took out her shawm, a very ancient double-reed instrument with a very temperamental mouthpiece. She played on it for a considerable time, then, truly worn out at last, she put the centuries-old instrument back in its case and gave herself over to slumber.

* * * *

Patma and Lui were waiting for her when she went to rehearsal the following morning. "Let's try the Mozart again, shall we? The *Vespri Confessore*. The breathing is too critical to get it wrong," said Lui to the women.

"No argument," said Patma.

"Agreed," said Carstairs.

Lui stared up at the ceiling. "Too bad our chorus isn't available. We'll need to rehearse their part shortly."

"The chorus is on duty," said Patma. "Perhaps after mid-day, we can arrange something."

Since most of the instrumentalists did double-duty as chorus, without the full consort, it would be impossible to perform the piece lacking a full complement of nineteen, and they all knew it.

Lui made an impatient gesture. "Well, let's make the most of the time we have, shall we?"

Carstairs had already moistened the mouthpiece and assembled her bassoon, and so she said, "Ready when you are."

"Very funny," said Lui.

Carstairs did not know what old-time saying Lui was referring to, but she manage to offer a quick grin, knowing that whatever Lui intended, he expected his witticism to be appreciated. She drew up a chair, turned on the music stand and tapped on the page of notes she was to play.

Patma did the same with her music stand, making sure that the light level was strong enough to show the marks she had made on the score.

"Err on the side adagio," said Lui as he adjusted his music stand and picked up his violin. "From the top. On four."

The first run-through went awkwardly, with occasional mistakes or loss of breath, but over six more repeats, the work improved significantly, and as Lui and Carstairs set their instruments aside and Patma turned off her music stand, they all felt that they had made real progress.

"Do you have duty tonight?" Lui asked Carstairs as she packed up the bassoon.

"Sorry, yes," she answered, remembering the Astrogator Calculator in her cabin. "But I'm off until afternoon tomorrow. If the rest of us are free, I can give you two standard time units without interruption."

"That could work," said Patma. "I have a busy morning, too. I don't know about the rest of us."

"I'll send a memo to them and see if we can manage another rehearsal in the next two days, in the smaller rehearsal hall, so we can all get the feel of it. We're not yet up to snuff, but we're getting there." Lui had wiped off his violin and was settling it into its case. "I'll let you know what we all decide before breakfast."

"Thanks," said Carstairs, for the first time having difficulties about the mission the captain had assigned to her. She had sworn to assist him, but her commitment to the consort was older than her promise to the captain. Perhaps she would have to speak to him about this unanticipated conflict, but not until she was certain that one existed.

* * * *

As Patma and Carstairs were leaving the smaller rehearsal hall, without warning The came rolling toward them. "Humans," The said as he grew near.

"Hello, The," said Carstairs, feeling almost clumsy in The's presence.

Patma looked around as if seeking a way to leave. "I'm one of the Environmentalists," she said, giving up escape for the time being.

"The vibrations you produced are hard to comprehend," The said, its translator sounding alarmed with this statement. "I have not been able to process them."

"They're not intended to be processed," said Carstairs quietly. "It is intended to provide entertainment. The piece was over five hundred Terra years old."

"What is entertainment?" The inquired.

"Some kind of presentation that provides pleasure or amusement or insight or inspiration," Carstairs attempted to explain. "Like the dancing and recitations the other species aboard offer to the rest of us."

"I don't understand," said The.

"I'm sorry you don't. This work we're rehearsing has been entertaining and inspiring Humans for centuries." Carstairs said, and Patma nodded.

"That's not ancient as Thes reckon time," said The, and rolled on past them to the door, spun around once, then left them.

"What do you make of that?" Patma asked Carstairs once The was out of sight.

"I don't know. The befuddles me." She turned toward her quarters. "I think we're getting the hang of the work, at long last. I'm glad that Lui was able to postpone our performance. We'll have a better concert with the consort," she added, wanting to convince herself.

"Now you sound like Lui," Patma said, turning down the opposite corridor and waving as she went.

* * * *

On the fifthteenth morning out, the captain summoned Carstairs to his quarters, his face clouded with dismay. "Sit down, Astrogator Calculator," he said before she had saluted.

Surprised by this unexpected courtesy, Carstairs did. "What's happened, sir?" she asked.

The captain gave the equivalent of a sigh. "I've been going over your calculations and I'm not liking what I see." The translator could not provide the tone of his voice, but his posture and lack of extruding tentacles told Carstairs that he was deeply fretful. "It is not the quality of your calculations, but what they reveal," he added.

"I find that disquieting, sir," she said, trying to remain calm.

"If you're correct, the implications are...terrifying," the captain told her. "I cannot review what you've provided without trepidation."

"Nor can I, sir," she said, a mixture of relief and dejection going through her.

The captain said nothing more for several ticks, then exclaimed, "We're seriously off-course, if you're right."

"That's what it looks like to me," Carstairs admitted. "Have you talked to The about it?"

"Not yet. I don't want to make The think that there's something this bad happening if The can't fix it. But it troubles me that The has issued no warning about the course drift." The captain paused once more. 'The hasn't said anything about our course in the last four days; I don't know why, but when I saw your last report, I began to feel distressed."

"What can be the cause?" she asked, a tightness developing in her chest. "And why wouldn't The report it?"

Three of the captain's extruded tentacles made a gesture of helplessness. "I've never known a The to behave like this. Humans are new to Worm-class ships, but if you were a problem, The would have reported it. There's an outbreak of fever among the Kyses, but the Medical Crew is addressing it, and I doubt that The can catch a disease from another species, let alone one that would interfere with The's sense of direction. We'll have to use second-rank Helmsmen for the time being, until the Kyses recover. I've been trying to think what else might have happened to The, and if it isn't The that's making this happen, then what else in the ship might be responsible for all this drift. Because it must be The or the ship that's keeping us off-course." He shifted in his hammock, his skin going from light mauve to dark blue, a sure sign of suffering. "I don't like to send for The, but I fear that I'm going to have to, and to ask The if there's any way we can get back on course."

In spite of her best intentions, Carstairs asked, "And if we can't correct course, what then?"

"I don't know," the captain said, and repeated, "I don't know." He withdrew all but one of his largest tentacles and said, "We have eighteen species aboard this ship—including you Humans—and every one of us are in danger." The captain changed color to a bilious green, and his array of eyes took on a distant look.

"That's what I was thinking," Carstairs said blankly, horrified at the possibilities that loomed in her mind.

The captain made a strange sound, one that Carstairs had never heard him utter before. Finally he went silent, and then his translator sputtered into life. "Perhaps the sentient monitors that run the ship are aware of this, but I do not have the coordinates to rectify the error on my own. We need The for that."

"But correcting the monitors is The's function, isn't it?" Carstairs felt the knot tighten in her chest again, stronger than before.

"It all comes back to The," the captain said heavily.

Cartstairs did her best to swallow her rising dread. "How can we find out about whatever is causing The not to do The's job?"

"Don't know," the captain said as if it were a mantra. "I'm deeply concerned."

Both Carstairs and the captain went silent, each of them caught up in hideous contemplation.

"I'll send a message to The," the captain said. "It won't be pleasant, but I need to address the problems before they get any worse."

"What about one of the Empathizers in the Environmental Staff?" Carstairs asked. "Can one of them find a way to determine what The is doing, and why The's doing it? That is, if The is doing anything?" This last afterthought was more pro forma than any real hope.

"It might be worth a try," the captain said dispiritedly.

Another hush settled over the two.

"I want you on the bridge in the afternoon, at your usual time," the captain said suddenly. "I'll speak with one of the Empathizers before then, and determine how this is to be handled."

"What about the crew?" Carstairs inquired cautiously. "Do they have to know what's going on?"

"If we can't get this dealt with without the situation getting out among the crew, then I'll have to inform everyone, but otherwise, we have to keep it secret, for the good of the entire ship." He faltered. "If morale breaks down, there is a risk of a breakdown in Reconciliation rules."

Carstairs blinked in astonishment. "Is that among your Reconciliation experience? A breakdown of Reconciliation rules?"

"Yes," said the captain. "It is. And the consequences were not at all congratulatory. It nearly ended my captaincy." With that, he made a motion with his one extruded tentacle and sank back in his hammock-chair, and did not watch Carstairs salute and leave his quarters.

* * * *

The Empathizer that Patma brought to Carstairs' quarters was a tall, soft-scaled creature, sloe-eyed and graceful as a willow. The Empathizer had to bend down its long neck in order to fit in the room. "I am S'sve," its translator announced as it found a place to sit on the floor.

"It's name is Ooo-thooo," Patma explained to Carstairs in a musical yodel.

"Ooo-thooo?" Carstairs asked, trying to duplicate the pitches precisely.

Patma said, "Flat the G a little."

Carstairs repeated the name with a quarter-tone flattened.

"Good enough," the S'sve translator siad. "I'm told you have some questions about The?"

"I don't know if you can answer them, or if you're ethically allowed to, but I've noticed The behaving...strangely. Ever since I came on board, it seems that I've drawn a lot of attention from The. Most of the time The has questions about the music we—" She broke off. "At least, the music I play. I don't know whether The likes it or dislikes it, but something about the music seems to affect The in an unusual way, to irritate or bother The, and I would like to know what the music does to The, so I can change my behavior and give The a chance to be able to deal with it, if that's possible." Carstairs ended on a slight sigh, knowing there was no turning back from this request, which she was making without first alerting the captain.

"An interesting problem, no doubt the reason for the anguish the captain is feeling," Ooo-thooo's translator warbled. "I will try to find the nexus of emotion that has created this situation."

"I would appreciate it if you would keep what you discover to yourself, and inform me alone," Carstairs told the S'sve.

"Patma let me know of your request, and so long as doing so does not violate any of my ethical requirements, I will give you my word to do as you ask," the translator wandered over three octaves of trills and cadenzas to provide Ooo-Thooo's response.

"That's good enough for me," said Carstairs, hoping fervently that it was.

The Empathizer tucked two sets of legs under it and leaned back a little, its breath whistling softly. "I believe I can do as you ask," it said nine tics later.

"Good enough," Carstairs repeated.

"I perceive that you are concerned for the safety of this ship and all who travel on her," the S'sve went on. "It is for that reason that I consent to this work; if you asked for personal gain or advantage, I would not have agreed to do this," the translator continued accompanied by quavers and whistles.

"Understood," said Carstairs.

Patma found a place on Carstairs' bunk to sit, and settled into it.

"I must concentrate," Ooo-thooo went on. "I ask you to be silent while I locate The and try to feel with The. Any abrupt movement or sound will interrupt my capacity to feel with The."

Carstairs pulled out the one chair provided for the room from its niche in the wall then sat down and waited, doing her best to stifle the rush of emotional strain that ran through her as she realized what a risk she was taking, asking an Empathizer to do its work without benefit of official order. She did her best to put her mind on something else, something that would not disrupt what the S've was doing, and chose rehearsing the Mozart piece in her head, breathing out the phrases that were so demanding.

Patma rested her head on the foot bolster at the end of the bunk and dozed.

A little more than a standard time unit later. Ooo-Yhooo let out a yelp that became a honk, opened its eyes on a gasp, the translator swearing ferociously. The Empathize rose to its feet and lurched around the small space in the center of the room, narrowly missing banging into Carstairs. When it came to a stop, the translator exclaimed, "The's insane!" And then fell over, panting in five-note mordants. After a short while, the S'sve got to its feet again and made an effort to communicate what it had felt from The. "That is what I felt. Madness, and a darkness of emotion that was obliterating all feeling but misery. I believe this shows a toxic reaction to your music."

Carstairs bit her lower lip; this was not what she had wanted to hear, but she made herself ask, "My music does that?"

"Human musical instruments do that to The. Thes do not have the…capacity to engage with the sounds your species regard as musical. There is a vibrational characteristic that to you is harmonious and enjoyable, but to The are like the screams of the tortured." Ooo-Thooo howled in sympathy to what its empathic meditation had revealed.

"That's awful," said Patma as if the words tasted dreadful.

"Why didn't The say anything?" Carstairs clenched her teeth as she waited to hear the answer.

"Because The is unable to assess what the music does to The."

Carstairs stared at the S've, her thoughts jumbled with shock and outrage at this turn of events. "You mean that it actually interferes with its direction function?"

"Among other things, yes," said Ooo-thoo in a mournful glissando.

Patma sat up, revulsion in her manner and her voice. "But other Humans have begun to serve aboard Worm-class ships, haven't they? There are Thes on all Worm-class ships,, but there's been no mention of problems."

"That may be true, but how many of you Humans have orchestras of any sizs on a Worm-class ship?"

"There must be something in the Access files that can inform you if yours is the first, and if it is, something will have to be done about it," the S've said in a wisp of a melody.

Carstairs consulted the Access files and glanced up at the ceiling above them, reading the answers presented. "There is a gamalon group on the *Time Tracker* but the other nine Human crews on Worm-class ships, have, for their entertainment component of service, chosen theatrical performances rather than musical ones." She sighed. "There are no other orchestras or consorts on any Worm-class ships."

Patma looked about in consternation. "But what can we do to…" Her voice trailed off.

Ooo-thooo considered all it had experienced in its empatheic investigation, and lamented, "I could find nothing that would reasonably resolve this impasse. You Humans cannot stay aboard without your entertainment duty fulfilled, and we cannot enter a worm-hole without The."

"Then we'll have to leave the ship," said Carstairs.

"But how will you get back to *Station 8, Quadrant 61?*" Patma asked, her voice shaking. "We're already off-course. We could end up drifting around in deep space for a long time, searching for the station."

Carstairs let her breath out slowly. "Well, we go, or all the ship gets lost in the worm-hole. I don't think we have much choice."

Ooo-thooo lowered its head and said on a single, dreary note, "I doubt that your absence will return The to sanity at this point."

"Do you mean that The's sense of direction will be permanently damaged?" Carstairs asked.

"Yes," said the S'sve. "I found no repair activity in The, no awareness of the distortion in The's directional perceptions."

"I have to inform the captain," said Carstairs, willing herself to get to her feet and take out the small Astrogator Calculator. "If you don't want to stay for what I have to tell him, you'd better leave now." This last was intended as a way to spare Patma and Ooo-thooo from any condemnation for the empathic meditation that Patma had arranged for Ooo-thooo to undertake with The.

Patma answered for them both. "We'll stay here. You may need some back-up."

Carstairs made no protest as she activated the small Astrogator Calculated and a signaled the captain on his esoteric link ro impart what she had discovered, ending with saying, "It seems to me that we Humans ought to remove from the *Star Treader* and hope that the evacuation craft can find its way back to *Station 8, Quadrant 61*. Maybe Tech Crew can find a way to fix The so that you can find your way back to the station, or go on to *Station 9* before the ship runs out of supplies, or—"

The captain cut her off. "That depends on where we actually have drifted, and what kind of distances we're talking about. For all I know, we may be beyond the Reconciliation."

This had already occurred to Carstairs, and she had already thought of a response. "Is there a way to send a message back to *Station 8* about The?"

"I don't know," the captain said wearily.

"Do you want the Humans to evacuate?"

"I don't know," the captain repeated. "Not yet," he added.

"What about The? If The is not functioning, is there any way to work out a course correction that The is not part of?" Carstairs asked desperately, afraid that the entire crew the *Star Treader* was doomed to wander in the vastness of space forever.

The captain was fatalistically silent, then said for a third time, "I don't know," and broke the connection with Carstairs.

THE INTERROGATOR

DARRELL SCHWEITZER

My badge, from one of those agencies most people barely know exist, got me past the guards without difficulty. I was ushered into the bare, underground room, where he sat at the table. I sat down at the other side, opened my briefcase, and reviewed the files I had with me.

Sunlight filtered in fitfully from a slit of a window. From overhead you could hear fair sounds of traffic. We were supposedly under New York, near Central Park.

"Doctor Leonard Tremblay—"

He looked at me sharply and said, "You can't kill me! I am too valuable. I know too much about <u>them!</u> I will never be executed, regardless of what you think I have done."

One hell of a way to start an interview, as anyone might have said.

"You <u>need</u> what I know," he continued.

"I am not an executioner," I said.

I shuffled through the files, pulled out a couple of exceptionally gruesome photographs, and showed them to him. He had no reaction at all, no apparent empathy.

"Doctor Tremblay, you are accused of some very serious crimes."

At that he sat up straight, folded his hands on the table-top, and said almost cheerfully, "Guilty as charged. What are you going to do about it?"

I sighed. "As I said, I am not your executioner. I am not here to <u>do</u> anything about it, because of course once an action has been committed in the past, there is nothing to be <u>done</u> about it. It is only possible to do something about the present or the future. I am here to understand."

"That is very logical, but we humans sometimes go on more than just logic—"

I continued, controlling my impatience. I did not <u>like</u> this smug bastard, as the common idiom would describe him. I made a note of that.

"Doctor Tremblay, you were a member of the Secondary Magnetic Expedition to the Antarctic, were you not?"

"Not mentioned in the published account. One of the also-was-there-in-the-crowd types. Third lieutenant sub-deputy aide."

"This is not a matter to joke about."

"Assistant biologist."

I made a note. "You were Doctor Blair's colleague," I said.

"I had been his graduate student. He'd kept in touch after I got my degree. I was honored that he asked for me to come with him."

"I didn't ask you, 'How did you feel about Doctor Blair?' yet."

"Sorry. You must understand that we humans sometimes get ahead of ourselves."

"Is that an attempt at humor?"

"No, just bad taste."

I made a note.

"So, how did you feel about Doctor Blair?"

"I won't say I loved him, but I had deep respect for him. He was smart. He had the right instincts, even when that instinct was to trust no one, even me. In the end, as you doubtless know, he trusted no one and went off by himself and locked himself in the shed."

"I have read the report," I said. "I know that by the time they got back to the shed, Dr. Blair was long longer Dr. Blair."

"And you believe that?"

"I do not think the report is a work of fiction."

"Wasn't it just too convenient the way the alien tissue samples melted down into their component molecules and the strange gizmos they found in the shed turned back into junk—like fairy gold it was, you know, the gold that seems to be a great treasure, but the next time you look at them, they're just dead leaves? Like that. In the fairy tales. But you don't read fairy tales, do you? Just reports."

"I have not had the time to read fairy tales."

"But we do. We find the time, at least when we're kids, when we are growing up. There's a time in our development when we are open to anything imaginative, when the boundaries between what is possible and what is not do not seem at all firm. Some of us even carry that into adulthood. It's called imagination. Creative people have it. But you, Mr.—you never did introduce yourself, did you? Make a note of that. It's what humans do. It sets the subject at ease—"

I detected that his heartbeat had increased, that he had begun to sweat. He was fidgeting. He pounded his fist on the table top. I assessed the threat level and determined that there was none. This was merely an emotional reaction.

"My name is Joseph Norton, Doctor Tremblay. Did that set you at ease?"

"Not particularly."

"Were you lying then, Doctor Tremblay?"

"Not particularly."

For a moment, he said nothing, just staring at me.

"I put forward to you, Joseph Norton, if that really is your name, if you even have a name, that what was in that report, what I've told the others before you, very much resembles the delusions of a madman, not a word of it true, not even this what I tell you now. A liar paradox, in other words."

"I am aware of the liar paradox, Doctor Tremblay. 'All Cretans are liars. I am a Cretan. Therefore I am lying about everything, even that Cretans are liars and I am one of them.'"

"Maybe that should be 'cretins'."

"Please clarify."

"Attempt at humor. Failed. Make a note of it."

I made a note of it.

Then I pushed one of the particularly gory photographs across the table to him. He picked it up and studied it for a while, then put it down again. "That was McReady," he said. "Only it wasn't. Liar paradox again."

"You hunted down and killed five members of the expedition. In each instance you tried to destroy their bodies with fire, acid, or both."

He tapped the photo with his finger. "Hell on the plumbing, to do that in a bathtub."

"You committed murder."

"Let us say that McReady and the rest were not themselves. I destroyed what they had become. It wasn't murder."

"I don't see the importance of this distinction."

"You wouldn't."

"Doctor Tremblay, I am going to be candid with you. Put my cards on the table, as the saying goes—"

"You're learning our idiom fast—"

"What I wish to learn from you is how you were supposedly able to recognize that your colleagues had changed. I have read the report. You have too, I am sure. It says that the extraterrestrial creature, if that is what it truly was, had been completely destroyed before any of you left the Antarctic. All of the dogs that were no longer dogs, the cows that were not cows, and the men who were not men, up to and including the late, lamented Dr. Blair. So I ask you to consider: Is it possible that everything you thought you perceived afterwards was a delusion, the actions of a man in shock after the horrific deaths of his companions?"

"You're asking me if I'm a raving paranoid?"

"Consider the possibility."

"Liar paradox. That is all I have to say about that. You figure it out. Take as long as you need."

He sat with his head in his hands. It took several minutes for me to get him to talk again. Then it was a long monologue. A tirade.

* * * *

"I don't think any of them came with us onto the steamer going home," he said, beginning slowly. "What walked up the gangplank were humans. I am sure of that. We had all been tested. We had destroyed the last fully developed monster in Dr. Blair's shack. Everybody had been tested one more time. Yes, we were mourning our lost comrades, but we also felt like men coming back from a war. <u>We had survived.</u> We were going home. We would see our loved ones again and get on with our lives.

"On the voyage back, there was almost a party atmosphere, but with a tinge of desperation to it, as if everybody still had to prove he was human. Barclay on the banjo and singing dirty songs at all hours. Men playing cards and drinking beer and watching movies and doing all those stereotypical things rough, tough explorer types do in their leisure time to distract themselves from really thinking about what had happened.

"I stood on the deck as we headed North, watching the Antarctic continent receding behind the ship, thinking that we would never know all its secrets, that we shouldn't have ever gone there, that some things are better left the hell alone. Which is not the correct attitude of an inquiring scientific mind, I will admit, but that was how I felt.

"The auroras looked odd, somehow threatening. I was afraid again. For the next few days and nights I kept mostly to myself. If anybody asked, I said I was working on my data. A lot of guys were like that, actually. Real scientists. Maybe we had beaten a hasty retreat from Big Magnet, but we brought our papers, our data, which is what any scientist would rescue from a burning house.

"It was a week later, or more—the air had grown warm my then; we were somewhere in the Southern Temperate Zone—that Henry Gould knocked on my door, came into my cabin, and confided in me. You don't know Gould. Another one of those also-in-the-crowd types, an aviation mechanic's mate. But he came to me, and he was worried, and the next night Gould brought Dr. Copper—the physician—along, and we three confided in one another, compared notes, and concluded that all this enforced jollity, or even resumed diligence with scientific work just wasn't natural. It was <u>too normal.</u> You know the joke about how you don't want to be too normal because that's not normal and then people will <u>know.</u> Well, we knew. We hadn't figured it all out yet, but we knew that the real Barclay never played the banjo so obsessively or that Norris and Benning were not that good at cards. Somehow monsters had gotten onto the ship with us, and very likely mankind and the whole Earth was doomed.

"So the following evening, after most people had gone to bed, we invited Barclay down to my cabin with the promise of some very special booze, and Gould put a sack over his head and I smashed his skull with a crowbar. Then Dr. Copper served as lookout while we bundled Barclay up onto the deck and over the side.

"Well that, I assure you, put an end to far more than the banjo-playing. The party atmosphere was gone. The only conclusion had to be that Barclay had snapped from the strain after the fact—think of it as something like battle fatigue—and jumped to his death.

"The rest of the voyage was quiet. Everybody was trying to be watchful and compassionate and looking out for the first signs that his buddy might be about to crack. A lot of us did our scientific work, as best we could, usually not in our cabins, alone, but in the common mess room. The place had the atmosphere of a very grim school right before final exams.

"Acting Commander McReady wrote most of his report then, the one you have seen. He passed it around to the rest of us for comments and additions. I contributed a paragraph or two myself. All the while I could not get it out of my head that this was a report by a Thing for Things, in a world of Things.

"Then Doctor Copper really did commit suicide. He called me into his cabin. He explained what a goddamned stupid thing we had done disposing of Barclay like that, how, if the world of men ever had a chance to survive, we had just decreased it by several orders of magnitude. Why? Remember how all the dogs had become infected—taken over—because they had tasted Thing blood? Well, if Barclay had been a monster, and we'd just tossed him over the side, alive or dead, when the crabs and fishes or even oceanic bacteria had gotten finished with him, they too would be infected—would become Things, large or small, swimming, flying, or just drifting until they had reached every corner of the Earth and every level of the biosphere. If Things are to be destroyed, it must be with fire or with acid. They have to be wiped out, every cell of them, or it does no good.

"Doc Copper sobbed as he told me this. He was shaking. I actually held him in my arms as if he were a child. He said it was his fault, inasmuch as he had gone along with our plan or even originated it. I actually wasn't sure whose idea it had been.

"Then he told me that he had already taken poison, and before I could do anything for him, he dropped to the floor in convulsions and died, frothing at the mouth. But he did not melt or turn into anything else. He died human.

"Well, that put an even greater damper on the rest of the voyage, you may be certain. The rest was positively funereal. No celebrations as we crossed the Equator. Some of what happened got into the report. But not what he had said to me, of course, or what we had done. No, that was a secret. I don't suppose there is any point in keeping it now.

"I think I spent the rest of the trip home in my bunk. The report says 'nervous breakdown,' doesn't it? Not quite the case. I spent that time dreaming. The dreams came from outside my head, I am certain, as if I were a radio antenna picking up faint signals that were getting stronger and stronger. I dreamed of the white wastes of Antarctica, and what it was like to lie beneath its ice there for millennia waiting, vaguely sensing—as if in a dream—the evolution of the world outside. I dreamed too, from the perspective of Things, as they infiltrated themselves into every human society on the planet and gradually took over. I saw their black metal cities rise above the ruins of ours, like Mountains of Madness. I saw them soaring in metal ships like swarms of enormous bees, spreading out to the stars. I saw them touch our sun and make it bluer and hotter, burning off most native life from the Earth except for what they chose to keep in reserve—for study perhaps, or as food.

"And when we got to New York, I was examined first by psychiatrists, but I kept my secrets from them. I was brought in, like the rest of the survivors—if that is what they still were—to testify before some very, very secret committees.

"I kept on dreaming. It was as if my mind were no longer my own, as if I were becoming part of something larger, more grand than an individual human being. But at the same time I hated that and feared and fought it.

"But how can a man fight his own dreams? And for how long?

"I think you know the rest. I knew I had little time left. Once I was able to work my way free, I sought out Henry Gould—who had retired from exploring and was hiding in an apartment upstate—explained to him the conclusions I had reached through impeccable logic and what I had to do as a result of them, compared notes with him on our dreams, and then killed him and dissolved his body in acid in his bathtub. It had to be done, you see. That is all I can say about any of my actions. They had to be done. I had figured it all out, you see."

* * * *

After Dr. Tremblay had stopped speaking, there were a few minutes of strained silence. I shuffled papers. I took the gory photo back from him and put it in my briefcase. I made some more notes. He just sat there, motionless, like a machine that had been turned off.

"The most obvious conclusion I can come to," I said, "is that you, and some of your colleagues on the expedition, succumbed to a mysterious group psychosis. To any objective, rational person, your entire testimony does sound, you must admit, completely insane."

"But as you well know," he said, "in science the obvious answer is not always the right one. We have long since discarded Occam's Razor for Occam's Swiss Army Knife. There are multiple possibilities."

"You claims are also illogical. There are numerous gaps in your reasoning. You have not reached your conclusions through valid means."

"Call that an intuitive leap. And there were the dreams. I would not expect your kind to understand."

"Why did you kill Henry Gould? To silence him about the murder of Barclay?"

"No. I killed him because he sneezed."

I took more notes, then said softly, "I do not see where you are going with this."

"You don't? I had figured it all out, you see. You are trying to trick me, or torment me, or maybe both, by the question you <u>did not ask</u>. I think you don't want to ask it because you already know the answer and you know I know, and I know you know I know, and so everybody knows and it would be redundant to explain away the eight-hundred-pound gorilla in the room, which is, if all those expedition members were human when they boarded the ship, how did the alien creature, or some element of it, get off Antarctica? We thought we really had extinguished the last of the Things when we cornered what had been Blair and then cremated all those bodies, but, we overlooked one detail, didn't we? It was right in front of us. It was explained when McReady and the others did their clever thing with the electric wire which made a drop of Thing blood behave like an individual being and leap out of a test tube. If each cell of the Thing can function as an individual creature, and slowly absorb other organic material to gain size and strength, how could we ever hope to stop it? It didn't have to devour men or dogs or cows to take us over. All it had to do was scratch its dandruff or fart or sneeze. Particularly sneeze. That's the perfect way, the innocuous way that nobody thought of, to get a few cells airborne, after which they were just lying in wait patiently in our lungs or on our skin and clothing until we let our guard down, and then, slowly, stealthily, those cells call out to other cells—in dreams, perhaps—and come together, and whammo! They take over the planet. That is what I figured out. I should have noticed it earlier. About the time we put Barclay over the side, Gould was sneezing a lot. I should have noticed. It's well known that after about a month in the Antarctic, nobody sneezes, because everybody at the base has already caught everybody else's colds and developed immunity to those particular strains. On the ship, on the way back, we had not yet been exposed to anyone but our own colleagues. There were no stops in South American ports. No fooling around with beautiful Latin women. But there was Gould, sneezing away. After a while, I noticed that the others were sneezing a lot too. Particularly Substitute-Commander McReady, who had taken over after Commander Garry had proven to be one of them. Aa—choo! It aroused my suspicions, I tell you, but I was too distracted. My head was filled with dreams. I couldn't concentrate well enough. It took me a while to work out the implications. By then we were in New York, sneezing away. Gould was sneezing too damn much. Even when I killed him, he was still sneezing. Aa—choo!"

I closed my briefcase, placed it on the floor, and folded my hands on the table. I leaned forward.

"And tell me, Doctor Tremblay, when you killed Gould, did he melt into a shapeless blob?"

"By the time I had him the bathtub and was pouring acid on him, he certainly did. Hell on the plumbing."

"But not before then. Not when he was merely dead."

"How could I be sure he was dead, and not filled with alien monster cells that he had been sneezing all over the place?"

"Either you are telling the truth, Doctor Tremblay, and the Earth faces an extraordinary peril, or else you are completely insane and you are a danger to your fellow men unless you are locked up forever."

"You want to keep some of us around, as breeding stock, for food, or for study, don't you? Start with me. I am a particularly interesting specimen. I know you are fascinated. Aa—choo!"

At this point I deemed it a strategic necessity to deliberately provoke him. An emotional response can be like the light from a stellar explosion. You can read much data in the spectral lines.

I got up as if to leave. "My God," I said. "I don't believe a damned thing you have told me. You have no secrets, Tremblay. You haven't figured anything out. You are merely a sniveling, pathetic psychopath. You have murdered several men quite uselessly. None of this happened. There was no monster in Antarctica. You somehow spread the contagion of your madness there too, murdered several more of your colleagues, and deluded the rest. This is useless!"

"That's not a very professional attitude, if you want to cure me, doctor," he said. He sneezed at me.

"I never said I was a doctor. I am not here to cure you," I said.

Tremblay sneezed again, deliberately, as if to ridicule me, then laughed. He pointed his finger at me. "Of course you're not, because you can't. You're one of them. You're an imitation, not a human being. I could see through you all along. Maybe you've already taken over the planet and are just keeping a few of us humans around for study. You're trying to figure out what makes us human. Is that it? Your individual cells make up a kind of collective, but you can't comprehend what it is to be an individual, not in the human sense, not a complete being rather than a mass of protoplasm pretending to be a complete being. You still want what we have that you haven't got. Is that it? Is that it?"

I turned to him sharply and pointed back.

"I posit, Doctor Leonard Tremblay, celebrated individual that you claim to be, a completely different hypothesis. What if you're the liar? What if you're the extraterrestrial monster pretending to be a man? Huh? What about that?"

He screamed at me, with a howl you wouldn't think a human throat could make, and his face began to shift, but only within the range of what his facial muscles allowed. It was a vivid emotional display, eyes wide, frothing at the mouth, as he screamed and screamed. For a brief while he became articulate again and said, "Then I'll have to reveal my true form and sprout a few tentacles and claws, and hypnotize you with my three burning, red eyes while I break this table into bits and club you to death with it before I rip your head off and dissolve the rest of you in my drool." And he screamed some more, rising to his feet, attempting to lift the table, to tip it over, straining with all his strength while he raged at me in a white-hot fury of indescribable rage.

But he could not lift the table because it was affixed to the floor. He could not tear my head off because he had no tentacles or claws, and in the end he just dropped to the floor, helpless and sobbing, as I pressed the buzzer and two guards came and took him away.

I must report that this session has been a failure. The experiment has yielded no results. The conclusion before us is that humans possess some quality that we, for all we perfectly mimic their physical forms and replicate their thought processes, cannot share. It as if there is another sense, beyond sight, hearing, taste, touch, smell, or even dreaming which enables them to somehow detect its absence in ourselves. I do not think they fully understand it themselves. They refer to it disparagingly as "madness" or "paranoia." It is a powerful weapon which we must add to our arsenal. Until then, we are not complete. Recommend further study.

In the meantime we dream of black cities rising, of the planet's sun changing color, and of our race, no longer the last survivors fleeing some unimaginable conflict deep in the universe twenty million years ago, but reinvigorated and renewed, soaring once more to the stars to conquer them.

"ACCORDING TO A RELIABLE SOURCE..."

ALLEN M. STEELE

ART BY MARC HEMPEL

A cold October rain was falling on the Hudson when the *Boliver* arrived in New York. From the front seat of his car, Scott watched the big Argentine freighter as it slowly came into port, hauled by tugboats the rest of the way to the dock. The longshoremen on the wharf were hunched over, hands in their pockets and the collars of their Navy-surplus pea coats turned up against the drizzle, as they waited for the ship to come in. It was the last light of day; along the waterfront, streetlights were beginning to come on.

Scott finished wiping his horn-rimmed glasses and put them on again, then turned to the younger man sitting beside him. "Look, if I'm right about this, we're going to have to work fast. It's not going to be what it's usually like when a ship comes in with some big-shot aboard. Even if any of the passengers want to talk to us, there's bound to be other guys running interference for them."

"Who are you talking about?" DeWitt was loading a film plate into the back of his Speed Graphics camera. "The cops? I thought you're pals with them, Scotty."

"I'm not worried about the cops. It's *those* guys." Scott nodded toward the line of Ford sedans parked nearby.

There were ten cars, coal-black and identical to one another. They'd shown up shortly after Scott and DeWitt did, traveling together as a convoy and parking bumper-to-bumper in the No Parking zone beside the dock. There were two men in the front seat of each vehicle, but so far only one man had climbed out, the passenger of the first car up front. He'd spoken briefly with the dock workers' foremen, who'd glanced at something the newcomer produced from inside his trench coat—probably a badge or another form of official I.D., Scott guessed—before nodding and turning away. Now the man in the trench coat stood near the longshoreman, umbrella open above his head.

"I'm guessing they're g-men," Scott said. "Here to pick up the survivors and take 'em someplace where nobody can talk to them."

"'Nobody' meaning us, right?" DeWitt slapped the film holder shut, then turned the camera around to check its flash bulb.

"Uh-huh. So it's not going to be like what we usually get, movie stars or ball players coming home from a vacation in Rio." As he spoke, Scott watched as the tugs pushed and pulled the *Boliver* the rest of the way in. Crewmen on the fore and aft decks were already tossing hawser lines down to the longshoremen. "Someone went to a lot of trouble to book passage for them on a freighter, not a liner," he went on. "They were trying to make sure these guys kept a low profile ... and they might have succeeded if the *Classic* hadn't been tipped off."

"Who gave us the tip?"

"The brother of one of the guys who was in Antarctica. That's what Casey at City Desk told me."

"Well, it looks like we're the only paper in town to get it." DeWitt turned his head to glance back through the rear window, then peered further up the sidewalk along the row of wharf-side warehouses. "Y'know, if it's such a big story, why didn't they call the *Times*, too? Or even the *Daily News?*"

Scott didn't have an answer for that, and he'd wondered the same thing. Among the half-dozen newspapers published daily in New York City, the *Classic* ranked at the bottom. A tabloid specializing in street crime, celebrity gossip, and political scandals, it was the kind of paper principally read by those who wanted their news as grisly and salacious as they could get it. But a story like this ... if it was true, then even the Gray Lady would put it on page one.

"I don't know," Scott said, "but a scoop is a scoop, so let's get something good for the bulldog." The freighter was motionless by now, the dock workers tying off the ropes. "You ready?" DeWitt nodded. "Okay, let's go."

As one, they threw open the car doors and jumped out. The man in the trench coat didn't notice them, but a police officer in a hooded rain poncho did. Turning away from the ship, he marched over to them and planted himself in their way. Even if the cop hadn't spotted DeWitt's camera, he couldn't have missed the yellow press tags both men wore in their hatbands.

"Not today, boys," he said, raising his hands. "Whoever you think you're going to meet, they don't want to talk to you."

"Really?" Scott asked. "All twenty-one of them? Because that's how many guys we hear made it out of Antarctica."

"Don't know how many there are, but that's not the point. No one's giving you an interview, and that's all there is to it."

The cop's attention was focused on Scott, which was good; it meant that he wasn't keeping an eye on DeWitt. And Scott knew how fast the young news photographer could be on his feet. DeWitt wasn't paying much attention to either him or the flatfoot. He watching the freighter; the gangway was being lowered, and although the passengers weren't yet in sight, it looked as if they'd be coming down any minute now. DeWitt wasn't going to wait for a waterfront cop to give him permission to do his job.

"C'mon, let them decide who they want to talk to." Ignoring DeWitt, Scott stepped a little closer to the cop. He already had a ten-spot folded and hidden within the half-closed fingers of his left hand. "Take your wife out to dinner and a movie tonight," he whispered, letting his hand brush against the palm of the cop's gloved right hand. "I hear the new Marx Brothers flick is pretty good."

"The old lady hates Groucho," the cop said quietly, but he made the ten-dollar bill disappear. "Okay … one picture, one question, and then you're outta here. Savvy?"

"Got it."

The cop nodded. "Wait here 'til they come down," he murmured just loud for both newspapermen to hear. "When they do. I'm gonna bend down to tie my shoes. That's your cue. I'll play dumb for a minute or so, but when I come up behind you and tell you to get lost, you get lost. No argument. Understand?"

"Sure thing, friend."

"I'm not your friend," the cop muttered, glaring at him, and Scott refrained from making the smart-aleck comeback that hovered on his lips. There weren't many New York cops who'd turn down a bribe, but it didn't mean they had to be proud of it. The Depression was over, or so it was said, but no one Scott knew was rolling in money. So the cop would take the juice, and in return he'd screw up just a little and let a couple of newshounds get by him.

Up on the ship's forward deck, just visible in the fading light, shadowed men were beginning to gather at the railing. As they appeared, Scott heard car doors opening and slamming shut. He looked around to see more men emerging from the row of parked sedans. All wore dark raincoats, their hats pulled low against the rain; if they weren't feds, Scott would have to ask if they had any Girl Scout cookies for sale. The g-men opened umbrellas and raised them above their heads as they moved toward the foot of the gangway ladder to meet the passengers as they came down.

The cop looked down at his feet, apparently noticed that his shoes were untied, and squatted down to do something about it. Scott nudged DeWitt, then both newsmen quietly stepped around the kneeling police officer. None of the feds noticed them. DeWitt had enough sense to keep his camera low until he was ready to use it, and Scott likewise kept his note pad and fountain pen clasped in his hands and out of sight in his coat pocket. Silently, pretending to be invisible, they came up behind the g-men, making sure they did nothing that would attract notice.

Scott watched as the *Bolivar's* passengers began walking down the ramp. None of them seemed to notice the weather; several were even bare-headed, and as they descended the gangway they looked about as wonderingly if the Hudson River waterfront and the luminescent Manhattan skyline belonged to another planet. Compared to Antarctica, a rainy October evening in New York must have seemed like Miami Beach. Yet no one smiled. In fact, it seemed to Scott as if he was seeing something again that he'd often seen when he was young reporter in France during the Great War, on the faces of American and British infantrymen coming back from the trenches of the front: a certain look of horror, the way men's eyes become when they've beheld something no man should ever behold.

Something had happened to them at the South Pole. Something awful.

The first ones had just reached the bottom of the gangway when, from the corner of his eye, Scott saw the nearest g-man look his way. The FBI agent, or whoever he was, studied Scott for a moment, then noticed DeWitt and his bulky rig. Once again, Scott wished that someone would hurry up and invent a camera you could hide in your coat pocket. The g-man tapped another fed on the shoulder, then cocked a thumb toward the two newshounds. Scott couldn't hear what they were whispering to each other, nor did he need to. In another second or so, he and Scott would be tossed out of there before either of them got a chance to do their jobs. So it was now or never.

"C'mon," he said to DeWitt, "follow me." And then they moved in, finding a hole amid the wall of umbrellas and darting through it before anyone could stop them. The feds were caught by surprise, some even stepping out of their way. Scott managed to reach the gangway in time to plant himself in front of the first guy to disembark from the *Boliver*, whom the reporter took to be the group's leader.

He was a big man, almost six and half feet tall, looking tough enough to wrestle polar bears or whatever the hell they got down at the South Pole. A face bronzed by a cold sun and even colder wind, framed by red hair and a coarse beard that had grown as long as a hermit's, turned toward Scott. He said nothing, but his cool grey eyes spoke a silent question: *yeah, so what do you want to know?*

"Scott from the *New York Classic.*" Scott had his note pad and pen out now, ready to jot down notes. "What happened down there? We hear a lot of guys were killed … fifteen, sixteen, something like that."

"We had thirty-seven men at Big Magnet and lost sixteen." The giant stopped walking; he looked straight at Scott, his voice deep and matter-of-fact. "That includes Garry, our commander."

"And you are …?"

"McReady. Second-in-command, expedition meteorologist." As he spoke, there was an abrupt pop just behind Scott, followed by a burst of light that made McReady wince. DeWitt had just snapped a picture; Scott hoped he was fast enough to reload the camera and get another shot before the feds confiscated his rig.

"That's almost half the people who were in your expedition," Scott said, and McReady nodded. "So how did they die? Was there some sort of—?"

"Okay, that's enough." The FBI agent who'd spotted him and DeWitt just a second ago had come up beside him. "G'wan, beat it," he growled, laying a hand on the reporter's arm to pull him away.

"Was there an accident?" Although Scott ignored the g-man, he was careful not to physically resist him or do anything else that could give the feds sufficient cause to put him and DeWitt under arrest. "Was there a fire or a—?"

"A fire. Yeah, sure, there was a fire." McReady spoke without conviction. One look at his eyes and Scott knew he was lying, and McReady knew that he knew.

"There's going to be an official statement made to the press." The g-man was pulling him away. "We'll let the *Classic* know when these men are ready to speak. Until then … *stop him, damn it!*"

Another pop and flash told Scott that DeWitt had managed to get that second shot. The commotion that followed, along with the curse snarled by the photographer, also told him that there would be no more. Before the FBI agent at Scott's elbow could haul him away, though, McReady stepped closer to the reporter.

"It's good to meet you, mister," the big meteorologist said, thrusting out his hand. "I hope we get to talk again soon."

Surprised, Scott clasped McReady's hand. It was big and sinewy and strong enough to crunch walnuts, and there was a small slip of paper concealed within the palm, just the same way Scott himself had slipped a ten-dollar bill to the cop. Scott let the note slip into his own palm, and McReady's left eyelid fluttered in a sort of half-wink, then they let themselves be pulled apart by the feds.

Scott tucked the note into his coat pocket and didn't touch it again. Back at the edge of the crowd, bookended by two g-men and the no-longer-cooperative waterfront cop, he silently observed the men from Antarctica as they were loaded, two or three at a time, into the row of sedans. Once they were all in the cars, engines were started, headlights came on, and the cars began to move away from the dock, windshield wipers slapping away the rain. Scott watched them go, then he and DeWitt returned to Scott's car.

"Get some good pics?" Scott asked the photographer once they were in the front seat of the Packard again.

"I'll know once I'm in the darkroom." DeWitt reached into the back seat for the leather bag he used for carrying his gear. Out came a chamois lens cloth that he used to dry his camera. "Sorry you didn't get in more questions. The feds really didn't want you to talk to that guy, do they?"

"No, they didn't." Scott found the note McReady slipped him and opened it. A single word had been written on it: *Metrolite*. He smiled, understanding its meaning. "But I'll be speaking with him again anyway."

* * * *

The Metrolite Hotel was located in midtown Manhattan, on Broadway a few blocks from Central Park. It wasn't as classy as the Waldorf or the Chelsea but neither was it a dump, and since it was also offered residential rooms for long-term guests, it was a good, low-key place for the government to park the expedition survivors while they investigated the matter at hand.

McReady must have known in advance where he and his people would be staying, which was why he'd written the hotel's name on a slip of paper and covertly handed it to the first reporter he met. That was Scott assumed, at least. Someone had managed to tip off the *Classic* and only the *Classic*, and it was a good bet that McReady was at the bottom of it.

DeWitt wouldn't be needed for the interview and he'd only be in the way, so Scott dropped him off at the *Classic* before driving crosstown to the Metrolite. He parked in the garage next door, but before he headed over to the hotel he stepped behind the car and opened the trunk. Inside were a couple of dark blue garment bags, the kind used by people who wore uniforms at work. Scott chose the one marked in chalk with a small letter "W" and took it with him.

He avoided coming in through the front door. The lobby was doubtless being staked out by g-men, and it was all too likely that they'd recognize him from the waterfront. Instead, he walked through the alley behind the hotel until he located the door used for kitchen deliveries. A few people in the kitchen looked up as he walked through, but no one paid much attention. Even though they wouldn't recognize his face, since he was carrying a garment bag and acted like he had every right to be there, they probably figured that he was a newly-hired staff member on his way in for his shift.

Which was exactly the impression Scott wanted to cast. He'd pulled this sort of gag before, when he wanted to get interviews from people who were holed up in hotels or hospitals. It was sleazy and unethical, but it got results. The other garment bag in his car contained a hospital orderly's uniform; the one he'd taken from his trunk held the sort of white tuxedo jacket, high-collar dress shirt, black trousers, and bow tie worn by a typical room service waiter. Scott changed clothes in a janitorial closet where he could stash his street clothes until he was ready to leave. He searched the bulletin board on the service corridor wall outside the kitchen until he located a clipboard holding a roster, several pages long, that listed the last names of hotel guests and their room numbers. From this, he learned that McReady was in Room 1207.

Scott loitered in the corridor, smoking a cigarette and pretending to be on break, until the kitchen's double-doors swung open and a cook pushed out that which he'd been waiting for: a room service cart with some guest's dinner to be delivered to their room. The receipt beside the covered platter stated that it was supposed to be taken to someone named Cooley, A., on the eighth floor. Well, A. Cooley was going to have to wait a little longer for his steak and potato. Shoving the receipt in his pocket, Scott wheeled the cart to the automatic service elevator and pushed the button marked 12.

On the way up, Scott removed his glasses and tucked them in his shirt pocket. He couldn't see very well without them, but he'd learned a while ago that, when he wasn't wearing them, no one except his wife and kids easily recognized him. And since he'd been wearing his hat as well when he and De-Witt had been down on the waterfront, it was unlikely that even an FBI agent would realize that a room service waiter looked an awful lot like an annoying reporter he'd seen earlier tonight. Or so he hoped. If this didn't work, he hoped there was someone at the *Classic* who'd come over to the court house and post bail for him.

But it worked. There was a g-man posted on the twelfth floor, but he was watching the guest elevators, not the service lift. He barely noticed Scott as he came around a corner and continued down the hall. The two men exchanged a silent nod, and Scott tried not to smile as he pushed the cart past him. For the agent's sake, he hoped that J. Edgar Hoover didn't find out that one of his men could be fooled so easily.

Luckily, the numbers on the doors were large enough that Scott could read them without his glasses. Just around another corner, he located 1207. He knocked on the door, and on his second try he heard its latch being unlocked. Then the door swung open and there stood McReady, looking both annoyed and slightly confused.

"I didn't order—"

"Shh!" Scott raised a finger to his lips, then whispered, "I'm from the *Classic* ... remember me?" McReady's eyes widened, and Scott hastily glanced back the way he'd come, making sure that the FBI agent hadn't followed him. "Hurry up and let me in."

"Yeah, sure." McReady hastily stepped aside and watched as Scott pushed the cart inside. "If that's dinner, then it's going to go to waste," he said as he closed the door. "Not hungry."

"Eat it anyway. It's going to look funny if you ordered a steak and didn't touch it." Then Scott noticed the bottle of Scotch on bureau, an empty glass beside it. It appeared that McReady had ordered room service already, only he was taking dinner in liquid form.

"Yeah, well ... if you've seen what I've seen, you'd have trouble with your appetite, too." McReady grimaced as he picked up the bottle and poured another couple of fingers of whisky. "Anyway, looks like my message got through to my brother and he called your paper."

Putting on his glasses again, Scott sat down on the bed. It was a small room with just one chair, and McReady had already claimed it. "All I know is what my editor told me ... something happened to an American scientific expedition to Antarctica, a lot of people lost their lives, and the ones who didn't were aboard an Argentine freighter called the *Boliver* that was on its way to New York. Aside from what little you were able to tell me before the feds hustled me out of there, that's all we got."

"That's because I didn't tell my brother much about it either. He lives in Queens. While the *Boliver* was at sea, I had the wireless operator send him a ship-to-shore telegram." A wry smile. "Back when we were kids, we worked out a secret code that only the two of us know. I told him to get hold of a newspaper here in the city and tell them to meet the ship at the dock. I figured that, if a reporter showed up, I could pass a message along if I could just get close enough to hand him a piece of paper."

"Well, it worked. I'm here." Scott hesitated. "Just one question ... why did your brother contact the *Classic*? Let's be honest, it's not the biggest paper in town."

"I dunno." McReady shrugged. "I don't read the papers, he does. I guess he likes the *Classic,* period."

That sounded like as good of an answer as any. At the very least, it explained why he was sitting here instead of a reporter from the *Times.* "All right then," Scott said as he pulled out his note pad and turned to a fresh page, "let's get started. I guess the obvious first question is, how on Earth did you lose sixteen members of your expedition?"

McReady said nothing for a few moments. He picked up his glass, rocked back his head, and killed the shot he'd just poured in one gulp. Then he picked up the bottle again and, taking a seat in the room's only chair, poured another drink of whiskey without offering any to his visitor. Scott waited patiently. He was familiar with this sort of behavior: it comes when a source wants to spill his guts to a reporter, but doesn't know where to begin.

Unexpectedly, a smile appeared on McReady's weathered face, the sort of smile that's ironic and without humor. "'How on Earth?'" he asked, repeating what Scott just said. "Funny you should put it that way ..."

* * * *

The feds caught him on the way back to the service elevator. It wasn't a total surprise. Scott had a premonition that they were onto him. Upon leaving McReady's room, while pushing the room service cart back the way he came, Scott passed the guest elevators and noticed that the g-man who'd been there a couple of hours ago was now absent. The hair on the back of his neck rose when he saw this, and in hindsight he should've abandoned the cart, doubled back to the emergency exit, and scurried down the fire escape to the alley. But he didn't, and so when he came around the corner, the feds were waiting for him.

Scott dropped the pretense the moment they nabbed him. In situations like this, the worst things a reporter can do are run away, resist arrest, or continue pretending to be whomever they'd been trying to pass themselves off as being. But easy surrender didn't stop the two g-men waiting for him from gloating.

"What did you do," asked the FBI agent whom Scott had seen earlier, "stick around for dinner? Shouldn't have stayed so long, pal ... that's what got my attention." He lifted the dinner tray cover, glanced at the untouched steak. "Waste of a good t-bone," he muttered in disgust. "Now *that's* criminal!"

The feds put the cuffs on Scott and led him back down the hall, past McReady's room to 1701, where they'd set up a base of operations. It turned out that the FBI had rented out the hotel's entire seventeenth floor, with every room either occupied by a surviving member of the Secondary Pole Expedition or otherwise left vacant. It was not a comforting notion to realize that, if the feds wanted to put the thumbscrews to him, they could do so with impunity; Scott doubted that any of McReady's fellow explorers would come to his rescue.

No, the best thing to do now was to cooperate, and hope that the feds would decide in the end that he was more of a nuisance than a menace.

There was already a senior FBI agent in the room, a fellow whom the other two respectfully addressed as Agent Marquette. Before they left again, presumably to resume guard duty by the elevators—this time, their chief told them to keep an eye on the service lift as well—Marquette didn't take any chances with Scott trying to make a break for it. Instead, he unfastened the handcuff bracelet on the reporter's left wrist, then refastened it to the radiator beside the window. He then searched Scott's tux jacket until he found what he was looking for, his note pad. Ignoring Scott's protests, Marquette lay down on one of the twin beds, propped his back against the headboard and put his feet up, then opened the little black pad and proceeded to study the notes from Scott's interview with McReady.

When he was through, Marquette closed the pad and tossed it on the bedside table. He folded his hands together on his belly and quietly regarded Scott for a minute or so, saying nothing. Scott responded in the same manner. The two men carried on a little staring contest, and it was Marquette who spoke first.

"So, Mr. Scott ... what should we do with you?"

"If you were smart, you'd let me go. I haven't broken any laws."

Marquette nodded. "You're right. There's not much we can charge you with except maybe misdemeanor trespassing, and impersonating a waiter is so trivial that I wouldn't waste a judge and jury's time with it. So, yeah, I'm inclined to take the cuffs off and let you go."

"Glad to hear it." The radiator was warmer than Scott liked, even on a cold and rainy night like this. His left wrist was getting hot and he was beginning to sweat.

"First, though, we're going to have a little chat. Namely, about what Mr. McReady has just told you and whether any of it belongs in that newspaper of yours."

"Of course it does. The people has a right to know—"

"No, sir … no, they don't." Marquette shook his head. "When it comes to matters where public safety is at risk, that so-called right to know takes a back seat."

"If the public is at risk, then why shouldn't they know?" Scott jabbed a finger at the note pad. "You've read what McReady told me. That … that *thing* he and his people found down there, the way it wiped out nearby half of their expedition … don't you think it poses a significant public risk? Particularly when it's something no one has ever seen until now?"

"I've read your notes, and I've already interviewed Mr. McReady and other members of his party. And there's nothing mysterious about it. A monster didn't kill all those people, Mr. Scott … a man did."

Scott stared at him. For a moment, he was unable to speak. "What?"

"You heard me. A man, not a thing from another world. Dr. Connant, to be precise."

It took a few seconds for Scott to recall exactly whom Marquette was talking about. Connant, the expedition physicist. The first person at the Antarctic base nicknamed Big Magnet who was killed and … *duplicated*, for lack of a better word … by the creature they'd discovered near the buried wreckage of an alien spacecraft.

"You've got the story mixed up, Mr. Marquette," he said, "Connant killed some of the others, sure, but he wasn't a man any more by then. He was the thing … one of the things … that assumed human form and then went about murdering anyone at the base they caught alone. Those victims were then duplicated themselves, since the thing was capable of splitting off part of its body and reproducing itself as a replica of its victim."

Marquette casually folded his arms together. "That's what you were told, sure, but do you realize how absolutely paranoid that is? A creature that kills someone, then imitates him so perfectly that it even *sounds* like the original? And then goes about killing and duplicating everyone else, even the sled dogs?"

"It wasn't just Connant." Straining against his handcuffs, Scott reached over to the bedside table, snatched up his pad, and flipped it open to the pages where he'd written the notes from his interview with McReady. "Commander Garry …Dr. Blair, the biologist … Kinner, the cook—"

"Yes, I know … they were all killed, allegedly first by the creature, and then again by the other expedition members when that blood test Dr. Copper developed exposed their true identities. And after they were killed, their bodies were burned out on the ice together with any organic remains they left behind, such as their bloodstained clothes. They shot the dogs, too, and even an albatross someone spotted circling the base."

"And you think McReady made all that up?"

"On his own?" Marquette shook his head. "No. I think he had help, all right … the worst case of mass psychosis anyone has ever seen."

"Aw, c'mon!" The newspaperman was incredulous. "You can't seriously believe all twenty-one of those men lost their minds, do you?"

"Why not?" The FBI agent shrugged nonchalantly. "It's happened before. Look what happened in Salem, Massachusetts, a few hundred years ago. Those men were isolated from the rest of humanity, living in close quarters at the edge of the world, in the harshest environment know to—"

"Sounds to me like you're hunting for rationalizations."

"And it sounds to me like *you're* hunting for a story that'll sell a lot of papers," Marquette no longer sounded as smug as he'd been. "But that's as irresponsible as shouting 'fire' in a crowded theater. If you write that story, Mr. Scott, and the *Classic* prints it, every nut case who reads it is going to come away believing that anyone they don't like … wife, husbands, children, co-workers, even their elected public officials … are actually monsters from outer space pretending to be human. You and the *Classic* will cause a panic, and more lives will be lost."

"That's not going to happen." But even as he said this, Scott realized that he wasn't persuaded by his own words.

"You don't think so?" Marquette shook his head. "I'm sorry, Mr. Scott, but I disagree. And I'm warning you right now, if the *Classic* runs that story the way you heard it from McReady, Director Hoover will take steps to make sure your paper is shut down and you personally are discredited. And don't think for a second that he can't or won't do that."

Scott said nothing for a moment. He'd been on the crime beat long enough to know that the FBI didn't make empty threats, particularly when it came to stories they want to have spiked. And reporters who lost their jobs at the *Classic* didn't usually find themselves working for the *Wall Street Journal* as their next career move. He'd be lucky to find himself handling classified ads at the *Daily News*.

"Okay, all right," he said, "so what do you want me to write instead? That Connant or Garry or someone else lost his mind, and that was enough to the other fellows over the edge?"

"No," Marquette said, shaking his head again. "Those men had families. Their loved ones don't need to know that truth if they don't need to. What you're going to say is that there was a fire. It started in the base kitchen as a grease fire that Kinner or someone else accidentally caused while working on dinner, and it swept through Big Magnet and killed sixteen men before the others got it under control."

"And what if those guys … McReady, Norris, Copper, or any of the other survivors … comes back later and reveals the truth?"

"They won't. Our people spoke to them while they were still aboard the *Boliver*. Everyone agreed to the cover story except McReady. He was the only hold-out, and now that we knows he's talked to you, I'm going to be have a little chat with him, too." A brief, flickering smile. "I'm sure that Mr.

McReady will come around and support the cover story. If he knows what's good for him, this is the last time anyone will hear that tale of his."

Marquette then rose from his chair and, stepping closer to Scott, extended his hand, palm up. "Your notes, Mr. Scott ... give them to me, please."

"Agent Marquette—"

"Mr. Scott, there is absolutely nothing you can say to me that will make me change my mind. And I'm not *asking* you, I'm *telling* you ... hand over your notes, now."

Scott hesitated. Then, realizing that he was never going to leave this hotel room with the note pad still in his possession, he reluctantly held it out to Marquette. The g-man took the pad from him and slipped it into his coat pocket.

"Very good," he said, a little more pleasantly. "Now, listen ... in about an hour or so, there's going to be a press conference downstairs in the hotel's main ballroom. Several members of the Navy and the scientific community will host it, during which they'll reveal the results of their preliminary investigation into the causes of the fire at Big Magnet. Since you've agreed to cooperate with us, I'll make sure that you're given a seat in the front row and that the first question goes to you."

Scott scowled. He wasn't satisfied with any of this, let alone the small favor he'd just been offered. Yet he knew that he didn't have much choice. It went without saying that, if his first question didn't have to do with a kitchen fire, things would go badly for him. So he said nothing and quietly nodded his head.

"Very good," Marquette said. "I think that covers everything. You can go now."

The FBI agent took a keyring from his pocket, found the one that unlocked the cuffs Scott was wearing, and used them to free the reporter from the radiator. Gently rubbing at his wrist, which felt as if it had been slowly broiled, Scott stood up from his chair. He headed for the door, with Marquette falling in behind him.

Scott was just about to lay his hand on the doorknob when another thought occurred to him. He stopped and thought about it for a moment, then he turned to Marquette again. "Say, there's just one thing I'd like to know ... off the record, that is."

"So long as it's off the record ..." Marquette didn't look as if he was very pleased to have the reporter pose a question to him, or at least not before the dog and pony show they were about to have in the ballroom downstairs.

"Well, if I remember correctly, McReady said that he, Dr. Copper, and Van Wall travelled across the ice to where they detected a magnetic anomaly about eighty miles southwest of the South Magnetic Pole. That's where they found what seemed to be an enormous craft ... a space ship ... buried about a hundred feet beneath the ice, and that it had apparently been there for millions of years."

"That's what Mr. McReady told me, too." Marquette was impatient to leave the room and get rid of this nosey reporter.

"Uh-huh. And when they tried to excavate it by planting thermite charges around the vessel, the charge reacted with something volatile like a fuel-tank, the explosion destroyed the ship."

"That's the story." Marquette's eyes became flinty and cold. "Scott, don't you go reporting this..."

"I won't, but there's just one more thing." Scott was doing his best to refrain from smiling, but he wasn't able to do so. "McReady said that, after they discovered the thing ... or monster, or alien, or whatever you want to call it ... and excavated it from the ice pack where it had fallen upon escaping from the ship, they discovered something else. Three more bodies, apparently no longer living but intact all the same, buried in the ice much like the first one. Do you remember that, Mr. Marquette?"

The FBI agent didn't reply. Instead, he continued to silently regard the reporter, not saying a word but carefully listening to everything Marquette had to say.

"So—" Scott didn't like the expression on Marquette's face, but there was no way to back down now "—if there are three more of those things down there, and they're like the one McReady and the other guys found and brought back to Big Magnet, then..."

He let his voice trail off, giving Marquette a chance to finish the thought for him. The FBI agent didn't speak for a minute or so. Instead, he looked away from Scott, gazing at nothing in particular as if trying to formulate an answer to Scott's unasked question.

"Since you're asking me about something we know to be untrue," Marquette said at last, "then your question is entirely hypothetical. And the FBI doesn't deal with hypothetical issues."

"But—"

"That will be all, Mr. Scott." Stepping around the reporter, Marquette opened the hotel room door. "And don't let me see that in your paper, all right?"

Scott didn't reply. Instead, he let Marquette escort him back down the hall to the elevator.

This story wasn't over. In fact, it was just getting started.

COLD STORAGE

KEVIN J. ANDERSON

Being assigned to an ultra-secret government warehouse deep in the Nevada desert wasn't as exciting as it sounded, but nobody chose a civil service job for the excitement. That was exactly the way Malcolm Hobbs liked it.

The work was interesting and engaging, especially on days when a new object landed on his desk. After he passed through the guard gates and security fences and entered the small cinderblock Unusual Object Intake Office, Malcolm found a plastic-wrapped package waiting for him.

The sturdy government-issue desk was painted seafoam green, and he had his own rolling chair on the linoleum floor. A metal file cabinet stood like a sentinel with gray fireproof drawers locked with combination dials and marked with classification tags. He glanced at the Uncle Sam calendar hanging on the wall, May 1950. Before considering the new package, he X'ed out the previous day with a black marker, as if it had been redacted and locked away. For the sake of national security, Malcolm did his best to forget everything he had seen, but some things he could never forget. It all went with the job.

He regarded the rectangular package, about fifteen inches on a side, wrapped and wrapped in several layers of plastic with hazard stickers on each layer. A standard Unusual Object Intake Form, in triplicate, was attached with cellophane tape. The form listed serial numbers and a chain of custody, but—as usual—gave very little real or useful information about the item in question.

Up and down the chain of command, no one did the slightest bit more than they were authorized to do. Malcolm was just a small cog in a very large machine, and he was on his own to figure this out.

He sat in the swivel chair, pulled a new government-issue notebook from the side desk drawer, and opened to a clean page. He sharpened his pencil, then began to record his observations. Malcolm would fill many pages with a thorough description of the item, and the logbook would then be stored in the fireproof, floodproof, and atomic-bomb-proof drawers of his secure file cabinet. After he was finished, the object itself would be locked away inside the gigantic government warehouse complex, where it would remain safe.

Once he finished his external observations, he took a box cutter from his top desk drawer and sliced the packing tape to unwrap the first sheet of thick plastic, only to find another layer of equally thick plastic and more hazard stickers beneath.

The warnings made Malcolm uneasy, but he was a loyal civil servant, and the government was here to help him. They had assigned him this job, and he knew they would never expose him to undue risk.

After making a few more notes, he cut through to the third layer, sawed through the thickest layers of tape yet, and finally exposed the actual object inside—a bound journal, a scientific notebook that was burned at the edges, battered and crimped as if it had been dropped out of a low-flying bomber. The broken spine had been taped to hold together the charred and bent pages. The bitter tang of soot rose from the book.

Gingerly, Malcolm lifted the cover with a creak of exhausted binding. The front page, marked in clear, confident handwriting, identified the journal as from "Antarctic Research Station, 1939," written by someone named Blair.

"What did you get today, Buddy?" said a voice that was altogether too loud for the hushed confines of the small office cubicles. "I sure don't want to trade with ya, though. I got cattle mutilations. Those are always fun!"

Flinching, Malcolm looked up to see blustery Glenn Romero, his lone coworker in the intake office. Instinctively, he covered the journal with the flat of his hand. "None of your business, Glenn. This is classified. Eyes only."

"Sure, but I've got eyes." He poked a finger at his face as if he meant to gouge out his orbs. "Were you expecting some bug-eyed monster?"

"I was expecting you to respect boundaries." Malcolm leaned protectively over the journal. "I take my security clearance seriously."

"Of course you do, Buddy. Nobody ever confused you for a fun-loving guy, but you're all the company I have in this dungeon."

In previous years, the Unusual Object Intake Office had employed many more workers. During World War II, even before the testing of the atomic bomb down in Alamogordo, New Mexico, the giant desert warehouse had been used to store dangerous and important items, including weapons stolen from the Nazis—the Spear of Destiny, some Biblical ark, spell books, magical artifacts, and numerous technological prototypes. One entire wing of the warehouse held super-secret materials from the Manhattan Project, as well as the far more destructive and even more super-secret Brooklyn Project. During the War, Malcolm often received as many as five mysterious artifacts in a single week. The work was dizzying and exhausting, not at all what he'd expected when he'd taken his civil service exam.

After the end of the war, they had begun to catch up, until the Roswell Incident in 1947 threw everything into turmoil again, forcing the intake offices to bring in an army of extra staff, with desks crammed together, diligent clerks filling drawers with classified records, and entire file cabinets rolled out and locked away forever. Now, three years after Roswell, the world had settled into a relative calm and the Unusual Object Intake Office had only himself and Glenn Romano to work on the backlog.

He hated Glenn.

The man had no personal boundaries, asking pesky questions, always snooping into Malcolm's work under the guise of "friendship," but Malcolm didn't want to be friends. This was a top secret installation, and Malcolm didn't even know who his immediate supervisor was.

The intake office building was no larger than a bunker and as secure as a bomb shelter, with thick cinderblock walls, no windows. His desk and Glenn's were at opposite sides of the main room. The only human touch was a little kitchen area with a refrigerator and a hotplate. Employees were allowed to socialize there, which Malcolm avoided whenever possible.

In the middle of the cinderblock wall near his desk was a large red button, prominent but untouched. Stenciled letters admonished NEVER CALL FOR HELP. Both he and Glenn knew that the red button was to be used only in extreme circumstances and would result in the termination of their employment and the revocation of their security clearance.

Though Glenn Romano was extremely annoying, Malcolm doubted a personality conflict warranted pressing the red button.

"I've got this new intake. You're interrupting my work."

"Sure thing, Buddy." Glenn slapped the painted wall with the flat of his hand. "Maybe we can meet at the commissary after hours, have a beer, let your hair down?"

Self-consciously Malcolm touched the short and receding stubble on his head. He liked his hair just the way it was.

Finally, he couldn't control his annoyance any longer. "You took my sandwich from the Frigidaire yesterday! Ham and cheese, just the way I like it. I went without lunch because of you!"

Glenn snickered. "I didn't eat your sandwich."

"It wasn't there. I looked."

The other man kept grinning. "Aww, I was just pulling a prank on you. Lighten up! Look in the bottom drawer. I kept waiting for you to say something, but you spoiled the joke." Glenn strolled over to his own desk to enjoy his new photos of cattle mutilations.

Malcolm turned back to the burned journal, wondering what had happened to the 1939 Antarctic Expedition. He'd never heard about it, which didn't mean anything. That was the whole point of this government installation. The journal had remained here, wrapped and untouched in the intake office for more than a decade. He would read it, cover to cover.

Before starting, he went into the kitchen area, pulled open the heavy door of the Frigidaire, and looked at the empty shelves where he had placed his sandwich yesterday. Determined not to go hungry again, he had brought a fresh sandwich this morning, sliced ham, Swiss cheese, and bright yellow mustard on white bread, wrapped up in butcher paper. Malcolm pulled open the bottom drawer designed for fresh produce, which was never used because here in the Nevada desert fresh produce was as rare as a UFO sighting.

Yesterday's sandwich was exactly where Glenn had hidden it.

In frustration, Malcolm snatched up the wrapped package and went back to the desk. He would eat the sandwich while reading the mysterious journal. Munching on the cold ham and cheese, he paged through the damaged book, careful not to get mustard on the paper.

Blair was the expedition's biologist at the Antarctic station, serving with dozens of meteorologists, geologists, engineers, radio men, support crew. Malcolm read with widening eyes about the discovery of an enormous alien spacecraft buried deep within the ice. From the description, the ancient ship sounded vastly larger than the more recent flying saucer found near Roswell, New Mexico.

During excavations, the team had found a hideous blue creature with three red eyes, also frozen in ice outside the ship. The alien inhabitant was certainly dead, especially since one of the diggers had accidentally cleaved its head with an ice axe when they chopped it out of the ice. When they had used thermite bombs to clear more of the ice sheet, they unintentionally vaporized the entire alien vessel.

A shame, Malcolm thought, since the ship would surely have been brought back here to Nevada to be stored inside the warehouse.

"You've got to see this, Buddy!" Glenn stalked over from his desk holding up a manila folder. He pulled out glossy black-and-white photos of mangled cattle, their bodily organs strewn across fields in Montana. "It looks like a combination of Dr. Mengele and some insane barbecue chef."

"We've already processed all the Mengele records." Malcolm looked up from Blair's engrossing journal, but quickly averted his eyes. "Hey, I'm not supposed to see that! It's not my project."

"Sure, sure," Glenn said as he wandered back to his desk. "Thought you'd find it interesting."

Malcolm went back to reading, turning one page after another as Blair described how the supposedly dead alien had thawed from the block of ice and come alive again...but more than alive. As the research crew studied it, they found that the alien organism was somehow infectious, a cellular chameleon that was much more than the three-eyed blue monster they found in the ice. The "alien" itself had infected the expedition members like a plague, taking over and mimicking one man after another. Something as small as a cell could spread the inhuman presence like a virus.

Malcolm kept reading, amazed. With all those expedition members crowded in tiny huts, shoulder to shoulder with no privacy whatsoever, how could they possibly remain in quarantine for an entire Antarctic winter? There would be no stopping such an insidious extraterrestrial invasion.

He was suddenly reminded of how he and Glenn were sealed inside a cinderblock office building in the middle of the desert, forced to work under conditions that were far too close for comfort. Malcolm shook his head, tried to get his thoughts back on track.

The journal described how the monsters subsumed one member after another, while Blair himself, a suspected alien, had been locked away in his own hut, isolated from everyone else. He had written this account, thinking that he was the safe one, while the crew turned on one another both through genuine alien violence but also with all-too-human paranoia.

Blair had huddled in his shack day after day. As his account grew more erratic and less rational, Malcolm thought the biologist might be suffering from cabin fever, slowly going insane. Then the writing itself became illegible, no longer the clear and concise letters from the opening pages, following the neatly ruled lines in the scientific ledger. The writing degenerated into scrawls and, chillingly, into a different language entirely—undeniably alien symbols conveying a message that no human was ever meant to read.

Malcolm swallowed a mouthful of ham-and-cheese and wiped mustard from the corner of his lip.

According to Blair's account, the alien presence was amazingly infectious. One little germ could transform a man into an extraterrestrial monster. At least the bubonic plague had required rats and fleas, but this silent invasion passed from person to person through nothing more than a touch. It was terrifying.

Self-consciously, he wiped his hand on a napkin, then froze, looked down at his fingers, at the pages he had been touching. He swallowed hard.

If Blair was contaminated when he'd written this journal, how long would the germs endure? Many disease organisms could not survive in the open air and stopped being contagious after only a minute or two. But this thing from another world had been frozen under the Antarctic ice for thousands of years, and it had thrived as soon as it was exposed.

Malcolm tossed the rest of his sandwich into the wastebasket, no longer hungry. He scrubbed his hands on his slacks and hurried to the lavatory to wash his hands, again and again, with hot water and soap. Finally clean, he heaved a sigh of relief. Next time he would wear gloves.

* * * *

The following morning, Malcolm passed through the guard gate and thick vault door, eager to finish documenting Blair's journal so he could be done with the unsettling story. He would fill out the Unusual Object Report and lock away this case once and for all. Flying saucers and little green men were far more palatable than a shape-shifting alien plague.

He went straight to the kitchen area and opened the Frigidaire to verify that his uneaten sandwich was still there from yesterday. Good, he was set for lunch. Just to be cautious, he slid it into the bottom produce drawer, hiding it. Maybe Glenn wouldn't notice.

When he entered the main room, he caught Glenn at his desk hunched over the charred journal, reading intently. His face bore a lascivious expression like a man staring at a pornographic pamphlet.

Malcolm squawked, "What are you doing? That's a breach of security!"

The other man had the decency to look embarrassed before he laughed it off. "I won't report it if you won't."

"I just might!" Malcolm snapped. He would have done so if he knew exactly where to file a complaint. He glanced at the red button on the wall—NEVER CALL FOR HELP—and sighed in frustration. "You're not supposed to be looking at my cases."

"I'll show you mine if you show me yours."

"No!"

Glenn offered a disarming grin that did not work on Malcolm. "We're co-workers, Buddy. We both have the same top-level security clearance." Trying to change the subject, he pointed down at Blair's journal. "That's an amazing story! I've been pawing through the pages, trying to get more information. You think it's real? Pretty hard to believe!"

Malcolm crossed his arms over his chest. "Think of all the things we've cataloged and placed into storage. *Everything* here is real."

With his bare hands, Glenn flipped the pages again, then closed the cover of Blair's journal. "That story reminds me of hoof-and-mouth disease, which I've been researching for my report. That's the official government explanation for the cattle mutilations, you know. Hoof-and-mouth disease is so deadly that if one cow gets infected, you can't just cull and quarantine the animal. The only way to be sure is to take out the whole herd." He nodded as if agreeing with himself. "The whole herd.

"Now, of course that's not the real explanation for the cattle mutilations, but the government is incinerating every carcass, burning an entire ranch to the ground and blaming it on wildfires. The ranchers who first reported the mutilated cattle are also suffering convenient accidents."

Malcolm backed away. "You're not supposed to tell me that."

Glenn tapped his finger on the closed cover of Blair's journal. "That's probably what happened to the 1939 expedition, extreme measures to stop the infestation. I bet the whole camp was burned to the ice, no survivors, no bodies, nothing left to salvage. Newspapers back in the day must have reported a fierce winter storm wiping out the station, condolences to the brave scientists, et cetera, et cetera. You know what I'm talking about, Buddy. We've both written stories like that ourselves."

"That's above my pay grade!" Malcolm said. "My job is to document the unusual object, fill out a report, and place it into storage. And you'd be well advised to do your job."

"Whatever." Glenn stepped away from the desk, rubbed his fingers together, then wiped them on his pants before he went back to his cattle mutilations.

Today, Malcolm pulled on a pair of latex gloves and turned the fragile pages with care. He filled half a notebook with his impressions of what he'd read yesterday, determined to make his report as complete as possible. Once Blair's journal went into cold storage, he wanted no excuse for anyone to touch it again.

In the journal, the biologist speculated that the infection rate might progress at different rates, depending on the host. The alien cells could seize and subsume any organic matter, not just the expedition members themselves, but also the cows at the research station, the sled dogs used for transport across the ice. Blair feared that a wandering gull might be infected, copied, and fly off to spread the alien infestation to the mainland.

The second time through, Malcolm read the speculations with increasing interest as well as skepticism. Since Blair had been quarantined and isolated in his shack, he was away from the rest of the camp. Therefore, how had he known the things he described as the camp fell apart around him?

Unless the alien cells that were taking over his body had some sort of connection with the others. Telepathy? An alien biological network? Maybe as he became more and more inhuman, Blair in his quarantine shack did know everything the other aliens knew.

Or maybe he was just a man losing his mind due to the isolation and the howling Antarctic wind.

Yes, that was the best explanation. Considering Malcolm's experience here in the government storage complex, though, mundane explanations rarely turned out to be true.

* * * *

That night back in his assigned employee barracks on site, Malcolm locked the flimsy plywood door then barricaded it with the single chair from his dinette table. He didn't want to talk to anyone, didn't want to go to sleep, but he couldn't stay awake.

He lay on his hard bunk, wide-eyed and listening to muted sounds through the thin walls. In the adjacent room, Glenn had a record player and was not shy about sharing his music. He played platter after platter, Nat King Cole, Bing Crosby, Guy Lombardo, the Andrews Sisters. Tonight, the music was at least comforting, and it was *human*. And Glenn himself was human, even though Malcolm didn't want his company.

He was hungry and queasy. That day, he had been so disturbed and distracted that he'd forgotten to eat his sandwich, so he left it in the refrigerator for the next day. Maybe he would have his appetite back then. His head throbbed. His ears had a ringing in them, possibly from the music next door.

Though still edgy, he finally dozed off, but the nightmares that came to him were far from comforting—vile dreams of monsters and spaceships. The cold emptiness of the universe was Earth's only real protection against all the terrors out there. Though he didn't dream in words or distinct images in his fugue state of sleep, Malcolm was overwhelmed by a surging loneliness replaced by intense anger, a need for conquest, a hunger to take over the world.

When he woke at dawn, those strange thoughts persisted, as did the headache, worse than an extreme hangover. He sat alone in the commissary and drank his morning coffee, shaking and confused. For some reason, his body was sluggish and hard to control, but the alien thoughts disturbed him more than anything.

Malcolm Hobbs was a civil servant, a quiet man; some might even call him meek. He had no delusions of grandeur. In fact, he had very few aspirations at all, and he was proud of it. He was comfortable with his role as a tiny cog in a big machine. He was not an emperor. If he took over the world, what would he do with it?

Thus, these thoughts clearly were not his own. They originated from outside his personality. Something alien.

He rubbed his hands together and washed them again furiously with soap and water. Was that sufficient? But if soap and water could kill an alien invasion, then surely the Antarctic research station would never have fallen.

What if the thing was inside him now? What if some alien cells had survived on the pages of Blair's journal? What if they had worked their way through his fingertips, penetrated his bloodstream, then swirled through his body, changing him cell by cell, organ by organ. Would he even know?

And what could the thing possibly want with him? He was isolated in the bleakest desert in the United States, a place as barren and isolated as savage Antarctica.

The answer dropped on him like a meteor falling from above. This government storage complex was no minor meteorological station. The top secret government warehouses held the most amazing artifacts, extraterrestrial technologies, powerful objects considered too dangerous for anyone but the U.S. government.

What if the thing wanted the Roswell spacecraft?

If the aliens spread among the workers here, they would have access to all the technology and resources they needed—not only to fly home, but to take over the Earth, even destroy it a dozen times over!

According to Blair, the alien organism could easily transfer from host to host without being noticed—not just human to human, but the sled dogs, the cows, everything in the research station had been infected. The alien cells could take over any organic substance.

What if an infected person got out of this installation? Even if the "human" were killed, the alien cells could jump to a desert rat or a tortoise, a rattlesnake, a beetle. The Nevada desert wasn't nearly as lifeless as it looked. What if the thing got loose?

Malcolm rushed off. He couldn't get through the guard gates, sally ports, and heavy vault doors quickly enough. He needed to get to his desk so he could seal away Blair's journal, along with its fully completed unusual object information form, forever!

He hoped he wasn't too late.

* * * *

Malcolm nearly collapsed with relief when he saw the journal still there in the middle of his desk. He had to finish the paperwork so the unusual object could be placed under even higher security deep in the warehouses, where Malcom need not worry about contamination.

He pulled on rubber gloves, then donned a second pair for extra security. The bland scientific journal looked so innocuous, like the lab reports he had written in college chemistry class, but he knew it contained a ticking biological bomb. The ringing in his head was so loud he couldn't concentrate.

He found the original layers of thick industrial plastic and wrapped the journal as tightly as he could, taping and retaping, scribbling *Danger! Hazardous Material! Danger!* in bold black marker. When that was done, he stuffed the bulky package into a lead-lined Top Secret courier packet. On the tag he wrote *Dangerous Material. Do Not Open.*

With shaking hands, he fumbled with the combination lock on the top drawer of his armored file cabinet. Due to his blurred vision, he had to try three times before he finally got the combination settings right. Malcolm stuffed the object inside the drawer, wedged it between thick manila folders about other mysterious artifacts he had worked on. When he slammed the drawer and spun the combo lock, at last he let out a sigh. He swept a hand across his forehead, smearing away beads of perspiration, and swallowed hard. His mouth tasted funny. He wondered if he was coming down with the flu.

Glenn barged in, whistling. He paused to give Malcolm a long suspicious look. "You okay, Buddy? You look like you went on a bender last night."

"I'm fine. It's all taken care of." Inside his head, he heard what sounded like faint and distant fire alarms ringing. He didn't want to talk to Glenn, couldn't stand to be around the man.

What if his office mate was infected? Glenn had smeared his sweaty hands across the pages, maybe contaminating himself. What would he do if Glenn was secretly an alien?

What if Malcolm himself was an alien?

He slapped a palm against his temple as if to jar his brain loose.

"Whoa, careful there, Buddy!" Glenn cried. "Don't hurt yourself."

Malcolm ran to the kitchenette just to get away. His stomach felt queasy, his body was shaking, and with a start he realized that he hadn't eaten since the day before. He had been so engrossed in filling out the report and documenting the terrifying journal that he had left his ham sandwich hidden in the drawer. Maybe that was all, low blood sugar, malnutrition...

Unreasonably ravenous, Malcolm pulled open the Frigidaire, ready to wolf down the sandwich right there. He just needed to eat.

But when he pulled open the produce drawer, he saw that the butcher paper wrapped around the bread had burst open, the paper tape split apart. The top slice of exposed white bread was pulsing and writhing. Startled, Malcolm recoiled.

Exposed to the light and the warmer air, the sandwich twisted, awake now. The neatly cut bread flapped open like the lips around a toothless mouth. The slices of ham churned and became alive.

Malcolm sucked in a breath to scream, realizing that the alien cells could invade anything organic…like ham, cheese, even mustard!

Before his eyes, the slices of ham grew needlelike fangs. The sandwich became a rabid, chomping monster. Long, thin tentacles flashed out, whips filled with mustard-colored blood.

Malcolm screamed and kicked the refrigerator door shut as the sandwich thing tried to escape from the drawer. The heavy door sealed and locked.

His heart pounding, his pulse racing, Malcolm staggered back. He heard a thump from inside the Frigidaire as the unearthly thing hammered inside its cold prison. He turned and ran.

He was isolated here in the office complex. Malcolm bolted to the main room, gasping for breath and trying to form words. He had screamed in the kitchenette, but now he saw Glenn patiently working at his desk, undisturbed, studying his cattle-mutilation photos as if enjoying them for breakfast.

"There's something weird in the refrigerator. It's trying to take over the world!"

The other man turned to him, and his eyes were strange. "You're acting a little odd, Buddy."

"Odd? The odd thing is in the produce drawer!"

Glenn rose to his feet, letting his swivel office chair turn slowly like a planet in a dying orbit. "Maybe you need a rest. You're not yourself."

"Nothing is the same!" Malcolm screamed.

Glenn took a step closer, consoling. "This is awfully strange behavior."

From the kitchenette behind him, Malcolm could hear the louder thumping and then a crash. The sandwich thing had burst through the seal and the lock, tearing open the refrigerator door. "Can't you hear that? It's escaping!"

"Come here, Buddy." Glenn's expression was unusual, as if he couldn't quite control his face.

Malcolm froze. "You're not acting normal, Glenn. I think you're—"

"Everything's fine, Buddy." Glenn reached out, but as he extended his arm, it kept growing. His fingers elongated into twisted tentacles. His hands split, and his chest swelled, reshaping itself to sprout a third arm that popped through the buttons of his shirt. All the appendages reached toward Malcolm, bursting with claws and suckers. One of Glenn's hands sported three red eyes.

Malcolm squirmed away as the Glenn-thing closed in. The sandwich monstrosity shambled out of the kitchenette, no longer resembling bread, deli meat, cheese, and mustard. It grew in bulk as if absorbing material from the air, and more tentacles lashed out as it approached Malcolm from the opposite direction.

Glenn's face melted, and his mouth dropped open, filled with fangs, yet still moaning in a quiet voice. "It's all right."

Pressed against the cinderblock wall, Malcolm expected to be torn to pieces as the monster grasped him, but the disfigured tentacle hand simply patted his shoulder. "It's all right."

Malcolm looked down to watch his own arm elongating as if the bones themselves had become thorns, as if the cartilage added extra inches. His fingers twitched and twisted with minds of their own, and one sprouted a bright red eye that peered back at his face.

Malcolm couldn't stop screaming.

The sandwich thing thumped into the room, joining them. Glenn's body split in half, sprouting fangs and claws in all the wrong places.

Malcolm's own throat was changing, his neck stretching. His corrupted vocal cords altered his scream into an inhuman roar.

But he saw the red button on the adjacent cinderblock wall. It wouldn't normally have been within reach, but his arms were freakishly longer now. They flopped about, but he could still control them…somewhat.

NEVER CALL FOR HELP.

Malcolm didn't care about losing his job or his security clearance. If there had ever been a time to push the red button this was it.

The Glenn-thing tried to stop him as it realized what he intended to do. The ham-and-cheese monster lunged, but not in time.

Malcolm hit the big red scary button.

A recorded woman's voice spoke calmly from the ceiling speakers, "Thank you for initiating the extreme decontamination protocol. Please stand by."

Alarm sirens went off along with rotating magenta danger lights, flooding the intake office with storm of racket and light. Ignited flame jets dropped down through the ceiling panels, bursting into bright orange fire at the same time as acid nozzles gushed a flood of caustic liquid.

As Malcolm saw a last burst of bright heat and searing chemical pain, he realized he was looking through a dozen additional alien eyes, all of which mercifully went dark in an instant.

* * * *

Being assigned to an ultra-secret government warehouse deep in the Nevada desert wasn't as exciting as it sounded, but nobody chose a civil service job for the excitement. That was exactly the way Dennis McGann liked it.

He was proud to have his top secret security clearance and glad to serve his country. This wasn't necessarily the most glamorous job assignment, but it would be interesting, no doubt about that.

Dennis was a new hire brought into the Unusual Object Intake Office. He and his new partner, a man named Wilson, had the office all to themselves, each with a sturdy government-issue desk and his own file cabinet. The office had plenty of elbow room, even a kitchenette with a new-model Frigidaire refrigerator. The cinderblock walls had a fresh coat of white paint.

"Nice digs," he said to Wilson. The other man just grunted and took a seat in a swivel office chair at his desk.

Dennis was pleased to see he already had a project waiting for him on his desk, a bulky lead-lined classified courier envelope. It contained a rectangular package, wrapped in layers upon layers of plastic. Someone had handwritten on the package label *Dangerous Material. Do Not Open*—obviously meant for someone at a lower pay grade.

Dennis had been brought in to document unusual objects, study them, and write reports. He intended to do a good job. He cut the layers of plastic and began unwrapping.

"Best get to work," he said aloud, receiving only a grunt from his office partner. Dennis opened the package.

GOOD AS DEAD

NINA KIRIKI HOFFMAN

When Lilian's husband came home to Norfolk, Virginia, from his scientific Antarctic expedition after seven months away, he brought his dirty laundry with him.

Lilian rushed to the store and bought Arthur's favorite food when she got the telegram saying his ship had come into port: big baking potatoes and fresh butter. The butcher sold her two steaks. Back home, she set the table with the good china and silver her parents had given her and Arthur when they had married two years earlier. She straightened up the living room, where she'd been doing mending for people in the neighborhood for extra money in the evenings, and she mopped the floor.

By the time he got home, the potatoes were almost ready.

"Oh, Arthur," she said in despairing tones as she unpacked his duffle in their bedroom. The stench wafting up from the furs and garments was enough to paralyze a parrot. Their wire-haired terrier, Asta, was as interested in the duffle as she often was in the manure the ice-cart and milk-cart horses left on the street. "Shoo," Lilian whispered to the dog, afraid Asta might roll in the filthy fur jacket Lilian had pulled from the duffle.

"Oh, Lilian!" Arthur grabbed her, hugged her, and swung her around in a foxtrot step. He had been able to wash on the steamer ship on the way home, and he smelled like coconut castile soap. "Isn't life grand?"

"Well, it's grand to have you home again," she said, "but I'm not so sure about your clothes."

"We washed our underwear at Big Magnet, but the outer garments—"

"They had no laundries on the ship?"

Humming "Life Is Just a Bowl of Cherries," he danced her out of the bedroom and into their living room, with its gramophone, cabinet radio, and fireplace. They had bought a house with a big living room just so they could dance. She laughed as her body remembered how well they matched tempo. They had met in a taxi dance hall. He had spent all his dance tickets on her that first night. He came back every Friday night until the night he brought the ring with him, and then she didn't ever taxi dance again.

They took three turns around the living room. He stopped, his arms still around her. "I had other things to do on the trip home," he said, and then let go of her. He lost his smile, and his gaze went past her into memory. Then he shook his head. "Good to have that behind me."

"What happened?"

He focused on her again, and his expression softened. He hugged her tight, then kissed her. "Honey, I can't tell you how glad I am to be home."

* * * *

"Do I smell something burning?" Arthur asked.

Lilian tightened her arms around him. He was so tense, not relaxed as he used to be when they danced. "Probably." She released him and went through the swinging door into the kitchen. She opened the oven and smoke poured out. "Oh no!" The bakers were charred. She hadn't started the steaks yet; Arthur always did the grilling.

He laughed. "We can go out," he said. "I'd love to take my best girl to a swanky place for dinner. Our rations down there were pretty darned basic. I've been dreaming of lemon meringue pie for months."

Lilian heaved a sigh and pulled the potatoes out of the stove with a big fork. She put them on a crockery plate near the sink. She'd cut them up later to see if anything could be salvaged. She put the steaks back in the ice box to keep. Good thing Asta hadn't gotten to them while she and Arthur were dancing.

"Asta," she said, suddenly.

Asta barked from the bedroom.

"Oh, no." Lilian rushed back to the bedroom to discover her fears had been realized: Asta was rolling around ecstatically on the stinking fur jacket from Arthur's duffle. "Bad dog!" Lilian cried, dragging the jacket out from under a wriggling Asta. "Can't we throw this horrible thing away?"

"That jacket saved my life. It was cold enough there to freeze flesh in a minute or two, honey. Sixty below zero. We spent a lot of time inside."

"Thank you, Jacket, for saving my husband's life," she said to the jacket. "For now, you're going in the storage shed." She stuffed it back into the duffle and hauled the whole thing out on the back porch, then put it in the shed with the washtub and washboard. She'd start the soak tomorrow.

She'd probably have to give the dog a bath, too, but the smell was much less pungent with the offending garment removed.

* * * *

She dabbed some Woolworth's perfume at her wrists and behind her ears, and put on lip paint. They walked to Granby Street in the cool April night and went to Arthur's favorite diner for supper. Arthur groaned with pleasure as he ate the meatloaf special, followed by his favorite lemon meringue pie. Later, in a night club with live music, when he had his arms around her on the dance floor, Lilian relaxed and leaned into him. He was warm, strong, and solid, and he smelled so male. She'd missed him so much.

They got home after midnight. "Asta? Do you want to go out?" she called as they entered the house.

The dog didn't bark.

Arthur laughed and pulled her toward the bedroom.

"Just a minute." She wriggled out of his embrace and went to close all the curtains. "Mrs. Milligan next door, I swear, Arthur, I've caught her in our yard peering in through the windows. Anytime, day or night. She's a menace to the neighborhood."

"A menace?" Arthur said, and laughed. "That old biddy? What menacing could she possibly do?"

"She makes up stories and tells them to all the meanest, most gossipy people on the block. And then—" Why had she brought this up? Lilian groaned. It had taken her three weeks to shrug off the story Mrs. Milligan had spread about Lilian having a man visiting her at night.

"Let's give her something to talk about," Arthur said, and tugged her to the bedroom, then unbuttoned her dress. She squealed and rushed to close the curtains before her dress slid off her.

"I've been dreaming of this," Arthur murmured as he stripped and followed her into bed.

"I have, too," she whispered.

* * * *

Later in the night, he woke screaming and thrashing. He pushed her away so hard she tumbled off the bed onto the floor. "You're one of them!" he screamed.

Her heart pounded. She had been sound asleep, and the shock of waking and being shoved out from under warm covers into cool air, the impact—she couldn't remember where she was or whom she was with. She lay on the floor, the cool night air reviving her, and tried to piece things together.

Arthur still thrashed in the bed. "Get away from me! Don't touch me! You're one of them!"

Shivering, Lilian wrapped her negligee around her. She'd heard one shouldn't wake a sleeper having a nightmare, but Arthur wasn't making sense, and he was in such distress. She turned back the covers as he fought with phantoms. "Arthur," she whispered, then louder, "Arthur!"

"Stay back! You've gotten the commander and the others, but you won't get me!" he screamed so loudly she was afraid Mrs. Milligan would hear.

"Arthur." She spoke sternly. "Wake up this instant." She took the glass of water she kept by the bed and poured it on his chest.

He jerked awake. "What?" he asked, and breathed as if he'd just run a race.

"You were having the most dreadful dream," she said. "What on Earth happened down there?"

"Lily," he said, and sobbed. He held out his arms, and she went into them. He hugged her so tightly her ribs creaked. "I thought I'd never see you again," he whispered into her hair. "We were all ready to die to save the world from—from—" His arms tightened, then relaxed. "But now…"

"You're home," she murmured, stroking his back.

* * * *

She got up early the next morning and put on her negligee, house coat, and slippers so she could boil water for coffee and check the chicken coop for eggs. "Asta," she called, because the dog always needed to be let out first thing; it was part of their routine. Asta wasn't waiting by the back door, and she should have been; Lilian hadn't let her out the night before. "Asta?"

The dog came out of the living room, shaking her head, then barked.

"Did you have an accident? You bad dog!"

Asta scratched at the back door and Lilian let her out into the yard. Lilian looked in the living room for a puddle or a poop, but found nothing. She grabbed the egg basket and followed Asta outside. Her hens had been laying well. Today she wouldn't have any extra eggs to sell to Mr. Elliott next door; she'd need them for Arthur.

Mr. Elliott was at the back gate, waiting. He was a much better neighbor than Mrs. Milligan. Gray-haired and stooped with age, he was a retired railroad man who lived simply, and was quick to help if Lilian needed someone to fix a misbehaving oven or a loose shingle. She gathered the eggs in her basket and walked over to tell him the news. "I'm afraid you'll have to find someone else with chickens. My husband's home."

"Is that who it is?"

"What did Mrs. Milligan tell you?"

Mr. Elliott smiled. "I don't ever believe her, but she's always entertaining."

"Would you care to hear what she's told me about you?"

His eyes sparkled. "What could be interesting about an old dog like me?"

"Honey?" Arthur, in his threadbare flannel robe, walked barefoot out the back door into the chilly morning.

"Arthur, this is our neighbor to the left, Mr. Elliott. Mr. Elliott, my husband, Arthur Vane. He's just come back from a trip to the bottom of the world!"

"Elliott," said Arthur, offering his hand. They shook hands. "We've met."

"Yes, of course," said Mr. Elliott.

"I've got fresh eggs, and I bought a loaf of bread at the bakery yesterday," said Lilian. "Excuse us, Mr. Elliott." She turned to go inside. Arthur followed her after a few murmurs to Mr. Elliott. "Asta!"

The dog rushed in ahead of her, and she poured some kibble for Asta in a bowl, then made coffee, toasted bread, and fried the eggs. Arthur sat and watched as she prepared him a plate. "You're a sight for sore eyes," he said, smiling.

"Thanks." She set the plate down in front of him and made one for herself. "I've got to get to work in half an hour. Will you be staying home today?"

"There's a debriefing at the naval base," he said. "We'll be studying all the data we collected for the next six months, at least."

"All right." She ate quickly and made him a sandwich to take to work. "Tell me all about it later."

* * * *

When she got home after her shift in the secretarial pool at the Ford Factory, Arthur wasn't back yet. On the back porch, she filled the wash tub with water and soap flakes and dumped Arthur's horrid fur jacket in to soak overnight, then snapped Asta's leash on and took the dog for a stroll.

The dog was behaving strangely. She didn't stop and sniff at every tree trunk, fence post, bush, and mailbox as she usually did, but walked head up, looking back and forth at everything around them.

The bulldog from the Petersons' house down the street was running loose. Asta and the dog had a growling relationship with each other that had never escalated to an outright fight. Today, the bulldog came up and growled at Asta, and Asta lowered her head. The other dog approached, and Asta nudged it with her shoulder. It yipped and ran.

Lilian frowned.

Mrs. Milligan was sitting on her front porch next door, and called out as they went by. She was thin, with a hawk nose, and hair so black it must come from a bottle. It crowned her head in a thick, braided coronet. She wore a sapphire blue gown, dark stockings, and polished black shoes, and she sat up straight, as though her righteousness gave her power. The knitting needles in her hands clacked away at something gray.

Lilian thought about ignoring her, but that was always a bad idea. She opened the white picket gate and walked up to the porch with Asta.

"Your husband's home?" Mrs. Milligan asked.

"Yes, ma'am." How I hate you, Lilian thought.

Asta stared up at Mrs. Milligan.

"It must be nice after such a long absence."

"Yes, ma'am." I wish you had a husband who would beat you every time you told a lie. And every time you tell the truth.

"What will you do with your other man now?" Mrs. Milligan's smile showed her small, pearly teeth.

"Why, nothing, ma'am." It was never any of your business in the first place. "Is that all you have to say to me, ma'am?"

"For now."

"Good day, ma'am." Lilian tugged on Asta's leash, and the dog finally turned around.

"How I wish she were dead," Lilian whispered to Asta after they'd rounded a corner. The dog looked up at her with bright eyes.

* * * *

Lilian and Arthur listened to "It's Dance Time" on the radio after supper, and tried all the fancy steps they used to dance. Arthur smelled of cigarette smoke and sweat. She held him close. He was still the best dancer she'd ever known.

She woke when his nightmares started, and eased out of the bed before he could shove her out this time. She took a blanket from the linen cupboard, went to the living room, and curled up on the couch.

Asta climbed up with her. She rested her hand on the dog's wiry fur. Asta's back was warm against her thigh.

In her dream, the dog spoke to her.

"I don't mean you any harm," said Asta in a warm voice that reminded Lilian of her mother's. "We worked too swiftly before. We had no strategy. Sometimes that's effective, but now it's time to put our second plan in place. We need…a friend. Will you be my friend, Lily?"

"We've always been friends, ever since you were a puppy," Lilian said. "But I never heard you talk before."

"I'm not talking now," said Asta, cocking her head to one side and then the other, the way she always did when she was considering something.

"Aren't you?" Lilian asked.

"Not out loud."

"Oh."

Asta licked her hand with a warm, wet tongue. "Be my friend, Lily." It was true: the voice didn't come out of Asta's mouth, but was somehow in Lilian's head.

"All right," said Lilian.

* * * *

She had a crick in her neck from sleeping sideways on the couch. It was Saturday, Lilian's wash day, since she worked at the Ford Factory on Mondays. Arthur slept late; he had the weekend off. After a solitary breakfast, Lilian heated pots of water on the stove and set up the wash tub and the mangle on the back porch. Today she had piles of clothes to wash—most of what Arthur had brought back with him, and all her own undergarments and her two work dresses. And that horrid jacket. After its long soak, it wasn't so terrible, only bedraggled. She didn't run it through the mangle, but she scrubbed it on the washboard so fiercely it shed some fur. She hung it on the end of the line farthest from the house.

When she turned around, Mrs. Milligan stood there.

Lilian startled. "Oh! You gave me quite a turn!"

Mrs. Milligan wore a scarlet dress today. It was starched and looked scratchy. She was taller than Lilian by a head, and seemed to enjoy looking down her nose at Lilian and everyone else. Mrs. Milligan said, "Your husband has been away so long. Perhaps he'd like to know what you did while he was out of town. I wonder if I feel like talking with him today."

"You don't," said Lilian. She had never seen Arthur in a rage, but he'd told her stories about fights he'd been in when he was younger. He'd been a boxer in college, and he'd gotten into trouble with the law a few times for street brawls.

If Mrs. Milligan told her about Peter, she'd be as good as dead.

"I wonder," Mrs. Milligan said, drawing out the syllables.

"What do you want?"

"I'll bring my wash over here, shall I?"

Lilian stared at Mrs. Milligan and ground her teeth.

"I'll come back for it when it's clean. I'll hang it on my own line when you're done. Unless you'd like to come over and do it for me."

Lilian lowered her gaze and stared at her roughened red hands against the washboard. Her head hurt. Probably from clenching her teeth so hard.

Asta barked. She darted toward Mrs. Milligan and growled.

"Leash your dog," Mrs. Milligan muttered, and backed out of the yard. She returned and dropped a basket of laundry over the gate.

Asta barked once at Lilian and raced to the fence. She stood watching Mrs. Milligan walk next door.

Lilian finished her own wash and hung it to dry on the line, then tackled Mrs. Milligan's. If only she had a box of the itching powder her little brother Paul used to torment her with, or a supply of frogs, or poisonous spiders. How she hated the woman's power.

* * * *

When she brought the basket of clean, wet clothes to Mrs. Milligan's front porch, the woman was nowhere to be found. Lilian knocked on the door, softly at first, then louder, but no one came. Muttering, Lilian went around back and hung Mrs. Milligan's clothes on the line herself. There must be something she could do to stop the woman ordering her around, but she wasn't sure what. She wished she could talk to Arthur about it, but that was the problem. Too long an absence made the heart grow fonder, and then weary of waiting. She had been so lonely.

She went home and made Arthur a late breakfast/lunch, and then they went to Ocean View Beach. Asta didn't answer her call when they left the house. Maybe she was sleeping. She would be sorry she missed the beach. She loved trotting along the water's edge, sniffing for new and disgusting things to roll in.

Chesapeake Bay was calm under the cool spring sky, and the beach stretched out in both directions, stirred by footsteps, empty of people. "Can you tell me what happened?" she asked Arthur as they walked along the water's edge. "The nightmares?"

He didn't speak for a while, staring out at the water and away from her. At last he said, "We discovered something amazing. I can't tell you much more about it—it's classified. It was exciting at first, though. And then…it killed half of us."

She gripped his hand. "Oh, Arthur."

"Killed half of us and made us all suspect each other. Broke our trust. We destroyed it, but—"

They walked a while without speaking.

"Where have you been spending the night? I woke up and you weren't there," he said presently.

"When those dreadful dreams take you, you punch. You pushed me off the bed. I didn't know whether to wake you, so last night, I didn't. I spent the rest of the night on the living room couch."

He turned and pulled her into his arms, resting his chin on the top of her head. "Oh, Lily. I'm so sorry. I wouldn't hurt you for the world."

"I know." She hugged him back, her cheek against his chest. What if half her friends had died? She thought of the other girls in the typing pool, and the couples she and Arthur sometimes went to clubs with or played cards with, the girls at the taxi dance club, and her childhood best friend Clara. She knew some of Arthur's colleagues from summer barbecues and Christmas parties. When he and the other men got to talking about their work, she and the other wives fled. She had liked most of the men, even if they talked about natural forces and numbers too much. "I'm sorry you lost your friends," she said into his shirt.

His arms tightened around her, then dropped to his sides. He took her hand and they walked again. "I guess we were in a war and didn't know it."

* * * *

She took all the laundry off the line and folded it when they got home, separating out the pile to be ironed. Then she glanced over the hedge and saw Mrs. Milligan's wash still on the line. Spiteful beast.

Asta scratched at the kitchen door while Lilian was making cornbread for supper. Lilian opened the door and the dog rushed in. She danced a little, then went to her food bowl and ate.

"Where have you been, you naughty dog?" Lilian asked.

Asta stared up at her with bright eyes, and dropped her jaw in a dog smile. Lilian knelt and hugged her. "Wherever it was, it doesn't smell horrid. Welcome home." The dog licked her cheek.

Someone knocked on the back door. She peeked around the edge of the curtain on the door's window and saw it was Mrs. Milligan again. Good lord, what could she want now? Lilian looked to see where Arthur was. He was in the living room, reading the paper, with the radio on low; Stan Kenton was reading the latest sports scores. She toed the doorstop away from the swing-ing door and let it flap closed, cutting off her view of her husband. Then she went to the kitchen door and opened it a crack. "What do you want?" she muttered to Mrs. Milligan.

The woman stared at her face.

"What is it? I have to make supper."

"I came to make peace," said Mrs. Milligan. She stooped to pet Asta, who smiled at her and shook all over with delight when Mrs. Milligan scratched behind her ears.

"What?" Lilian looked at her dog, who routinely growled and barked at Mrs. Milligan. Sometimes Lilian gave Asta dog biscuits to encourage her.

"I won't be threatening you anymore, my dear. I hope we can be friends." Mrs. Milligan held out a hand. Lilian stared at it, and then finally shook it, though she suspected this was a trick.

Mrs. Milligan's hand was warm, her clasp gentle. "Thank you for clean-ing my clothes," she said.

"Sure." Lilian wiped her hands on her apron. "Excuse me."

"Of course." The woman turned and walked down the back porch steps. Lilian closed and locked the door behind her, then turned on the gas stove so she could heat a pan she could fry hash in.

"Well, Asta, that was strange, wasn't it? Why do you like her now?"

Asta barked, turned around three times, and lay by the stove, resting her muzzle on her front paws.

* * * *

That night, after she and Arthur had made love, she slid out from under the covers and pulled on her nightgown.

"Don't go, honey. You don't know how much I've missed hanging onto you in the dark."

She hesitated, then slipped back into bed and into his embrace. His arms were cabled with muscle, his chest padded with musky fur. He rolled onto his back so she lay half on top of him. She laid her head on his chest and listened to his heart. His breathing was quiet as he held her. She relaxed into sleep.

She woke to a storm. "Get off me, you vampire, you monster! You got the others, but you won't get me!" Arthur shoved her away from him and she rolled off the bed onto the floor again. Her head thunked against the wooden floor boards. She landed badly, barking her elbows. She lay on the floor and cried silently while he fought with the covers and screamed. She crept from the room.

In the bathroom, she studied her elbows and painted Mercurochrome on the bleeding scratches. She took an aspirin for her aching head, then retreated to the living room couch again, curling up with Asta.

* * * *

Asta was in her dream again. "You don't have to worry about Mrs. Milligan anymore. She's a changed person."

"All right." Lilian stroked along Asta's jaw and scratched behind her ears. "Does anyone really change?"

"Oh, yes," said Asta. "I've changed, too."

"Yes, you have." Asta didn't pull on her leash as much, jerking Lilian's arms nearly out of the socket when she saw a squirrel or a bird. She was much more well-behaved on their walks, not even barking at other dogs or cats but just brushing against them, and she hadn't chewed up a couch cushion or a shoe in two days.

Arthur had changed. Everyone had changed but Lilian.

"Arthur can change again," Asta said.

"His nightmares frighten me."

"I'll make them go away."

* * * *

Sunday morning, Lilian and Arthur met in the kitchen. His eyes had dark shadows under them, and his shoulders sagged. "Did I hurt you?" he asked.

She held up an elbow to show him the red stain from the Mercurochrome. "Only a little. It wasn't you, it was the floor."

"The floor!" he cried, and pulled her into his arms.

"Come on, honey," she said after a moment. "I've got to get ready for church. Are you coming?"

He shook his head. "I didn't sleep well last night."

"Go back to bed. Maybe the nightmares won't bother you in the daylight."

He kissed her and went back to bed.

* * * *

Some of Lilian's friends from the secretarial pool invited her out after church. She went, figuring Arthur could use extra time to sleep.

Over pastries at the tea room, Mary McReady said, "How's Arthur? Mac came back so—so strange."

"Did he tell you what they discovered? Arthur has terrible nightmares," Lilian said.

"Mac's staying mum," said Mary. "Classified."

"Arthur said a lot of men died."

Mary's gaze sharpened. "That's more than Mac's said. No wonder he's been so gloomy. Between bouts of excitement."

"Excitement?" Lilian said.

"They made some major discoveries down there. Mac won't say a word beyond that."

"Arthur yells in his sleep, but it's about vampires and monsters."

Mary touched Lilian's hand. One of the other women spoke about a recent film she'd seen, and they let the subject drop.

The house was silent when she let herself in. "Asta? Arthur?" she called.

The dog barked from the bedroom and came racing out to greet her. "Who's a good dog? Who's a good dog?" Lilian knelt to rub the dog's ears. Asta yipped and danced around her. "That's right! It's you! Where's Daddy?"

Asta ran to the kitchen and Lilian followed. Asta barked at her empty food bowl. "Arthur didn't feed you? Poor thing, you must be starving!" She filled the bowl, then looked in the cupboard for ingredients for supper. "Arthur?" she called. She went to the bedroom door and looked in. Her husband was covered with a sheet and blankets; even his face was hidden.

"I don't feel well," he said from under the sheet. "I need to rest a while longer."

"Oh, dear!" She stepped over the threshold. Should she take his temperature? Feel his forehead? Bring him aspirin and water?

"Don't come any closer. I don't want you to catch this," he said, muffled.

"Is there anything I can get you?"

"Not now. I'll let you know when I feel better. Could you close the door?"

She went out, closing the door gently.

She put together supper, not sure whether he would eat.

Later, he came out of the bedroom wearing only his skivvies, looking tired, pale, and rumpled. She had made a pot of chili, and it was still warm on the stove. He gave her his half smile, the one she'd fallen in love with, then came over and kissed the top of her head. "Hey," he said. "Everything will be all right now."

She put her hand on his forehead. No temperature. "How's your appetite?"

"Just dandy. Is that chili I smell?"

She dished up a bowl for him and sat with him while he ate. Afterward, they danced. He had lost the tension that had tightened his shoulders, and he was an even dreamier dancer than he'd been before. Every step was in perfect unison, and just when she was thinking he might dip her, he did. As though he could read her mind.

He held her tight after they made love. "You don't have to leave tonight. I promise," he said.

She sighed, not sure whether to believe him. Then she snuggled close.

He was right. The nightmares were gone.

THE HORROR ON THE SUPERYACHT

MARK MCLAUGHLIN

"Okay, we're here!" Warren Piedmont said, lifting the latch of the passenger door. "Be sure to put on your gloves. Models, you go first. Each of you, please grab an equipment case on your way out."

Capheen was the first to step out of the silver luxury helicopter, onto the frozen surface of Antarctica. Or rather, the *slushy* surface—it wasn't as frozen as she'd thought it would be.

"Shouldn't it be a lot colder than this?" she shouted into the vehicle. In addition to a black-leather equipment case, she also carried a lumpy leopard-print purse, slung over her left shoulder.

"Of course!" replied Piermont. "Why do you think we're here?"

The rest of the models—Dilektibl, Anemone, and Tymebomb—followed Capheen. Piedmont helped Quentin, the photographer, to carry out the remaining cases.

The group walked toward the burnt remains of the nameless camp. Behind them, the helicopter rose into the air. Everyone stopped to watch it fly off.

"Oh!" Capheen cried. "He *is* coming back, isn't he?"

Piedmont laughed. "Certainly! Do you really think he'd abandon us here?"

"How long is he going to be gone?" said Dilektibl with a worried pout.

"Like, I hope he doesn't forget about us!" whined Tymebomb.

Piedmont scanned the group and sighed with exasperation—the models were staring at him with worried frowns. He flashed what he hoped would be construed as a reassuring smile. "I promise you, we're going to be fine! Let's take a moment to go over the game plan one more time, okay?"

The models and the photographer all nodded. Dilektibl was curvaceous and red-haired, while Anemone was tall and slender, with blue-green dreadlocks and no eyebrows. Tymebomb was a lean, muscular young man with a thick shock of silver hair. Capheen was the most exotic member of the group. Her face, arms and cleavage were tattooed yellow and black in a tiger-stripe pattern. Quentin Slay, the photographer, was a chubby young man with a thick blond beard.

The models wore stylish snowsuits, gloves and boots in various fluorescent colors, as well as full makeup, foundation and all. The makeup was to be expected, since they were the top beauty icons of Sceptir Fashions, one of the world's most prestigious lifestyle brands, founded by world-famous designer Emil Sceptir. The team looked expectantly toward Piedmont, marketing expert and supervisor for the project.

"As you all should *already know…*"—Piedmont turned to Capheen for a moment as he said those words—"we're here for the big 'Save Antarctica' photo shoot. People need to see that this whole continent is starting to thaw out! So, we're going to shoot pics here at this old research base. Later, I'll call the pilot with a special transceiver and he'll take us back to our nice big yacht." He turned to the photographer. "Quentin, could you start setting up over there, in front of the biggest building? Everybody else, please help him with the equipment."

Capheen kicked at the slush with a hot-pink boot. "I always thought Antarctica was frozen solid. I guess I don't get how this whole 'global warming' deal works."

"Why did you agree to be part of this campaign?" Piedmont said.

"For the publicity—and the money, of course."

"Well, you were right earlier: Antarctica *is* supposed to be a lot colder. It used to have seasonal thaws, but never like this. Right now, this part of the continent is as warm as a late-winter day in the Midwest, with spring just around the corner. Ice is melting faster than ever around the coastline, and as a result, beaches worldwide are being covered by rising water."

Capheen nodded. "Okay, I get what you're saying … but how is a photo shoot going to fix anything?"

"We're building public awareness. Sceptir Fashions is involved with a lot of high-profile causes. It makes us look like we care for the Earth. And I suppose we do! It's the only planet we've got." He smiled warmly at Capheen.

Suddenly, a high-pitched *yip* sounded from within the model's purse. The smile faded from Piedmont's lips. "*Tell me* you didn't bring that animal of yours with you," he said.

"I didn't bring that animal of mine with me," Capheen said with a defiant shrug. She reached into her purse and pulled out a black chihuahua. "He was having a nice cozy nap in there. Guess he woke up!" Once the dog saw the light of day, he squirmed out of her grasp and began to scamper across the slush.

"Now, don't get mad," Capheen said. "I thought it would be cute for him to be the first chihuahua to visit Antarctica! I was going to keep him in my purse, but since it's not so cold, he can run around and get some exercise."

Piedmont rolled his eyes. "Let's go join the others."

Quentin was already shooting the individual models as they posed among the burnt ruins, taking care not to smear ashes on their snowsuits.

"How did these buildings burn up in the middle of Antarctica?" the photographer said. "It doesn't make any sense."

"When we came up with this project," Piedmont said, "we spent weeks flying around in the helicopter, trying to find a locale in this crazy slush that was even remotely interesting. It was a miracle we found this place. We know it was a research base, because … well, what *else* has ever been built in Antarctica? A shopping mall?"

Anemone shook her head sadly. "So much destruction in the middle of nowhere…. How *creepy*."

"It's a mystery, that's for sure," the supervisor said. "It must've been some kind of secret project. It has to be from a long time ago, back when America had one president."

Tymebomb tilted his head to one side. "There used to be *just one* president? Like, how can one person do a mega-job like that? Even the three we have *now* doesn't seem like enough."

Dilektibl, who had been wandering by herself, rejoined the group. "I've been looking around," she said. "I noticed something kind of weird."

Anemone looked around nervously. "*Everything* here is kind of weird. What did you notice?"

"It's hard to explain," Dilektibl said, "Looking at the scorched areas, I don't think everything was burned *at once*. Some spots look more faded … older. It's like they set fires here and there, and somebody came back much later and burned it up some more."

Anemone's eyes grew wide with fear. "Maybe there was some kind of disease here. I hope we're safe!"

"If you folks don't like hanging around this place, we'd all better hurry up," Piedmont said, nodding toward Quentin.

"Capheen, I haven't shot any pics of you yet," the photographer said. "Stand over by those beams. Stare into the distance, like you're worried about the planet."

The tiger-tattooed model hurried into position. "Hey, does anyone see Yippy? He's around here somewhere," she said.

"Like, you brought that stupid rat-dog?" Tymebomb said, shaking his head. "I hope he freezes to death. Once he starts yapping, he won't shut up!"

"So why isn't he yapping now?" Anemone said. "Quentin already has plenty of shots of me. I'll look around for Yippy."

Anemone looked for half an hour, but couldn't find the dog. Capheen and Dilektibl took over the search, since Quentin wanted to get some shots of Anemone and Tymebomb together.

Piedmont walked toward Capheen, to scold her about bringing the chihuahua, but then noticed that she'd started to cry. Clearly she already felt bad enough. He decided to join the search for Yippy. The photo shoot was nearing completion, so their top priority was finding that stupid dog.

Suddenly he saw a quick movement out of the corner of his eye. He walked toward it and saw a small, wagging tail, protruding from under some scorched boards. He lifted one of the boards and saw Yippy—chewing furiously on the partially burned, decayed remains of a frozen sled-dog. Like the surrounding slush, the sled-dog was thawing. The dead tissue was horribly freezer-burnt from countless years of freezing, thawing, and refreezing. And yet the hungry chihuahua was gnawing on it as though it were sirloin steak.

Piedmont saw that the chihuahua was feasting on the sled-dog's bowels. Looking closer, he saw dead intestinal worms in the rotten, fleshy mix.

"Yippy, you are revolting!" He picked up the dog and pulled it away from the corpse. He tucked the chihuahua under one arm and pushed the burnt boards back on top of the dead sled-dog. He then carried the dog back to the others.

Tymebomb was the first to see him. "Look! Like, he found the rat-dog!"

"My *baby!*" shouted Capheen. She rushed toward Piedmont and pulled the dog into her arms.

"Capheen, don't let it—" But, Piedmont didn't utter his warning quickly enough.

The chihuahua began to lick the model's face.

"*Peeeuuw!*" the model cried, laughing. "Yippy, you need a mint! What in the world have you been *eating?*"

* * * *

Once their work was finished, the helicopter returned to take the team back to *Her Highness*—the Sceptir superyacht, cruising off the coast. It was a truly massive vessel, with a spacious helipad that allowed the helicopter to come and go with ease.

Once they were aboard the superyacht, Capheen let everyone know that she would shampoo Yippy, since he had somehow "picked up an awful stink!" Piedmont had decided not to tell her about the chihuahua's gruesome meal under the boards.

While Piedmont and Quentin were talking about the day's results, Tymebomb came up to them, all smiles. "Wow! Like, that was a real adventure!" he said. He swept an arm toward the female models, who were fawning over Yippy. "We're going to our rooms to take showers, and later, we're gonna meet up in my room for drinks. I make a killer Manhattan! You guys want to join us?"

Piedmont shook his head. "I appreciate the invite, but I'm way too tired."

"Same here," Quentin said. "I'm going to sleep like a log tonight."

"Like, that's funny!" Tymebomb said. "Logs don't need sleep!"

The next day, they all met mid-morning on the sun deck for brunch. Piedmont was the first one to show up, followed by Quentin. The superyacht's buffet was laid out full English breakfast-style, including black pudding and fried tomatoes, along with an elaborate Bloody Mary bar.

"What a spread!" Quentin said. "But, I'm more of a dinner person. I can't even *imagine* eating that much so early in the day."

"Yeah, I'm not a big brunch person, either," Piedmont said. "I'm sure our models won't be eating much. You know how models are! Dilektibl might have a plateful, but I'll be surprised if any of the others even nibble on a slice of toast."

Both men prepared small plates of food and sat at the table. A few minutes later, Capheen, Dilektibl, Anemone, and Tymebomb showed up, walking together in a tight, silent group. Piedmont was surprised to see that none of them had bothered to apply any makeup or hair products. He also noticed, they seemed to have unusually *intense* looks in their eyes. Maybe they were hungover.

The models moved to the buffet and loaded their plates ridiculously high—mostly with meat dishes. They sat down at the table, and without saying a single word to ether Piedmont or Quentin, began to devour their food ravenously. Never before had the supervisor seen anyone eat with such bestial hunger.

"Are you folks okay?" Piedmont asked. "You're really wolfing down that grub!"

Tymebomb glanced toward them, his mouth filled with blood pudding. He simply nodded before returning to his overloaded plate.

A young blonde crew member walked onto the sun deck. "Good morning, everybody! I'm Jessica," she said with a perky smile. "Sorry I wasn't here to meet you." She moved closer to Capheen. "I wanted to tell you, I saw Yippy running around down below. I tried to see if I could catch the him, but he was too fast for me. Could you please try to keep him in your room? I wouldn't want the little cutie to get hurt!"

"Don't mind the dog," Tymebob said.

"Yes, it just wants to look around," Capheen said.

"'It'?" Quentin echoed.

Capheen stared at him without a word, an oddly blank look on her face.

"You called Yippy 'it,'" the photographer said. "You always call your dog 'he.'" He pointed to Tymebomb. "And *you* call Yippy the 'rat-dog.'"

"What are you trying to tell us?" Dilektibl asked, chewing ferociously on a fat sausage.

"You are observant, Quentin. But you should mind your own business," Anemone said, matter-of-factly.

"In what area of the vessel did you see Yippy?" Capheen said to Jessica.

"Like I said: down below," the blonde said. "Near the crew members' rooms."

"Good," the striped model said.

"Hey, none of you have made yourself a Bloody Mary yet!" said Jessica. She walked over to the Bloody Mary bar and began to prepare cocktails for the group.

"We do not want any…." Capheen said, but clearly there was uncertainty in her voice. "We do not … want…."

"Come on now!" Jessica said with a laugh. "My goodness! Who are you and what have you done with Capheen?" She laughed again, louder this time. "You've been onboard plenty of times before. I know my girl Capheen and she hasn't refused a drink in her entire life!"

Jessica brought a Bloody Mary to the striped model. It was an exceptionally large cocktail, garnished with a celery stalk and a slice of dill pickle, as well as green olives and chunks of bacon on a skewer.

"I really should *not*…" Capheen said, just before she took the glass and chugged down the savory beverage.

"I want one, too!" Tymebomb yelled.

"So do I!" Anemone shouted.

Dilektibl slapped her palms against the table repeatedly. "Me! Me, too!"

Jessica returned to the bar and made more drinks as quickly as she could. The models left the table and swarmed around Jessica, eager to receive their drinks as soon as they were prepared.

Piedmont watched as the models swilled down the Bloody Marys. He had seen them drunk before, but this was something else altogether. The models were squealing and grunting like pigs! He had no idea what was going on with them.

Piedmont finished his meal and left the table. Quentin followed close behind. They did not bother to say goodbye, and the others did not acknowledge their departure.

Once they'd reached the deck below, the photographer said, "What is *up* with them? They're acting so weird this morning."

"*Something's* going on, that's for sure," Piedmont said. "They had drinks last night, and now they're having way more. And they weren't wearing make-up! That's the first time I've ever seen any of our models without makeup."

Quention looked out toward Antarctica. Even as he watched, a massive chunk of ice fell from the edge of the continent into the ocean. "Look at it! The place is thawing out right in front of us," he said. "Even the *air* is warm, and it's still early. We could be wearing swimwear right now, as far as the temperature is concerned." On the coast, another huge chunk tumbled into the water.

"Maybe that's the problem," Piedmont said. "Our models are tired of seeing so much slush and snow. It's so sad and dreary. They're party-people and they aren't having any fun. They're stressed out!"

"I have an idea," Quentin said. "Let's do a shoot on the sun deck this morning, while they're still tipsy. We'll bring 'em more shots. Models partying as Antarctica melts! They can wear their best swimwear. I'll get the coastline in the picture behind them. Those would be fabulous pictures. They'd really capture how warm the weather has become down here."

"I'm not sure if we'd be able to use those pictures," Piedmont said. "The head-honchos might think they're too frivolous."

Quentin shrugged. "So what if they do? Even if we can't use the shots, at least everybody had fun at the shoot."

Piedmont grinned and nodded. "I like how you think! I'll tell the models to get into their swimwear. And you—go get your camera! You'll need help setting up, so feel free to ask some crew members. See you up on the sun deck!"

* * * *

Within an hour, the brunch furnishings had been cleared away from the sun deck and Quentin's equipment was set up, thanks to Jessica and two cabin boys. The models had returned from their rooms, wearing their best swimwear. Capheen wore a leopard-print one-piece, and Dilektibl's scarlet bikini was lightly trimmed with black lace. Anemone's bikini featured cyan and navy-blue stripes, while Tymebomb kept it simple in a silver swim-thong.

Jessica found some beach balls and soon the photo shoot was underway. "I wish I knew where all the other crew members were," she said to Piedmont. "Half of them are nowhere to be seen."

"Now that you mention it," the supervisor said, "I haven't seen little Yippy this morning, either. Though I recall, you said you'd seen him down below."

"Yes, but only for a few seconds," Jessica said.

"I want this to be a festive shoot," Piedmont said, "so could you prepare a couple trays of tequila shots? Make sure there's plenty of salt and lime wedges."

Jessica smiled, nodded, and hurried off to see to the task.

Piedmont walked back to the photo shoot. The models were tossing beach balls back and forth, but it was clear that their buzz from the brunch Bloody Marys was quickly wearing off.

"People! Don't tell me you're done for the day!" Piedmont said. "Let's see some energy!"

"How long are we going to be trapped on this boat?" Capheen said. It occurred to Piedmont that somewhere along the way, she had become the spokesperson for the models.

"You *do* work for Sceptir Fashions," Piedmont replied. "Is there some other place you'd rather be?"

"We want to be around people," she said. "Lots and lots of *people*. Millions! You are right: we work for Sceptir Fashions. We need to leave this place and go to Sceptir headquarters in New York City."

"I don't think I've ever seen you this *forceful* before," Piedmont said. He noticed Jessica and a cabin boy approaching with trays of shots. "Ah, here we are! I told Jessica to bring more refreshments. I think this trip has been stressful for everyone. A whole continent covered with slush is pretty depressing … enough to fray anybody's nerves. Here's some more joy-juice to lift our spirits."

He noticed that as the tequila drew closer, the models' eyes grew wider and they began to lick their lips, like thirsty beasts. They sure were craving the booze this morning!

Once again, the models guzzled down the alcohol, every drop, in record time.

"More!" Tymebomb cried. "Bring us more!"

"They'll bring more, no worries!" Piedmont said. "In the meantime, start tossing those beach balls! Laugh, dance, have some fun! The sooner we get some great shots, the sooner we'll head for New York!"

The models began to hoot and squeal with gusto. The sounds they made as they partied hardly seemed human. "Yes! Off to New York!" Capheen cried. Quentin began shooting, jumping back and forth among the models to capture the best images.

"Make sure Antarctica's in the background whenever possible!" Piedmon called to the photographer.

"No problem!" Quentin replied. "It's a big continent! I can't miss it!"

Piedmont heard sounds from the far end of the sun desk. He turned and saw several crew members silently approaching—led by Yippy, who walked slowly and deliberately. Capheen saw the chihuahua, but did not rush to pick up her pet. In fact, Piedmont noticed that she actually *nodded* in a sudden, jerky way toward the dog. Was it his imagination, or did the animal *nod back?* The crew members seemed to have oddly intense looks in their eyes, like the models.

"Jessica!" Piedmont yelled. "It looks like we have more guests. Double that last order of tequila. Or better yet, triple it!"

A moment after Piedmont uttered those words, he began to wonder if he was doing the right thing. He was beginning to feel unnerved … perhaps even frightened. The current situation was simply unnatural. The models just weren't themselves anymore—and neither were those crew members who'd joined the party. He decided he should keep his distance from the party, in case things got ugly.

He couldn't figure out what was happening, but one factor did seem to connect the odd goings-on. It was as though everybody who'd come into contact with Yippy had changed … after the chihuahua had eaten that decayed meat. On Antarctica, he had held the dog for a short time, but he'd been wearing gloves.

Did the chihuahua have some sort of mad-cow disease? Mad-*dog* disease? *Rabies?* Maybe it was something else altogether … some condition that humans could contract.

The crew members began to suck down the tequila, while the models drank their shots two at a time. He saw Quentin have some shots, as well as

Jessica and the cabin boys. He did not dare to have any tequila himself. He needed to stay sober so he could monitor this bizarre situation. He felt that it would soon take a turn for the worse.

He didn't have to wait long.

The models stripped off their skimpy swimwear. The drunken crew members also shed their clothes.

"Whoa, steady now!" Jessica shouted. "I'm seeing *waaay* too much skin! I know it's a party, but let's keep it rated PG, okay?"

"Yeah, I don't take X-rated pics!" Quentin said.

Suddenly, squirming clusters of tentacles shot out of the naked bodies of the models and the crew members. The slick tentacles wrapped around Jessica and the cabin boys. Dilektibl made sure that Quentin received an extra-special hug. Tentacles shot out of Yippy's body as he jumped into the hideous fracas.

"Get your ass over here, Warren!" Capheen cried, laughing uproariously. Her eyes blazed as red as fire—and there were three of them now.

"Yeah, come join us!" Tymebomb called. "Don't let this pretty lady have *all* the fun!" He drove two wriggling tentacles down Jessica's throat.

"It's a party, honey, and you're invited!" Anemone winked at the supervisor, just before wagging an impossibly long blue-white tongue at him.

Piedmont turned and ran until he reached a stairway to a lower level. As he'd watched the grotesque bacchanalia, something had *clicked* in his mind. Now that he had the facts, after seeing them *firsthand*, things were starting to make sense.

Obviously, that scientific base in Antarctica had been taken over by some horrible creature … something alien and monstrously aggressive. It took over other life-forms, infected and *converted* them. People had tried to burn the monsters to death—maybe more than once, based on what Dilektibl had said she'd seen. Yippy had eaten some meat from a sled-dog that had been infected, long ago. The meat must have infected the chihuahua.

He gasped as he remembered Capheen's words: "We want to be around people. Lots and lots of *people*."

He kept running down stairways until he found himself standing near the prow of the superyacht. He looked around but couldn't figure out where to go next. Should he go down into the lower levels and hide? Or, maybe he could find the helicopter pilot. Then they could fly off and—

Suddenly he remembered, to his despair, that the pilot had been one of the crew members following Yippy. Piedmont had no idea how to fly the vehicle by himself.

A new thought came to mind. Maybe he could escape in the tender. The tender was a smaller boat, housed in an internal dock, that was used whenever travel between the superyacht and a dock was necessary.

He had used the tender before on two previous photo shoots, both in Hawaii. He'd even been instructed on how to drive it. The boat had contained food, water, and medical supplies. There was also a communications system, so that crew members operating the tender could stay in touch with both the superyacht and its destination.

Clearly some sort of evil intelligence was behind the transformations—an intelligence that had access to the knowledge of its victims. Once a victim was converted, the new creature became part of a sort of team, bent on world conquest. The team had probably already figured out that the captain of the superyacht would need to be converted. So, trying to find the captain wouldn't do him any good.

But, many members of that monstrous team were now drunk. Distracted. Perhaps they had not yet realized that he could use the tender to escape.

Piedmont found a door leading down to the level where the tender was kept. He descended the stairs quickly and quietly, listening to make sure no one else was nearby. After a while, he could discern the faint but unmistakable scent of marijuana smoke. As he drew closer to the tender, he could hear that was the vessel was occupied. Once he'd reach the level of the dock, he slipped into the darkness under the metal stairs.

On the tender, two young male crew members were being assaulted by a trio of tentacled, humanoid creatures with blazing red eyes. The two men had obviously popped into the tender to share a joint, only to fall victim to the invading monstrosities.

Piedmont tried to think what he could possibly do to save the men, but it was far too late for heroics. All he could do was wait in the shadows. Maybe after the crew members were converted, the attackers and victims alike would depart and he'd be able to use the tender.

It appeared that the creatures were able to sprout body parts with relative ease. They had covered the men's mouths with flat, flipperlike appendages to muffle the screams. One of them had grown a small, crooked arm ending in a pincer to hold the wrist of one of the men.

Piedmont watched in horror as the creatures slid clusters of sinuous tentacles into their victims. The men writhed in excruciating pain at first, but as time passed, it became hideously clear that the humans were *adjusting* to the ordeal. At one point, the pincer relaxed its grip on the victim, who did nothing to fight back.

As Piedmont waited for the completion of the grotesque acts taking place in the tender, he looked around to see if he could spot any possible weapons, in case one was needed. He noticed, in a hallway to his left, a door marked SECURITY. The metal door was halfway open and the lights were on in the room. That had to be where those two crew members worked.

The creatures seemed to be fully absorbed in their actions. So, he decided to take a chance. Maybe there were weapons in that room. He dropped to his belly and moved, as slowly as possible, out of his hiding place. He crept down the hall and before long, he was able to crawl into the Security room.

Once inside, he stood up and looked around. The walls of the room were covered with security monitors, showing various areas of the superyacht. He was dismayed to see that creatures were attacking the remaining crew members throughout the vessel. He searched the room but could not find any weapons. But then, firepower probably wouldn't be a high priority aboard a private superyacht in the fashion industry. In a drawer, he found a cigarette lighter, so he took that. It wasn't much, but it was better than nothing.

On one screen, Piedmont noticed a curious sight: walking along outside the executive conference room, he saw a handsome, silver-haired gentleman in a black silk robe. The old man smiled as though he didn't have a care in the world....

Piedmont looked more closely and suddenly recognized the old man. He was designer Emil Sceptir, owner of the superyacht and of course, the entire company. He had given Piedmont a warm handshake on his first day, years ago. He recalled that the old fellow had told him, "I'm sure you'll do a fabulous job. If you ever decide to switch jobs, you can always be one of our models. You're very handsome."

Piedmont glanced outside the door. The tender was now empty. Creatures and victims alike had moved on. Of course, now the victims were creatures, too.

He hurried out of the Security room—and up the stairs. He wanted to escape in the tender, but he couldn't possibly do it without trying to bring Emil Sceptir with him. The route to the executive conference room was pretty much straight up some stairways, without too much rambling. With luck, he'd be able to run up and find that kind old man without encountering any of the creatures.

Once he'd reached the top of the stairs, he stepped cautiously out onto the deck. Fortunately, there was no one else to be seen in that area. All he needed to do now was take another stairway to reach the upper level.

Suddenly, Tymebomb staggered out of a side corridor. He had sprouted several smaller arms of various lengths, and each held a different bottle. He'd also grown several thick-lipped, misshapen mouths—all the better to drink with.

"There you are!" Tymebomb roared. "Why'd you take off? Don't you like me, buddy?"

Piedmont looked at the bottles—rum, cognac, high-proof grain alcohol. "You're quite the party monster. Those are some powerful refreshments you've got there."

The model poured more liquor into his mouths, splashing booze all over his body. He reached toward the supervisor with his longest tentacles. "Don't be shy! Let me give you a back rub!"

Piedmont noticed a newspaper sticking out of a nearby trash canister. He grabbed the paper, set it on fire with the lighter he'd found, and threw the flaming mess onto Tymebomb. The flammable fluids covering the model burst into blue flame.

Tymebob squealed like a wounded hog. He lurched from side to side, beating at the fire with his tentacles and extra arms. But he hadn't let go of the bottles, so all he managed to do was cover himself with broken glass and more alcohol.

Piedmont pulled a fire extinguisher out of its wall bracket. He hit the living nightmare over the head with the metal cylinder, and then used it to shove the creature away from him. As Tymebomb staggered off, Piedmont used the extinguisher once more to push him over the rail. The flaming horror screeched with rage all the way down to the ocean.

The supervisor rushed back to the stairway that led to the executive conference room. At the base of the stairs, he looked up—and saw Emil Sceptir coming down.

"Thank God!" Piedmont called, smiling. "You're still okay!"

Sceptir returned the smile. "Well, of course I'm okay! Why *wouldn't* I be okay?" When he reached the lower level, he looked closely at the supervisor. "You're Warren Piedmont, aren't you? We're certainly having a noisy day. I keep hearing the strangest hubbub, coming from here, there, and everywhere. Must be some kind of party!"

"Actually, we're right in the middle of a crisis situation. You obviously don't know about it. When did you come aboard?"

Sceptir laughed. "I've been here since the trip began! But I've kept to my cabin, since I wanted to catch up on some work. Jessica has been taking care of me. Wonderful young lady! Now please, tell me about this crisis you mentioned."

"You wouldn't believe what's going on. It's so horrible!" Piedmont said. "We just need to get in the tender and *go*, sir. Right now, before it's too late!"

"Please, calm down. Nothing can be *that* bad." The old man laid a hand gently on Piedmont's arm. "You're simply under a lot of stress, that's all. You know what you need? A pet! Pets always bring out the best in us. Our inner gentleness and serenity. Why, just last night I was playing with the cutest little chihuahua, and now I feel much better!"

So saying, Sceptir opened his black robe and embraced his screaming employee with writhing tentacles.

APOLLYON

G. D. FALKSEN

On the plain below the monastery, the laborers struggled knee-deep in mud and oil, digging new wells and cutting channels to coax the thick black liquid from the earth. It seeped out naturally all across the island, but the oil that came unbidden was never enough for the alchemists. So the men had to dig, and pile, and haul the stuff until now the whole of the rocky shore was stained by it.

Markos wrinkled his nose as he watched the scene from a window. He knew the stench of rock oil so well that he had almost forgotten what it was like to smell clean air. Even the salt air of the Black Sea was drowned out. Eight months they had been trapped on the island, exiled at the command of the Emperor until the work could finally be finished. Absolute isolation for absolute secrecy, that had been the decree.

He was drawn from his musing by angry voices from across the room.

"You must not rush things, General," began old Theodoros. The gray-haired alchemist wagged one boney finger at the stern-faced General Andronikos. "This sort of work is complicated, it takes time...."

"Time!" snapped Andronikos. His cheeks were red with anger behind the thick black beard that covered his chin. "Time is a luxury that we do not have, old man! When this damned venture began, you swore to me that you would require three months to perfect the formula. It has been almost a year."

"General, please—"

Andronikos flicked a hand at Theodoros to dismiss him. The general's anger often outstripped his patience for the complexities of alchemy. He turned to Markos.

"What do you say, boy? How much longer until the liquid fire is ready?"

Markos looked away from the window, bristling at the general's dismissive words. At twenty-three he was half the age of Andronikos, but hardly a boy.

"As my master says, it is a matter of time, my lord," Markos replied, his tone obedient and humble. He was angry, not stupid. "We have tested so many different formulae, it is inevitable that we will get it right soon."

"How hard can it be to pump naphtha through a siphon?" Andronikos demanded.

Markos grimaced. Very hard, in fact. The weapon's pump mechanism was proving even more difficult than the formula itself. But there was no reason to alert Andronikos, who would only rage all the more at yet another setback.

"Respectfully, my lord, it is one matter to spray oil at an enemy's ship. It is another to make that oil stick, or to ignite upon contact with water, or even to fly far enough that one's own fleet is not threatened. As it stands now, we are half as likely to drench our own ships...."

"Then correct the problem," Andronikos snarled. "I have promised the Emperor liquid fire, and you two are expected to deliver it."

"Yes, General," Theodoros began timidly. "We are aware of the urgency."

Andronikos turned his back on them and gazed outside, across the dark rolling sea. Markos sighed. There was a speech coming, one that he had heard dozens of times already. Behind Andronikos's back, he mouthed the words as the general spoke them. It was the same every single time.

"For centuries," Andronikos said, "liquid fire has protected the Empire against its enemies, from the Saracens to the Rus. But in our darkest hour, the secret was lost and when the Latins betrayed us, our navy was helpless against them. That must never happen again. We are beset on all sides by enemies. Even now, the Turks swarm across Anatolia. Should they reach the Bosporus, liquid fire may be the only thing that stands between them and Constantinople." Andronikos turned back to them with a dark look in his eyes. "So I ask again, when will it be ready?"

Markos and Theodoros looked at one another. Neither wanted to be the one to speak. As they both hemmed and hawed around the fringes of an answer, there came a distant shouting from the oil fields. Markos went to the window and looked out. There was some commotion among the laborers at the far side of the island.

"What is that noise?" Andronikos demanded.

It was an opening for escape, and Markos gladly took it.

"I know not, my lord, but I will investigate at once."

* * * *

Markos hurried from the monastery, eager to be away from the oppressive place. The monks had abandoned it a two hundred years ago, and Markos didn't blame them. It was squat and shadowy, and it had smelled of oil even before the workers started digging the wells. Now, it was unbearable, and seepage had contaminated the cellar with equal parts oil and water.

Most of the laborers were still at their work, hauling the oil out of the ground for Markos and Theodoros to use. A few of them had come from the mainland with Andronikos's soldiers, but most were the fishermen who lived on the island, pressed into service in exchange for food and water and the promise of future pay.

Fishermen. There were no longer any fish for them to catch. After months of runoff from the wells, the local wildlife had quit the shallows, and Andronikos had ordered all of the fishing boats burned to preserve security. The only way on or off the island was the supply galley that arrived twice a month with food. So the fishermen had become diggers, trading their nets for shovels and fish for naphtha.

A brisk wind struck Markos as he crossed the field. In the distance, he saw a familiar figure running in his direction: a young woman with long dark hair and a wide mouth that seemed always eager to smile.

"Helena!" Markos called, waving both hands to get her attention.

There came the smile, so broad and genuine that it almost hid the sunken hollows of Helena's cheeks. Food was rationed, and the soldiers always had their fill before the villagers.

"Markos!"

Helena sprinted to Markos's side and grabbed his hand in both of hers. She looked around quickly to be sure that no one was watching them, and stole a kiss from him. Markos blushed. For four months they had been together, and still he was giddy every time she looked at him.

"Helena, I..."

But Helena had no time for sweet murmurings. She gripped Markos's hand and pulled him along after her. "Come, you must see this! Thomas has found something!"

Markos laughed and stumbled as he tried to keep up.

"What has your fool of a brother done now?"

"He's not a fool!" Helena protested. "You must not call him a fool! And besides, he has found a fallen star!"

"A...what?"

"A fallen star. I know it must be one, because it is as bright and silver as any of the ones in the sky."

"I do not understand," Markos said.

"Come, you'll see."

Markos followed Helena to the far end of the oil field, where a new well was being dug. A few diggers stood around, their mouths open in wonder. They were pointing and murmuring to each other in nervous tones. As Markos approached the well, he saw why. At the bottom of the hole rested a large, silver shape, like half of a dome swallowed up by the rock. It looked like it had been encased in rock, until some ancient disturbance had broken open a fissure above it, revealing it to the soil and waiting to be unearthed by the hands of men.

Markos just stood and stared for a little while, his mouth agape like the diggers.

"So? What do you think?" Helena asked breathlessly.

"I don't know what to think," Markos confessed.

Helena's gangly brother Thomas crawled out of the pit, wiping dirt from his hands.

"Ah, Markos!" he exclaimed. "Look what I have found! I'm going to be rich!"

Helena scoffed at her brother. "The general won't allow you to keep it, you know. And what are you going to do? Pull a boulder out of the ground and roll it across the sea to Constantinople? Who is going to buy it from you?"

"Bah!" Thomas dismissed her words with a wave. "It's not a boulder, it's a room!"

Markos stared at him, and then glanced at the dome. "What?"

"Look, you can see the door."

Thomas pointed to where some of the men were straining to force open part of the silver wall with picks and shovels. The metal creaked and groaned, until finally a door sprang open with a tremendous clang. Two of the workers lost their footing and were flung into the dirt. Cursing like a sailor, Thomas scrambled down into the pit to help them.

"Stay here," Markos said to Helena.

Helena gave him a look. "You know that I won't."

Markos sighed. "I know."

They descended a wooden ladder and joined Thomas at the doorway. The air that drifted out from inside the dome was stale and peculiar, half the odor of a cold cellar and half the stench of heated metal, though how the two could coexist was beyond Markos.

Now at the threshold of his prize, Thomas became hesitant. "What do you suppose is in there?" he asked.

"You didn't wonder that before you opened it?" Helena asked her brother.

"Well, I..."

Markos ran his fingertips along the edge of the doorway. It was perfectly smooth. Impossibly smooth, in fact. It was hard as well, harder than silver had a right to be. The banging of the picks and shovels had left no mark at all. Mighty was the smith who had forged this.

As the siblings argued behind him, Markos went through the doorway. Inside was a small, cramped chamber, dimly lit by the light from outside. Markos suddenly wished that he had a lamp, but the workers were careful not to bring any fire onto the oil fields. Still, it was bright enough for his purpose.

The chamber was perhaps the size of a small boat, or an especially large carriage. Just inside the door, Markos saw a kind of table wedged against the wall, and something resembling a chair in front of it. The table and the nearest wall were covered in flat, glossy tiles colored pitch black. Most of them were badly cracked. In a small depression at the side of the table, Markos saw a pile of strange waxy paper. It was covered in markings that might have been language, but certainly wasn't Greek.

Some instinct of self-preservation told him not to touch anything.

The only other object in the chamber was a tall sheet of glass built into a metal frame. Markos could half see his reflection as he approached, but there was something else behind it: a dark shape nestled inside the container. It was hard to make out any details. The inside of the glass was covered in frost, which distorted his view. Markos reached out his hand and held it near the surface. The glass felt cold to the touch, like a church window on a winter's night.

"What is this place?" Helena whispered, as she joined Markos. She gasped in wonder, expressing Markos's own sentiments with excitement rather than apprehension. "Did the monks build this?"

"I do not think so," Markos said.

He took Helena's arm and drew back from the glass. Everything in the chamber was strange, but it slowly dawned on him just what this last curiosity might be.

"We should leave."

"Why?" Helena asked.

Markos pointed at the glass. "That is a sarcophagus, and this is a tomb. I am certain of it."

Thomas pushed past them, holding a pick in his hand. "A crystal coffin in a silver tomb? Someone rich is buried here! Like a pharaoh of Egypt!"

"Thomas, wait—" Markos exclaimed.

Thomas did not listen. The light of greed danced in his eyes. He jammed the point of his pick into the edge of the sarcophagus's lid and started pulling with all his might.

"Thomas!" Helena shouted at him, angry and disgusted. "Grave-robbing? Do you have no shame?"

"I am not going to be a fisherman all my life!" Thomas retorted.

With a few loud grunts and a strong pull, Thomas yanked the pick backward and the sarcophagus snapped open. A draft of cold air rushed out and stung Markos's nose and cheeks. He brushed his face, and heard Helena gasp in fright. Thomas made a similar noise, more of a gurgle than a gasp. The pick hit the ground with a loud clang.

"What is it…?" Markos asked, rubbing his eyes.

No one answered, and no one had to. With the lid open, the figure inside was clear to see. Markos had expected a corpse, but the corpse of a man. The thing that reclined against the back of the sarcophagus was nothing of God's Creation. The figure was short and squat, with four gangly arms and fingers shaped more like the tentacles of an octopus than the digits of a hand. It was blue in color, with flesh that better resembled the viscus body of a sea beast than anything that walked the earth. Three red eyes set in its head gazed blankly into the distance, and in place of hair its hideous form was covered in oddly curving protrusions that put Markos in mind of worms burrowing into the soil.

"What is that?" Helena asked.

Markos had no reply to give her.

Thomas slowly leaned in and peered at the monstrous cadaver. "That… It is a statue, isn't it?"

Again, Markos could not find his words. He just shook his head.

"It must be a statue," Thomas continued, trying to convince himself as much as the other two. "Those eyes are rubies, yes? And the body is some kind of stone. It must be."

"I don't think so, Thomas," Helena said. Her voice sounded hoarse.

Finally, Markos forced himself to speak. "Out. We have to get out."

He grabbed for Helena and Thomas, and pulled them out of the chamber with feverish urgency. Some instinctive part of his brain told him to flee, and he obeyed. Panic seemed the most reasonable response to such a sight. Once he was in the sunlight again, the fear ebbed a little. Markos leaned against the earthen wall and rubbed his face with one hand, while Thomas collapsed to his knees, mumbling again and again that the thing in the sarcophagus must be a statue.

"That was not a statue," Markos whispered.

Helena held onto Markos's arm and cast a hesitant look back toward the chamber. "It was not," she agreed. "What are we to do?"

Markos thought about it for a little while. He was half tempted to bury the thing again, to leave it forgotten under piles of soil and rock. He was equally tempted to drag the thing out into the light and examine it in detail. As much as it horrified him, his curiosity was driven wild by the sight of something so impossible. Such a creature could not have been made by God, and yet it existed.

Still, that decision was not his to make. There was a strict hierarchy on the island, and he knew better than to violate it.

"We tell the general," Markos said, "and the general will call Father Cyril, and hopefully one of them will have an explanation."

* * * *

Andronikos was where Markos had left him, still ranting to poor Theodoros about the preservation of the Empire and the unacceptability of further delays. Old Theodoros dithered like always, mumbling excuses that failed to address to very real restrictions and setbacks the research faced. Better to hem and haw about water in the oil, than to admit that they were attempting the impossible: to recreate a formula known only in legend, with barely any hint of where to begin. Any one of the dozen compounds they had already devised might actually be the sought-after mixture, and yet they had no measure to evaluate it with other than Andronikos's outlandish expectations.

But no matter. There was a more pressing issue. At first, Andronikos and Theodoros both listened to Markos's report with skepticism. Only after Markos insisted, did Andronikos summon Father Cyril, and together the four of them went to the pit to see the truth of Markos's "mad ravings." Theodoros grumbled all the way, and Andronikos, though silent, did nothing to hide his displeasure.

Markos led them to the chamber. His heart began pounding as he stepped through the low doorway. His hands trembled. He was a reasonable man and prided himself on keeping his wits, but there was something deeply unnerving about the figure in the glass sarcophagus. It was surely nothing of this earth, and its very unnaturalness made Markos sick and dizzy.

"So," Andronikos murmured, "you spoke true, boy." He cleared his throat like he wanted to be sick, but had too much dignity to give in and do it.

"Mother of God…" Cyril whispered, crossing himself as he saw the body. Markos, Andronikos, and Theodoros followed his example. The priest peered at the body and shook his head slowly. "This is… This… What is it?"

Andronikos grunted. "That is the question I would put to you, priest. You are a man of God. How can this *thing* exist? Do not tell me that this abomination crawled through the Garden of Eden, or that Noah brought two of it upon the Ark."

Cyril reached out to touch the body, but then he shuddered and drew back his hand. He crossed himself again. "'And I looked, and behold a pale horse: and his name that sat on him was Death, and Hell followed with him.'"

Cyril's voice quaked with fear, the same thing felt by the rest of them. Markos clutched his hands to keep from shivering. The chill that had enveloped the sarcophagus before was now completely gone, replaced by the lingering warmth of autumn. Even the frost on the body was melting, and droplets of water trickled to the floor.

"Does the Apocalypse mention a blue horse?" Markos muttered, seeking humor in blasphemy, and finding a little comfort in it.

"What was that?" Andronikos asked.

"Nothing, my lord."

Father Cyril set his face firmly, and clutched at the heavy cross around his neck. He turned back to Markos and the others.

"We all know what this is," he said. "There is no point in pretending otherwise. This creature is not of God's earth. It is an abomination, a fallen angel cast from Heaven. 'They were ruled by a king, the angel of the bottomless pit, whose name in Hebrew is Abaddon, and in Greek Apollyon, the Destroyer.'"

"A devil, then," Andronikos mused. He scratched at his bearded chin and grimaced. "I never believed I would see such a thing in my life." He paused. "Why doesn't it move? Is it dead? Can a fallen angel die?"

Cyril shook his head. "No, certainly not." However sure his pronouncement, the priest did seem unsure about the other half of the question. "It… slumbers, of course. Banished from Heaven and flung into the earth, it waits for some evil purpose to awaken."

The four men all considered his words, and as one they took a step back from the body.

"What are we to do?" Markos asked. "Should we…um…" He cast around for the most probably means of killing a devil. "Burn it?"

"Surely not!" Cyril exclaimed. He quickly silenced himself, and cast a nervous look at the sarcophagus, fearful that his loud voice might stir Apollyon from its slumber. "Anything we do to it might awaken it."

Andronikos grabbed Cyril by the arm. "Then what exactly are we to do?"

For the moment, Father Cyril had no answer. He looked at Theodoros for help, but Theodoros had no answer either.

"Perhaps we should just bury it and hope that it stays asleep," Markos suggested.

The three older men answered him with more or less identical looks of patronizing distain.

"Shut up, boy," Andronikos said. He turned back to Cyril. "Well?"

Cyril clasped his hands and exhaled. "There is only one thing to do. We must exorcise it. I will perform an exorcism and banish the creature to Hell."

"Have you ever exorcised a demon before?" Andronikos asked.

"I have never even seen a demon before," Cyril confessed, "but I know how it is done. I will pray that the Lord give me strength to cast out this evil."

Andronikos nodded. "Good. Get to it."

"What? Now?" Cyril sputtered. "It is almost sundown!"

"I will have some lamps brought, and you can exorcise it over night." Andronikos leaned over and looked Cyril in the eyes. "I do not care how it is done, but I want that thing gone! Exorcise it, burn it, bury it, it makes no difference to me. But I will not spend two nights on the same island as that monstrosity!"

Markos said nothing, but he agreed with Andronikos's words. The only thing he questioned was the methodology. Surely, it would be better to just cover the silver chamber with heaps of rock and dirt until nothing could possibly climb out again, devil or otherwise. It wasn't that he doubted the power of exorcism, he simply refused to believe that it could possibly work.

* * * *

That evening, Father Cyril went into the chamber alone to perform the exorcism. A few of Andronikos's soldiers stood guard at the top of the pit to ensure he was left undisturbed, and they eyed each other nervously, as the sunlight faded. Several of the workers lingered near the pit, trying to catch a glimpse of what was happening, though in the end this proved impossible. There was no way to observe the exorcism without venturing into the pit itself, and Andronikos had forbidden anything that might distract Cyril.

Markos, still harboring misgivings, stole away from the others and looked for Helena. He found her by the shore, watching the sun setting over the Black Sea. She glanced at him as he approached, and flashed a smile.

"So that is that, I suppose," she mused. "Our brave priest will banish that horror back to Hell, and life will return to normal."

Markos put his arms around Helena and gazed at the sea with her. "So it seems. By tomorrow, it will be as though your brother never dug up that tomb. Imagine: the strangest episode of my life over and done with in half a day."

Helena laughed. "You sound disappointed."

"Nothing of the sort, my love," Markos replied. "I'll admit, that horrible thing intrigues me, but it is a monstrous curiosity. I know better than to indulge it, just as I know better than to put my hand in a fire. To be honest, I wish that thing had never been unearthed in the first place. I fear it will haunt my dreams tonight."

"Mine too," Helena said. Silence drifted between them, growing with the lengthening shadows. After a little while, Helena touched Markos's cheek and looked into his eyes. "Markos... When all of this is done, and you return to Constantinople...."

"Yes?"

"You are going to take me with you, aren't you?" Helena sounded hesitant and uncertain, like she feared giving voice to the question would somehow make it impossible.

Markos held her tighter and kissed her temple. "Of course, my love. As I promised, when I leave here you will come with me as my wife."

"Good," Helena murmured, resting her head against Markos's chest. "I do not think I could bear to life the rest of my life on this island, and certainly not without you."

Markos smiled at her. "I do not wish to live in a world without you, Helena. You bring me a kind of joy I didn't know could exist. It is as simple as that."

Helena chuckled softly, and seemed pleased. They stood together for a little while, watching the darkness creep across the sea.

* * * *

Markos slept fitfully that night. At first his dreams were of Helena, and of the life they would have in Greece once they could finally leave the accursed island. But quickly, they turned from his future happiness to visions of the demon in the silver tomb. He saw its hideous blue face, writhing with worms that were its own flesh. Its red eyes stared blankly ahead, frozen as if in death, but still they bored through him, gazing into his very soul. Cyril's words echoed in Markos's slumbering mind:

A king, the angel of the bottomless pit.

Hour after hour, he tossed and turned, only half sleeping yet unable to wake. When the morning light finally roused him, he found himself drenched in cold sweat. Markos cursed loudly as he crawled from his bed. This was going to be a bad day. He could feel it.

Despite his doubts about the exorcism, he went straight to the pit to see the results. His skepticism did not invalidate the power of the divine. When he arrived, he found a whole crowd of people standing at the edge, waiting for Cyril to emerge. The soldiers kept the onlookers back. It wouldn't do to disturb a holy man in the middle of casting out demons.

Two of the soldiers were well known to Markos: Ioannis and Georgios, who were often tasked with helping the alchemists test new formulae for the liquid fire. Markos joined them and exchanged uneasy greetings. Having spoken, all three of them looked back into the pit nervously. The tension in the crowd was almost physically uncomfortable, and that was just what had grown from rumor and speculation. None of the frightened on-lookers had even seen the devil in the tomb. Perhaps that was worse. Markos was haunted by what he knew it looked like, but the soldiers and the workers were free to imagine all manner of horrors even worse than the corpse in the glass coffin.

"Any word from Father Cyril?" Markos asked.

"Nothing," Georgios said. "No one has been in or out except that girl of yours."

"Helena?"

Georgios nodded. "Brought Father Cyril some breakfast, oh 'bout an hour ago. Said he was sat there on his knees praying. Didn't even notice her."

Ioannis glanced toward the back of the crowd and pointed. Markos looked and saw Helena waiting there, leaning against a dead tree as she watched the pit. The sight of her soothed Markos's nerves, and for a little while banished the troubling thoughts that had invaded his dreams.

"Ask me," Ioannis added, "I think she just wanted to sneak a peek at the exorcism."

"Can you blame her?" asked Georgios. "None of us have even seen one done before. I've half a mind to go take a look myself!"

"Don't you dare." Ioannis jabbed a finger at his comrade. "Stick to your post. I have no wish to get into trouble on account of your curiosity."

Markos quickly excused himself before the two soldiers could start bickering over who was more likely to get who into trouble. He stole away to the back of the crowd and sidled up to Helena.

"So, has Father Cyril made any progress?" he asked knowingly.

Helena grinned at him, but she shrugged at the question. "Who knows? He didn't notice his breakfast when I brought it. I hope that's a good sign."

"Better than if he got up and started eating."

"I'm sure he can pray and eat at the same time," Helena said with mock seriousness. "Our priest is very talented."

Markos snorted. "I wonder what is taking so long. I would have expected him to be finished by now."

Helena gave Markos an irreverent smirk. "Perhaps he is wrestling with the Devil."

"Mm." Markos's reply was noncommittal. He was still unnerved by what he had seen the previous day and by the dreams that had followed, and he felt ashamed of it.

"You are handling this very well," he noted. "Aren't you afraid of that monster?"

"If it were alive, yes," Helena replied. "But it was dead, and I have seen dead things before."

"Those tentacles and that flesh…" Markos was speaking more to himself than to Helena. The particulars of the creature's physiology had been especially pronounced in the dream.

Helena shivered, but she refused to show fear, and as she so often did, tossed it away with a flippant comment.

"I am a fisherman's daughter, Markos. I *have* seen the dreaded octopus before."

Markos scoffed at the analogy. "I wish it were just an octopus, or some beast of the sea. But that thing is not of our world.…"

His words trailed off as Father Cyril emerged from the tomb, with his hands raised in triumph. Markos and Helena pushed their way forward to the edge of the pit, to hear the priest's pronouncement.

"It is done!" Cyril declared. "The demon is vanquished! There is nothing more to fear!"

The workers began to murmur with excitement, pleased at being saved from an evil that had only appeared the day before and none of them had seen. The soldiers were more stoic in their expressions, and they remained silent. At the edge of the pit, General Andronikos gazed down at Cyril with folded arms and a cautious expression.

"Well done, Father," he called. "Tell me: what has become of the fiend? Should we burn its body now?"

Father Cyril looked astonished at the question. He motioned to the tomb and said, "There is no need, General. It is gone, banished back to Hell. Come and see for yourself."

Andronikos nodded. After some consideration, he climbed down the ladder and approached the tomb, one hand resting on the hilt of his sword. Markos, for his part, felt his heart grow calmer at the news. The devil gone? He had to see it for himself.

Markos followed Andronikos and Cyril into the tomb. It was silent and still. The sarcophagus that had interred the monstrosity was completely empty. Markos stared at it for a while, dumbfounded. The devil had simply vanished into thin air. The exorcism had worked.

"Incredible…" he gasped.

Andronikos's response was more practical and less overawed. "Good. The men can return to work."

"Of course." Father Cyril looked especially pleased with himself. Pride was a sin, but under the circumstances he could be forgiven for indulging it.

"What should we do with the tomb?" Andronikos asked. "Bury it?"

"Probably the best course of—" Markos began.

"No, I would advise against that," Cyril quickly interjected. "The demon is banished, but there may still be a touch of evil that lingers here. If we rebury this place now, it will bring misfortune upon the venture. Perhaps this is why there have been so many setbacks. In a day or two, I will return and cleanse this place of whatever evil remains. But for now, I fear that I am far too weary after my struggle with the beast."

Markos began to protest, to point out that the delays were caused by the sheer complexity of the task, not by some lingering demonic aura haunting the island. He was cut off by Andronikos.

"That would seem to make sense," the general agreed. "I will trust your judgment in these matters. Whatever must be done to speed the work along, will be done."

As he spoke, Andronikos looked at Markos, without any pretense of subtlety. Markos gritted his teeth to keep from saying something foolish. He was glad that Cyril had dispatched whatever foul fiend had inhabited the tomb, but the exorcism was not going to make the tedious process of alchemy go any faster. Of course, Andronikos would fly into a rage if Markos said it aloud.

"With your permission, my lord, I will return to Theodoros and resume my work," he said.

Andronikos nodded. "Good. Get to it, boy. And tell Theodoros, the two of you had better start producing some results!" Having dismissed Markos, he looked back at the sarcophagus and addressed Father Cyril. "And you are certain that...thing...will not return? It will not conjure itself up from the depths of Hell some night?"

"Certainly not, my lord," Cyril assured him. "Exorcism springs from the power of God, not man. No devil is strong enough to withstand it." There was a pause. "Although..."

"Although?"

Cyril smiled. "Perhaps, just to be safe, you might wish to join me in the chapel for prayer tonight."

"If I must," Andronikos grunted. "I have never been much of a man for prayer. I find the concerns of this world more pressing."

Markos didn't care to remain behind to hear them discuss the respective merits of prayer and the sword. Besides, he had work to do. Though Andronikos hid his fear well, he had been as frightened by the demon as Markos. That kind of fear would not sit well with an old soldier like Andronikos. Any more delays, and he would start venting his nerves upon Markos and Theodoros.

Helena was waiting for him at the top of the pit. They stole away from the crowd, and lingered near the edge of the hill. They were still in plain sight if anyone cared to look at them, so Markos was careful to keep his behavior appropriate. Helena was not his wife yet, and he would best remember that.

"Well?" Helena asked breathlessly.

"The devil is gone," Markos assured her.

Helena exhaled in a gush of relief. "Thank the Lord. That thing haunted my nightmares last night."

"Mine too," Markos said. "Half the time it felt like the devil was there with me, hovering above me in the dark. I'm glad there will be no more of that tonight."

"Markos," Helena murmured, brushing his hand with her fingers. It was subtle. No one would notice, but it conveyed the tenderness it needed to.

"Yes?"

"Will I see you tonight?"

Markos frowned sadly. "I don't think so. Andronikos wants results. He was berating us about the delays yesterday. After *that*," Markos nodded toward the tomb, "I've no doubt he will wish to be finished and off the island as soon as can be. I fear he'll be a harsh task-master. I need to at least make some progress before I can go sneaking out at night."

"I could always sneak in," Helena suggested. Her eyes twinkled at the idea.

"Sneak into the monastery?" Markos nearly laughed aloud at the idea. "The soldiers would catch you in a moment." He took Helena's hands, and turned so that no one in the crowd could see it. "No, my love, I fear there is no choice but for me to lock myself away with Theodoros until the work is done. I want to be off of this island as soon as can be, and with you at my side."

"Mmm, then I suppose you are going to be as impatient as the general," Helena said.

"Yes, but for very different things," Markos replied. "Once we have the formula, Andronikos can return to Constantinople in triumph and have his audience with the Emperor, whereas I just want an audience with you in a home of our own."

The two of them traded a smile and gazed into each other's eyes, and Markos felt certain that all would finally be well.

* * * *

He spent the day and the night in the workshop, barely sleeping or eating. It helped distract him from his memories of the devil in the pit. The beast might be gone, but the image of it lingered in Markos's mind. He imagined every shadow stalking him in the candlelight. Every hint of movement he saw from the corner of his eye was transformed in his mind into a suggestion of the hideous creature.

Theodoros was not particularly understanding of Markos's feverish pace of work. He grumbled when he retired to bed with Markos still awake, and did so again when rose to find Markos already mixing fresh chemicals. Half the time, Markos didn't even bother listening to what the old man was saying. He just wanted the work to finally be done so he could get away from the island that stank of oil and harbored the corpses of fallen angels.

Markos skipped lunch on second day, the better to keep an eye on the experiments. He had a pot of naphtha on the table in front of him, and was agonizing over the exact measurements of the chemicals being mixed in. Liquid fire had to burn even when drenched with water, stick fast to its target, and spray far enough to threaten only the enemy. So many mixtures could do any of them, or even all to a degree, but none so far had met Andronikos's demands.

He yawned and stretched his neck as he heard the door open. A glance told him that Theodoros had returned. The old man had gone to dine with Father Cyril, and likely to enjoy the company of someone more sensible than his frantic apprentice.

"How is Father Cyril?" Markos asked, still focused on his work.

There was no immediate reply, but he heard Theodoros close the door. The alchemist crossed the room with a soft shuffling noise. Markos thought nothing of it.

"If it had been me wrestling with the devil, I'd be a wreck even now," Markos continued.

He didn't mention that he still was a wreck himself, still haunted by just the sight of the fiend in the glass box. He turned in his chair to say more, and froze. The devil in the sarcophagus stood behind him, right where Theodoros had been. Right where Theodoros was. Markos saw the last vestiges of Theodoros melting away and reshaping into the demon Apollyon, like clay molded by a potter.

Theodoros was the devil and the devil was Theodoros. It stood there, with blue quivering flesh and burning red eyes, and four hands that were not hands, outstretched to catch him. If he had not turned, he would be even now caught in its grasp.

Markos screamed and bolted from the chair. His heart pounded inside his chest, threatening to burst in its frenzy of terror. His eyes grew wide and he stared dumbly at the monster facing him, approaching him.

Do something, he screamed to himself. *Do something or you will die!*

One tentacled hand caught his arm and pulled him in. The others grabbed for other parts of him: a shoulder, a leg, his throat. Markos thrashed and pulled away before the thing could strangle him. His hand found a knife on the table, and suddenly Markos forgot everything in the world but that single weapon and the thing in front of him.

The tentacle hand finally got a grip on his neck as Markos grabbed the knife. He wanted to panic, and knew that to panic would be his death. The devil would choke him until he was too weak to fight back. It would crush the life from him and pull his soul into the abyss! Well, if he was to be dragged to Hell, he would give a good account of himself along the way.

Markos drove the knife into the demon's eyes. He stabbed again and again, all the while writhing and fighting against the hands that were not hands and the fingers that were not fingers. Within moments, the three red eyes were eyes no longer. The devil seemed not to have expected such fanatical resistance. It let out a hideous shriek, like nothing born upon the earth, and pulled away. Markos slashed at the tentacle around his throat and forced it off. Next, he hacked at the hand grasping his arm until it finally released him.

The devil scurried backward, shrieking and shaking its head. A noxious green fluid tricked out from the gashes across its face. The creature paused in the middle of the room and turned in all directions, as if listening for Markos. At each hint of noise, it lashed out with one of its horrid limbs, in case its victim had approached close enough to attack again.

Markos shuddered and struggled not to lose his mind. The most sensible thing he could do, he reasoned, was to laugh, and scream, and jump out of the window. Suddenly nothing in God's Creation made any sense. The devil had been banished, yet here it was. It had occupied Theodoros's form, but now Theodoros was nowhere to be seen, not even his lifeless body. Could the creature even be killed? If a priest's exorcism was useless against it, what could Markos do with a knife?

His gaze fell on the pot of naphtha. It was still incomplete, far from liquid fire, and that was assuming the current formula was even close to correct. Still, oil was oil. Markos grabbed the pot and flung it at the devil. The contents splattered all over it, and the devil snapped its head toward Markos. It snarled and chortled, and then it sniffed the air. It was hard to gauge any sentiment on its contorted face, but its posture stiffened. It understood what had happened.

Markos grabbed a candle and tossed it into the pool of oil at the devil's feet. The naphtha ignited instantly, and the creature burst into flame. It wailed horribly and thrashed around, fumbling for a means of escape. As it stumbled toward Markos, he grabbed his chair and beat it back desperately.

The fire was quick and powerful, and in due course the devil collapsed into a heap. Its body melted into a kind of thick fluid, but this burned just as well as solid flesh. Eventually, there was nothing left but a stain of char across the stone floor.

Markos collapsed onto the ground and vomited. His chest kept heaving even after his stomach had emptied itself, until at last his body was too exhausted to continue. Markos curled into a ball and lay there, quaking less with fear than with an utter inability to understand his own existence. His mind turned circles upon itself trying to understand what he had just seen, and coming up with nothing. Nothing in the world made sense any more, and that prospect seemed better than any possible explanation a rational mind could conjure.

* * * *

Markos did not know how long he lay there. He vomited again at some point and didn't remember it. At last, he uncurled himself and rolled onto his back. He gazed at the ceiling and reminded himself that this was not a dream. This was the world, and he was alive in it.

"Get up," he whispered. "Get up. Get up. Get up."

On the fourth recitation, he managed to sit. On the seventh, he forced himself to his feet. The air smelled disgusting, a mix of charred flesh and charred something else entirely. The thing that had once been Theodoros was gone, burned into an unidentifiable heap of ash. But was that the end of it? Could devils be killed so easily with fire?

Markos clutched his head and fought the urge to wail in despair. He felt like he was going mad. Cyril had banished the demon, and yet the demon had returned. And poor Theodoros! Had that thing been the old man all along, possessed by the unholy, flesh twisted into such a monstrous form? Or had the thing that returned merely worn Theodoros's face as a disguise?

Stop. Don't panic. What must be done?

Father Cyril. The priest would know what to do.

Markos looked down at the knife in his hand. It was covered in a sickening yellow-green fluid that couldn't possibly be blood. Markos wiped it clean on a rag, and then threw the rag into the fire in disgust. Was the devil gone, or had its spirit broken free with the destruction of Theodoros's body? Might it possess another hapless person? Might it attack Markos again on his way to Father Cyril's chamber?

Fire at least would destroy the form of the possessed. Markos filled some flasks with naphtha and tucked them into his leather bag. He approached the door, and had to spend another minute forcing himself to open it. Each time he reached for the handle, he had a vision of the devil and his hand pulled back as if stung.

Markos shook his head. No, he would not be a coward. People were in danger. Helena was in danger. He couldn't let the others end up like poor Theodoros.

The hallway was deserted. Markos quickly hid the knife inside his bag and hurried toward the cloister, where the soldiers were housed. Father Cyril was there too, in a set of rooms next to the chapel.

As Markos reached the end of the hallway, a figure in a hood and cloak darted in front of him, hurrying in the opposite direction. Markos threw out his hand to catch the person before they could collide, and without thinking, he also reached for his bag and the knife inside it.

Thankfully, there was no call for it. Helena stopped short and pulled back her hood, her eyes wide with surprise at the sight of him.

"Markos!" she exclaimed, her voice barely above a whisper.

"Helena? What are you doing here?"

Helena looked bewildered at the question. "I came to see you. I thought you would be in your workshop." She reached up and touched his face. "My God, Markos, have you slept? You look terrible!"

Markos caught Helena's hand and pulled it away from his face. After the near-death struggle with the devil, he shuddered at the thought of being touched, even by her.

"I have been working," he explained. "But what about you? What are you doing here?" Markos looked into the cloister and saw soldiers on guard. They had probably seen her. "You could get into a lot of trouble if Andronikos finds you!"

Helena laughed. "No, it is fine, Markos. Thomas and I came to see Father Cyril. Thomas has been having nightmares, so we thought he should unburden himself with confession. And I..." Helena grinned at Markos as her delicate fingers played with the folds of his tunic. "I thought perhaps I would go and see you."

Markos sighed in despair. If the devil truly was on the loose, the monastery was the last place Helena should be.

"You shouldn't have come, Helena! It isn't safe!"

"What? Why not?"

"Because the devil is not banished," Markos replied. "It is *here*!"

Helena turned pale and drew back. "What...?"

They were interrupted by the arrival of Ioannis and Georgios, and a third soldier called Simon.

"You! Girl! What are you doing here?" Ioannis snapped at Helena. "You were supposed to remain in the chapel until your brother is finished with confession."

"Oh, I, um..." Helena stammered. She blushed modestly and cast a shy glance at Markos. "I simply wanted to say hello to Markos."

Simon snickered. "Yeah, I'm sure you did." He gave Markos a knowing nudge. "I like a good 'hello' now and then."

Markos looked Simon dead in the eyes and said, "The devil is loose in the monastery. It just attacked me in the workshop."

"W-what?" Simon stammered.

Ioannis and Georgios traded looks and began asking questions that Markos didn't have time to answer. He pushed past them and hurried across the cloister toward the chapel. Helena raced after him, with the soldiers close behind her. It was probably the exhaustion as much as fear, but Markos was frantic. He could think of nothing but reaching Cyril. The priest would have to know how to banish the demon forever. The alternative was unthinkable.

The chapel was empty, and the door to Cyril's private chamber was closed. Markos tried it and found it latched. He banged on the door with his fist and shouted Father Cyril's name.

"What are you doing?" Georgios demanded. "Father Cyril is at prayer!"

"It doesn't matter! This is more important!" Markos snapped. He banged on the door again. "Father Cyril! I must speak with you!"

Ioannis caught his arm. "Markos, what do you mean 'the devil is loose in the monastery'?"

"Just that," Markos said, still pounding his fist on the door.

From the other side of the door, he heard Cyril shout angrily, "Yes! Yes! I am coming!"

The door opened and the priest stuck his head out, looking furious at the disturbance.

"I am at prayer..." Cyril began.

Markos did not let him finish. He force the door open and pushed past Cyril. The priest sputtered and shouted for Markos to leave, and Markos clasped his hands in penance for the intrusion.

"Father, you have to perform another exorcism," he said.

"What?"

"The devil was not banished like we thought. It just attacked me in the workshop. It had possessed Theodoros, and..." Markos paused and looked around the room. It was sparse, like everything in the monastery. "Where is Thomas?"

"Thomas?" Father Cyril gave Markos a curious look. "Why would he be here?"

That was odd, Markos thought. Hadn't Thomas gone to confession?

"Oh, because he came for confession," Cyril said, as if just then realizing what Markos meant. "We finished a few minutes ago and I sent him away. Now, if you will please leave me in peace, I have my own prayers to complete."

He began pushing Markos toward the door, shooing him and the others out.

Helena took Markos by the arm. "We should go. We can look for Thomas."

"No! No!" Markos shoved everyone away from him and forced his way to the center of the room. "Father Cyril, the devil is still on the island. You must exorcise it again!"

Father Cyril looked at Markos sternly. "That is ridiculous, Markos. Look, Theodoros told me you have not been sleeping. Your thoughts are playing tricks on you. Go back to your room and rest, and stop all of this foolishness."

"No, you don't understand," Markos insisted. "Theodoros, he... He was possessed. He attacked me. The demon attacked me pretending to be Theodoros!"

There was a long, uncomfortable pause, and Markos realized what he had just said. He was suddenly conscious at the three soldiers standing close to him. They were all exchanging looks. Georgios put his hand on the hilt of his sword.

"Markos, what have you done?"

Markos pulled away from them and drew back, trying to find the words to explain.

"It was not Theodoros, it was the devil!" he insisted. "Blue flesh, blood-red eyes, claws and tentacles... I had to kill it with fire. I didn't have any choice!"

The soldiers drew their swords, and Markos knew that it was all over. They thought he was insane and he had murdered Theodoros. He looked at Helena, silently pleading for her to understand. Helena just shook her head, a distant look in her eyes.

"Come quietly, Markos," Ioannis said. "If you killed Theodoros, the general will want you alive. Don't make this difficult."

Markos looked at Father Cyril. The priest fell to his knees and began to pray, beseeching the Almighty for the preservation of Markos's soul. It confirmed what the soldiers already thought.

Markos kept backing away until there was no more room left. The soldiers continued to advance, moving cautiously in case Markos threw all sense to the wind and attacked them too. Ioannis was right: with Theodoros dead, Andronikos needed him alive to finish the formula, but he had no illusions about what would happen to him once the work was finished. He could spend the rest of his days mixing chemicals in a prison cell.

He passed Cyril's bed and pressed against the wall, hemmed into the corner.

Cyril glanced up from his prayer and his eyes widened. "Don't just stand there gawking, grab him!" he shouted at the soldiers. "Get him away from there! He is dangerous!"

Markos tensed and put up his hands, ready for a fight he couldn't possibly win. As he did, he turned and saw a shape on the floor behind the bed, concealed from the rest of the room. It was Thomas, but only part of him. Thomas's body was missing from the waist down, along with half of one arm. The division was clean and precise, like flesh and bone had simply melted away into nothing. No tearing, no cutting, just gone.

"Oh God!" Markos screamed. His body convulsed at the sight. Ioannis grabbed him, and Markos did not put up a fight. Instead, he just pointed at the corpse.

"What are...?" Ioannis looked. "Oh God!" he echoed in horror.

Georgios joined them and recoiled as he saw the body. Simon fell to his knees and was sick.

Ioannis released Markos and slowly knelt by Thomas's remains. "I don't understand. What has happened to him? What killed him?"

"The devil in the pit," Markos said.

"Where is the rest of him?"

Markos had no answer. "Destroyed, with hellfire perhaps?"

"But if he was killed here..." Ioannis said.

They both looked toward Father Cyril. Now it was the priest's turn to back away, retreating toward the door.

"No you don't!" Ioannis shouted.

The soldier pushed Markos aside and charged at Cyril. The priest turned to flee, but Ioannis caught him by the shoulder and pulled him back. Cyril turned, and suddenly he was no longer Cyril. Markos felt a dizzy sickness fill his head as he watched Cyril's face melt away and transform into the devil's writhing blue flesh and burning red eyes. Cyril's whole body followed, lashing out with tentacles and claws, snarling in desperation.

Ioannis howled in pain as he was struck, but he was a good soldier and he knew his business. He grabbed the thing that had been Cyril and stabbed it again and again with his sword. Georgios and Simon rushed to help him, and together they hacked the demon to pieces, until it lay in a sickening heap on the floor. The soldiers stumbled away, gasping for air.

Simon sat on the bed and put his face in his hands. "Lord preserve us, we have killed a priest!" he cried.

"I think it was the devil that did the killing," Markos said, approaching the body cautiously. "That thing was no longer Father Cyril."

"That is what happened with Theodoros?" Ioannis asked.

Markos nodded. "The very same."

"Do you think the devil traveled from Theodoros to Cyril?" Georgios asked nervously.

"Maybe." Markos wasn't actually sure, but suddenly he was being regarded as the expert on the matter. "Or maybe Cyril was possessed during the exorcism, and he conjured an entirely new devil up from Hell to possess Theodoros."

Simon looked up, ashen-faced. "If that's the case, who is to say it is only the two devils? Anyone could be possessed. Any one of us!"

"My God, you are right," Georgios agreed. He drew his sword and held it out to keep the others back. "Any one of you could be possessed! Perhaps all of you!"

Helena looked at him sternly. "Don't be stupid. And put that thing away before you hurt yourself." She looked at Markos. "We must all be fine. If any of us were possessed, why didn't they help Cyril?"

"Ah, she makes a good point," Ioannis agreed. "Still, what about the others? What about the garrison and the workers?"

Simon whimpered softly, and muttered what the rest of them were thinking: "How can we know who among them is possessed?"

Markos shrugged helplessly. "The only man who could have answered that was Cyril."

He looked at the hideous corpse on the ground and grimaced. So much for seeking a priest's advice. They were now adrift in a world of fallen angels and the darkest of unholy things, and he had no idea how to combat this evil.

Suddenly, there was another matter to concern him. As he looked upon the body, Markos saw its severed hand twitch. For a moment, he was certain it was his imagination taunting him. How could a limb, even a demonic one, move once it had been separated from its body? And yet, it did indeed move.

As Markos watched, the hand clenched and wriggled its fingers, and then began to crawl away as though its body were still attached and struggling to flee.

"Look!" Markos shouted, pointing at the hand.

Ioannis stared dumbfounded, mumbling an oath. Georgios cursed, Helena gasped, and Simon was sick again. Markos ran to the hand and kicked it away before it could escape under the bed. In that time, Ioannis came to his senses, and stabbed the thing with his sword. He lifted it into the light, and the thing continued to squirm.

"This is not possible," he said, staring transfixed at the horror at the end of his blade. "Not possible at all."

Markos grabbed the blade from him and flung the hand into the hearth fire. The appendage squirmed all the more as it burned away. A piercing shriek issued from the dying flesh, though it had no mouth with which to scream. Finally, it succumbed and stopped moving, as the cozy fire rendered it to ash.

"Did that just happen?" Ioannis asked.

Markos handed his sword back to him. "It did. There is no question now. We must burn the devil's body, every last piece of it."

"I don't understand," Simon moaned. "How can that be possible? How can a severed hand move?"

"It was controlled by the devil that possessed Father Cyril's body," Markos said. It was the only explanation he could think of.

Georgios shook his head in disbelief. "Impossible. Why would the demon go into the hand? Perhaps you were seeing things. I didn't see it move. Did you?" he asked Helena, who gave him no reply but a cold stare.

"Maybe there are many demons," Simon offered, picking himself up from the floor. "Legion, like in the Bible. One demon for every limb, for every portion of the body. Cut off the hand, the demon in the hand tries to escape...."

Simon was rambling, but in the chaos of his words, Markos found the germ of an idea.

"Maybe indeed," he said. He raised a finger as an idea blossomed in his head. "And if that is so, then that is how we can tell that someone is possessed!"

"What?" Georgios exclaimed. "You're talking nonsense."

"You mean cut off a hand and see if the devil in the hand tries to escape?" Ioannis asked. He exhaled and stared at the fire. "That is a steep price for confirmation."

"Maybe not a whole hand," Markos agreed.

Ioannis shook his head in disbelief. "Just a finger?" he chided. "No Markos, this will not work. We cannot be chopping limbs off our comrades in the hope that one of them is possessed!"

Markos scratched his head. There was more of an idea lurking in there, waiting to be coaxed out. Not hands, not fingers, then what?

"Blood," he cried, as the idea came to him. "What if there are devils lurking in the victim's blood? If we could bleed one out, it would be trapped, and it would try to escape."

Ioannis made a face. "I won't lie and pretend it's a good plan, but I suppose I would rather try that before I start cutting my fingers off."

Georgios scoffed at the idea. "And I suppose you expect us to bleed ourselves dry while you stand there and watch, eh? How do we know you're not possessed too? You might be running us in circles to keep us distracted."

"Hey, just a moment!" Ioannis exclaimed. "Markos is the one who warned us about the demon in the first place."

"Exactly! The perfect way to draw suspicion away from him!"

Markos threw up his hands. "Stop! Please!" More calmly, he said, "I will go first. I don't know if it will work, but as Ioannis says, I would rather try this before cutting off fingers and toes."

He took out his knife and cleaned it again, holding it to a candle flame for a while to be sure that every last trace of the devil had burned away. Then he cut a small gash in his forearm, and allowed his blood to drip onto a metal plate from Cyril's table. He bandaged his arm as the others gathered around.

Markos pondered what to do next. Should he stab the blood? Would that threaten a devil lurking there? Not that he believed there were any devils in his own body, but he needed a method they could use for everyone on the island, and this way he proved that he was treating himself no differently than the rest of them.

"Well? What now?" Ioannis asked.

"Um." Markos frowned. He picked up the plate and held one of the candles close to it, until the heat upon the blood was unmistakable. As he expected, nothing happened.

Georgios scoffed. "A lot of good that did."

Helena sighed and touched Markos's hand. "Markos, please stop hurting yourself. This isn't going to do any good. Maybe if we pray, we can force the devils to reveal themselves."

There was a pause, and then Ioannis pushed up his sleeve. "No, I'm willing to try this. It's better than any idea I have."

"You cannot be serious!" Georgios said.

"I'd rather shed some blood than lose a hand," Ioannis said. "I have bled in battle before. This is nothing."

Markos nodded. He dumped the plateful of blood into the fire and cleaned both it and the knife. Best to leave no trace after each person was tested. He cut Ioannis's forearm, and the soldier bled onto the plate just as he had done. Markos held a flame to the blood as before, and the result was the same. Nothing.

"This is stupid," Georgios declared, as Markos cleaned the plate and the blade again. "If you will excuse me, I'm going to report what has happened to the general, and hopefully he will know what to do. It's obvious that you don't!"

The parting comment was for Markos, and the barb in Georgios's words made Markos frown, ashamed at his failure. In truth, he had no way of knowing whether this would work at all.

"No," Ioannis said firmly, grabbing Georgios by the shoulder.

"What did you say?"

"None of us have an answer to this, but at least Markos is trying to find one. If you wish to be so rude about it, you can go next."

Georgios pushed Ioannis away. "I am not going to dignify this madness! We need leadership and prayer, not bloodletting!"

Ioannis took the knife from Markos and held it up to Georgios's face.

"You are going next, Georgios. Do it yourself, or I'll do it for you. And you won't like it if I do it."

"Well, what about Simon? What about the girl?" Georgios protested.

"They'll go after you," Ioannis said. "Now get cutting."

Georgios grumbled some more, but he pulled back his sleeve and made the cut. After bleeding onto the plate, he drew back and folded his arms angrily.

Markos took the plate and held the candle to the blood. At first, it was as before: nothing worth noting. The blood grew hot, but it was only blood. Suddenly, the pool of blood began to wriggle of its own accord. Small tendrils reached out, lashing at the candle, only to pull away again, fearful of the heat. Markos tilted the plate to force the blood to pool next to the flame. Instead, the liquid defied all sense of reason, and began to crawl away from the candle, up the metal incline.

"Do you see that?" Markos shouted.

"I do!" Ioannis replied. The soldier turned toward Georgios, only to find that Georgios was already halfway to the door. "No you don't!"

Ioannis and Simon rushed Georgios before he could flee the room. They grabbed for him, but by now the demon that had possessed Georgios had given up all pretense. Human flesh erupted in a torrent of blue wriggling tentacles and hooked claws. Red eyes bubbled out of Georgios's forehead as his body twisted and reshaped into the unholy form. He struggled, but as with Cyril, the soldiers knew their business. They had swords and armor, and they hacked the devil that had been Georgios to pieces.

Dumbfounded, Markos barely had the sense to throw the living blood into the fire before it could crawl its way off the plate. As the second demon's corpse fell to the ground, Simon rushed to Markos's side.

"Test me! Test me!" he cried frantically. "I don't want to become one of those things!"

Ioannis slumped against the wall, breathing hard from the fight. "I don't think it works that way. If you were possessed, you'd know it. Georgios was doing everything he could to dissuade us. I should have seen it."

"He said I was mad and stupid for suggesting we do a mad and stupid thing," Markos replied. "I would be more suspicious if he'd said anything else."

He tested Simon's blood, and like his and Ioannis's, it proved to be ordinary. That was good. So far, only one of them had been possessed, and the test was proven to work. Markos turned to Helena, but she was nowhere to be seen.

"Helena?" he asked aloud, rushing to the door. Helena was gone, and the chapel was empty.

Ioannis and Simon joined him at the doorway.

"You don't think...?" Ioannis began.

Markos's heart sank, and his stomach grew sick. "Why else would she leave?" he asked.

"But how? When?"

The muscles in Markos's face tightened. "You said she brought Father Cyril breakfast that morning?"

"Yes."

"There is your answer." Markos closed the door and secured it. He wanted to rush after Helena, to beg her for proof that his worst suspicions were not true. That was foolish, and he didn't intend to be foolish now. "I am going after her. When I return, test me again."

"But you're not possessed," Simon protested.

"When I return, test me again," Markos repeated. "If anyone is ever separated from the group, they must be tested again. We don't know how the possession happens. Out of sight invites danger."

Ioannis nodded. "Agreed." He motioned to Simon. "We'll burn the bodies and start checking the rest of the garrison. I hope this thing hasn't spread far."

"One person at a time," Markos said. "Never let yourselves be outnumbered."

"What about General Andronikos?" Simon asked. "Shouldn't we warn him?"

Ioannis gave his comrade a grave look. "The general went to prayer with Father Cyril right after the exorcism. We must assume he is possessed as well."

"Surely not!" Simon protested.

"Surely he is," Markos said grimly. "The general, Father Cyril, and Theodoros are the three most important people on the island. They were all compromised, there is no doubt." A thought came to him and he muttered a curse. "If Theodoros and I finally managed to perfect the formula, Andronikos would shortly find himself in a private audience with the Emperor. What a triumph it would be for the forces of Hell to place an agent of their wickedness upon the throne of Rome."

Simon crossed himself. "God preserve us!"

"So," Markos continued, "you must treat everyone like they are possessed until you know that they are not. Even me when I return, understood?"

"Understood." Ioannis clapped a hand on Markos's arm. "Good luck. I hope you don't die."

"Me too," Markos said.

He picked up Georgios's sword, which had been abandoned in the fight. Clutching his bag close to him, Markos steeled his nerves and went out into the cloister. He ducked out of sight before the other soldiers could notice him carrying a weapon around. No good would come of alerting any of them now, even those who were not possessed. As Markos crept along the wall, he caught sight of a figure in Helena's hood and cloak ahead of him, moments before it darted into one of the adjoining corridors. Markos stopped himself from calling her name, and hurried in silence to the doorway.

There was another glimpse of the figure as it ducked into the stairway leading down to the cellars. It was Helena. She paused just long enough to see him and for him to see her. She knew that he was following her, and she was leading him along intentionally.

In his heart, Markos knew the truth. Helena was possessed and she was leading him into a trap, and yet he couldn't stay away. He grabbed a torch from a wall sconce and descended into the cellar. Again, he was given just enough time to spot Helena, before she vanished into the shadows to his left. Markos grimaced. He was meant to follow her, to run along from glimpse to glimpse until he was cornered somewhere.

Well, he was having none of that. If the devil wanted to corner him so badly, it could do so on his terms. Markos turned to the right and hurried through the dimly lit cellar into a store room that he knew well. It had once contained wine, but now the barrels were filled with oil, some for storage and others containing the results of failed formulae. It was familiar ground, and that gave Markos some very small measure of comfort.

He placed his back against the far wall of the room and waited. Minutes dragged past, and Markos soon lost track of the time. There was nothing but him and the stench of oil, the flickering shadows, and the beating of his heart. Had he been mistaken? What if it really was Helena? Perhaps she had lured him there to comfort her in secret, or to relay some news she didn't trust the others knowing? Had he made a mistake?

Helena appeared in the doorway, her face marked by that familiar, too-wide smile. Markos had always delighted in seeing it before. It did not delight him now.

"Clever Markos," Helena said, slowly approaching him. "Knowing a trap when one is set for you."

She stopped in the middle of the room, as the figures of Andronikos and two of the garrison soldiers entered behind her. One of the soldiers closed the door and secured it behind them, in case Markos had any illusions about escape.

"Not so clever," Andronikos noted. "He avoids one trap, only to corner himself here." He grinned, and even in human form it was horrible to see. "I know your mind, boy. You thought it would only be her."

"Yes," Markos confessed, tightening his grip on the sword. He certainly hadn't expected to face four of them. One alone would be challenge enough. Markos began to panic.

Helena frowned at him, sad and sympathetic. "Poor Markos. Just close your eyes and it will all be over soon. I promise, I do not wish to hurt you. But with Theodoros dead, you must become one of us."

"So I can finish the formula," Markos said. "So that Andronikos can meet the Emperor. So that you can do *this* to him!" Markos waved his sword at the four of them.

"Yes," Helena answered. "Your Emperor, your Patriarch, every high and mighty lord of your Roman Empire will become one of me."

"Why?" Markos cried. "Why are you doing this to us?"

The laugh that issued from Helena chilled him to the bone, and was made all the worse as it was echoed exactly by Andronikos and the soldiers.

"Because I must get off of this pathetic planet. I have been conscious for two of its days, and already I despise it."

"I don't understand," Markos said. "The earth is not a planet. It is the earth."

Andronikos scoffed at him. The general advanced a pace, and the soldiers went with him. Markos raised his torch and sword menacingly. He was little threat to them, and likely they all knew it, but he wouldn't allow them to take him without returning some injury. And they seemed to sense his certainty as well, for Andronikos hesitated, and so did the soldiers. Their courage seemed to have faded, and along with it their obedience to their commander. Markos snickered at this realization. It seemed the demons all feared death, and none wished to be sacrificed for the sake of the others.

"I have neither the time, the patience, nor the wish to explain the vastness of the cosmos to you, boy," the general said. "It would be a wasted effort, like explaining mathematics to an ant."

Markos bristled at Andronikos's dismissal. The insult was nothing compared to the fear he felt, but even so it made him angry and that strengthened his resolve.

Helena gave Andronikos an irritated glare, and then just as quickly offered Markos a gentle smile.

"Your planet is one of many," she explained, "just like mine. There is no divine vastness in the sky, like you imagine, nor devils in the depths of the earth. Simply space: darkness unending, punctuated here and there with spots of light, and worlds revolving around them. Worlds like yours and worlds like mine, although the difference between my planet and this place would be like Constantinople compared to a hovel. Put simply, I am trapped here and I wish to leave. That is all."

"Then leave!" Markos snarled. "We want nothing to do with you!"

Helena sighed. "If only it were so easy. Had I the means of building a spacecraft, I would depart this wretched place at once, but you don't even have the basic materials for me to use."

"What?"

"You Romans believe that you are the greatest civilization on your entire planet, and you cannot even *fly*!" Helena laughed. "You have no *computers*, no *rocketry*, no *electricity*. You have nothing for me to use."

Markos felt his head spin. Helena spoke in plain Greek, but phrases she used felt out of place, like she had to jumble together concepts to explain things beyond Markos's knowledge. Thinking machines? Flying towers? Captured lightning? Each explanation made less sense than ignorance.

"You want an explanation?" Helena asked. "It is this. I will replace your Emperor, your Patriarch, your priesthood and your nobles with myself. Through them, I will transform your entire society into a vehicle of technological progress. I will drag your species into modernity, so that within my lifetime you can build me a vessel that will free me from this place!"

She gazed at Markos, and Markos shuddered to see Helena's eyes looking into his. "I only want to go home," Helena pleaded. "Is that truly so wicked of me?"

Even though he knew better, Markos felt his heart soften. His ears heard Helena's gentle voice, and the genuine sorrow lurking there. She was lost in this hellish place, and she needed him to help her escape.

It was almost enough to distract Markos as one of the soldiers crept toward him from the side. Almost, but not quite. Markos snapped out of the trance and quickly pointed his sword at the soldier. The thing had already begun to change, its fingers extending into long tentacles ribbed with barbs and claws. But again, at the sight of the sword and the torch, it hesitated.

"We tried it your way," Andronikos said to Helena. "Now we do it my way." He pointed at Markos and advanced cautiously, mirrored by the soldiers step-by-step as they formed a semi-circle in front of him. "Close your eyes, boy, and die without a struggle. You will not like how death comes if you resist."

Markos glared back defiantly. "I will take one of you with me, at least. Maybe more. Which of you wishes to die first?"

There came that hesitation again, but this time Andronikos shrugged it away and motioned the soldiers forward again.

"I will take my chances."

Markos felt the fear of death well up inside of him. He wanted to scream, to cry, to beg, to plead for his life. His instinct was to think that he didn't want to die. But as that thought passed through his mind, he suddenly realized that he no longer cared. Living or dying didn't matter now. All that mattered was stopping this evil before it could hurt more people. It had to be stopped here on the island, and if that meant his death, Markos would pay that price.

He threw the torch onto the ground at Andronikos's feet. The general scrambled backward as if afraid. The soldiers froze too, and Helena drew back from the rest of them.

"What are you doing...?" Andronikos began.

In truth, Markos hadn't come there with a plan, but now one blossomed to life in his mind. Fire. Oil. A closed door and a stone room. He ran to the nearest barrel of naphtha and forced it open with his sword. Andronikos was shouting for him to stop, as if the general knew the contents of Markos's mind as soon as Markos did. It was a curious notion that Markos had no time to ponder. As Andronikos and the soldiers rushed at him, Markos tipped the barrel over and a wave of thick, foul oil spilled out to meet them.

Andronikos scrambled back to keep clear of the thick black liquid. One soldier slipped and fell to his knees, though as he fell his entire form shifted into the monstrous blue creature. It caught itself with its tentacles and tried to rise, moments before the oil reached the torch and the whole pool ignited.

The air was filled with heat and smoke, and the horrible high-pitched wail of the demons as they burned. Both soldiers were caught before they could run, and writhed in the flames as they died. Andronikos abandoned all pretense as he fled from the wall of fire, transforming into his demon body and shrieking in fear. Across the room, Helena ran to the door and forced it open, disappearing into the cellar. Markos knew he couldn't reach her, but at least he could keep Andronikos from escaping too.

Markos ran to the next barrel and broke it open. The thing that had been Andronikos advanced on him, lashing with its tentacles. Claws tore Markos's flesh, and he scrambled away, bleeding and gasping amid the smoke. As Andronikos came at him again, Markos reached into his bag and flung the bottles of naphtha at the devil. Andronikos seemed almost to smile at him, as its tentacles swatted the bottles away one at a time. They tumbled to the ground and there was the audible sound of glass cracking. The contents seeped out all around Andronikos, mingling with the oil from the barrels, and together they created an unbroken chain.

Torch to oil to devil.

The wall of fire reached Andronikos in a violent rush, faster than the devil could react. There was barely time for its blood-red eyes to fix on Markos with an almost human expression of hatred. He was supposed to die in that room. The devil was supposed to live.

The fire engulfed Andronikos.

Markos grabbed his sword and ran for the door, barely ahead of the fire. It clawed at him from behind, threatening to overtake him if he slowed for a single moment. Markos reached the cellar, and slammed the door shut. Choking and gasping for air, he slid down onto the floor, unable to stand any longer.

Keep moving.

Markos began to crawl for the stairs, all the while willing himself to get up even though his body refused to obey. It was all too much, but if he stopped there, he would surely die. There was no knowing how far the fire would spread in the stone building, but the cellar would soon be choked with smoke.

He reached the top of the stairs and collapsed. Unconsciousness took him soon after.

* * * *

Markos woke in the chapel, surrounded by soldiers. He sat up with a fearful gasp and put up his fists. The soldiers looked at him like he was crazy, but one did reach for a sword. Ioannis came into view and motioned for the man to put away his weapon.

"You're safe, Markos," Ioannis said. "You are among friends."

Markos looked around fearfully. "All of these people? They're not possessed?"

Ioannis shook his head. "We have tested every one of them. Two devils, both dead now. The rest are men."

"Test me!" Markos demanded, offering his arm.

Ioannis looked confused. "Do you think you're possessed?"

"No, I know I am not," Markos said.

"Then why...?"

"Because you don't know it! That's the rule: everyone is tested whenever they rejoin the group. No exceptions."

Ioannis nodded. He gathered a knife, a basin, and a candle, and performed the test. Even though Markos was certain he remained himself, he felt a pang of uncertainty as he waited for the blood to either boil or react. If he was possessed, would he even know?

He breathed a sigh as his blood remained still.

"See? I knew you were yourself," Ioannis said.

"Did you, though?" Markos asked. It was a joke, or at least both of them chose to take it as one. They chuckled together, and found it better than admitting whatever doubts they had harbored.

Ioannis motioned to the cloister. "There was a fire raging in one of the storerooms when we found you. What happened?"

"Andronikos, Helena, two more soldiers," Markos said. "All devils."

"Dead?"

"Helena escaped," Markos replied. He frowned and looked down at the floor. It wasn't Helena. He had to remember that it wasn't Helena.

"I will get some men and go looking for her."

"No." Markos shook his head. "Finish the garrison and move on to the villagers. I will find Helena."

"Should we test you a third time when you come back?"

"Yes." Markos didn't voice his certainty that he wasn't coming back. Instead, he laid a hand on Ioannis's arm and said, "The supply ship is due here in a day or two. We must have this contained before it arrives."

"Agreed."

"When you see its sails on the horizon, test everyone again before it docks. Everyone."

"You truly believe that's necessary?" Ioannis asked.

"When I was in the cellar, the devils spoke of possessing the Emperor and the Patriarch. We cannot risk them escaping this island."

Ioannis thought of something and frowned, suddenly even more worried than before. "What should we say to the crew? We've lost several men, including our commander, our priest, and the alchemist. The imperial court will want answers, and I don't think they are going to believe stories of demonic possession. I don't want to escape all of this, only to be executed for murder."

"Say there was an accident. The oil caught fire and the dead died trying to put it out. It's a better way to be remembered than what happened."

"Better than the truth, I suppose," Ioannis agreed, sighing heavily.

* * * *

Markos said his farewells to the soldiers before leaving the chapel. He didn't let on, but he did not expect to escape his next encounter alive. A part of him was at peace with that.

He took his borrowed sword, a lamp, and a bucket from Father Cyril's room. He needed more oil, and after the fire in the storeroom, there was precious little of it left. The soldiers watched him cautiously. None of them could understand why he was going alone, risking his life and inviting suspicion upon his return. Well, that was fine. He didn't plan on returning.

On the way to the demon pit, Markos filled the bucket with oil from one of the wells. The tomb that had held the demon needed to be destroyed. It was a single-minded task he could focus on, which freed him from the weight of everything else that had happened that day.

Helena was inside the tomb when he arrived. She sat on the floor, an expression of abject resignation on her face. And it was still her face that the devil wore, though the hellish form began to creep through in other places. Her hands had become the strange tentacle-fingered appendages, and they held a pile of the curious waxy paper Markos had seen stacked by the table when the tomb was first opened. He had thought little of them then, but it seemed they were of significance to the devil.

Helena looked up as Markos entered and set the bucket down on the floor. She laughed. It was still Helena's laugh, but it was bitter and dejected. Markos's heart twitched at the sound. He wanted to rush to her and comfort her, even though it was not Helena sitting there.

"You survived," she said.

"I did."

"I assume the others are dead."

"They are," Markos replied.

"And now you have come to kill me." It was a statement, not a question, and strangely, it was spoken with acceptance rather than fear.

"I don't want to kill you," Markos confessed.

Helena grinned. It was angry and cruel. "Oh no? Or do you mean to say, you don't want to kill me while I am *wearing her face?*" The devil laughed again. "I could simply transform into myself, make it easy for you. You'll have no qualms about killing me then."

"I never wanted to kill anyone," Markos said.

"But you did when you had to," Helena mused. "You have learned something about yourself."

"I have learned a great deal." Markos turned his eyes heavenward. "I've learned that there are things up there that I cannot imagine, and that I will probably never understand. You spoke of other worlds...."

"More numerous than the stars in the sky," Helena said.

"And I will never see them. I have devoted my life to understanding the mysteries of Creation, and you have revealed to me the inescapable fact that most of them will forever remain beyond my grasp. And I would be at peace with that if Helena was still alive. Now that she is gone, I have nothing. You have shattered my world and left me with *nothing!*"

The devil scoffed at him. "You knew her for less than one of your planet's years. Don't pretend it was more profound than it really was."

"I loved her!" Markos shouted. "She was good and kind and clever, and she deserved better than this! Better than to be transformed into your puppet!" Markos felt his cheeks grow wet with tears. "Why did you kill her? She had done nothing to you!"

"Expediency," Helena replied softly.

"Andronikos, I can understand. Father Cyril, I can understand. Theodoros, even me! But why *her?* What use could her death possibly be to you?"

Helena sighed and leaned back against the wall, staring off into the distance.

"I was on a transport vessel passing through your star system. There was a malfunction and we became trapped in your planet's gravity. The ship had only one working escape pod, and I took it." Her tone became hard and determined. "I did what I had to do to survive." The hardness died away in a bitter laugh and she said, "It seems it was a wasted effort. The pod launched too late. It couldn't escape the gravity well. But I didn't know that. Once aboard, I followed procedure and put myself into cold sleep. The next thing I knew, I was here."

Again, she spoke in proper Greek but the words and phrases she used were confusing to Markos, hinting at even more secret knowledge that would forever remain beyond his reach.

"I expected to be rescued by my own kind. The first face I would see once I had thawed would be familiar, blue, three-eyed. *Normal.*" Helena scowled.

"Instead, I awoke to the sight of a grotesque, two-eyed monster with spongey pale flesh, kneeling in front of me and wailing in a hideous unnatural voice."

"Father Cyril," Markos said.

Helena nodded. "What was I to do? I confess, my mind was not entirely together at the time. Freezing and reviving every cell in one's body does take a toll, even being adapted for it. I killed him, and I ate him, and then I made a copy of myself in his image."

It took Markos a few moments to grasp what she had said.

"Copy? That was never Father Cyril?"

"It was never any of them. They were all me, and yet not me. Cells of my cells, arranged in perfect mimicry."

"Then why Helena?" Markos demanded.

The devil shrugged. "I had just finished making the Me-Cyril, when I realized that I couldn't copy that form too. There couldn't be two Cyrils walking around. Your species is clever enough to notice a thing like that. And then who should enter, but your dear friend. Pretending to bring the priest food, but really she was curious, and that curiosity killed her. I ate her and I became her." She grinned and spread her arms dramatically. "In a way, 'tis like she never died."

"You are a monster!" Markos shouted.

"Are you a monster for eating a cow or a goat, and wearing its skin?" Helena asked. The question sounded sincere, though it was cruel and no doubt calculated to offend. "It doesn't matter anyway. All my labors have been for nothing."

The dejected tone in her voice gave Markos pause. "What do you mean?"

Helena threw the handful of waxy paper at Markos. The sheets scattered across the floor of the tomb, their words as meaningless as when first Markos had seen them.

"Status reports," Helena said. "The pod was very diligent. Every year it reported on my vitals, the state of the systems, and the surrounding environment." She picked up one sheet and pointed to it. "Oh, look. Still buried under dirt and rock."

Helena allowed the paper to slip from her fingers. "They said the pods were made to last, but I never understood just what that meant. The reports only stopped when the main systems finally shut down after five thousand years."

"Five...thousand?" Markos was certain he had misheard.

"Five thousand. And that is only as long as the computers lasted. Main power died. Reserve power died. I would have died too, if the cold sleep chamber hadn't remained sealed. To put it frankly, I have absolutely no idea how long I have lain here. Thousands of years? Hundreds of thousands? *Millions?*"

Helena's voice was distorted with uncertainty, tinged with madness at the very contemplation of such a thing. She rose to her feet and fixed Markos with a furious glare. Her eyes glinted, and green began to fade into stark blood red.

"Answer me!" she screamed. "How long have I been trapped on this planet? Does my civilization even *exist* anymore?"

She collapsed to her knees and her whole body sagged from the weight of despair.

"Am I the last of my kind?"

Markos had no answer.

Helena's face darkened with impotent rage. "I should take my revenge on you. I should stride across your world like a scourge, consuming every last living thing that draws breath, until there is nothing left alive here but me! Untold billions of me, exactly me, perfect copies of me! And that way…" Her voice choked. "And that way I will no longer be alone."

Silence filled the tomb, and slowly Helena forced her expression to grow hard and cold again. "Forgive my outburst. Your kind are sentimental. Something happens when you copy a creature cell by cell, neuron by neuron. Fragments of the original seep through. It seems that this fragment is terrified of being abandoned."

"How can you be so callous about murder?" Markos snarled. "My heart would feel for your plight, but you have killed and eaten innocent people! You wanted to enslave us! You fear being the last of your kind? And yet in the next breath you speak of slaughtering every last person on earth! How am I to have sympathy for that?"

Helena looked down at her hands, which remained caught between the forms of human and devil. "There is no sympathy to be had. It is an illusion, a fantasy in a cold and uncaring cosmos." She looked up at him, her expression suddenly calm, serene even. "You came to kill me."

"I did," Markos admitted.

Helena thought for a bit and then nodded. "I think I am ready to die."

Markos tightened his grip on the sword. He still didn't trust the devil. It obviously knew his mind, knew his soft heart. All of this might be a plot to put him off guard.

"I have all of your Helena's memories," the devil said. "They are very strange. She imagined that there is an immaterial world waiting beyond this one."

"She did," Markos agreed.

"My people have traveled to the furthest reaches of space, but we have found no evidence of any such world." Helena looked at Markos and asked, "Do you believe it exists?"

Markos emptied the bucket of oil across the floor of the tomb, and picked up the lamp.

"I suppose we will find out together," he said.

THE MONSTER AT WORLD'S END

ALLAN COLE

Deception Bay, Antarctica
Latitude: -62° 58' 22.19"
Longitude: -60° 38' 59.99" W
20XX A.D.—The Cusp of Winter
Temperature: -50 (F) -45 (C

* * * *

I must escape.
Escape what?
Escape this place.
I must get out.
Out of what?
Out of here.
Where is here?
I'm not sure.
Confused.
Head swimming.
I think they shot me with drugs.
They? Who are They?
I don't know. Beasts of some kind.
Things.
They have two legs like us. Two arms like us. Hands with five digits. Faces, lips, eyes, ears. Mouths that make sounds.
Word sounds?
Possibly... Yes, I think so.
The sounds are loud. Angry.
Who are they angry at?
Me.
They push close. Shout in my face. Wave objects at me. Objects that can harm.

Threats, then. But why are they threatening you?

I don't know. Last cycle they wheeled a Thing into the place where they keep me.

It was naked. Female, unlike the others who were white males. Dark hair. Dark skin.

She didn't move. She didn't breathe. Her eyes were closed. Her throat had been cut and there was blood everywhere. So much blood that I knew she had to be dead.

They shouted at me. The smallest Thing, whose face and head were hairless, brandished a sharp object and screamed at me.

Screamed?

Yes, and jabbed at my eyes.

I tried to turn, but another Thing—taller and hairy—held my head and shouted encouragement at the other. At least I think it was encouragement. The sound he made was like this: "Dewit! Dewit!"

Each time the small one jabbed the blade point came closer to my eyes. Closer. And closer.

Suddenly, I realized the blade was my own knife. It had been a gift from Kaarla. Black anodized with intricate engravings.

Where did the Thing get it? I'd lost the knife several cycles back when they were chasing me. I guess he found it.

The hairless Thing waved the knife before my face.

Malice eyes.

Grinning. Like the rictus grin on the corpse.

And the hairy Thing shouted, "Dewit! Dewit! Deewit! Dewit!"

Then I saw the light change in the small Thing's eyes.

I thought: *This time he will blind me.*

I managed to jerk my head aside. The blade missed my eyes but slashed my forehead. Blood sheeted. Blinding me. I tried to wipe it away, but the manacles stopped me.

The hairy Thing keened.

I shook blood from my eyes, spattering them. They jumped back. Sounds of disgust. Scrubbing away my blood like I was diseased.

They came at me. Angrier. Strong hands caught my head. The hairy Thing again. The small one approached, brandishing the blade.

Close. So close. Breath foul with hate.

I thought—this time he is going to cut out my eyes.

Fear and anger gave me strength. I pushed my head closer despite the resistance of the hairy Thing's strong hands.

Readied my teeth.

They are long and sharp.

Thinking: *I will bite this Thing, if I can. I will rip off his face, if I can. Kill him, if I can.*

Unbidden, my talons arced out. When he saw them the Thing's eyes fear-flashed.

Stepped back.

Eyes narrowing.

I saw decision in those eyes.

Hate in those eyes.

He would strike first.

A step forward—knife raised.

A shout.

A sound like: "Stawp!"

The small one turned. With a start, the hairy one released his grip. The shout came from the third Thing. A forgotten presence. The third Thing was taller than the others. Narrow face. Eyes pale. Commanding eyes.

Motioning them away. Made sounds like, "Kuum heer." The voice was low. Compelling.

They joined the tall Thing by the door. Quarreling. My tormentors shouted at the third Thing. He seemed to argue back, but kept his voice calm. Measured. Authoritative.

The leader?

Yes. I'm sure of it.

The shouting stopped. But not the anger. Snorts of disgust. Murderous looks at me.

But for the moment, the crisis had passed.

The Things shrugged on thick red parkas. Shoved their legs into insulated red trousers.

The tall Thing escorted the others from the room, letting in the cold wind. I shivered.

Will I ever be warm again?

The door shut against the wind with difficulty. The lock clicked in place.

I sagged against my bonds. Alone with the dead Thing. Blood and gore and rictus grin.

Sightless eyes...

Accusing?

Yes, accusing.

Was she blaming me for her death? For cutting her throat?

I don't know. Probably.

Do the Things think you killed her? Is that why they are angry?

Yes. It must be so.

Did you?

Kill her?

No.

Well... Possibly.

My memory is...

But the knife... I'd lost the knife... so how could I have killed her?

THE MONSTER AT WORLD'S END, BY ALLAN COLE | 165

Hard to remember.

My mind was awhirl from the drugs I'd been shot with. The last moment of clarity was just before the green-tipped dart struck. Then time collapsed into itself until I was unsure when or where I was.

The Things caught me not far from my base camp. It was a foolish error. A stupidity likely to have cost me my life and doomed our mission.

I had been carrying away some accumulated trash. I'd be in the open ten minutes tops. Bury the trash and dash back into the shelter for a little breakfast.

Then they were upon me. Hunters popping out of nowhere. Electronic eyes lighting up. Proximity alarms squealing, in a mechanical display of victory.

I dodged and there was a Pop! Pop! Pop! as they fired their dart guns.

I ran. Digging in with my ice striders. I am strong and tall with long legs that carried me faster than their tracks. But I couldn't shake them. No matter how hard I tried. No matter the tricks I played or the traps I laid. They kept coming with the never-wavering confidence of machines.

They chased me for several cycles. Hunters on tracks that raced across the ice and snow. Two sky vehicles that followed wherever I ran.

Wherever I went, the hunters were on my heels, alerting the Things piloting the flying machines. No matter how well I hid myself their sensors managed to find me.

Even so, I ran and kept running. Legs numb. Heart hammering. Clouds of labored breath streaming behind me. Heralding my presence wherever I fled.

With each cycle I grew weaker. The intense cold burning calories I couldn't afford to waste.

And then the dart struck and it was over.

Thinking back on it—reliving the ordeal—I finally fell asleep.

Hanging in my bonds, it was a troubled sleep.

Sudden cold brought me back. Cold and the sound of wind howling down from the mountains. The wind's freezing breath finding gaps around the window and door, chilling me to the very bone.

Door?

What was happening with the door?

Were they coming back?

I heard the lock click. Raised my head to see, but my eyelids were glued together with dried blood.

The door opened.

A blast of freezing air.

It slammed shut.

I heard someone approaching.

Pounding heart.

Sweat soaked palms.

It was a Thing.

The Thing came close. A sweet smell, quite unlike the foul, unwashed odors of my tormentors.

A light voice. A gentle voice.

Do I detect sympathy?

I tried to open my eyes.

Useless.

Slumped in my bonds.

Dispirited.

Emptied of all hope.

The Thing moved away. I heard it bustle about. Cabinet doors opening and closing.

Then... Was that running water?

Mouth desert dry. Tongue swollen. Parched throat closing over. I made a sound. I didn't mean to. It was the first sound I had made since I was captured.

The sound of running water pulled it from me unbidden. My desperate thirst overruled my pride. The sound I made was a croaked plea.

The footsteps came near. I sensed a presence. Then a warm, wet cloth closed over my face.

The Thing wiped the blood away. Slowly my eyes came open. At first, I saw nothing but the out of focus wet cloth and I gripped it in my teeth and desperately sucked it dry. The cloth pulled against my teeth. Gently. The Thing made an imploring sound and I released the cloth.

Now I could see the new Thing. Like the corpse, she was a dark skinned and female. She was about the size of my small tormentor. Except slender. Limbs graceful. Black curly hair falling in waves to slim shoulders. Heart-shaped face. Large dark eyes.

Unconsciously, I made the croaking sound again.

Pity turned to understanding. The new Thing turned away and went to a sink. Turned a lever and water streamed. She filled a vessel and brought it to me.

Held it out.

I tried to reach, but the manacles restrained me.

Another groan.

My desire for water was agony.

She nodded understanding and lifted the vessel to my lips.

Drinking.

Gulping.

Choking.

Water, precious water, spilling down my chin. I sucked the vessel dry compelling yet another unbidden groan of frustration. The vessel was repeatedly refilled. I drank all I could hold, swelling up, flooding my cells until I finally had enough.

The Thing wiped wetness from my face. Made a sound. A questioning sound. Then motioned—hand to open mouth.

THE MONSTER AT WORLD'S END, BY ALLAN COLE

Meaning dawned.

Was I hungry?

I nodded. Desperate. Please! Trying to convey just how hungry I was. The last time I had eaten was well before I left the safety of home.

A long time ago.

Impossible to know exactly how long in a place where sunlight is endless for many revolutions of the planet the Things called Earth. Followed by night as dark as uttermost space for many revolutions more.

The Thing moved to the corner, opening a small cupboard door and rummaged inside.

With a shock, I realized the corpse was gone. I had slept through the drama of opening and closing doors, freezing blasts of wind, Things moving about, throwing vicious glares. Threatening noises.

Exhaustion had shut away the world as if I had died. For a crazy moment I wondered if I had.

The small Thing rattled implements. I smelled cooking odors. It returned with a tray. On it was a vessel brimming with a dark brown liquid. It smelled delicious. Saliva flooded my mouth.

Soup?

What kind of soup? I don't care, just give me that soup.

A spoon carried a portion to my lips. Gratefully, I accepted it. The soup was sweet and nourishing, coating my tongue and warming my belly. She spooned up more and I eagerly took it in. So fast that it dribbled down my chin.

She laughed. It was the first time I had heard one of them laugh. It was a pleasant sound.

She paused to wipe my chin, then made a sound. A word.

"Chklette," she said "Gud chkelette,yas?"

A definite question. But what was she asking?

"Gud?"

Did I want more? Is that what she was asking?

I nodded and opened my mouth. It must have been the right answer because she fed me more and didn't stop until the spoon clicked against an empty bowl.

She patted my lips clean with a cloth and stepped away. I felt a sudden desire to speak. To thank her.

I said, "Gud."

Her eyes widened. Did she understand me? Had I made the proper Thing sound?

Emboldened, I said "Chkelette gud. Yas?"

She laughed. Then opened her mouth to speak, but before she could there was a sudden rumbling and the floor lurched.

Plaster and dust fell.

Cupboard doors crashed open.

A sound like an explosion.

Then another. Closer. More violent. The floor bucked under us. The small Thing fell against me. I tried to catch her—to help—but the manacles restrained me. Her body was soft. Trembling with fear. She was so close I was able to stroke her head. Whisper comforting words.

A sudden start as frightening awareness sank in. She gasped, pushing away from me.

Eyes wild and fearful.

I shook my head, wanting to say, "No, no. I won't hurt you." Waving my hands. Manacles clattering. But my voice and the clatter only seemed to make her more afraid.

She backed away.

Hesitated. Then calm returned. I saw a smile, realizing Things can smile too. Before, I had only seen anger. Hate. And the corpse's grin.

Another explosion shook the building. Followed by more rumbling and lurching—cupboard doors slamming shut. Soon we were covered in plaster and dust.

The small Thing made an angry sound. But not at me. She glared at the door, muttering under her breath. Face taking on stubborn look. Angry resolve.

Resolve to do what?

I wish I knew. Was it possible we shared similar worries?

Interesting.

She pulled on a parka and went to the door. Opened it, struggled to hold it against the buffeting wind. Then she slipped out and was gone.

The lock clicked into place and I heard footsteps hurrying away.

I was alone in my prison again.

Despair gnawing back to the surface. A nasty little animal with small, sharp teeth. Weary, I leaned against my bonds.

My heart jumped.

What was this?

Did the bonds gave way?

Once again, I leaned forward.

Testing.

A definite slackening.

Breath quickening, I pushed harder. Behind me a groan of complaining metal.

Bear down. Push and push and push… bolts screeching in their sockets. Push more. Harder. Sockets tearing.

I wrenched with all my strength and I ripped free.

Falling face first. Somehow I caught myself just in time. Hands and wrists taking the sudden shock of weight.

I allowed myself to sink to the floor. I had been on my feet for a long time now.

Rested a moment. Heart a joyous race.

Fear returned.

Had they heard the tearing metal? Were they coming? The small hairless Thing will kill me if he finds me like this.

I listened. No sounds but wind beating against the walls of my prison.

I rose to my knees and I turned to see what I had accomplished. To my delight, the bolts holding the chains had been ripped from the wall. Wind knifed through a large hole where the chains had been connected. And I realized that the explosions and the combination of my weight and the Thing's had done the job.

On my feet, I inspected the hole. It was about the size of my head. I gripped the edges and pulled with both hands. It resisted at first, then gave way.

Not large enough, and the edges were sharp, cutting my fingers. I found rags by the skink and wrapped my hands.

I gathered all my strength and pulled.

A frighteningly loud shriek, and then icy wind blasted through the enlarged gap. Now my shoulders would fit through. I poked my head out, wind biting my nose and cheeks.

The way was clear for my escape.

But the chains?

What about the chains?

And the manacles?

I pulled at them. No use. I searched the room for a key. Heart trip hammering. The Things might return at any minute.

Nothing.

Very well. The chains and manacles must remain for now. Ripped up rags made ideal pads for the manacles. Gripping with both hands, I experimentally swung the chains.

An excellent weapon.

I found a thick musty blanket in a corner. It was double thick, padded and insulated. Rummaging in a drawer near the sink, I found a large sharp blade with a wooden handle.

Another weapon.

First, I used it to make a holes in the padded blanket. Worked my head through. Much better. I was warmer now.

I wanted to rush out before I was discovered, but I steeled myself. To stay free, to stay alive, I needed supplies. Without high calorie food I would soon exhaust myself. Then it would be a race between capture or death on the ice.

The room was a jumble of castoffs. I found a few tools that looked useful, including a heavy hammer and chisel. Better still, I found packets and cans with pictures of what appeared to be food. Also, two large insulated flasks. I filled them with steaming hot water from the tap.

In the corner, I found a old sled with heavy tarps and ropes to lash them in place. Now I had the means to transport an increasingly heavy burden.

Then, wonder of all wonders, I came upon my ice striders tossed in a corner.

Problem: how to fit all this through the hole? I tried to enlarge it. Pulling with all my strength. The screech of tearing metal frightened me. If they heard, they would come. If they came, I was dead.

I lifted the chains. Swung them experimentally. I would kill some of them first.

But that satisfaction was false and only lasted a foolish bloodlust moment. I had to guard myself against selfish emotions. If I die, all of us were threatened.

A loud explosion rocked the prison.

Then another—*Boom!*

And another—*Boom!*

Then a whole series of explosions: *Boom! Boom! Boomboomboomboomboom!*

Fighting to keep my feet I struggled with the metal siding. Ripping and tearing. The ear-piercing sounds covered by the explosions.

Finally, I was done.

Now there was room enough for the sled. Shouldering the chains, I grasped the harness and stepped out to face the wind. It whipped at my makeshift coat. Icy fingers stabbed the flesh beneath. From experience, I knew it was many degrees below the freezing point of water.

I looked around. There was only ice and snow. In the distance I saw a long, low building. It was crouched at the edge of a bay, whose wind-whipped waters were blanketed with floating chunks of ice.

The bay was empty except for an enormous, startling green iceberg. It was like a work of art, framed by towering mountains covered with thick ice. I had seen many bergs during my sojourn here. All shimmering with glorious colors. Green and gold and blue and white so pure that it was difficult to believe one's own eyes.

I scanned the area. Not a single Thing in sight.

To get a better look I eased closer to the edge of the shack that had been my prison. I nearly fell over a metal object protruding from the ground. It was painted a bright red. Presumably to keep dimwits like me from stumbling over it.

I looked closer. The object appeared to be the end of a large pipe with a heavy metal cap. There was an aperture in the cap. I leaned close to sniff at it.

Familiar.

A fuel of some kind.

Then it came to me. It smelled like the exhaust of one of the flying machines. Aviation fuel? Sniffed again. Yes, I was sure of it.

There was a small shed next to the pipe. I opened it, hoping to find something useful. But the only Thing inside, other than gauges and switches, was a large wrench. It looked like it was meant for the fitting on top of the pipe. I had no use for it, or anything else, so I shut the door.

Looking down the hill, I saw two of the flying machines parked in an enclosure with open double doors.

Still feeling brain-fogged, I toyed with the notion of trying to disable the machines, but gave it up when I realized just how foolhardy that idea was.

I gave my head a violent shake.

Damned drugs.

I crept to the edge of the shack for a better look. Nothing but the iceberg. There was an acrid smell on the wind. It was the distinctive odor of an enormous colony of flightless birds. I'd investigated the colony before the Things arrived. The birds were tubby little creatures about as high as my knee. They were black and white and had stubby wings. They looked clumsy when waddling about on two legs.

The birds tended nests made of piled rocks. Usually one or two large eggs rested in the nest, which the birds warmed with their bodies. I had witnessed fuzzy babies cracking through their egg shells with the help of their parents. Those birds, so clumsy on land, were amazing acrobats in the sea, scooping up food they would later regurgitate into the gullets of their ever-hungry young. They defecated a pink liquid, which covered the breeding grounds. That was what I smelled when I emerged from my prison.

I heard their distinctive cheeping. Thousands of birds calling for their mates and young among an immense crowd of what appeared to be identical birds. How did they ever find one another? Looking closer, I could see tens of thousands of little figures hopping around in a vast colony near the base of a mountain of ice. After six winters in this place the little animals still charmed me. During my visits they paid no attention as I moved among them. Sensing that I was no threat.

They had never seen my like before, so how could I possibly be a threat? So unlike the Things who had also never seen my kind before, but immediately feared me.

To them I was so fearful that they spent days in the biting cold hunting me with their machines until they finally ran me to ground and shot me with a dart gun. Then hauled me to their base and locked me in chains. I wondered what they had planned for me, beyond torment.

A deafening roar hammered my ears as another explosion rocked the earth. I clung to the side of the shack for support.

And then an enormous mass of ice ripped away from the mountain and crashed down with a force so tremendous it nearly knocked me off my feet.

Only the oversize ice striders kept me upright.

Then more ice broke free. A gathering avalanche poured down the mountainside and to my horror, the avalanche obliterated the entire colony of birds, before spilling into the sea.

A moment later the door of the building burst open and a group of Things raced out. They were bundled against the cold in thick red parkas and trousers. They seemed excited. Waving their arms and shouting.

At first I thought they'd discovered my escape.

I shrugged off the harness and got ready to run. Losing the supplies would be devastating. But they were so close I'd never be able to outrun them while hauling the sled.

Then it came to me: They weren't shouting in anger.

But in glee.

I wondered what manner of beings these creatures were who found joy murdering tens of thousands of helpless little birds and their nestlings.

Looking up at the area the thick ice had covered, I saw bare black rock. Now, instead of bird droppings I smelled another familiar stench.

Oil?

Yes, that was it.

Oil.

Black liquid poured down the mountainside, fouling everything in its path until it streamed into the pristine waters of the bay.

Already bodies of dead fish were floating to the surface and washing ashore. A big black mass of a creature struggled to the beach. It collapsed, gasping for breath. Its flippers moving weakly as it tried to drag itself from the foul water.

I'd seen its like before—beautiful animals with glistening brown fur and large dreamy black eyes.

One of the Things walked out to it, carrying a long black object.

Realization: It was the one I had come to think of as My Thing. The gentle female with black skin. She took a small box from her parka, sorted it through it, then withdrew what looked like one of the darts I'd been shot with. She loaded it into what I now recognized as a dart gun.

The creature on the beach moaned, flippers barely moving. My Thing straightened. Took careful aim. A long hesitation. Then she pulled the trigger and there was a sharp report.

The creature jumped.

I saw a slender dart with red stabilizers hanging from its throat. Another sharp report. Another dart piercing its body.

For a short time, the creature moaned. Flippers moving as if it thought it was swimming.

Then it gave a long sigh and fell still.

My Thing lowered the dart gun and walked slowly back to the others. Their excited jabbering continued. They had talked during the entire incident.

Only pausing at the sound of the shot. Some of them glanced at the scene, then continued on as nothing had happened. Totally indifferent.

Shouldering the harness, I slowly retreated to the other side of the shed. Then I set off, taking care to keep the shed between me and the Things.

Soon, I came to a place where there was no cover. I'd be exposed for a hundred meters or more.

Leaning forward I caught a glimpse of the Things. Still talking excitedly. The small, hairless tormentor was among them. I saw him pass a flask to his hairy friend, who drank greedily and passed it back.

Standing apart from the others, I spotted My Thing. She seemed isolated from the others both in attitude and skin color. I wondered if she was the only female among them? If so, she was isolated by gender as well.

Then it came to me that the others might blame her for my escape, even though it was the explosions that had freed me. If so, I was sorry for that. It seemed a cruel way to repay a kindness. A rare commodity in this frozen wilderness.

Once again, there was nothing to be done about it.

I crouched there—waiting in the freezing wind. First my ears and nose, then my fingers and toes grew numb.

After a time, the Things went inside. My Thing was last—hesitating for a long moment. Turning to look at the oil-befouled corpse on the beach. Then the great heaps of oil-fouled ice and rock where the colony of birds had been.

Her head slowly turned to look in my direction. There was a pause—as if she sensed my presence.

I crouched lower, expecting a cry of alarm.

Then she seemed to shake off whatever had captured her attention and went inside. The door shut behind her.

I jumped to my feet. Shouldering the harness, I threw my weight from side to side, breaking the runners free of the ice. Then I dashed for the cover of a jumble of boulders.

A moment later I was safe from view. I paused for breath and to calm my racing heart. Then I started off again. Burning kilometers with a survivor's stride. Running a hundred paces. Walking fifty. Repeat. A hundred, then fifty. And so on.

I couldn't head directly home. It was vital that they didn't discover my base camp, where I have labored for six long winters and summers. It was well hidden and stocked with supplies and sophisticated tools and weapons. I would need them to complete my mission and file my long-overdue final report.

The wind was fiercer now. To my delight, dark storm clouds boiled on the horizon. A storm would delay any search. If so, I could take a more direct route home.

As I paced, I used the position of the sun to help guide me. The sun was nearing its lowest point just now. Soon, it would be winter when the blackest of black nights would descend on the land. Driven by gravity the winds would blast down the mountains onto the icy plains at speeds up to 300 kilometers an hour. The cold would deepen to an unimaginable hundred and thirty degrees below zero, or more.

In other colonies, flightless birds would huddle together for warmth. At regular intervals, the birds on the outside traded places with those closer in so every one of them would have a chance to live.

But this cycle the storm never came. I had been counting on it to delay the search. The luck that began with a gift of water and the soup the Thing called "Chklette" ended with my escape.

Just as I feared, the hue and cry began within a few scant hours. They pursued me relentlessly with their flying machines and powered ice sleds. Even more dangerous were their mechanical hunters. They were about waist high and were equipped with powerful laser guns and sophisticated sensing devices that seemed able to track me no matter how well I was hidden.

I eluded them for several cycles, going to ground whenever I caught sight of them.

Then one cycle I felt safe enough to breakfast on a soup made from a packet of nasty-smelling powder mixed with hot water, which I boiled in one of the flasks with a heating element. It was nothing like the delicious Chklette My Thing had fed me. Never mind the taste, my belly complained that what I had eaten was not enough, so when I trekked on I was paying poor attention to my surroundings.

That carelessness almost cost my life. As I moved around an ice cropping I almost fell over one of the hunters.

It appeared to be at rest. It was making little beeping sounds and it had a solar umbrella arrayed to recharge. Fortunately, it was also paying poor attention to its surroundings.

Very slowly, I shed the harness and lowered it to the ground. My intention was to abandon the sled before I was noticed and get quickly out of there.

Then one of my ice striders bumped against something. The scraping sound was so miniscule that at first I thought I was safe.

But the hunter caught the sound. In a scant millisecond the solar array furled and shot out of sight. At the same instant the turret whipped about and the muzzle of its laser gun came up.

Before it could fire, I lashed out with my chains. The desperate blow struck with such force that it bent the muzzle.

Still, the hunter tried to fire, but the effort failed. It tried again and again and there was a mad clicking noise with each attempt. Going, clickclickclick-chilc.

Seeing it helpless, my spirits soared. Then my temper blew. All that pent-up anger from so many hours of torment and hunger and thirst exploded.

The hunter had found me.

Too bad for the hunter.

I slashed at the machine. Over and over. Pummeling it with the heavy chains until it was nothing but a ruin of metal and exposed wiring that sparked feebly.

Finally, there was a shower of sparks and the hunter was still.

I was so exhausted I dropped to my knees.

Then I started laughing.

Within seconds the laughter became uncontrollable. I laughed until my ribs ached and I was bent over gasping for breath.

Then I wept.

Tears streaming.

Gobs of snot.

Choking on my own hysteria.

On my own despair.

On my own desolate loneliness.

Finally, I rested my head on my knees. Gradually, I gathered my strength. Grabbed two big handfuls of snow and scrubbed my face clean.

Took a deep breath and then rummaged in the sled until I found the hammer and chisel. I sat there on the sled and started hammering at the links. So desperate to be free that for a long moment of near insanity I didn't care if they found me.

I hammered away. Sitting there in plain view while the flying machines traced a relentless pattern that came close, but somehow kept missing me.

Finally, I was free.

I stood up with only the manacles on my wrists. I dropped the chains, then strode away on my ice walkers, leaving the sled behind, carrying only a small bundle of supplies.

Time passed.

The relentless hunt continued.

Hunger gnawed at my belly.

It became impossible to quench my thirst, or make more soup. I didn't dare stop long enough to thaw out a flask full of snow, so I had to make do with hasty scoops stuffed into my mouth. Eking out so little water that it was hardly worth an ice-burned tongue.

I found my base camp with little time to spare.

First, came the roar of the snow cats.

Then. The whop, whop of flying machines.

Proximity alarms blared from the hunters closing in from all sides.

I was traversing a broad beach blanketed with black rocks. The beach was warm from volcanic activity. Steam rose in thick clouds that obscured me. I'd chosen the area partly because of this, and partly because of the strange magnetic field that my instruments had detected. The field served to blind my pursuer's devices. The area also offered a rare luxury: a grotto with a pool of water hot enough to bathe.

Suddenly, a flying machine popped into view and headed my way.

Even so, I was sure they hadn't spotted me yet and I made a mad dash for the grotto, diving into the water just in time. Vanishing in the delicious steam as the machine roared overhead.

I held my breath until my lungs were ready to burst, then surfaced just long enough for a breath.

The sky was empty, but the proximity alarms of the hunters sounded all around me and I heard the voices of Things coming from a snow cat that had stopped on the beach.

I went under again.

Waiting.

Waiting.

Lungs burning.

But still I waited.

When I could stand it no longer, I was forced to surface. The sounds of the hunt were still all around me and down I went again.

The hiding game went on for an hour or so, until finally I surfaced to be greeted with nothing but the sound of the wind and the waves crashing against the beach.

I crawled out, limp from so much time in the water. The skin of my hands and fingers so wrinkled it made me smile.

I slipped out of the padded blanket and then my clothes and spread them out over warm boulders. With the sun blazing through a cloudless sky I knew they'd soon dry.

Nothing stays wet very long in this strange but beautiful land the Things named Antarctica. Moisture evaporates instantly. Even the snowflakes seem dry. At so many degrees below the freezing point of water the flakes won't melt. You just brush them from your shoulders like dust. The snow on the ground just remains there. Piling up, snowstorm after snowstorm until it is as impenetrable as ice and many kilometers thick.

Enjoying a rare moment of leisure out of the cold, I checked for injuries. My torso was a mass of bruises from the beatings the small, hairless Thing had administered while his bigger companion held me. Other than several scrapes and ribs more prominent than usual from being denied food for so long, I seemed to be in decent shape.

The cut on my forehead wasn't infected. No surprise there. Infections are rare in this land where it is too cold for most bacteria to survive. Another good sign: my skin had a healthy sheen, black as the volcanic rocks on the beach.

When my clothes were dry enough I pulled them on. Then donned the padded blanket, which was still uncomfortably damp. With luck, I'd be wearing it for the last time.

I set off and soon I spotted the towering pile of enormous white bones that marked my destination. I lost sight of them for a moment as I moved through a warren of boulders.

When I emerged, the beach was in full view. The bones were the skeletal remains of hundreds of gigantic beasts that were scattered about with no thought, much less care.

When I first found the place, I thought I was hallucinating. It was if I had stepped into a child's nightmare. A cruel tale told by a bored creche nurse to bully her little charges into an early nesting time.

Once I got over my initial shock, I realized I was looking at the remains of enormous mammals. Their bleached pelvises towered over me. On all sides were huge backbones, shoulder bones, and spinal columns many meters long. And there were rib cages big enough to stand up and walk around in.

At first I was puzzled by the absence of leg, or arm bones. There were so many of the beasts that their absence was mysterious. Did whatever creature that preyed on them particularly favor legs, eating them bones and all?

Which made me wonder about the size of their predators. I shuddered at the thought.

It turned out to be a foolish one. Not far from that graveyard of giants, I came upon a wind-battered building. It had the look of a long abandoned facility of some sort. Although in this land nothing ever truly rusts or is reduced to ruins. Looking inside, it soon became apparent that the facility had been built by small, but no less deadly, predators.

Things had built this place.

Things had killed all those animals on the beach.

The building proved to be an old factory where Things had processed the giants. Gutting them and stripping them of fat and flesh until there was nothing left but morsels for birds to pick at until only sun-bleached bones remained.

With the instruments at my base camp it took little extrapolation to realize just how staggering the slaughter must have been. The appetite for those poor creatures was such that surely their very existence as a species must have been threatened.

But that was in the early days of my mission. When my heart was full of hope and I saw promise, despite the warnings of my mission mates that were trickling in from all over the globe.

Later I saw several of the giant animals surface in the bay. They were magnificent creatures. My marine listening devices recorded the songs they sang to each other and I soon came to realize they were animals of great wisdom and intelligence.

After a little more investigation, and consulting with my mission mates I learned just how few had survived during the days of that great slaughter. Since then their numbers have grown smaller with each passing cycle. For a time, my mission mates reported similar findings in non-Thing life all over the globe.

The appetite of the Things was so voracious that only a favored few creatures seemed to thrive.

We found that everywhere they go the Things excrete so much waste and burn so much fuel that it is overwhelming the rivers, the oceans, the mountains and the plains and the deserts and the very air they breathe.

Still, my mission mates and I held to our hopes.

I suppose it is the nature of our kind to cling to such ephemeral hopes. It has been so long since our own world was turned to cosmic dust we can't imagine that all sentients don't treasure the planets they are fortunate to inhabit.

Otherwise, how could we have clung so long to the singular goal of finding the one place where we could end our search and settle peacefully among the native inhabitants?

It had been our dream that Earth was such a place.

To begin with there had been twelve of us. We were spread strategically across the planet. We had all been specifically educated and trained for the mission.

Over the centuries, many missions had been launched. For one reason or another they had all failed. Each failure had been a costly blow that ended in many deaths and the squandering of precious supplies.

Our leaders said by cruel necessity this mission would be the last. No one seemed to have the heart to continue. Much less risk the precious supplies these missions required. Great age had taken its toll on our ships, equipment and hydroponic farms. Even the seeds we'd carried away when we fled the orphaned exoplanet that destroyed our world were failing to germinate.

Soon, our storerooms will be empty.

Our species doomed.

When my mission mates and I began we were brimming with energy and optimism. Our initial reports sang Earth's praises. We were told that with each report the spirits of our families and friends rose to giddy heights.

Unfortunately, the doomsayers among us have been growing in power. They have urged us to just take the planet and be damned to the sentient overlords. But such a thing is against our nature. And has always been so. I feared if we chose that path it would be at the cost of our very souls.

My mission mates were of the same mind and we worked diligently, repeatedly risking our lives for the good of the cause. Then reality sank in. As perfect a world as this planetary body must seem, its sentient overseers appear to be intent on destroying it.

Even so, for a time we thought this frozen continent to the south might offer a solution. It is of no use to the Things. Yet with our technology, we could live here and flourish.

We could exchange vast knowledge they are centuries from achieving in return for permission to peacefully settle here. To make a home in a place other than uttermost space where it seems we are doomed to wander until there are no more of us.

That was to be the conclusion of our final report.

A report now long overdue.

Then my mission mates began vanishing.

One by one their regular communications stopped. Operative after operative lapsed into a silence that I knew must have been forced.

Kaarla was the last.

In her final communication, she feared she'd been discovered and was being hunted.

She said they were close.

So very close.

But she said she'd located a better place for a base camp safe from prying eyes.

In her last message Kaarla said: "We are the last best hope of the people, brother mine. Be on guard. And stay safe."

Then I heard no more.

Nothing but the static of stars like our own that vanished from the universe long ago.

Her loss shook me to the core. Kaarla and I had been lovers once—back during the latter days of our training.

Our love was fierce.

Beyond mere passion.

It burned brighter than any Starfall celebration. Then, as quickly as it had enveloped us, it flamed out. But unlike most failed love affairs we were neither angry or felt betrayed.

Instead, we became fast friends.

Actually, it was more than mere friendship. We bonded together like twins. Each feeling the emotional ups-and-downs of the other no matter how far apart we were.

It was an uncanny connection. Almost telepathic.

I didn't need the absence of her regular communications to know in my heart that she was gone.

One sleep period, a searing—almost unbearable pain—brought me out of a deep sleep.

I shot up from my cot gasping for breath.

Then another wave of pain struck.

And another.

And once more.

So terrible I fell to the floor.

I remained there for a long time, dragging in precious air. Then the pain vanished, leaving me feeling empty and drained.

It was then that I knew my sister was gone from me forever.

My lover, my friend, my sister and the last of my mission mates was dead. Even worse, I realized everything now rested on my shoulders.

Then they found me.

Hunted me relentlessly.

Until I was brought to ground.

Later, when looking into the eyes of the small, hairy Thing I came to believe I was seeing pure evil. When his companion in evil gripped my head for the blinding I thought all Things must be like this.

They all must be evil.

How else to explain it?

But after meeting the female Thing I regained a modicum of hope. I retained it, despite the disaster that killed the colony of birds. It became stronger still when I witnessed her act of mercy when she ended the pain of that poor struggling creature on the beach.

We shall see how that all plays out in the end.

When the long winter's night comes, I will investigate one more time. Until then I will rest here. Regain my strength and formulate a plan. And then I will decide if these Things are worth saving.

There was no one to welcome me home when I finally reached my base camp. It was a shelter made of special thermal material, arranged in a jumble of boulders. A holo device provided camouflage so cunning that even if a Thing were standing right next to the entrance he wouldn't be able to see that anything was amiss.

The moment I entered the warmth of the heaters enveloped me. I dropped my gear. Threw off my makeshift coat and fell into my cot without bothering to undress.

I just pulled a thermal blanket over me and slept.

Hours passed before I reentered the world. I was awakened with a start. Heart racing. The chill of evaporating fear sweat. The whop, whop, whop sound of a flying machine hovering overhead.

Had they found me?

What was that?

There!

Tracks grinding against stone.

The beep, beep, beep of electronic sniffing just beyond the camouflaged entrance.

A desperate clumsy search for a weapon.

Finally!

Fingers closing on a gun.

I backed into a corner—weapon aimed at the door.

Ready to fire.

To escape I had to get a jump start.

I'd shoot through the door, then charge straight out, catching them unawares.

A spray of automatic fire, then run for it.

With luck they wouldn't catch me.

But if they did...

If they did...

At that moment I determined to take my own life before I'd let myself fall into their hands again.

Then, just as I decided to fire and rush the door, the sniffing ended. And the sound of the flying ship moved away.

I collapsed in relief.

So close.

So very close.

I pulled myself together. Washed under a clever little showering device with soothing hot water that lasted for seven minutes on extra hot. Fifteen if lukewarm.

I chose the extra hot.

I pulled on clean clothes and heated a container of my favorite stew. I ate it out of the pot and washed it down with a mug of high calorie brew.

My first order of business was to get rid of the blasted manacles. They were a constant reminder of my captivity. A little file from my dental emergency kit did the trick. Then I settled down to wait for the endless dark of winter.

Two cycles later, food, sleep and restlessness led me to change my mind.

And there was another factor.

The blood tests I ran in my little lab revealed that the drug they'd shot me with was meant for animals much larger than myself. No wonder my brain had been so clouded. My thinking so jagged.

It was remarkable I was even alive.

Now that my mind was clear, I realized that although winter's darkness might be safer, I needed light to learn what was really going on. What was their true goal.

Oil?

Unlikely.

It was too simple an answer. And with time running out for my people, I needed the answer fast.

Kaarla and the others had reported a plentitude of oil in places easier and cheaper to exploit than this wilderness where the ground is locked in ice many kilometers deep. And where the elements made travel and movement impossible during the long winter's night.

It had to be more than just oil.

I prepared carefully. Filling my knapsack with the barest essentials so it wouldn't slow me down if I had to run.

Actually, it wasn't a matter of "if," but "when."

With all their resources it was only a matter of time before I was discovered. Then they'd be on me like a fury.

I armed myself with two weapons. Three, if I counted the knife I wore in a belted sheath. It was a poor replacement for the one Kaarla had given me. The foolish thought came to me that I could hunt down the hairless Thing and take it back. I surprised myself with the joy I felt imagining how good it would feel to kill him.

That was quite unlike me. But I suppose that is what happens when you are in the company of Things too long. Thoughts of murder and destruction become ordinary.

Balancing the sheathed knife was a fazergun with adjustable focus. It could be dialed to take out a single target, or multiple targets if they weren't too far apart. It was light weight, fit easily into my hand and could only be fired by its owner.

For long range I carried a Lazzerus rifle. It was under 60 centimeters long, was fitted with a powerful scope, and fired rounds with adjustable explosive power.

One setting meant death for one.

Another, the deaths of many.

I had another weapon that could only stun. But I had neither room in my pack or compassion in my heart to carry it.

When I felt rested enough to proceed, I set out for my enemies' base camp. I took a roundabout route and approached from the far side of the main building.

To my surprise, none of the hunters were patrolling for me. Better still— the alarms and traps the Things had set were so simple I easily bypassed them.

I approached along a narrow beach that ran past a jagged cliff face that rose out of the sea a hundred meters or so from their base.

The silence was eerie. Nothing but the booming surf. What was I missing? Then as I crept around a bend I saw the damage the explosions had wrought and realized that what I was missing were the sounds and smells of the normally busy colony of wingless birds.

There was nothing left of the million or more breeding pairs that had once made the place their home but mounds of oil-fouled rubble.

The oil had stopped flowing and in the middle of the field I saw four poles with red flags speared into the ground marking an area about four meters square.

I checked for spy cameras, spotted two hidden on either side of the beach. Soon, I determined that they were inoperable. Their batteries were dead— drained by the stress of intense cold. A storm had swept out of the sea not many hours before and with the wind chill factor the temperatures would have dropped to 130 degrees below zero.

It was balmy today. The wind light. Temperature about twenty degrees below zero.

Birds were out in force. Hundreds of them wheeling in the sky, or squabbling amongst themselves in their cliff-side nests. There were easily a score or more species of birds who dwelled there, ranging in size from tiny creatures that could fit in the palm of my hand, to their larger cousins with wingspans of two meters or more.

I'd noted previously that each species favored certain areas on the cliff face to build their nests. Each group took possession of a specific strata and never encroached on the others.

Staying alive is difficult in this harsh climate—so perilous—that the birds chose peaceful coexistence over inter-species warfare.

Which is exactly the sort of arrangement my kind wanted with the Things.

The question in my mind was whether the damage the Things were causing was so vast that in a few short years the planet will become uninhabitable for any species.

If that's what happens my own people are doomed. Because Earth is the last best place within reach. If we are denied a place here, we face a long and torturous death with the wails of starving children the last sounds we heard.

A great horn blared. The blast was so sudden, so loud, that I feared I'd been discovered.

I dropped to the ground so quickly I banged my chin against the ice. Even so, I had the presence of mind to unsling my rifle. Cautiously, I raised my head, scanning the area through the rifle scope.

I settled on the building first. The only sign of activity was steam rising from an exhaust stack.

The horn sounded again.

This time I was ready, and I traced the sound to a strange ship anchored in the bay. It was a surprising sight. The last time I'd seen a ship was when the Things had arrived at winter's end. That ship had been sleek, as if meant for luxurious travel. This one had seen better times. Crates of equipment were stacked on the deck. A large crane was fixed to the bow. I wondered what the Things were up to.

There was another blast of the horn, and this time it was answered. A long, loud blast emanated from the building.

A moment later the front door opened and red clad Things emerged. I could clearly see My Thing among them. She was on the edge of the group.

I centered the scope on her face. She looked troubled. Even a little frightened. I saw her flinch and push away from the group.

Moving my scope, I spotted the pair she'd stepped away from with such alacrity. And there were my old companions in torment: the small hairless Thing and his taller companion. They appeared to be mocking her. My Thing grew angry. I saw her shake a finger at them, but they only laughed more.

The Thing I took as the leader spoke to them. I couldn't hear the sounds he made but I was fairly certain he was admonishing them. Even so, I could tell he wasn't putting much effort in it. They nodded, but when he turned away I saw them roll their eyes.

The hairless one wagged his tongue at My Thing. For some reason I took it as an obscene gesture. My Thing turned away and tried to ignore them.

The group walked toward the beach. In the bay, I saw several small boats being lowered from the strange ship. They were crowded with equipment and

Things clad in white cold weather gear. The boats sped for shore and a few moments later they landed.

Two of the visitors approached the shore party, while the others unloaded the boats.

One of the visitors wore red epaulets on his shoulders. He extended a hand to the land group's leader. They clasped hands and a lively discussion ensued. The acted like friends. The leader of the land group called out to the hairless one and his companion. They trotted up, carrying knapsacks stuffed with equipment.

After a few words were exchanged, they all moved over to the oily rubble, fastidiously picking their way through the worst of it until they reached the red flags.

Soon the knapsacks were unpacked, a clear sheet of plastic spread on the ground, and the hairless Thing scooped up a shovelful of rocks and dumped them on the plastic sheet. Meanwhile his companion hooked up the visitor's leader to a device consisting of earphones, a black box and a long, red-tipped wand.

The visitor gave the leader of the land group a questioning look. He appeared to laugh, then made a deep, flourishing bow, then waved his hand as if to say, "Proceed."

The visitor shrugged and passed the wand over the rocks. Immediately the black box lit up with madly winking lights. Even at a distance I could hear clicking noises.

The visitor was so surprised he took a step back. Through the scope I saw nervous laughter. Then he passed the wand over the rocks again. Once again the box lit up and it went cliclclickclickclick.

For some reason this caused a great deal of excitement and back slapping. The visitor fished out what I took as a com unit because he immediately began speaking into it. His excitement was such that I could hear him shout something that sounded like, "Phantaztik!"

A few minutes later the two groups trooped into the building. The last one was My Thing. I saw her look back at the red flags, then give a sad shake of her head.

As I watched her, I felt an odd sensation. A prickling at the back of my neck. It wasn't unpleasant. Just a gentle sort of probing.

Then My Thing's head suddenly came up. Her eyes cut to where I was hidden. Something stirred inside me. It was almost like those odd moments of near telepathy that I once shared with Kaarla.

My heart wrenched.

I missed Kaarla so.

Finally, My Thing shook her head. The feeling vanished and she stepped through the doorway. A moment the door closed.

I waited for a long time, making sure they were settled. Then, just as the cold was making my wait almost unbearable, I heard the raucous sounds of celebration coming from the building. To my delight, it sounded like they'd be busy for at least several hours.

I crept from cover and carefully made my way to the red flags. I studied the rocks spread out on the plastic sheet. There was nothing obvious to cause such joy. I pawed though the rocks until I had a nice sample. Then, just to make certain, I scanned the area with an instrument and recorded a rough estimate of the scope of their find.

Burning with curiosity, I hurried home. I was hungry, so I put something on to heat while I cleaned the samples, then slid then into the analyser. The answer came not long after I finished my meal.

Unfortunately, my instincts had been right.

It wasn't about oil. It was about a substance with 92 protons and 92 electrons. It was definitely radioactive, although mildly so.

Very well, what the Things had discovered was a rare element that was undoubtedly valuable. But was it valuable enough to mine in a place with such a hostile climate? To find out I had to chance another trip to their base camp.

Also, I was troubled by the position My Thing had found herself in. From the way the hairless one behaved, I sensed she was in danger.

Then I thought, but what if she was?

What did that have to do with me, much less the overriding importance of my mission?

Whatever the situation, it was my duty to just shrug it off. Ignore it.

Still.

Still.

I repacked with even greater care. Stripping the weight down to the barest necessities so I could add a few more measuring instruments.

The celebration was still going on full blast when I returned. Voices were louder. Music blared. Meanwhile, a group of Things from the ship were unloading several small boats. I watched for a long time to get some clue of their purpose.

They were unpacking crates right on the shoreline. Lining them up and using crowbars to rip them open. I wondered why they were performing the work here, instead of loading the crates on power sleds and hauling them to the building, out of the elements.

To my horror their purpose soon became clear.

Each crate contained one of the hunters. When the visiting Things were done I counted at least two dozen. Even more disturbing, the moment their tracks hit the ground the hunters came to life.

Motors firing up.

Red eyes blinking to life.

And then, one by one they set off toward a long low, metal building. Two workmen stood at the open door of the shack, checking off each hunter as it made its way inside.

I was so shaken by this development I sank to the ground, not feeling the intense cold. With that many hunters my capture was practically guaranteed.

The glittering eyes of the hairless Thing jumped into my mind. Threatening me with my own knife. Jabbing at my eyes, while his companion held my head in a vise-like grip chanting, "Dewit! Dewit! Deewit! Dewit!"

I remained there for a long time.

Gathering my nerve.

Renewing my purpose.

Steeling myself for what I had to do next.

By the time I had recovered the beach was empty. The boats had returned to the ship, carrying broken up crates.

I approached the flags with care. My weapons at ready. I kept my eye on the building's entrance while I worked, taking readings and running preliminary calculations.

Determined to kill any Thing unlucky enough interrupt me.

I worked quickly. I had to get this information back to my base camp for my final report. My final recommendation.

Now, for the rest of it.

I found a back door to the building.

It was unlocked.

The sounds of celebration poured out when I opened the door. I waited, stretching my senses to their fullest. All the noise came from the front of the building where the Things were gathered.

There was no one about as I crept through the hallways, peeking in rooms as I went.

As I approached one door I heard footsteps coming down the hall. Quickly I ducked into the darkness inside. The footsteps continued, but sounded a little odd. Faltering. Someone was stumbling about, bumping into walls. The footsteps paused outside the door. Then there was a horrible retching sound. Someone sputtering. A long silence followed.

The Thing moved away. I peeked outside and saw a disgusting mess on the floor.

Thing vomit.

The sight and smell made me nauseous. What nasty creatures these Things were.

As I turned away, I nearly knocked over some sort of free-standing object. I steadied it, making sure it was upright, and stepped away.

When I shined a pinlight on the object I nearly jumped out of my skin. And I found myself gaping at one of our kind.

It was so realistic I almost blurted a greeting. Widening the beam, it was obviously a replica.

A replica that had my face.

There were red marks on the "body" that at first, made no sense. Then I realized they were marking my major organs.

Killing targets?

No doubt about it.

The only way they could have gleaned this information was by physically examining one, or several of us.

A sob caught in my throat, imagining the agony my mission mates must have suffered.

And Kaarla. My dear sister of the mind.

For long seconds I could barely breathe.

I flashed the light around the room. On the walls were a series of large photographs. They were grainy, and blurred. They were pictures of me on the run. The Things must have snapped them while they were hunting me.

On one wall was a large map of the surrounding area, with tiny flags marking various locations. They had been charting sightings of me. Soon it became apparent that they were closing in on my home.

A large red circle took in the beach of giant bones and the volcanic area.

It was only a matter of time before they narrowed that circle and cornered me. And with those new hunters the time I had left was frighteningly short.

This had to end soon or I was done for.

More determined than ever, I moved on.

I came to another room where there was an immense diorama of the bay and the land surrounding it.

The whole center of the diorama was a replica of a vast mining enterprise. Nothing was left to the imagination. From the gigantic black crater that encompassed the landscape, to the giant machines that dug the pits. As well as the smaller ones that would crush the rock, and process the radioactive ore.

The mine ran all the way down to the bay, where miniature freighters waited for small boats heaped with ore.

A vision of the avalanche that destroyed the colony of flightless birds flashed into my mind. Then the image of the poor oil-befouled creature My Thing had put out of its misery, while the other Things watched, amused, or just indifferent.

I recorded images of the diorama and considered what to do next. I quickly decided I had all that I needed. It was time to return to my base camp and make my final report.

If I could remain free long enough to transmit it, that is.

I retraced my steps. In the background I could hear that the celebration had reached a crescendo.

The noise was so loud I nearly missed a voice coming from a nearby room. It was a familiar voice and had a desperate pleading sound to it. A frightened sound.

It came from a closed door with light streaming through the gap in the threshold.

Drawing my side weapon, I moved closer to the door. Placed an ear against it. The voice was more distinct.

It was My Thing.

Then I heard other voices. The mocking tones of the hairless Thing. Then the voice of his companion.

Chanting, "Dewit. Dewit. Dewit"

Cautiously I cracked open the door.

Through the gap I saw the frightened face of My Thing. The hairless one had her pushed onto a bed.

He held a knife to her throat.

My knife.

Then everything became frighteningly clear.

This how the other female Thing had died.

A death they had blamed on me.

I pushed the door wide and stepped in, kicking it closed behind me.

A frozen tableaux.

My Thing sprawled on the bed, clothing ripped and in disarray.

The hairless Thing bent over her, knife pressed against her throat so hard a trickle of blood ran down to her torn blouse.

The tall, hairy Thing, an audience of one.

Delighting in the fear and torment.

Calling out "Dewit. Dewit. Dewit."

I made the same sound their leader had made when I had been their captive.

I croaked, "Stawp!"

They whirled. Eyes registering shock when they saw me. I know how I seemed to them—a living incarnation of their worst nightmares.

I was taller.

Much taller.

And big.

Much bigger.

I was so angry I knew my eyes burned as yellow and hot as the sun. In anger, the lips of my kind instinctively draw back, displaying long, sharp fangs. And just as instinctively our talons arc out, blood red against black skin.

In my wrath, they have never in their lives seen a monster such as me.

I took a step forward and there was a sudden foul odor as the hairless one's bladder gave way.

The other held up both hands.

Puny shields against my burning hate.

Another step, and the foul odor increased as his bladder followed suit.

I laughed, taking evil pleasure in their fear.

Then I shot them both.

First the hairless one.

Then his friend.

My Thing came upright, pulling her torn blouse together.

THE MONSTER AT WORLD'S END, BY ALLAN COLE | 189

For a moment I feared she saw me as a monster as well. I made an effort to make myself less threatening. Talons vanishing. Fangs covered by my lips. I hunched down, trying to appear smaller. Like one does with a frightened child.

I wanted to tell her, "No. Please. Don't be afraid. It's only me."

But I hadn't the words.

I started to turn.

I'd have to run.

She was so frightened she'd surely raise the alarm and I'd have scant minutes to escape.

And then she rushed to me, throwing her arms around me and burying her face in my chest. Weeping, and mumbling a stream of words I had no hope of understanding.

I stood there awkwardly. My hands dangling fools at my side. Finally, my arms closed around her. I stroked her hair. Whispered words meant to calm her.

Gradually her heartbeat slowed, and she pushed against me. But gently so.

I released her, and she took a step back. She looked in my face. Our eyes met and although we couldn't speak a word of each other's language, we suddenly understood.

I felt that familiar tingle in my mind. She shivered and rubbed her arms and I knew that she felt it too.

Kaarla had the exact same shiver and goose bumps on her arms when we were together. As did I.

Then, coming down the hallway I heard approaching voices.

Panic welled.

I had to get out of here.

Run.

I had to run.

I wrested Kaarla's knife from the hairless Thing's dead hands and shoved it into my belt.

Then I gripped the doorknob, ready to fling it open. I would kill as many as I could, then escape in the confusion.

But then My Thing placed a hand on mine. I looked down at her. She shook her head, then placed a finger against her lips.

Silence.

She wanted silence.

I nodded, and she reached over and shut off the light. Then ever so quietly, she locked the door.

A moment later the footsteps stopped just outside. The doorknob turned slightly as someone tried to open it, then found it locked.

A moment later someone called out in a low voice. I looked at My Thing and again she shook her head again. Finger pressed firmly against her lips.

Then another Thing called out.

This time My Thing answered, but in a low, sleepy voice as if she'd been awakened.

A tap at the door. Someone entreating. Pleading.

My Thing replied in a voice full of irritation. The kind I used when I was sleepy child, whining for my creche nurse to go away and let me sleep.

After a long tense moment, the footsteps and voices retreated down the hall.

I looked at the bodies sprawled on the floor, then at My Thing. I made motions—what should I do? I pantomimed tying her up, so no blame would fall on her.

A violent shake of her head. She tugged hard on my sleeve. Pointed at herself, then me. And then outside.

I was incredulous.

Pantomimed question: *You want to go with me?*

She nodded: Yes. Pantomiming: *Hurry. We must hurry.*

I shook my head. Made motions: *Impossible. Too dangerous.*

She grabbed both my hands in hers and stared into my eyes. Looking long and deep. There was a tingling at the back of my spine. A whirl of images flooded my brain. It was like being with Kaarla again—the sister of my mind.

It came to me that My Thing might face imprisonment or even death if she stayed behind. She trusted no one here. They all either meant her harm or were indifferent to her fate.

After a long moment, I relented. I nodded. Then urged her to make haste.

She jammed a few belongings into a pack, pulled on cold weather gear, then grabbed a pair of ice striders and motioned—*Let's go.*

We had no trouble getting out of the building. The Things had been too consumed with their revelries to be bothered to set a watch.

When we were safely outside, I looked around. It was bright and sunny. The skies a clear blue. The air was crisp and had a quality to it that I've never experienced before. Especially after a lifetime of breathing recycled shipboard air.

How to say it? Well it was delicious. Food for the lungs and the brain.

A sudden burst of energy.

My mind buzzed with ideas and plans.

The Things would come for us soon. And they would come with a fury. Doubly so, because now they would not just be hunting me, but My Thing as well.

I looked down the hill to the shed where they kept the hunters. Just beyond was the shelter that housed the flying machines.

I remembered a game we played where the ultimate challenge was to pin a minor game piece in front of a more important one. If your opponent moved the minor piece, the important one was doomed. But, if she didn't, the game was over. Leaving no choice but to sacrifice the important piece and hope for a miracle recovery.

Motioning for My Thing to follow I ran to the shed where I had been imprisoned.

I found the pipe I'd nearly tripped over. I turned to the shed and then groaned when I saw that some clever Thing had thought to secure the door with a heavy lock.

I grasped the lock and pulled.

It didn't give.

I tried again. Pulling with all my strength, which is considerable.

It started give way and there was frighteningly loud screech of metal as the screws holding the lock in place started give away.

Then stopped.

They would go no further.

A tap on the shoulder and I turned to see My Thing holding a long metal bar.

She motioned me aside, jammed the tip of the bar between the lock and the door of the shed and gave a mighty heave.

A loud SCREECH! and the lock fell to the ground.

We both looked around to see if anyone had heard us.

Nothing besides the sounds of the party.

I grabbed the wrench, fit it to the aperture, and heaved. It stuck for a moment, then came free. The smell of aviation fuel grew stronger and I heard bubbling deep within.

Turning to the shed, I examined the gauges and dials. I saw what appeared to be writing on a metal plate, with red pictographs showing what I took to be operational directions.

I sighed. This was hopeless, By the time I deciphered the directions we'd be in chains, or dead.

My Thing pushed me side. She looked at directions, glanced at the pictographs, then spun several dials.

She motioned for me to move away.

I took two steps back.

My Thing wriggled her fingers.

More.

Two more steps.

A snort of impatience, then more finger waggling.

I almost laughed. It was a nervous reaction that drew glares from My Thing. Clearly, this was a female who had no use for slow-witted beings.

I got well back and she pulled down a lever, jumping away as she did so.

A geyser of fuel burst from the pipe.

My Thing scrambled to where I was and we both ran for shelter as the aviation fuel shot out of the pipe.

We watched from cover as the fuel pooled around the pipe. Clouds of steam rose from the frozen ground.

Soon a river of fuel was running down the hill, flooding the area where the hunters were kept. Then rolling on to envelop the place where they housed the flying machines.

When the whole area was saturated with steaming fuel, I hoisted the Lazzerus rifle to my shoulder.

Dialed in the most explosive force.

And fired.

A sheet of flame erupted that was so intense we were momentarily blinded.

Soon as my vision cleared, I grabbed My Thing and started running.

We ran as fast as we could. Ice striders ripping up frozen ground. With my long legs I would soon outpace her, so I grabbed a hand and pulled her along. She came willingly. Pumping her legs as fast as she could to keep from being dragged along the ground.

And then there was an explosion so great it hurled us into the air.

I landed on my back. So stunned I didn't move for long seconds. A faint voice penetrated the ringing in my ears.

A tug at my sleeve.

I opened my eyes to find My Thing kneeling over me. She urged me to look and I sat up to see what we had done.

The homes of the flying machines and the hunters were fully engaged. Flames shooting up. Black clouds of smoke rising to the sky.

My hearing cleared, and I heard shouts. My Thing was pointing, and I turned to see Things pouring out of the building.

Hysterical confusion reigned for long minutes, then the leaders of the two groups got their underlings organized to start fighting the fires.

A moment later, there was an explosion, and one side of their quarters burst into flame. Now they concentrated on that fire, letting the others burn. It was either that or face the most severe environment on the planet without food or shelter.

Every bone in my body ached. I fell back when I tried to rise. My Thing didn't seem to have been affected as much and helped me to my feet.

We set off for my base camp. Slowly at first. Then, as my muscles warmed up, and the aches and pain diminished, we moved faster.

Behind us we heard shouts, and then another explosion.

We slowed, husbanding our strength.

They wouldn't be coming after us soon.

As we made our way, I ran over my preliminary findings. I would confirm them when we reached home, but even a cursory look at my device's screen staggered the imagination.

The proposed mining site contained at least thirty-five thousand metric tons of Element 92.

THE MONSTER AT WORLD'S END, BY ALLAN COLE | 193

Ripping it from the earth would create an environmental nightmare. Just one more nightmare to add to the Things' crimes against their own planet.

Tens of thousands of square kilometers of landscape ripped apart.

Whole mountains leveled to get at the ore.

The waters of the bay despoiled for a thousand years or more.

Sea life and birds dead and dying by the millions.

And the only pristine continent on the globe would be destroyed forever.

In my heart—no, not just my heart, but my entire being—I knew the Things would continue their destructive practices until the entire Earth was unfit for life of any sort.

Me and my kind have been star wanderers for many centuries now. And never in all that time have we come upon such monsters.

As we trudged across the ice I glanced over at My Thing.

She smiled at me. Teeth sparkling in the sunlight. Her ebony features so bright and gleaming that it was as if she were saying grace.

And I thought, *I don't even know her name.*

* * * *

"We're not all monsters," Eva said.

I said, "So far, you seem to be in the minority."

She sighed and lapsed into silence, contemplating the iceberg floating serenely in the otherwise empty bay. In the sunlight it shone a deep emerald green, so compelling you could stare at for hours, your mind awhirl with dreamy thoughts and images.

We sat on a large couch we had rescued from the blackened ruins of the place the Things had called home. They left in a hurry after I burned them out.

A translator rested between us. Little green lights winking when she spoke. Red lights for me. Theoretically, the sounds emanating from it perfectly imitated the tonal nuances of whoever was speaking.

To me, her voice was gentle and sweet. I don't know how mine seemed to her. At least she didn't flinch when I spoke.

She said, "What do you call yourselves? Your species, I mean. If that's the correct terminology to use for beings from another planet. Another star system."

I frowned. "Call ourselves?"

She grimaced. "Don't do that," she said. "It's scary when you make that face. Your whole forehead comes forward and your lips curl up in the opposite directions."

"What's so scary about that?" I asked.

"Well," she said, looking embarrassed, "Your teeth are really long and sharp. And your jaw juts forward like...well... I don't know... It's just scary."

She ducked her head. "I'm sorry," she said. "That's not very professional of me. My only excuse is that I'm just not used to it yet."

Then she looked up at me. "What about me? I must look scary to you sometimes. Tell me the truth. Am I ugly?"

It was probably rude of me, but I couldn't help laughing. The red lights winking like mad, trying to interpret the uninterpretable.

"One question at a time," I said.

"Answer number one, we call ourselves The People. For that's what we are—people."

She nodded, and I went on. "Answer number two: no, I don't find you ugly. Your body is well formed. Your skin a healthy black. Your features nicely proportioned. Your eyes are clear and full of intelligence. And your teeth, although rather small, are pearly white."

I paused, then added. "I'd suppose you'd be considered rather beautiful in the eyes of your own...people."

She laughed at my little joke. It was a peasant sound. The little green lights winked rhythmically. Visual music.

Then I asked a question that had troubled me since we fled together. "Why did you come with me, Eva? You could have blamed the deaths on me. After all, I was the one who killed them."

She hesitated, getting her thoughts in order. She'd probably been asking herself the same question since we'd set the entire facility ablaze and fled.

Finally, she said, "At first it was partly out of panic. Hank and Jerry were going to rape me and kill me. Just like they did Shawntelle. They planned to blame you. They boasted about it. Thought it was a big joke.

"We were the only women in the group, you know. Also we're both black. Lesser human beings in their view, and probably most of the others. Although they'd never admit it."

I almost asked how someone could be a "lesser being," but guessed that question was much too complicated a subject for the moment.

She said, "But the real reason is that I am a biologist. As a scientist I grabbed at the opportunity to study a life form from an entirely different world. To learn if Darwinian evolution is a universal phenomenon. If life develops similarly throughout the cosmos."

I chuckled. "We have a saying—'Curiosity slew the reek.'" The translator beeped. Stumped by the word. I said, "A reek is a little animal about so..." I spread my hands, trying to indicate size and looks.

She laughed and grabbed my hands, pulling them back together. "We have the same saying," she said. "'Curiosity killed the cat.'"

Then she looked at our clasped hands. It was the first time we had touched. After a moment, she gently pulled hers back.

"That's always been my problem," she said. "Curiosity. It's landed me in trouble more times than I care to admit. Curiosity is what led me to this place and my current predicament."

"I don't understand," I said.

"Jobs for female scientists are hard to come by," she said. "Doubly so for black female scientists. So when the opportunity to join this expedition arose, I jumped at it. Not just for the money, but for the chance to study the wildlife at the bottom of the Earth.

"When I got here, I immediately fell in love. I've never known a place of such beauty. The birds and animals are incredible. The way they cling to life in the most difficult and dangerous climate on the planet. It really made me appreciate what all forms of life will endure just to stay alive."

"And the land itself boggles the mind. Here in Antarctica all directions are North. And every year consists of a single day, divided into six months of summer when the sun never sets. And six months of winter when the sun never rises."

"But it was a mining expedition," I said. "It had nothing to do with science. Much less a scientific study."

"Well, Shawntelle and I didn't know that," she said heatedly. "They fooled us with pretty words about their noble intentions to save the planet. Also, there was a mixture of nationalities: American, British, Russian, German and Chinese. Making its purpose seem international. That appeared to add dignity to the effort.

"What Shawntelle and I didn't realize is that we were the only scientists among the group. The others were miners and engineers and people whose only interest is business.

"We were their façade. A carefully constructed and publicized façade to hide the fact that their intent was to violate international law.

"They were betting that their discoveries would be so enormous, so valuable, that greed would overcome complaints by anyone except the most extreme environmentalists. And everyone mocks them, anyway."

"What did you do when you found out what they were really up to?" I asked.

"We hit the roof," Eva said.

The translator went crazy at that. Lights blinking red and green. It has trouble with idioms.

Eva got it before I had to explain. She wiped the air with an open hand. As if scrubbing the words away.

"We were really, really angry," she said. "We made our views known in no uncertain terms. Art—the leader of the expedition—tried to calm us down. To 'see reason,' as he put it. He swore a percentage of the profits would go toward environmental concerns."

I snorted. "There is no way mere money could fix the damage."

"Well, we knew that," Evan said scornfully. "We refused to go along. We said we were going to report it. But when we tried to use the radio, they stopped us. Put a lock on the door of the communication center and forbid anyone but authorized personnel to enter."

"Did you try to circumvent Art?" I asked. "Find a way to communicate another way."

"We certainly did," Eva said. "Shawntelle stole a satellite phone from the supply room. She was going to report it the other day, but then she went missing. Art said she must have been lost in a white out and made a big a deal about sending out search parties. Then they... They..."

Eva fell silent. Her face pale. Eyes brimming as she remembered.

"It was horrible," she said. "Horrible. They said... They said..." She looked at me. "They said you had killed her."

"The first time I saw your friend," I said, "was when they wheeled her corpse into the room."

"That's what I figured," she said. "Shawntelle was no fool. She wouldn't have wandered from the barracks during a white out.

"Besides, some of the others warned us to shut up. They said they'd heard Art tell Hank and Jerry to talk to us. To put the fear of God into us."

The translator rebelled at that, but I had no trouble guessing the meaning.

"Hank and Jerry were Art's enforcers," Eva continued. "They were like his private cops to keep order. We all knew they were nothing but crazy thugs. That they were drunks who never bathed or did a lick of work, other than strong arm people who were foolish enough to publicly disagree with Art. They were always trying to catch Shawntelle and me alone. And made snide sexual comments and gestures when the thought no one was listening.

"Apparently, the theft of the satellite phone was discovered. There were cameras. Hidden cameras we didn't know about. We flipped a coin to see who would steal the phone. We were like little schoolgirls, giggling over being so...so..."

Eva choked up and couldn't go on. Her eyes brimmed, threatening to over flow.

I remained silent. Realizing one comforting word or touch would unleash a torrent of weeping. If she were like Kaarla, instead of thanking me, she'd feel resentful. So I waited while she gathered herself, taking deep breaths. Then she smiled her thanks at me, and continued.

"I suspect that when they went to talk to Shawntelle—on Art's orders— the situation got out of hand. Power went to their booze-addled heads and they raped and killed her. I'm sure Art knew what really happened. But he was afraid of them. You could tell. He always deferred to Hank and Jerry. No matter what they said or did, or how much they drank. So they concocted a story and blamed you."

"Murder, I might have been guilty of," I said. "But never rape. It isn't just that I'm not inclined to commit such an awful crime. But it would be a biological impossibility. How to put this... I don't have the necessary equipment."

"I realized that," Eva said. "Although I didn't know they were hunting you until just before your capture. When I saw the pictures, and learned about the strange beings that had been discovered in other parts of the globe, I knew we were talking about sentient beings from another world. And then I saw you when they brought in your unconscious body.

"Right after that Art blamed Shawntelle's murder and rape on you. I knew then he was lying. This time I didn't say a word. I was afraid the same thing would happen to me. But I'm a terrible liar. I must not have covered it up very well. Hank and Jerry started acting even weirder around me. Giving me creepy looks.

"Then, the other day... During the party..." She shook her head at the memory. "If you hadn't shown up I would have been next."

I thought about that a minute. Considered her position. I said, "I'm sure you panicked when you insisted on coming with me. Figuring that Art would get someone else to kill you. Or do it himself. It was the only way to continue the cover up."

Eva nodded. "I didn't panic," she said. "I'm not the kind to panic. But in the heat of the moment it seemed the best thing to do."

"The problem," I said, "is that now that you are here with me there may be no going back. What of your friends? Your family?"

She looked at her feet. "I have few friends. And as for family..." She shrugged. "Mine are all dead. The last of them were killed one summer in Chicago during a murder spree."

Eva's head came up, realizing what she'd said. "But that doesn't mean all of us are like that," she said. "We're not all murderers. Monsters."

I said, "My entire experience with your kind is one of murder and acts of monstrosity. The attacks on you and Shawntelle are just the latest examples. Such as the colony of flightless birds—"

"Penguins," she said. "They're called penguins."

I nodded. "Penguins... Then the bones of the giant animals dumped in that mass graveyard on the beach—"

"Whales," she said. "A shameful tragedy. And I'll admit that although most countries have banned the practice, whale hunting still goes on."

I shuddered. "I know how they hunt," I said. "They'll go to any extreme to capture and kill their prey."

Eva patted my hand. "I'm so sorry," she said. "I can't imagine how terrible it was for you."

I waved it away. I wasn't looking for sympathy. There were more important matters at stake than reliving threats to my own worthless hide.

I said, "My mission mates reported a host of similar crimes against nature. Then they were hunted down and killed without sense or reason. None of them harmed any of your kind. Or threatened to do so."

"They are afraid of you," she said. "There is nothing more dangerous on the face of the Earth than a frightened human being.

"As for the rest—your other accusations—those depredations are the fault of a greedy, deliberately ignorant few who have seized power over the rest of us."

I looked at her for a long time. Then I asked, "But who gave them that power in the first place? And who allows them to retain that power now?"

She hung her head. And in a voice so low the translator strained to deliver the words, she said, "We did."

Then her head came up and she looked me full in the face, dark eyes flashing.

Defiant.

And she said, "We did, damn it! And it's true, we keep repeating that error time and time again. Even though it is painfully obvious what is happening to our world. Air so polluted it is unhealthy to breathe. Water so poisoned that our own children are getting sick and dying. Devastating storms and fires…"

Her voice trailed off. She drew a deep breath. Then she pointed at the startling blue sky. With winter near, the sun was low on the horizon. And I could plainly see an enormous pale yellow halo directly overhead. It seemed to vibrate and I could see darkness just beyond. As if I were looking at outer space.

"That is a hole in the sky," she said. "A hole created by us. And we're leaking atmosphere like crazy. Not long ago it was starting to heal, then we resumed doing the greedy practices we had all agreed had to stop."

I nodded and settled back. "There it is, then," I said. "The answer to your own question. The crimes against nature committed by your fellow beings are monstrous.

"So they must be monsters.

She leaned forward, face desperate, eye pleading, "But don't you see, we're all so afraid."

Once again she grasped my hands. "Just like you are afraid. You told me yourself your people are on their last legs. Without Earth as your new home you are all doomed. And so you are terrified. Understandably so.

"So terrified that your leaders are seriously considering that the only answer is euthanasia. Wiping out the entire human race to save yourselves."

"And your planet," I said. "As well as all the other life forms who dwell on Earth." A great sadness settled on me. I sighed, then added, "Your kind won't be missed, you know.

"If the other life forms on this planet could applaud, the sound would be beyond deafening."

Eva squeezed my hands harder. I was surprised at the strength of such a tiny being.

She said, "If you do this, you'll become just like what you are accusing us of being.

"Monsters."

Her words struck me like a physical blow. She was right. At this moment our leaders were weighing the fate of the human race.

If we attacked there would no warning. Although we could win any war, without surprise on our side we would suffer so many losses it would unconscionable. Bring our numbers so low our very existence would be in doubt.

I said, "It's not up to me. I have no control over their decision."

"Please don't wash your hands of it," she begged. "Speak for us. And let me speak. All I ask is a chance.

"I know I'm a nobody, but at least try to convince them to hear me out. And I'll speak to others. People more important than I am. And in turn, they know even more important people."

I felt confused. Helpless. I sighed, and she released my hands.

And I thought, what was the use?

Then I recalled another time when I was confused, helpless and devoid of hope. Then an act of kindness restored that hope with a gift of clear, cold water.

I reconsidered. Thought of the many hours Eva and I had spent together. She was a remarkable woman. Kind and gentle and incredibly intelligent.

Surely, she wasn't unique. A human anomaly. Surely, there were others. Possibly many others.

Would my people listen?

I don't know.

Should they listen?

I don't know that either.

I looked out at the pristine waters of Deception Bay. As my eyes took in the shimmering emerald green iceberg, I saw a little penguin in a comic waddle to the edge. Once there it dived into the bay and literally flew through the water.

"So graceful," Evan murmured. "And beautiful. How could something that looks so funny be so beautiful?"

As I watched there was a whooshing sound, and a geyser of water shot into the sky. Painting glorious rainbows.

Then I saw the waters gently part.

An enormous gray shape surfaced.

A whale.

Magnificent and in its own way as graceful as the little flightless bird.

"Beauty comes in all sizes, does it not?" Eva said in a low voice.

As the whale glided through the water, I imagined it was observing me from through one great eye.

"She looks so wise," Eva murmured.

"Infinitely so," I replied.

"It's as if she held the secrets of everything—past, present and future," Eva said.

I felt a tingling sensation, as if the whale was trying to speak to me. I strained all my faculties trying to catch what she was saying. Then she spouted water and went under, her tail slapping the surface of the bay, as if in farewell.

Eva said, "Could you feel it?" She tapped her head. "Up here, did you feel it?"

"Yes," I said.

"I think she was trying to talk to you," Eva said.

"You mean to us," I said.

Eva shook her head. "No, to you. She was speaking to you."

"What did she say?" I asked.

"You know," Eva insisted. "You know."

I sighed. "She said, 'Welcome, brother.'"

And at that moment I knew what the future would hold.

AUTHOR'S NOTE

This story way inspired by Angus Erskine, Richard Rowlett, Peter Harrison, and Sabina and Dennis Mense who helped us appreciate the beauty of the seventh continent and the fortitude of our fellow lifeforms who dwell there during our expedition to Antarctica in the summer of 1989.

THE MONSTER AT WORLD'S END, BY ALLAN COLE | 201

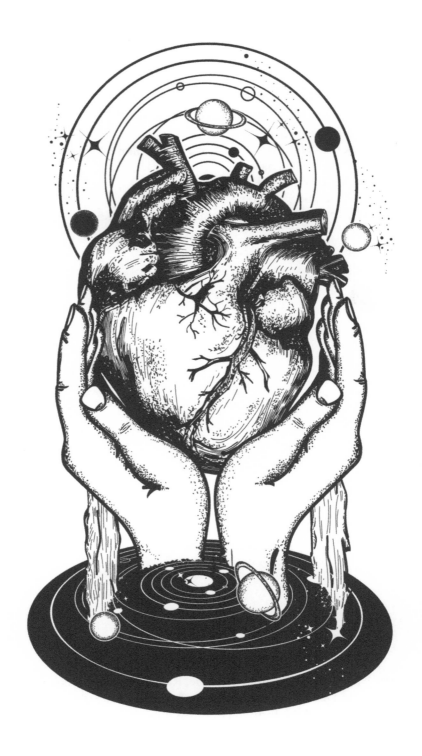

THINGMAKER

PAUL DI FILIPPO

On the late afternoon of December 7, 1941, Senator Harry Truman arrived at the secret government establishment dubbed "Thingmaker" in a discreet Nash 600 sky-sled that appeared to be a standard Washington, DC, taxicab. Behind the wheel of the floating vehicle sat a youthful fellow with dark wavy hair and a long oval face featuring an aquiline nose above full lips. Looking back over his shoulder at his passenger, the driver received a positive nod. He maneuvered the controls of the sky-sled in response, so as to cause it to sink slowly onto its undercarriage bumpers as they made contact with the pavement.

The building before which the car settled, an innocuous and shabby warehouse-type structure with its windows boarded up, stood in the shadow of the Nehi Bottling Plant at 1923 New York Avenue in the Ivy City district of the nation's capital, a zone devoted to light manufacturing, gas stations, railyards, junkyards, and other rough utilitarian structures of modern civilization. Today, a Sunday, the famous soda pop enterprise was dormant, and there was little traffic, vehicular or pedestrian. The day was sunny, and in fact a high temperature of ninety degrees had been recorded, now dwindling as the evening approached.

The driver emerged from the Nash. Out on the street, he proved to be only in his smooth-cheeked mid-adolescence, despite affectations to maturity. Although dressed informally—colorfully printed cotton sports shirt, gabardine slacks, rubber-soled tennis shoes—he still carried himself with a military alertness. Abetting this impression was a pistol tucked into his trousers waistband at the small of his back. He keenly sized up the sparse traffic, being sure to look overhead as well, for other sky-sleds, then spoke to his passenger in a voice that bore a hint of Texas twang.

"It's all jake, Senator. Climb on out."

Harry Truman levered himself out of the curbside door. The well-known politician today wore a lightweight tweed suit. At the age of fifty-seven, his hair had noticeably thinned from its youthful richness. His trademark round wire-rimmed spectacles caught a glint from the sinking sun. Perspiration dotted his brow.

The driver had joined Truman on the sidewalk. "Where's the door?"

"Around back," said the Senator, indicating an alley between the warehouse and the adjacent building.

The driver regarded the passage suspiciously.

"I'll go first."

Truman chuckled. "One would imagine you were scouting in the ruins of Berlin, Audie."

"Yeah, well, maybe I was too young to get into that scrape. It was over before it hardly began. Had to haul myself out here to the War Office just to find some action. Then what job do they give me? Babysitting a politician. No offense, sir, but that's just how I see it."

"Your description, while unflattering, is mostly accurate."

"'Preciate your understanding, sir. Anyhow, I stalked a lot of critters back home in Farmersville, and if I didn't shoot them before they saw me, we didn't eat that night. So I always figure that it's a good thing if you can see your opponent before they can see you."

Truman seemed thoughtful when he said, "Assuming one can always recognize friend from foe."

Audie registered a bit of puzzlement at that remark, but did not follow it up. Instead, he moved to the mouth of the alley, which was well lit by the fading daylight and offered no places of concealment, save for a couple of dented galvanized trash cans behind which perhaps a Munchkin from *The Wizard of Oz* might be able to crouch. After making great show of his inspection, he beckoned Truman to follow. The pair quickly traversed the brick corridor with its assorted litter: the wrapper from a Chicken Dinner candybar; a takeout menu from the famous China Clipper restaurant; an empty bottle of Lucky Tiger hair tonic, and one of Ancient Age whiskey.

At the end of the alley a board fence, separated from the rear of the building by a few feet, allowed them to turn left. On this far side of the warehouse, they encountered the door: a rusting iron facade with a padlock and chain that seemed immovably soldered to the entrance by time.

"You sure this is the right door?" Audie asked.

Truman said nothing, but instead merely knocked in a complex pattern.

A door-sized section of the brick wall, adjacent to the fake door, pivoted outward. A Marine with a rifle awaited them. Senator Truman showed the soldier an identification card, and the visitors were allowed entrance. The wall swung silently shut behind them.

The interior of the warehouse belied its exterior, comprised entirely of modern textures under bright overhead lights—at least in this large anteroom, which featured crisp checkerboard linoleum floors, a steelcase desk, and three futuristic looking wooden Eames chairs.

Behind the desk sat a young dark-haired woman, more striking than beautiful, in the uniform of a WAC—complete with a large Webley Mk VI .455 calibre revolver in a well-oiled holster. Her somewhat haughty features failed to completely mask a warm and concerned soul. A nametag on the breast of her uniform read COL. K. SUMMERSBY. She smiled at the newcomers—a contrast to the unrelentingly stern visage of the Marine—and Audie made sure to beam back. When she spoke, she revealed British origins.

"Welcome, Senator."

"You're looking lovely, as usual, Kay. Life with Ike must be agreeing with you."

"Oh, he's a tad mardy, griping at how peaceful the world is these days. Old soldiers, you know. But he's basically a dear. Still, I shouldn't detain you with household talk. You're here to see Doctor Delbrück, I assume. He's expecting you."

"Yes. And if Doctor Luria could spare some time to accompany us as well, I'd be grateful."

"I'll see if he's available."

Using the intercom on her desk, Summersby received confirmation from both Delbrück and Luria that they would soon be present to receive the visitors. An inner door to the rest of the mysterious warehouse beckoned, but a second stern Marine kept vigil by it, not offering admittance.

After a minute or so the door swung open into the anteroom, and two men strode through. Any observer could discern by their labcoats and savant's demeanors that they were scientists of some stature.

Truman took the time to introduce his companion, producing a smile of pleasure from the boy.

"Doctor Delbrück, this is my chauffeur and all-round general factotum, Audie Murphy."

Delbrück proved to be a skinny fellow in his mid-thirties with a wry and puckish face and a wing of dark hair sloping across his forehead. His German accent layered his impeccable English.

"I'm very pleased to meet such an accomplished youngster. Call me Max."

"Aw, shucks, I ain't so much, nor so young!"

"And this is Doctor Luria."

His black hair trimmed short and adhering to a high line above his wide forehead, Luria resembled a continental movie star, such as the newcomer Rossano Brazzi. And in fact, his speech showed Mediterranean origins.

"*Ciao, ragazzo!* Any friend of the Senator's is a friend of Salvador's."

The introductions over, Truman was quick to assert the urgency and importance of his visit.

"Gentlemen, as head of the Senate Committee on Wolf-Rayet Technology, I'm here to make one final inspection tour before we render our decision on the continuation of your project."

Delbrück and Luria straightened their shoulders and looked hopeful but wary. The German scientist said, "We will show you everything again, of course, and answer any questions in full. You already have all our written reports and records."

"Your forthcomingness is admirable, professors. But I should warn you that the votes are trending against your research."

An excitable Luria responded intemperately. "*Madonna mia!* What is the problem, Senator? Are you and your comrades blind to the potential benefits of our discoveries? Have you not seen how vital and important the other technologies from the Garry Expedition has become? Why, atomic power and anti-gravity have revolutionized our world in just three short years, ever since those heroic explorers returned with the goods from the South Pole. And they allowed the Allies to put a quick end to the Axis powers, shortening a war that surely would have killed millions. But even those life-saving innovations are trivial in comparison to what we offer here!"

Truman nodded somberly to acknowledge the truth of Luria's protest. "Yes, the United States monopoly on anti-gravity and the neutron-beryllium power sphere, shared with her partners, did bring those bastards Hitler and Tojo and *il Duce* up short. Pardon the aspersions on your native lands, gents, I know where your true sympathies lie. But no matter how revolutionary, those gadgets were just that—gadgets. What you two are working on is the stuff of life itself."

"And thus its greater potential for good!"

"I don't deny that, Doctor Luria. But it's a double-edged sword. The potential for harm, should the technology ever escape your built-in restraints, is immense. You know the men of the Garry Expedition suffered great losses and barely avoided total annihilation."

An impatient and curious Audie interjected a question. "What're you talking about, Chief? I know Commander Garry lost some of his crew and all their dogs during a brutal storm in 1938. But you can't rightly associate a faraway force of nature like that with something going on right here in Washington—can you?"

The three men looked at each other significantly, and then Delbrück said, "Is the boy cleared to receive the true story?"

Truman looked fondly at the lad. "He's one hundred percent loyal to his country, and smart enough to keep his mouth shut. He's bound to hear a lot as my aide-de-camp. So I'll take responsibility for his silence."

"Very well, then." Delbrück assumed a lecture-hall mien. "*Herr* Murphy, the reality of what transpired at the South Pole is otherwise than you and the general public have been led to believe. The official story explains that the Garry Expedition uncovered an alien spaceship, and retrieved from the wreck the technologies of antigravity and atomic power, all before the ship was destroyed by a foolish misuse of a thermite heat source. This is a conflation and omission of the real events. What those men took from the crashed interstellar vessel was not any kind of technology, but rather a frozen alien corpse. Or so Doctors Blair and Copper assumed. But the corpse came alive, and proved savage and lethal, exhibiting strange abilities of mimicry derived from a destructive possession of its victims. This 'thing from another world,' if I may so call it, was just on the point of either escaping to civilization or exterminating the humans—or both—when it was finally defeated by the bravery of the men and an ingenious tactic. They eradicated all contagious traces of its body, then turned their attention to the aftermath of its secret doings, when it had been sequestered in a hut. Secretly roaming the base, it had replicated from local parts both the antigravity mechanism and the neutron-beryllium power source before it died, as well as a simulation of its native environment in an outbuilding of the camp—a simulation that revealed its preference for the light of a blue-white star. These stars are classified as Wolf-Rayet types, and so we have adopted that general term to distinguish the alien technology."

Audie absorbed the radical revelations with his quick intelligence, then asked, "Well, what's the secret third technology that's you're hiding here? The Chief said something about 'life itself.'"

Luria gave the answer to that question. "The thing was a creature composed of infinitely malleable protoplasm—what we call totipotent cells. If it managed to insinuate the smallest traces of itself into a living creature, its alien protoplasm would rapidly replicate and replace all the original material of a being, while retaining both surface and cellular appearances. To all eyeball and instrumental tests, the creature reproduced itself as a perfect duplicate of the subject. But in reality, the victim would be a scion of the alien, an heir in disguise. In a way, just as green algae can fission into daughter cells, so the thing would have reproduced itself on the coattails of its victims, while wiping out the integrity and identity of the original host."

His eyes big as saucers, Audie said, "Jeepers, it's a good thing they wiped out all traces of that monster." When the scientists said nothing, the boy's eyes narrowed. "Or did they?"

Senator Truman chimed in. "Bright boy! Yes, the Garry Expedition felt sure that they had neutralized every iota of the thing. If they hadn't been certain, they would never have risked coming home and infecting us. And upon their return, all the experts did in fact deem them clean. And they were. But the monster survived, back in the Antarctic, in a most unlikely host. What the men had not reckoned with was the presence of polar microorganisms, bacteria living just beneath the snows. Drops of blood from the slaughter of the infected dogs penetrated the snow and infected these microrganisms. The thing from another planet could do nothing in these primitive vessels, but it remained alive. It was Doctors Delbrück and Luria here—two of our most brilliant biologists—who theorized this might be so. And the next expedition to the South Pole brought back core samples that proved their theory correct."

"Are you saying that you've got living bits of this monster here in bacterial form?"

Luria smiled proudly. "Much more than that, *ragazzo*! But we waste the Senator's valuable time in talking. Let us conduct the necessary tour, so that he might return to his committee with a positive report, and save our project that offers so much possibility of alleviating mankind's ancient sufferings."

With a nod to the stony-faced Marine, the two scientists led the way through the inner door, which swung shut tightly behind them.

The party found itself in a corridor whose walls, floor and ceiling appeared to be all stainless steel, apparently formed into shape from a single plate, with but a lone double-welded seam running down the middle of the ceiling. The metal chute conveyed the sense of travelling through some industrial network of pipes.

"Nothing permeable, no means of even the smallest particle escaping," said Delbrück. "We have complete confidence in the harmlessness of our charge, but even so, we take these incredible precautions."

Ahead a massive door like that of a bank's vault intervened. It had to be unlatched by the spinning of a wheel, and was able to be dogged shut from either side.

"A kind of airlock between the subject and the outer world. There are several more."

True to the scientist's word, the group passed through additional airlocks. The final one opened onto a view of a large room that constituted the bulk of the warehouse's cubic center.

This inner sanctorum was sharply illuminated. Again, all vertical and horizontal surfaces were bright metal, as if in a lounge built for robots. Central to the room, various pipes and tubing and effectuators ran into and out of a large glass sphere, big as a cottage. The sphere in its cradle featured a platform around its equator. Banks of instruments, attended by a handful of technicians, occupied much of this platform. Various apparatuses protruded into the sphere, through tightly gasketed openings.

Several more Marines, their rifles held ready for action, were stationed around the lab.

But these details were not what would immediately draw the eye of any observer. It was the incredible contents of the sphere that commanded all rapt gazes.

Inside the glass bubble, a mass of ivory protoplasm like a gigantic tapioca or blancmange, not quite enough to fill the entire enclosed space, roiled and churned as if agitated by propellors. But no such mechanism existed: the thing twisted and seethed, bubbled and pullulated under its own quasi-muscular impulses.

The quartet of newcomers crossed the gleaming stainless steel floor to the platform that surrounded the sphere, climbing the four steps that led to the banks of instruments. The technicians looked up briefly from monitoring their gauges and dials and uttered brief greetings, before returning to their vigilance.

Having seen this alien spectacle before, Truman was not completely taken aback, although even his face registered glimmers of a requisite awe. But Audie experienced a vertiginous sense of confronting the unthinkable. Drawn to the surface of the glass sphere like a rabbit sucked into a snake's ocular orbit, he was unprepared for a sudden unexpected change in the undifferentiated convulsing mass.

The protoplasm closest to Audie's face sprouted a cluster of three malevolent red eyes and a beak-like orifice surrounded by writhing blue worms!

Audie jumped away and instinctively reached behind his back for his gun. The Marines all snapped alert, pointing their rifles at the boy. Luckily, Truman intervened swiftly, catching Audie's arm in mid-reach and repositioning it away from his weapon.

The lad wiped the spontaneous freshet of sweat from his brow and said, "Holy cats! I ain't never been so shaken by anything as I was by that! Not even coming on a nest of rattlers in my bare feet! But you don't gotta worry. I don't aim to take no potshots at that creature—so long as you got it pent up safe like that."

Delbrück and Luria actually seemed proud of their captive monster, and amused at Audie's dissipated fright. The former said, "The enclosure is indeed escape-proof. But more than that, the monster is now harmless."

"How's that? You mean it can't take over a person no more?"

"No," Luria said, "it can't. For one very good reason. We have rendered its predatory genes docile. Max and I, along with invaluable help from our peers Thomas Morgan, Edward Tatum and George Beadle, have discovered how to shut off the expression, if you will, of its virulence. Oh, it might smother you with its sheer bulk, if it fell atop you. But its former ability to conquer by ingestion and replication is banished. But its new harmlessness is far from all we have achieved. Much more to the point, we have discovered how to control and shape expression within these totipotent cells."

"I don't rightly understand."

"A demonstration will convey our achievement more clearly than words."

Delbrück turned to one of the technicians. "Joe, initiate the Leghorn Sequence, please."

Inside the glass ball, a mechanical arm, tipped with a hypodermic needle, descended from above. All eyes were drawn to the needle, and Audie noticed a hitherto-unseen feature of the spherical cage. A glass box protruded both inside and outside the sphere. The inner mouth of the box was open to the protoplasm, while the outside face of the box was sealed with a door. Another instance of an airlock.

The needle plunged into the white gelatinous blob. Instantly, as if in utter obedience, the thing budded off a piece of itself, and spat the disconnected segment into the box. An inner door slid down, capping the little chute. Luria walked to the airlock and, opening it, removed the segregated bit, about as large as a brick, with a pair of forceps.

"Joe, the torch, please."

The technician clicked alight a small propane torch and played the flame over the detached mass.

"Are you aiming to kill that piece of the critter?"

Delbrück smiled. "Not precisely. This sample is already inert."

A very familiar aroma began to permeate the room.

"Is that—is that *chicken*?"

"Good nose, *ragazzo*." Joe ceased flaming the sample, and Luria waved it in the air to cool it. "Anyone care for a taste? No? Too bad. But it is past my lunch."

Luria plucked off a piece of the alien-sourced meat and popped it into his mouth. Delbrück did the same. "We have all enjoyed several such meals, without suffering any consequences other than a full stomach. All risked only after extensive animal testing, of course. We now have much better indicators of alien possession than the primitive immunity blood tests rigged up by Doctor Copper during the Antarctica crisis. And we affirm with absolute certainty that the monster's flesh is one-hundred-percent non-invasive."

Looking humble, pleased and serious all at once, Luria added, "Senator Truman, Mister Murphy—you have just witnessed an end to human hunger and starvation on this planet. With this artificial meat, endlessly replenishable and infinitely variable, we have conquered want and privation."

"What's this here jello-mold critter feed on?"

"Anything organic. Grass clippings, seaweed, even sewage. All turned into healthy edible products."

Audie gagged a bit at that last named contribution to the thing's diet, before recovering his aplomb. "Well, I guess what goes around's gotta come around."

Luria and Delbrück focused on Senator Truman now. "Senator, don't you agree that this achievement alone is sufficient justification to continue our project?"

Truman cupped his chin mediatatively. "I know there's over two billion people on the planet, and that's a lot of mouths to feed. Not that I see the population numbers going much higher than that anytime in the next century or so. But we've got this smart fella Norman Borlaug working on the problem, and he thinks he's got it licked by conventional means. So why do we need to invest in all this far-out technology, even with minimal risk? And besides, you've got the extra barrier of convincing folks to eat this foreign stuff. Once they know they'll be chowing down on converted roadkill and dead plow horses, say, you've got a major public-relations and marketing problem on your hands."

Delbrück sighed and looked to his partner, who nodded affirmatively. "All right, Senator, we are not quite ready with this development yet, but we feel we need to bring it center-stage to convince you of how invaluable this new Wolf-Rayet technology is. Mary, please initiate the Valentine Sequence."

A female technician worked the controls that sent another needle jabbing into the protoplasm to deliver its cargo of instructive tailored enzymes and proteins and chromosonal fragments. As before, the captive thing responded by forming its totipotent cells into a specialized unit, which it deposited into the transfer chute.

Luria had donned a pair of surgeon's gloves. He reached into the glass box and removed the output of the thing.

There in the biologist's cupped latex hands quivered a human heart, tinted with the natural colors of humanity. It beat for half a minute, disgorging residual tank fluids from its arteries, before it shivered to a halt.

Audie whistled in awe. "You gents got yourselves an all-purpose thing-maker there!"

Delbrück's gaze was both dreamy and practical, even a shade messianic. "Healthy, functional, a universal match for any blood type, and nonantigenic. If we had the surgical procedures perfected for transplantation—and studies such as Carrel and Lindbergh's *The Culture of Organs* are already leading the way—and if all operating rooms were equipped with a small-scale version of this tank, organ failures would become an archaic abomination of the brutal past. New kidneys, lungs, livers—all on demand."

Luria chimed in. "Not only internal organs, but limbs as well! New arms and legs that might not even need to be surgically attached, but which might attach themselves upon command!"

Truman at first was speechless. But, recovering his wits, he said, "Doctor Delbrück, Doctor Luria—I am a Baptist because I think that sect gives the common man the shortest and most direct approach to God. But I'll be god-damned if I can figure out what the Good Lord would think of this unholy idea of inserting monster parts into a person. Maybe the deity would approve, maybe not. He's already allowed his creations to perform some amazing feats that would have counted as blasphemy in other eras. But I do think you've just raised more obstacles to approval of your project—and big ones—instead of removing some."

The two scientists were plainly marshalling their further arguments in favor of the revolutionary technology when a new development precluded all talk.

The boom of a huge explosion sounded from the rear of the warehouse, shaking and rattling the inner chamber. The Marines instantly responded with practiced moves, taking up defensive positions with their rifles aimed at the only entrance.

Audie leaped in front of Truman, his gun in his hand.

"Get down, Senator! This ain't no playtime!"

The scientists and technicians activated controls that dropped a heavy metallic curtain around the thingmaker tank. Then they crouched as best they could behind the control kiosks on the platform.

The wait seemed to last forever, although it was only half a minute or so, but then came a second explosion at the inner door, sending acrid smoke and flying debris into the lab.

Gunfire rattled from both sides of the engagement. Flat on the decking, Truman practically felt Audie's booming pistol in action. Again, time stretched during the battle. Then the gunfire ceased—and Audie fell atop the Senator!

A Marine approached the platform. "It's over now. Are you folks all okay?"

"No!" Truman said. "We have a man down!"

He levered Audie's body off, and kneeled to investigate.

The boy was still alive, but suffering from a large deep chest wound.

Truman heard the protective curtain rattling upward, and Delbrück shouting, "The Patch Sequence!"

Luria dropped down beside the stricken lad. Somehow he found the courage and bravado to grin at Truman. "Allow me to introduce myself. The most famous never-matriculated undergraduate of the University of Turin medical school." He began ripping away Audie's shirt.

Delbrück raced over with his hands full of protoplasm. He tossed it to Luria, who slapped it down on Audie's chest like a mustard plaster.

The totipotent cells went straight to work, integrating themselves and rebuilding the shattered bones, flesh and organs, becoming human in color, shape and texture. In almost no time at all, Audie was sitting up, a slightly dazed yet competent and cogent look on his face. He placed a hand tentatively on his breastbone, regarding the invisible repairs with quiet astonishment.

"Jeepers! Sure hope this don't mean all my kids are gonna have three red eyes and blue catfish whiskers!"

In a few moments the thingmaker had produced a half-dozen more all-purpose patches, carried in spare Erlenmeyer flasks. Thus equipped for instant first aid, the two scientists, Truman and Audie followed the Marines on a path back out to the reception area. They paused first to examine the bodies of the fallen attackers. Contrary to any expectations that the invaders might have been uniformed soldiers of a hostile nation, they appeared to be native Americans of a certain type, that class known as the "gangster" or "underworld" figure: hard-nosed mugs in flashy suits, armed with tommyguns.

Once attaining the reception area, they discovered a scene of chaos. The outer door had been blown away. The lone Marine on guard had been mercilessly cut to pieces, too far gone for even thingmaker fixes.

Across Summersby's desk sprawled another gangster, facedown, this one unarmed and dressed with more panache.

A Marine flipped the body over.

Truman exclaimed, "I know this yegg from when he testified to Congress! It's Bugsy Siegel!"

At the sound of his name, the mobster opened his eyes, took in his audience, and spoke in a grating whisper. "Truman, you bastard... Cut off my radium-atomite sales to Mussolini... Knew you had something big going on here... Figured you owed me a share..."

Siegel lapsed back into unconsciousness. Truman said, "Get him fixed up. The US government is going to want to hold this pissant responsible for all this mess."

Audie shouted from where he was squatting behind the desk. "It's Miss Summersby! She's still breathing!"

In a brief time both Summersby and Siegel were once more hale and hearty. Her trig uniform all in disarray, Summersby got to her feet, still instinctively clutching her huge Webley revolver. Siegel glared at her with traces of reluctant approbation at her courage.

"Thought the bitch was dead on the floor, but she took me out when my back was turned."

Summersby holstered her sidearm. "One does not go skeet shooting every week since age twelve for nothing, nor endure the Blitz as an ambulance driver without mustering some resilience."

The exterior phone line proved to be intact, and soon the warehouse was flooded with troops and police and high-level politicos. Everything got sorted out with speed and precision.

After Siegel had been led away and all the corpses removed, Truman turned to Luria and Delbrück.

"Professors, this is no longer a safe or secret site for your project. I suggest we get you set up in a more secluded place. We have a facility in Los Alamos, New Mexico, that we're not using for anything. I think it would be just right for Project Thingmaker."

Audie piped up. "Much as I like working with you, Chief, I might ask to be assigned to help these guys. After all, I gotta pay back my pound of flesh, don't I?"

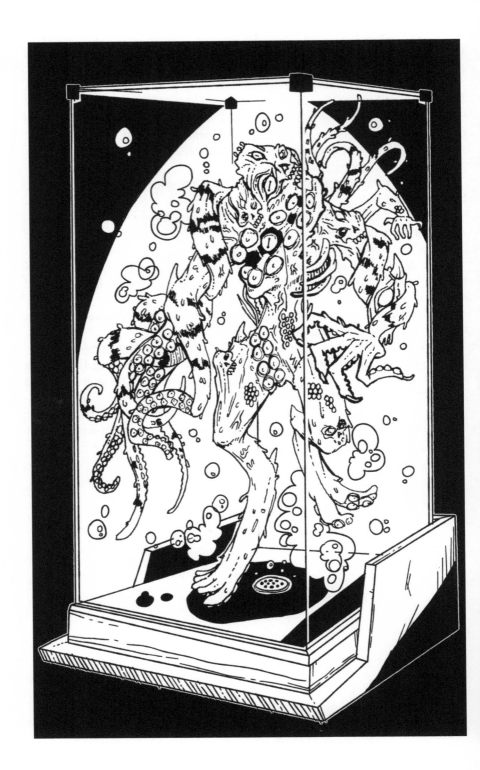

THE NATURE OF THE BEAST

JOHN GREGORY BETANCOURT

The Thing in the glass cage paced, as it had done every day for the last month, flowing from form to form as it did. Tentacles, claws, fingers—a vaguely human face giving way to bluish, sheeplike fur—shimmering scales to feathers to prickly, gray-green skin—and on to other, even stranger forms.

This process was something out of my worst nightmare, yet I could not look away. It was my job: observe and record—and try to establish contract.

I checked the camera mounted on the table before me. The red light glowed steadily; still recording. The analysts at home base, who would watch after my shift when I hand-delivered the recording on a secure thumb drive, were going to love *this* session. I'd seen bits of at least two or three creatures we hadn't catalogued before.

Then faint whispers started in the back of my mind: *Open the door. Open the door. Open the—*

I slapped the red button on the control panel in front of me, and the steel floor of the cage delivered a jolt of electric current. The Thing yelped, spasmed, flipped onto its back, and writhed. The voice in my head shut up. I released the button, and the Thing withdrew to the far corner. Sulking, no doubt. There, it grew a very human-looking eye at the end of long, multi-jointed stem. The eye stared at us, not blinking. But then, it never blinked.

"You heard that?" Paul Jarman, my assistant, asked from behind me. He had a soft step; I hadn't realized he'd come into the observation room.

"Yeah." I shuddered as the Thing's eye-stalk pulled back into its body. A dozen additional limbs sprouted along its torso. Had it settled on a new form?

"Don't like it getting into our heads," he muttered. "Ought to kill it and be done."

"You know it's too valuable," I said. But secretly I agreed with him. "We have to get through to it. Find a way to communicate. To negotiate."

He snorted. "Only way to beat them is to kill them. Can't negotiate with something that wants to eat you." He studied the Thing. "Does it know we can't open the door?"

"Would it keep asking if it did?"

"Guess not." He dropped into the office chair next to mine, spun it in a circle, then stopped facing me. He held out a large white envelope.

I took it. "New orders?"

"New orders."

The envelope had DR. IAN GRAHAM written in black sharpie on the front. I slit the red security-tape with my thumbnail, then pulled out a single sheet of paper. Department of Home Defense, today's date, and all the other usual stuff. I tracked down to the instructions. *Assessment 38. Rewards and incentives.*

"They've got to be kidding," I said, as I skimmed our instructions. "I think they want us to train it!"

"Good dogs get treats?" Jarman snorted. "How do you train *that*?"

"It's too smart for training."

"More like too stubborn." He shrugged. "Refuses to bend an inch. Why keep trying to escape? Why refuse to make any effort to communicate?"

"Too smart or too stubborn—does it matter? It's the nature of the beast. You get the same result either way."

I glanced at the Thing, which had now settled on the form of a large, brown, armor-plated lizard with twelve legs and a pointy, thick-boned skull. Interesting. I hadn't seen this one before. I glanced at the camera—red light blinking, still recording—and leaned forward. What now?

Without warning, it charged straight at us, striking the wall head-on. *Bam!* It was clearly audible through the two-inch-thick glass. The Thing staggered, then backed up and charged again. *Bam!* And again. *Bam!* And again. *Bam!*

It wouldn't get through, of course. It had to know that. And yet it still kept trying. Why? Why not learn from its mistakes?

"Can I?" Jarman's hand hovered over the electric shock button.

I sighed. "Be my guest."

His finger stabbed down. The Thing howled, spasmed, withdrew to the far corner of its cell. There it hunkered down, grew three more eye-stalks, and regarded us. Again, no eyelids. Maybe it didn't like to blink.

I reread our instructions. *Protein in exchange for verbal interaction.*

Protein? What sort of protein? It had to mean meat. Maybe…a lab rat? If so, we'd be seeing incisors and long, naked tails in its transformations from now on.

If it cooperated. Which, of course, it wouldn't.

Clearing my throat, I read the memo aloud to Jarman, who snickered. He also knew it wouldn't work. I could see that.

"Ready?" I asked.

Jarman nodded and switched off the microphones.

I leaned forward and read the script aloud: "I know you can hear and understand me. This will be easier for all of us if you cooperate. As a sign of good will, if you adopt a human form to communicate with us, we will provide you with 8 ounces of protein in a form you can digest."

Silence. The three eyes stared. No change.

I continued: "If you do not cooperate, you will be punished. Take my advice, you will be much happier if you make an effort to meet us halfway." Nothing.

I looked at Jarman. His index finger hovered over the shock button. When I nodded, he pushed it.

The Thing began to scream.

* * * *

So it continued, day after day, week after week, in four-hour shifts. Jarman and I relieved Dr. Chang at 10 A.M., and Dr. Rodriguez relieved us at 2 P.M. I didn't know the other teams. Since the Thing never slept, it had keepers on duty 24 hours a day. We had established a monotonous pattern of question-and-punishment, as we hammered at its will around the clock. Eventually it had to break.

I always paused to compare notes with both Dr. Chang and Dr. Rodriguez as we relieved each other. Neither of them had made any progress, either. Our sessions with the Thing were not so much variations on a theme—there were no variations—as a series of elaborate tortures imposed on another sentient creature. Each carefully worded script we read to it ended the same way: in screaming and pain.

"God, I hate that thing," Jarman told me on Day 72.

"Me, too."

"Think how many there would be if we hadn't captured it? Thousands!"

"More like thousands of trillions," I said idly. I'd done the math. "That's how we know we've got them under control. Everyone on the planet would be a Thing by now if we hadn't stopped our friend here. And probably every dog, cat, bird, and fish, too."

"If it gets loose—"

"It won't."

The whispers started in my head again: *Open the door. Open the door. Open the door—*

Jarman looked at me, eyebrows raised, and I nodded.

He pushed the red button, and he kept it pushed long after the voice had stopped.

"Die already," he muttered. "Die already and be done."

Killing the Thing would have ruined both our careers. I pulled his finger from the shock button.

"Not today. Not on our shift. Stay on mission."

I watched the Thing crawl to the far corner and curl up into a ball of writhing yellow worms. Another new form. It sprouted a pair of eyeballs and trained them on us.

If looks could kill...both Jarman and the Thing would be dead.

* * * *

The questioning dragged on.
Eight weeks.
Ten weeks.
Eleven.

* * * *

On day 79, I had just finished saying, "If you adopt a human form and speak with us, we will provide you with an extra ration of water," when Jarman grabbed my arm.

"Look!" he cried.

I glanced up from the page and gasped.

The Thing was gone. A naked man now stood in the glass cage, muscular arms folded across his well developed chest. His had short black hair, mud-brown eyes, and a strong chin. He appeared perhaps twenty-five years old. I noticed a puckered white scar on his right shoulder, another long scar along his left thigh, and a third on his abdomen where his appendix would have been. He was staring straight at us.

"Can you understand me?" I asked.

When it spoke, a faint Texas twang colored its voice, distant and tinny through the speaker.

"Of course, Dr. Graham."

I swallowed hard. "You know my name. How?"

"I have been studying you."

Jarman reached out and killed the microphones. He covered his mouth, as if the Thing might be reading lips, and said, "Don't you recognize him?"

He did look familiar, but... "Should I—?"

"That's *Varnas*, the guy it killed. Looks just like him! The photo's in his file—"

"Get it."

He ran from the room. He was back in a minute with a blue file folder, which he threw down on the table in front of me. *Staff Sergeant Vitas Varnas*, it said.

"See? That's him." He poked a finger at the photograph taped to the front.

Nodding, I said, "I believe you're right."

The Thing had been captured while absorbing an off-duty sergeant in New Jersey. Our analysts had decided it wanted to infiltrate the Picatinny Arsenal in Dover, where Varnas worked. Luckily, it had been discovered by sanitation workers in a parking garage in mid absorption. They trapped it in a steel dumpster until help could be found.

I looked closely at the Thing, then down at the picture. It *was* Varnas, down to the smallest detail. No doubt the real man had those same scars. If I hadn't seen the Thing in its other forms, I would have thought it *was* Varnas. It would have fooled his wife or mother.

Varnas—rather, the Thing that looked like Varnas—stepped to the edge of its cell and opened its mouth, saying something. I couldn't hear it with the microphones off. I wasn't sure I *wanted* to hear it.

I turned my back so it couldn't read my lips. Better safe than sorry.

"Call HQ," I told Jarman. "Tell them it's talking. This is out of our hands now."

"Right."

As he scrambled from the room to let our superiors know, I swiveled around to face the Thing again and flipped on the microphones. I didn't want to speak to it, but this was my job. I took a deep breath.

"You look like Staff Sergeant Varnas," I said. "Is that what we should call you?"

It shrugged. "If you wish. Is Dr. Rodriguez there?"

I glanced at my watch. "She's not due for another ten minutes. Why?"

"You will understand when Dr. Rodgriguez arrives," it said. "I have something to say to all of you."

"We do not have the authority to negotiate. You must wait for our superiors."

"There is plenty of time for them. I am not trying to negotiate with you, Dr. Graham."

At that moment, I heard Helen Rodriguez's voice. She was speaking urgently to Jarman in the hallway. Luckily she had arrived early today.

"We did it," I said, facing her as she strolled through the door. "We made contact."

Her steel-gray hair had been pulled back in its usual tight bun, and her white lab coat was spotless. She gave a curt nod.

"Well done," she said.

Rare praise, indeed. Normally she remained cooly remote with colleagues, treating us like so many lab rats. I often gave thanks to the gods of Homeland Security that I'd been paired with Jarman instead of her.

She joined me at the control table, taking in the creature that now looked like Sergeant Varnas. Her assistant, Juan Fox, trailed in with Jarman. Everyone stared at the Thing in its new human form. You could have heard a pin drop.

The Thing smiled. It was not a pleasant expression.

"Too smart or too stubborn to be trained," it said, settling its gaze on me. "You said that was our nature. You were wrong, Dr. Graham."

This could be a breakthrough—everything we had all been waiting for. But what did it mean? The breath caught in my throat.

I felt Rodriguez's hand on my shoulder. She leaned forward, too.

Raising my chin, I looked into the Thing's eyes. "Tell me, then—what *is* your nature?"

"Patience." I caught a hint of smug, alien superiority in its tone. "Time is *our* ally, not yours. Conversion is a game of numbers."

Then an alien voice filled my head with whispers: *Sleep... Sleep... Sleep...*

Automatically, I reached for the red button to shock it. But Dr. Rodriguez's hand on my shoulder grew hard and heavy, pushing me back down in my chair. Like a warm molasses, her arm began to melt and spread across my neck and chest and mouth. I tried to jerk away, but couldn't move, couldn't breathe—

Sleep... Sleep... Sleep...

Then I realized it was Rodriguez in my mind, not the Thing in the cage. A chill went through me. I couldn't move—couldn't breathe—

Like a puppeteer playing with a marionette, Dr. Rodriguez jerked my body backwards, over the chair and to the floor with inhuman strength. My head tilted; I glimpsed ceiling tiles before she loomed over me.

Her lab coat swung open, and as I watched, powerless to stop it, her torso split down the middle. Tentacles with fish-hook barbs reached toward me. They snagged my flesh, began pulling me toward her, *into* her. There came no pain. I floated far from myself, an observer rather than a participant.

No, no, no! This couldn't happen. I couldn't allow it. I struggled through the fog, like a heavy sleeper trying to rouse mid-dream.

"Paul!" I managed to gasp. My assistant had to do something—had to get help—

With the last of my strength, I kicked, tried to twist, almost wrenched an arm free. Somehow, I turned my face away from the Thing that had been disguised as Dr. Rodriguez.

"We don't need billions," Varnas was saying from what seemed an impossible distance. "Not at first. We only need the ones in charge of the herd."

My eyesight dimmed. I couldn't fight off sleep much longer. Far, far away, as though down a long, dark tunnel, I saw my assistant standing open-mouthed by the door.

Run! I tried to scream. No words came out. *Run, Paul! Run!*

Paul Jarman didn't move. He, too, must have been paralyzed by the siren song playing in his head.

He didn't begin to scream until the Thing that looked like Juan Fox reached for him with dozens of lashing white tentacles.

Lightning Source UK Ltd.
Milton Keynes UK
UKHW010629070122
396770UK00001B/94